"NEWMAN REALLY KNOWS THE TERRITORY."
—William J. Caunitz, author of *One Police Plaza*

Action-packed, atmospheric, and totally authentic, Christopher Newman's novels of the NYPD go behind the badge and into the hearts and minds of New York's cops . . .

More praise for *Dead End Game*, the newest Precinct novel featuring Lieutenant Joe Dante:

"[A] GRIPPING NEW YORK CITY COP DRAMA . . . lots of hard-boiled humor."
—*Kirkus Reviews*

"A GRITTY AND BELIEVABLE POLICE PROCE-DURAL. The characters are a fascinating urban cornucopia . . . Newman's writing keeps events moving at a crisp pace, yet he manages to incorporate impressive detail."
—*Library Journal*

"A STRONG AND UTTERLY ABSORBING BOOK . . . Newman's revelations offer surprise after surprise and build toward one of those climaxes that make readers cancel dinner dates, ignore ringing telephones, and postpone sleep . . . A WONDERFUL ACHIEVEMENT."
—Peter Straub

"HIS SCENES—of street warfare, inside police politics, high-end hustlers and low-end shooters—MOVE AT A TERRIFIC PACE."
—Lawrence Block

DEAD END GAME

CHRISTOPHER NEWMAN

BERKLEY BOOKS, NEW YORK

DEAD END GAME

A Berkley Book / published by arrangement with
the author

PRINTING HISTORY
G. P. Putnam's Sons edition / July 1994
Berkley edition / February 1995

ISBN: 0-425-14564-6

BERKLEY®
Berkley Books are published by The Berkley Publishing Group,
200 Madison Avenue, New York, New York 10016.
BERKLEY and the "B" design
are trademarks belonging to Berkley Publishing Corporation.

PRINTED IN THE UNITED STATES OF AMERICA

10 9 8 7 6 5 4 3 2 1

Prologue ∎

WILLIE CINTRON WONDERED IF HE WAS LOSING HIS EDGE. He was exhausted as he rolled off her, and that confused him. It wasn't the physical fatigue of exertion he was feeling. He could barely keep his eyes open. It was long after curfew, he had the game of his life to pitch tomorrow, and he shouldn't have had that last drink. There was a meeting scheduled for eight-thirty—far less than a good night's sleep from now—and he needed to salvage as much shuteye as he could in order to be alert. But what kind of righteous stud would he be if he just ignored her now, let himself be pulled into the depths of slumber? As that fatigue surged over him he fought it with a determined shake of the head.

"You have such strong hands," she purred.

He reached to touch her hip, to drag a heavy hand along it. She stirred. The flesh beneath his fingers shifted slightly, but he could hardly feel the smooth nakedness of that sweet elliptical curve. God, why was he so tired?

"You're 'underfuh, too," he murmured. "The bes'."

The throb in his loins, all that was urgent a moment ago, was now a distant sensation of no particular consequence. He'd done her better than she'd ever been done in her life, so where was his glow of satisfaction? He liked to savor this moment, to bask in the warmth of gratitude. So why was he unable to find the strength? He couldn't even turn his head to meet her eyes. Instead, his eyelids closed on a view of the ceiling, and he was powerless to lift them. His final effort saw him suck breath deep into his powerful lungs, before his thoughts drifted into fog.

As Willie lay on his back, snoring slightly, his bedmate reached to prod his rib cage with a fingernail. She stared intently at his face, but saw nothing. Perfect. There they were, surrounded by rumpled bedclothes and a hotel room littered with a dozen empty beer bottles, an ashtray overflowing with butts, and clothes tossed over chairs. She couldn't have set the scene better by design. He'd been so eager to strut his stuff he almost tore his pants getting out of them.

She stole from the bed and dressed quickly before removing the works from her purse. Willie had killed all the lights in the room and opened the drapes, letting the colorful glow of Times Square below create the atmosphere. She closed those drapes now, pulled on a pair of latex gloves, and switched on a nightstand lamp. She'd touched those two drink glasses, both his and hers, touched the rum and Coke bottles, too. One at a time she wiped them clean. Then heroin from a folded paper packet was dumped into a spoon lifted from the lounge downstairs. Into that, she dripped water from the tap in the bath, barely enough liquid to absorb so heavy a hit of the drug.

The flame of a match helped accelerate the dissolving process. When the liquid was clear, her latex-gloved fingers set the spoon on the nightstand. There, she dipped the tip of the needle into it. Slowly, the warm solution was drawn up into the barrel of the syringe.

It hadn't been so bad, jumping this kid's bones. She'd had better, but she'd also had a lot worse. The lousiest ones were always so pleased with themselves that the act made her physically ill, nauseous. At least this guy hadn't been like that. All he'd wanted was to impress, to prove himself. Too bad it was wasted on her. Another woman might have appreciated all that frenzied enthusiasm.

Once she tied off his upper arm, she probed the inside of his elbow for a vein. The needle went in easy, not prompting so much as a twitch from her peacefully slumbering victim. Then she slipped the tie loose and, with slow, steady pressure, pushed the plunger to the end of its run.

As soon as she plucked the needle free, she lingered only long enough to set the syringe beneath his hand. Before she could avert her eyes and rise, she saw the first of that massive dose hit his brain. His expression was peaceful no longer. He suddenly grimaced with subconscious agony while his fingers grabbed up the syringe in a white-knuckled fist. Rather than watch the sheen of sweat break out to coat his rigid physique, she stood and walked to the window. There, with the curtain held aside, she stared down at Times Square.

Even at that late hour, the confluence of Broadway and Seventh Avenue teemed with wee-hour revelers. This was the ever-beating heart of the city that never slept. To Willie Cintron, the garish light thrown by a horde of neon billboards was atmosphere.

When she turned back to the room, he lay still on the bed, his face frozen in grotesque evidence of his pain. She pulled off her gloves and moved to the door. Outside it, life went on.

Chapter ▪ *1*

THE LITTLE FINGER ON TERRY MARSHALL'S RIGHT HAND
was swollen stiff when he hauled himself from bed that
October Sunday morning. Yesterday, in game six of the
American League Championship Series, Paul O'Neill had
foul-tipped a David Cone slider. The ball hooked the extended little finger of Terry's throwing hand, tearing and
dislocating it. For one moment of nauseating pain, Marshall
had squatted there behind the plate, trying to determine how
serious the injury was. He'd dislocated fingers at least a
dozen times in his major-league career. Early on, he was
content to let a trainer pop an injured digit back into place.
Later he'd learned to grit his teeth and do it himself—shake
it off. He'd cultivated a reputation for being a "gamer," a
guy who could handle the pain and keep on playing. Yesterday, he'd be damned if a dislocated pinky would spoil
his chance to help make history. Without a pause, he swallowed deep, dropped that hand out of sight between his
thighs, and grabbed the injured finger to jerk it hard. Two
pitches later Cone caught O'Neill looking at a slider that
nipped the low, outside corner of the strike zone. O'Neill
went down on strikes, the Yanks went down to the Royals
3-2, and the ALCS went down to today's seventh and final
game. Two weeks ago, sportswriters across America and
Vegas oddsmakers were counting the Kansas City club out

in four, maybe five games. Today, with Willie Cintron on the mound for the Royals—22-5, 2.13 ERA—the bookies stood a good chance of taking a real bath.

"Wha . . . ? Time is it?"

The buxom blonde Marshall had met in the Marriott Marquis lobby bar last night rolled over in confusion, trying to get her bearings. She squinted up at the stocky, muscular catcher, her mascara smeared beneath one eye and face puffy with sleep. Terry crossed to the tiny hospitality refrigerator and dug out an ice-cube tray as he answered.

"Time to shake a leg, babe. You want the shower first, you got five minutes."

He knocked cubes into the little wet-bar sink, wrapped a half dozen in a bar towel, and then wrapped his injured little finger. He was scheduled to meet Willie Cintron and their manager for breakfast, to go over the Yankees lineup one more time, talk about who was hot at the moment and who was not. If he wanted to play today and go on to the World Series, Terry knew he had to get the swelling in that finger down. The skipper liked the rapport Willie and Terry had developed, but he wasn't a fool. If he thought the injury would affect Marshall's throwing or how he swung the bat, Terry would be scratched in a Kansas City minute.

Marshall's bedmate—Terry was awful with these groupies' names . . . Debbie?—threw the blankets back and swung her long legs over to plant feet on the floor. Terry noted that her gargantuan breasts had looked a lot more impressive contained in body-hugging Lurex than they did now, unbridled. Still, she'd been an eager partner, and what more could a guy ask of a one-night stand?

"You gonna take me to breakfast?" She screwed a fist into one eye socket, rubbed, stretched, and yawned. "I'm starving."

"Got a meeting, babe. Sorry," Terry tossed over his shoulder as he crossed to draw back the curtains and see what sort of day New York had in store.

"Whadabout later? After the game? Am I gonna see you again?"

Marshall thought about his wife Tina and daughter Tiffany back home in Overland Park. He'd met Tina much the same way as he'd met this woman last night, but Tina was in the right place at the right time. This one wasn't. Tina was also a *real* blonde, with a build on her that was the genuine goods, stem to stern. No doubt Tina suspected his continued infidelities on the road. It was something they never talked about and probably wouldn't, at least so long as Terry continued to bring home a million-two per year. Tina enjoyed the life she lived, and her status as a major-league ballplayer's wife.

"I doubt it, babe. Win or lose, we got a team flight out right after the game. You going to use that shower, or am I?"

The day outside looked crisp and clear. Morning traffic clogged the Times Square intersection of Broadway and Seventh Avenue, just to the south. The garish neon billboards coloring the surrounding skyline suggested this might as easily be Tokyo as the heart of the Apple. Everywhere Terry looked, the brand names of Japanese electronics products dominated.

Debbie pouted while crossing to the bath as Terry started for the bedside phone. Cintron was famous for sleeping through hotel wake-up calls. Their breakfast meeting was set for eight-thirty, downstairs in the coffee shop. The team bus was scheduled to leave for Yankee Stadium at noon, for a three o'clock nationally televised start. With his finger starting to numb from the cold, Marshall flexed it gingerly, lifted the receiver with his glove hand, and punched in Willie's number.

▪ ▪ ▪

Marriott Marquis housekeeping employee Angela Travers had a routine. Its goal was to get as many of the rooms assigned to her cleaned before the staff's ten A.M. coffee break. When she came on shift at eight o'clock, she'd pick up a computer-generated checkout sheet from desk personnel. Weekdays, she could count on most guest traffic being business people. Up and out early. She did all their rooms first. By the time she finished them, the rest of the guests were usually on the move.

Weekends were a different story. Half the guests in the hotel were suburbanites doing the city on special-rate packages. They tended to sleep late, leaving the Do Not Disturb cards hanging until an indecent hour. They seemed to enjoy leaving their rooms like pigsties—towels soaked and wadded up on the bathroom floor, bedclothes in a heap on the carpet, little treats like spent condoms and tampons hiding under the beds. Angela understood anger, but didn't understand what these affluent suburbanites had to be so angry *about*. Hell, they didn't work this shit job.

Matters were even worse this particular weekend. Angela had a baseball team in her sector. On a scale, these sports clowns weren't as bad as a rock-and-roll band, say, but they didn't measure a whole lot higher, either. They were cocky little kids who made too much money and got too much attention. They expected to be treated like royalty and managed to forget their humble roots the instant the IRS took its first half-million bucks. Angela was grateful they were playing a pair of weekend day games here in New York. That meant they had to get out at a reasonable hour.

As she pushed her cart down the sixteenth-floor corridor, a majority of doorknobs sported those hated privacy cards. The occupancy printout indicated only five of the floor's thirty guests had checked out. She parked out front of one of those—1726—and inserted her passkey into the lock set.

Behind the next door down the hall she heard the telephone start to ring.

When Willie Cintron failed to answer his phone after fifteen rings, Terry Marshall pulled on a pair of sweatpants to step across the hall and pound on the staff ace's door. As Marshall left his own room he heard the toilet flush and water start to run in the shower. It was eight-ten already and Willie wasn't the only guy who had to shake a leg. Their manager was a stickler for punctuality, figuring for what they were being paid, his players could at least be on time. Terry hoped his last night's amusement took a quick shower. The fewer doors he had to break down this morning, the better.

There was a cart parked outside the room next to Willie's as Marshall lifted one hamlike fist to roust him. The Dominican Dazzler had his Do Not Disturb sign out, like most everyone else. Last night, the New York native had entertained his brother and some cousins from the old neighborhood. Hopefully, he hadn't gotten wasted. Getting Willie to move might require a maid's passkey. Terry was thankful he wouldn't need to travel far to find one.

Angela Travers was startled, looking up to see a solidly built, bare-chested black man enter the room where she was stooped over, making the queen-size bed.

"Excuse me?"

Angela straightened in a hurry, reaching to tug down her skirt. "The extra towels is on my cart. What room you in? I gotta mark it down."

"It ain't towels I'm after." The intruder had advanced far enough into the room that Angela could see he was barefoot, too. "My buddy in seventeen twenty-eight and me have a meeting at eight-thirty. I can't get him to answer his phone or his door. Late for a morning meeting is a heavy fine. You mind?''

She should have guessed. Stud built like this *had* to be a ballplayer. A Kansas City Royal.

''You just called there? You sure he's in? That phone must've rang a hunnerd times.''

''Trust me. He could sleep through nuclear attack.''

Angela started around the edge of the bed while digging for the key ring in the front pocket of her smock. ''We ain't s'pose to do this, y'know. What position you play, handsome?''

''Catcher.''

''You guys surprise a lotta people this year. Mosta the bookies in *my* neighborhood.'' She paused to raise an index finger and tap the air between them. ''Marshall, ain't it? *Terry* Marshall?''

The big man nodded. ''I'm sorta in a hurry here, miss.''

''Angela. Call me Angie. Everyone does. You had a couple good hits in yesterday's game.''

He nodded. ''Double and a single. Two RBIs. Three forty-two for the series.''

She shrugged again, heading into the hall. ''Hate to see the Yanks lose it at this late date. Then again, you all took the same road, right?''

One door up, she reached to insert her passkey. ''You're sure this is him?'' She lifted a fist to pound on the door when Marshall nodded impatiently. ''Mister . . . ?''

''Cintron.''

''Mr. Cintron? Housekeeping! You got a friend out here says it's urgent.'' She paused to look back over her shoulder. ''*Willie* Cintron?''

''That's right.''

''He be blazin' hot of late.'' Angela marveled. ''Damn.''

''Been blazing hot all year,'' Marshall countered. ''And his wallet's gonna be a thousand bucks lighter, you don't let me in there to drag his ass outta bed.''

Angela turned the key in the knob while conjuring up an image of Willie Cintron—a tall, lanky left-hander from down in the islands somewhere. She imagined him wrapped around some hot Latin lady, unwilling to break it off before he'd finished his business. She pushed the door open, prepared to get herself an eyeful.

Chapter ■ 2

AS HE STOOD THERE LOOKING INTO THE DEAD FACE OF this year's likely American League Cy Young Award winner, New York medical examiner's pathologist Rocky Conklin could think of nothing but the waste. Conklin had planned to spend that Sunday afternoon in front of the set, watching the Yankees try to salvage their playoff hopes against the surprisingly scrappy Kansas City Royals. Instead, he'd be spending this particular afternoon doing a rush autopsy . . . on the Royals' best hope of pulling off the baseball upset of the decade. To Conklin's practiced eye, that hope had died in the wee hours of Sunday morning. Willie Cintron, the twenty-one-year-old Dominican native who grew up in the Washington Heights section of Manhattan, had apparently overdosed himself with an intravenously injected drug. His corpse lay stretched naked on his room's queen-size bed, his eyes bulged grotesquely and his tongue protruded slightly from between grimacing teeth. The beautifully gifted young athlete had died with a syringe clenched in one fist and his head thrown back in an attitude of mortal agony. There on the nightstand beside him, a square of white paper lay unfolded, bearing only the slightest dusting of an unidentified white powder. Along with it, a hotel-plate Marriott spoon, blackened on the bottom side, and a single burned match.

When he watched Willie Cintron throw that marvelous two-hitter in game three of the ALCS, Rocky thought he'd never seen such pure and natural body mechanics. It was like watching the slow-motion uncoiling of a bullwhip, then the strike of a cobra. Everything worked in concert, fluid grace combined with awesome power. Conklin—himself only a mediocre schoolyard athlete in his youth—found it incomprehensible that anyone with such a gift would risk it so selfishly.

"Look pretty much cut-and-dried to you, too?"

Conklin glanced up, prodded from his ruminations, to confront the eager-beaver visage of Manhattan South Homicide Task Force commander Captain Frank Ottomanelli. One of the new breed of Patrol Guide boy scouts, the captain was ambitious and going places, another wannabe commissioner. A glamour gig like command of Manhattan South Homicide was a feather to be worn at a jaunty angle in his cap. The suit was as slick as any mayoral aide's, and a pair of wire-rim spectacles gave him just the right intellectual air. The thinking man's cop.

"What's so cut-and-dried about the most dominant southpaw in the American League spiking a vein with gutter-dreg dogshit and killing himself, Captain? Why would a man in his position *do* a thing like that?"

"I thought asking those questions was my part of the job," Ottomanelli countered. "From you I need a time and cause of death. Any unusual circumstances. To me it looks like he partied too hearty. You find evidence to the contrary, please let me know."

Conklin reached down and lifted a dead arm. It was still loosely wrapped with the necktie used to tie it off. "Unusual, Captain? Tell me what *you* see." It was Cintron's right arm. His glove arm.

"What? I see a spent spike in his hand and the delivery hole in his vein, big as day."

"And nothing strikes you as odd about that?"

"About what?"

"That delivery hole, as you so poetically put it."

Ottomanelli shook his head. "Why should it?"

Conklin turned the arm one way and then the other. He then lifted the left and manipulated it in much the same manner. "You see any others, Captain? I don't. That's sort of odd for a junkie, don't you think?"

Frank Ottomanelli frowned at the clean condition of both the dead man's arms as Rocky moved on to examine between Willie's toes and behind his knees. They, too, were clean. Indeed, with the exception of a crude, faded heart-shaped tattoo between thumb and forefinger on the dead man's right hand, the skin of the front of his body was virtually unblemished.

"Who said he's a junkie, Doc? Man was set to pitch the biggest game of his career. Who knows what sort of pressure he was under? A twenty-one-year-old kid, in a spot like that? Maybe he faltered, looked to buy himself a little courage in a bag."

Conklin wasn't having any. "And the night before the biggest game of his career, he decides to *shoot* that dope? He wanted courage, he could have snorted it just as easily."

Ottomanelli had already made up his mind. "That guy who found him? The catcher—Terry Marshall? He says Willie did some partying last night, with his brother and some other guys from the old neighborhood. You think they *snort* their smack up on Dyckman and St. Nick Avenue?" He paused to point at the syringe pried from the dead man's hand. The rusty red of Cintron's backwashed blood was visible between plunger and needle. "Up there, that is the primary tool of the trade."

New York *Daily News* sports columnist Barry Zajac was already at the ballpark that Sunday morning when he heard the news. Word had gone first to the city desk at the *News,* and then spread like wildfire. The Yankee locker room, where the players were starting to trickle in, was buzzing with it. After yesterday's defeat, their mood had been somber, despairing almost. They'd thrown everything they had at the Royals and could do nothing to thwart Kansas City's relentless surge back from a two-game deficit. The Royals had won three of the last four games, playing faultless baseball. They'd only narrowly missed winning game five when Montgomery hung one a little too high in the ninth inning. Danny Tartabull drove it halfway to the Harlem River, and with Don Mattingly already on board on a junk single, the Yanks had managed a one-run, ninth-inning comeback win.

Dave Anderson of the *Times* delivered the news to Zajac upstairs in the press box. Afterward, Barry sat in one place a long time, too numb to speak. Anderson and the others present knew of Zajac's special relationship with the dead man. They gave him wide berth out of respect for his loss. It was five years now since Zajac first met the sixteen-year-old pitcher with the flamethrower arm. At the time Willie Cintron was tearing up hitters all over the city league while wearing the uniform of George Washington High in the northern reaches of Manhattan. A Dominican immigrant, he had been raised by a father who worked as a garment-district deliveryman and a mother who worked in a sweat-shop as a seamstress. At home, he'd watched an unflagging work ethic get his parents nowhere but older and more beaten down. On the mean streets of Washington Heights, Inwood, and Harlem, he'd learned the ethic of territorial imperative, of bad-ass streetcorner posturing. There, a crude order was enforced by violence.

It was his athletic gift that made Willie Cintron stand out from all the other kids in his hopeless world. The first time Barry Zajac ever saw him throw a baseball, he knew he'd witnessed something most sportswriters never see in a lifetime of hoping. He'd discovered a diamond in the rough, a gold nugget the size of his fist. At sixteen years of age, Willie Cintron was close to having it all. He had the pure velocity of a ninety-plus-mile-an-hour fastball and uncanny control for a kid so young and raw. He'd yet to perfect his curveball, and it still looked better than ninety percent of the stuff being thrown at the Triple-A level. He was hitting at a .375 pace and had a good defensive player's quick reflexes and pure animal instincts.

One week after Zajac first saw Willie Cintron play, Willie was arrested for grand theft auto. He'd been busted joyriding with his brother and a cousin. That was when Barry decided to make Willie his personal project. Before Cintron left New York at eighteen to play as a number-one draft choice in the Kansas City Royals farm system, he and Zajac saw each other on at least a weekly basis. Barry became a voice of hope, daring Willie to dream. Barry challenged him, chastised him, and cajoled him when necessary. He showed Willie Cintron a bigger world than Willie ever knew existed, and once he saw it, Willie sprouted like a seed kicked from barren to fertile soil.

"I heard about Willie, Barry. I'm sorry."

The familiar female voice was soft and consoling. Zajac glanced up to find local sports-radio beat reporter Marcy Larsen. She laid a hand on his shoulder and squeezed. "It's so hard to believe."

Barry shook his head. "I don't believe it, Marce. A fucking heroin overdose? Willie hasn't so much as smoked a joint in over five years."

"I know. It seems crazy. But it's what we're all hearing."

He closed his eyes and sucked a breath deep, trying to calm the turmoil in his stomach. "It *is* crazy. There's something they're not telling yet. That kid was on top of the world, Marce. Unbeatable. If there were any doubters left after game three, he would have convinced them today. I'm supposed to believe he stuck a needle in his arm the night before the biggest game of his life?''

''The rumor I hear says he was partying with old friends. His brother and some other guys he grew up with. You know what sort of pressures those situations can create.''

Zajac shook his head, vehemence behind it. ''Bullshit. He drew the line between that world and this one the day he left New York. His old crowd played a dead-end game, and nobody knew the score better than Willie did.''

Detective Lieutenant Joe Dante said good-bye to Captain Rosa Losada in the International Terminal Building at Kennedy Airport, and Rosa glanced at her watch. She nodded back toward the security check they'd just bypassed, using their shields.

''You don't have to wait here with me, Joe. You'll be late for the game.''

Until recently, Rosa had worked as the deputy commissioner of public information's executive officer. She'd enjoyed a rapid rise in rank, but ultimately missed the challenge of working the street. Today she was second-in-command of the Manhattan district attorney's investigation squad and was headed to Brussels for an Interpol symposium on international terrorist networks. It wasn't an assignment generally associated with her current job description, but Police Commissioner Anton Mintoff thought her the best-qualified representative the department had to spare. NYPD's smooth liaison with various United Nations embassies throughout the city was a crucial link to the success of this conference. With her public-relations background, Captain Losada was elected to carry the ball.

''I've got an hour,'' Dante countered. ''How's it feel to know you'll be missing a Royals–Giants World Series?''

''Oh, it's breaking my heart.''

The prospect of watching Kansas City and San Francisco battle it out for the Series title didn't thrill Dante either. He'd grown up in a Brooklyn neighborhood that never forgave Walter O'Malley for moving the Dodgers to Los Angeles. Just a week ago the possibility of seeing a New York team in the series again excited: the right coast versus the wrong coast, hot dogs versus sushi, hustle versus hype. Today, it looked like Willie Cintron would serve up all the hot dog the Yankees could eat, and humble pie for dessert.

"But duty and vacation call, Dante," Rosa continued. After the four-day symposium, she had plans to visit an aunt and family in Barcelona, maybe head south from there to a beach. "What I hear, everything in Europe costs an arm and a leg. Don't expect more than a T-shirt."

Over the past five years of their on-again, off-again relationship, they'd endured a number of separations, most of them voluntary. Today they maintained separate residences. Many nights they went their separate ways. And while neither had made a declaration of undying exclusivity, it was the age of the AIDS virus. Exclusivity had become an easy habit.

"Remember to pack your rubbers?" he asked.

Rosa's eyes narrowed as she shook her head. "I'm not the one with the rampant testosterone problem, buddy boy."

"In other words, only a couple. Just for emergencies."

"Smallest package they sell is a box of three. There's a store in the Village now, you can get them that even glow in the dark."

"You sure you got to take this flight? You're getting me all excited here."

She smiled a smile that never failed to melt his heart and reached to trace his face with her fingertips. "What was it we Catholics used to say? Something about avoiding the *occasion* of sin?"

"Ex-Catholics," he corrected. "And it's the *near* occasion. Anything out of arm's reach is free game."

She chuckled and kissed him before starting to turn away. "You feel any uncontrollable temptations, tie a knot in it."

Exotic-car dealer Miles Berga met Debbie DeLong on the Rupert Place sidewalk outside Yankee Stadium. The sight of her gave him the same hot jolt of pleasure it always did. It had been three days since he and the swimsuit model last spent time together, three days spent in a rising state of panic over how the Yanks were doing and how much Miles had riding on this series. It had also been three days he spent sharing a bed with his wife. He needed a hit of Debbie in the worst way and felt his skin prickle with goose bumps as she pressed herself hard against him and slipped her tongue into his ear. Needed it bad, considering the state his nerves were in. In fact, if it weren't for the field-level box seats one of the Yankee players had given him, he might have dragged her off to do her right then. Instead, he let a hand drift over the tight denim sheathing her backside and put on the most optimistic face he could muster.

"God, I've missed you, baby."

She rolled her eyes and affected boredom. "Sure you have, Miles. You heard about Willie Cintron?"

That evoked a grin. "What do you think? It's enough to swing it back around?"

"That's what I like about you, speed. You're such a sentimentalist." As she said it she kissed him on the cheek and turned to lead him through the throng toward the stadium entrance.

"How can I be anything but nuts right now?" he asked. "This was the one gonna buy me some breathing room."

With an arm draped around his waist, she patted him affectionately on one hip. "Could be it will yet. It still ain't over and the Royals just blew a tire. Try not to forget what you promised, okay?''

Miles produced his two tickets and handed them to the attendant at the turnstile. ''I *can't* quit gambling, baby. It's in my blood. Like a drug. You can't understand the rush it gives me.''

She smirked in return as they joined the crowd headed for field-level seats. ''I know all about rushes, speed. And it's your wife you promised to stop gambling. You promised *me* you'd divorce her, but you ain't done that, either. You said you'd introduce me to those players who bought the hot rods from you.''

Miles squeezed a little fanny and grunted. ''You make me wonder what you love me for, Debbie. My friends and fast cars or my winning personality. Considering this state I'm in, I'd be more interested in heading for your place after the game.''

She stuck her tongue in his ear again, her breath hot around it. ''Stop worrying about your state, Miles. You're gonna be a quarter-million-dollar winner. You let me have my fun, I'll make sure you have yours.''

Joe Dante was in a hurry. He'd waited until Rosa was called to board her flight, and had just half an hour before the first pitch was thrown in game seven of the ALCS. The chief of detectives and his wife had invited Joe to join them in their box, which meant fighting Sunday traffic from the far reaches of Queens to Yankee Stadium in the South Bronx. To make it before the national anthem was played would be no mean feat.

Dante's car was in a multilevel parking structure two hundred yards removed from the TWA international terminal. A construction project forced him through a maze of plywood-fenced walkways, the sound of his hurried steps echoing with jungle-drum insistence. The mercury loitered in the low fifties and the sun sparkled in a bright blue sky. It was an ideal October day for baseball. Dante considered the chances of a Yankee win with Willie Cintron throwing for the opposition. Then his thoughts turned to Rosa leaving for two weeks as a jet roared skyward, directly overhead. Theirs was an odd relationship. Both were too fiercely independent to make cohabitation possible. They'd tried and failed. Still, they kept drifting back to each other.

Dante entered the first level of the parking structure, and it was several seconds before his eyes adjusted to the relative gloom. Midway through the Jewish High Holy Days, many stalls stood empty. Joe had taken advantage and parked his Nissan 300 ZX close to the exit ramp and attendant's booth. Halfway up the first rank of cars he spotted a well-dressed woman with neatly bobbed gray hair, one aisle over. Paused behind a Jaguar, she dug into her pocketbook and failed to notice a slender black man pop up between two cars behind her. Another strolled toward her down the row of parked cars ahead. The national anthem, Willie Cintron's flamethrower fastball, and everything else on Dante's mind went south. An old, familiar sixth-sense alarm was going off.

"Aw, shit," Joe muttered to himself. This wasn't happening. Not on his day off. It was no use reaching to the small of his back, either. He'd left his Walther PPK locked in the glove box.

By the time the tall, skinny black man in the ill-fitting brown suit approached to draw abreast of the woman, she'd extracted her keys from her purse and was turning toward the Jaguar's driver-side door. Triggered by her key-ring remote, the car emitted a happy chirp and unlocked automatically. Then the strolling man swerved, threw out an arm, and slammed her in the throat. Joe was just starting to move, heading toward them between parked cars, when the force of the blow knocked the woman hard on her fanny.

Armed, Dante would have yelled to freeze them. Bare-handed, he had no choice but to go in quick and quiet. The woman was on the ground choking as the man who assaulted her plucked the car keys from the pavement and hurried to jerk open the Jag's driver-side door. His buddy moved around the car and grabbed the choking woman by the hair. As he tried to drag her out of the way, Dante ran at him in a crouch.

From twenty yards away a voice screamed something unintelligible as Dante made contact, driving his shoulder into his target just above the left hip. It slammed the man into the back of the Jag with bone-breaking force. He sagged, instantly out cold as Joe backed away and reset his feet. The guy with the keys had one foot inside the car when Dante launched. Hands planted on the Jaguar's trunk lid, Joe vaulted over the roof just as the taller man was starting to duck. Joe's hands created a pivot point, his momentum whipping his feet back to front in one smooth, airborne sweep. The heel of his left foot caught the target above the right ear. The man's eyes went glassy as he was thrown against the top edge of the open door.

Something fell from inside the tall man's jacket and clattered to the pavement while Joe leaped atop him and hammered his midsection with close-quarter elbow punches. Joe was backing away from his retching opponent when the assaulted woman finally found her voice and began to scream. He spotted movement from the corner of one eye. From the opposite direction of the tall man's initial approach, a third black man now raced toward him, a pistol in one outstretched hand.

A shot rang out, pulverizing the glass in the Jaguar's rear window. Joe dove for the ground, rolled hard for the cover of a Ford Explorer's undercarriage, and was jabbed in the small of the back by something sharp. Trying to slide from view, he groped at the hard object in his way. His fingers closed around the barrel of what felt like a revolver.

Feet appeared as Dante dragged the gun across his stomach, his knuckles scraping against the Explorer's underbelly. He managed to get his fingers wrapped around the gun butt, his thumb tugging back the hammer as the weapon cleared his right hip. He could tell by the weight it was something medium-framed. The caliber, and therefore the wallop it packed, was anyone's guess. He just prayed his gift horse was loaded.

The new arrival yelled something to his fallen accomplices. As the screaming Jag owner tried to rise to her knees, Joe saw one of the man's feet leave the ground. The woman grunted and flopped onto her side, gasping and clutching at her ribs. Joe lifted the gun parallel to the pavement. What was that language? Its tongue-clicking, guttural rhythm had to be African. There was a ring of Ghanaians reported to be working the urban areas of the northeast, hijacking cars at gunpoint.

The man moved cautiously. In the last few seconds his partners had been incapacitated. Pack animals had trouble with independent action, and this guy was all alone now. A knee appeared, then a hand reached toward the pavement for balance. The gun hand appeared simultaneously with the man's head as he peered beneath the Jag. From the car opposite, Joe reached to touch the back of that head with the barrel of his newfound gun.

"Twitch and I blow your fucking head off."

The man froze. "I—I put gun down. Yes, boss?"

"I'm not your boss, asshole. I'm your worst fucking nightmare. Don't put it down. Open your hand and let it drop."

Chapter ■ 3

WHEN CHIEF OF DETECTIVES GUS LIEBERMAN ENTERED Commissioner Anton Mintoff's office at ten o'clock that Monday morning, he was still riding the disorienting high of seeing his Yankees squeak into the World Series. Indeed, the entire city was jubilant about that eleventh-hour deliverance.

"Come in, Chief," Mintoff greeted him. "Meet Barry Zajac. You're no doubt familiar with his column."

In the presence of civilians from outside the job, the PC invariably addressed Gus by his title. It had something to do with his screwy paramilitary view of how the job should be run. Familiarity—or the appearance thereof—was certain to breed the contempt of outsiders.

Gus crossed to shake hands with the popular sportswriter. "Mr. Zajac? I'm a great admirer of your work, on and off the paper."

Zajac's often acerbic column was enjoyed by nearly a million New Yorkers every day. In recent years he'd worked with a number of area sports stars to organize clinics in the city's ghettos. Among those stars, Lieberman knew, was Willie Cintron. By all accounts, those clinics were a tremendous success.

The sportswriter who shook Lieberman's hand looked tired. Boyish in the byline photo run alongside his column,

Zajac looked decidedly old this morning. Gus guessed he was in his early fifties. A thick head of curly hair with only a peppering of gray helped belie those years.

"Mr. Zajac has misgivings about how Willie Cintron met his fate yesterday," Mintoff announced. "Considering his unique relationship with the man and the history of that friendship, I think it best we hear him out."

Lieberman assumed a seat alongside the sportswriter. "Big Tony"—as the rank and file had tagged Mintoff—contemplated the two of them across the surface of a desk Gus thought too massive for the room.

"How about you bring Mr. Zajac up to date, Chief?"

"I've read the homicide commander's report pretty thoroughly," Lieberman told Zajac. "Postmort findings were consistent with a heroin overdose. Our Crime Scene Unit did a more exhaustive job on the room than usual for a suicide. They found the residue of at least two marijuana cigarettes in the trash can, and more ash on the carpet. Cintron and any other occupants of that room had consumed two six-packs and half a bottle of rum."

"How much alcohol was in *Willie*'s system?" Zajac fired back.

"Not enough to make him drunk, but some."

Zajac nodded. "And no evidence that he smoked pot. Am I right?"

Lieberman eyed him steadily. "Which means what to you?"

"It's all consistent with who Willie had become, Chief. The heroin is what I'm not buying. I can't deny it was in his bloodstream. That's what killed him. What I question is *how* it got there."

Gus frowned. "You're suggesting he was murdered?"

"I'm more than suggesting it, Chief. I'm sure of it. The Willie Cintron I knew would no more stick a syringe of that poison into his arm than you would." Zajac shifted in his chair to better face Lieberman. He leaned forward. "Did you ever see that kid pitch? Believe me, Willie knew the *value* of his gift. He knew what his life would have been without it."

"Murdered by who?" Lieberman pressed.

Zajac collapsed back into his chair and sighed. "That I can't tell you. Or how, for that matter. I only know he didn't kill himself."

"Because he knew the value of his gift." Now Gus leaned forward, his thick-fingered hands spread toward Zajac in a gesture of sympathy. Lieberman's heavy-shouldered fifty-six-year-old frame carried the weight of too many business lunches and ceremonial dinners. He refused to forsake his fondness for cigarettes—Carlton low-tar, at his wife's insistence—and a stiff scotch or two at day's end. "Has it occurred to you that the pressure mighta been too much for him, Mr. Zajac? This twenty-one-year-old kid with the weight of an entire season on him? Maybe he couldn't *handle* all that pressure."

Zajac's eyes flashed fire. "You come from a neighborhood like he came from, you have a whole different respect for life's pressures, Chief. Baseball was a *game* to Willie. Period."

"For which he was paid over a million bucks a year."

"And next season even more, Chief. He was scheduled to negotiate a new contract. The way he was pitching, the sky was the limit. Three, maybe even four million. A kid with that to look forward to *kills* himself?"

Mintoff stepped into it here. "Our investigation found nothing inconsistent with the ME's cause of death, Mr. Zajac. The toxicology analysis says the heroin was unusually pure. That scares me. Makes me wonder how many more guys will turn up dead from this particular batch of dope in the next few days."

"What if someone *meant* to kill him?" Zajac countered.

"But why?" Mintoff asked.

Zajac's look of exasperation made a nice preface to his words. "You're aware of the Vegas oddsmakers' spread on this year's ALCS, Commissioner? The Yanks were favored four to one. By yesterday's game, the Royals were favored three to one. When Willie died, those odds fell to almost dead even. Do you have any idea how much money was at stake? With a New York team as one of the contestants?"

Mintoff frowned. "You're suggesting what? That gambling interests may have wanted him dead?"

"It's an interesting thought," Gus mused. "Frankly, one that hadn't occurred to me."

Encouraged, Zajac held his ground. "The city that lands the World Series stands to make tens of millions of dollars, gentlemen. That means *individuals* stand to make millions."

"I still think it's farfetched," Mintoff told him.

"Willie Cintron didn't kill himself, Commissioner."

Lieberman stopped him before this back-and-forth could escalate. "Okay. Say we respect your reservations, that we agree to have a couple detectives do some digging. You're prepared to keep a lid on your suspicions for a few days, Mr. Zajac? Avoid making mention of them in your column?"

Zajac met him eye to eye, his gaze unwavering. "How many days, Chief? And what sort of detectives? Glue-factory candidates who'll only go through the motions? If I'm going to sit on my hands, I need your assurance that you're serious."

Lieberman glanced to Mintoff. "What? A week?"

Mintoff's reluctance was clear as he shrugged. He hated being forced into corners, and that's where he found himself now.

"I've got a few ideas about who, Mr. Zajac," Gus continued. "You want assurances about the quality of their work? You'll have to trust me when I say the glue factory's still a few years away."

Commissioner Anton Mintoff had a lot on his plate this particular Monday morning. It was an election year, with the mayoral race up for grabs. The incumbent wanted to put his success in revamping the police department center stage, to subject it to some sizzling, high-wattage scrutiny. While Mintoff hated being put on the spot, it did beat the alternative. If the mayor was ousted next month, Big Tony would be on the next bus behind him. He knew a dozen hard chargers who would gladly take the reins from him tomorrow. If he could do anything to avoid a changing of the guard, he'd do his damnedest.

And now this. Just what he needed. When the door closed behind columnist and sports-clinic do-gooder Barry Zajac, Tony stared at his chief of detectives across the top of steepled fingers. Lieberman looked a little too comfortable sitting there, and that irritated. No matter what happened politically, Gus was married to an heiress, a woman who would keep him in handcrafted Italian loafers and Mercedes seat leather deep into his golden years. Gus didn't need the job, neither for his ego nor his wallet. Tony often wondered what sort of sick mind took itself to work in the cesspool of New York City crime every day, just because he loved the work.

"So talk to me, Gus." He kept his tone controlled. "One word of a Willie Cintron homicide investigation leaks to Zajac's competition, I've got George Steinbrenner, the commissioner of baseball, and presidents of both leagues crawling up my ass. To say nothing of the TV network."

Steinbrenner was the often outspoken owner of the Yankees, and Gus had no trouble understanding Tony's concerns. "Then we do it quietly. Put out some feelers. Locate the brother. Determine who the other homeboys were partied with Cintron Saturday night. Maybe look into this gambling angle a little.''

''A sports-betting scandal of that magnitude?'' Mintoff complained. ''It's just what we need, three weeks before an election.''

Lieberman held his ground. ''You gotta admit it's possible, Tony.''

''You think Zajac held back a little, just to see how hard we'll work? That he's already heard something?''

Gus shrugged. ''There had to be thousands couldn't afford to lose that bet, plenty of them who were into it pretty deep. How many, I got no idea.''

Mintoff watched Lieberman dig out his cigarettes. ''So who are your horses, Gus?''

Lieberman spun the wheel of his Zippo, eyes steady ahead. ''You *know* who, Tony. His exploits out at Kennedy yesterday were the other story in this morning's papers.''

Mintoff shook his head hard. ''Nuh-uh. Absolutely not. The man draws headlines like shit draws flies. I want a media spectacle? I'll hire Marla Maples to dance naked in the lobby.''

''If it's homicide, there's no way we can avoid that kinda spectacle, Tony. I want to see Joey on it.''

Mintoff's guts were clamoring for that first Di-Gel of the day. There wasn't much about Lieutenant Joe Dante that *didn't* irritate him. Yes, the son of a bitch was good. He couldn't deny that. The problem was, Dante invariably ended up doing things his own way. The term ''loose cannon'' didn't approach him. He was a loose M-1 tank. And if the truth be known, Dante's life-style rankled Tony as much as anything. He didn't trust a man who was still single at the lieutenant's age, a man who had no mortgage or kids to put through college. Mintoff counted on those things to mellow a cop, to give him pause. Rumor had it that

Dante was seeing Rosa Losada again, the best-looking woman Mintoff knew, on or off the job. After making lieutenant just to cut himself a certain amount of command-chain latitude, Dante persisted in refusing to take the captain's exam. Rather than play the game and move up the ranks to some cushy desk job like most cops with his skills would, Dante preferred to work the street. To hear him tell it, he had everything he wanted, right where he was.

Stalemate. Lieberman was the best chief of detectives a PC could ask for. Gus was tough, fair, above reproach, and above all, results-oriented. Under his command, the Detective Bureau ran like a well-oiled machine. Right now he was also probably right.

"What if Willie Cintron *was* murdered?" Lieberman continued. "You think a man like Barry Zajac is gonna let this one lay until after the election? He could give a rat's ass about who wins. He turns up evidence on his own, or already has some in hand, he can make us all look foolish. We want him as a friend, Tony. Not as an enemy."

Zajac was a crusader. Mintoff knew that. Zajac's fires burned brighter and longer than most people's. A week from now he was likely to show up asking for an accounting. If anyone could get them something on short notice, it was Lieutenant Dante.

"I want your man on a leash, Gus. One so short I can hear him strangling, trying to draw breath."

Mintoff would swear the corners of Gus Lieberman's mouth twitched in a smile.

Chapter ■*4*

LIEUTENANT BEASLEY "JUMBO" RICHARDSON WAS AT HIS desk in the eleventh-floor Special Investigation Division offices at One Police Plaza. As part of a two-man troubleshooting task force at SID, Richardson and his partner, Joe Dante, saw themselves as the division's garbage collectors. A Sanitation Department Penalty for Dumping sign was mounted on the partition outside their office. Still, the threat of a five-hundred-dollar fine did little to stanch a steady flow of foul-smelling case files. The garbage collectors were the last hope for unsolveds and untouchables. If they couldn't recycle the information contained in those files, it was dumped into the desolate limbo of the Detective Bureau's forever-open files. Technically, an unresolved case stayed open in perpetuity. In truth, any investigation in those files was ninety-nine percent dead.

It went without saying that Richardson and Dante always had more work on their desks than two men could handle. Their mandate allowed them a fair amount of latitude as to where they focused. Periodic meetings with Chief Lieberman helped define that focus. This morning, Dante had been summoned to just such a meeting. Jumbo was tidying up when Joe returned.

The two-hundred-twenty-pound black detective eased back in his chair and laced the fingers of those huge Oscar

Peterson hands behind his head as Dante paused to fill his mug from the Mr. Coffee.

"So?"

"You're gonna love it." Dante crossed the crowded cubicle to his own desk, set face-to-face with Richardson's, and sat. "You know Barry Zajac? The guy with the smart-aleck sports column at the *Daily News?*"

Jumbo nodded. "Too cute for me, mosta the time. Don't tell me he's buggering little boys at them clinics he organizes."

Dante chuckled. "Better. He refuses to buy Frank Ottomanelli's suicide conclusion in the Willie Cintron investigation. He thinks somebody killed him."

"Based on what?" Jumbo lowered his hands to the edges of his desktop and unconsciously started tapping out a little rhythm with his fingers.

"Based on how well he says he knew Cintron. I gather he and Willie were close, had been for five or six years. He refuses to believe there's any way in hell Cintron stuck that spike in his own arm."

"So maybe someone else did it for him. The squeamish ones do it that way all the time."

Dante sipped from his cup and shook his head. "I'm getting this all through Gus, but the way Zajac tells it, the kid was a kinda born-again square." He outlined the sportswriter's misgivings and described the forensic and autopsy findings. "Only a point-six alcohol level in his bloodstream. That's with the Crime Scene Unit finding the empties from two six-packs and a half-consumed bottle of rum. Couple joints were smoked in there, too."

"Funny company for a health nut to keep, don't you think?"

Joe set his coffee down and shrugged. "He spent his whole life around that crowd, Beasley. Unless he wanted to completely cut himself off from his family and friends,

I imagine there's a certain amount of that shit he put up with.''

Richardson, a former fat man who'd lost a hundred pounds on a supervised diet, stopped drumming his fingers and shifted his still-considerable bulk forward in his chair. He'd lost the weight, but certain things like nicknames stick with a cop all his life. "So how do we fit in, Joey?"

"As long as Big Tony agrees to dig around, Zajac has promised to keep a lid on it. Gus thinks he may know something he ain't saying and might even be useful to us. Still, Tony's nervous about this." He paused to grin. "With the Yankees in the Series now and Cintron dying the night before that deciding game, he's afraid this makes the news, all of major-league baseball's gonna crawl up his ass."

"Wearing cleats, I hope."

Joe chuckled. "Gus wants us to take it slow, go in as quiet as we can. Talk to Zajac, see where he can point us and what he might be sitting on. Needless to say, Big Tony is less than enthused about our involvement."

A smile to match Dante's lit Richardson's battered countenance. "I'm hurt, Joey. What is it? A crisis of confidence?"

Barry Zajac was in his office at the *Daily News* on East Forty-second Street when a staff assistant showed the two detectives to his door. As they entered he got that same feeling he experienced in the presence of professional athletes. Barry was diminutive in stature, barely five foot four and a hundred forty pounds. Like many cops from pre–affirmative-action days, these two were big guys. The black one, while an inch or two shorter than his white partner, had to outweigh him by a solid twenty pounds. Very solid. The white guy, on the other hand, was built tall and rangy like a pro cornerback. With his wide, square shoulders and slim hips, he had the lean look of a man who stayed in excellent shape. It wasn't until Zajac shook hands with him that he noticed his knuckles. Those were a seasoned karate fighter's hands. Barry guessed both men might be every bit as formidable as they looked, and he was relieved. Could it be that Commissioner Mintoff was a man of his word, after all?

The white guy introduced them. "Mr. Zajac? I'm Detective Lieutenant Dante and this is my partner, Lieutenant Richardson."

Zajac's recognition of the speaker's name was instantaneous. The story of his mixing it up with a gang of car thieves had made page three that morning. He shook hands with Richardson and watched the way both men took note of their surroundings as they sat. There were several sports-writing awards framed and hung on the wall behind his desk. Alongside, he'd hung photographs of himself and various New York sports celebrities. There was also a citation from the city, commending him for his ghetto sports-clinic work. Lieutenant Dante eyed a photo of Barry and Willie Cintron, standing together in the stern well of a deep-sea fishing rig. There were other boats crowding the Florida marina behind them.

"His first spring training, Lieutenant. The Royals took a good look and sent him down to Double-A. He had a change-up that was unhittable, even back then, but trouble finding the strike zone with it."

Dante nodded and let his gaze meet Barry's eyes. He was a good-looking man, Zajac thought. Dirty-blondish hair, a good, tough jaw, and cool blue-gray eyes. The color of a stormy sea.

"Tell us why you don't think he killed himself, Mr. Zajac. Specifically."

Barry outlined the same reservations he'd detailed to Commissioner Mintoff and Chief Lieberman. Before seeing them that morning, he'd made a few calls to confirm certain suspicions. It still wasn't time to play that hand. Not yet.

"As far as who he was with the night he died? All I know is he had dinner with his agent. The president of an Hispanic food distributor was there, too. And somebody from the network. Willie'd signed with the food people to do some commercials. Later he had a couple friends from the old neighborhood up to his room. You've probably already seen that in your homicide squad's report."

"Any idea what the dinner was about?" Dante asked.

Zajac shook his head. "Some public-service campaign the network is doing. That's all I know."

"What about these old friends?" Richardson asked. "You ever meet any of them?"

"I can only guess. The guys he used to hang with were a pretty tight-knit bunch. His brother Hector, for one. A couple cousins, but it's hard to tell who is and isn't related up there. *Everyone's* an uncle or a cousin."

"It says in the file that at least one player from the Royals dropped in on them. You talk to any of them?" Richardson wondered.

Zajac shook his head. "They were on a bus to the airport almost as soon as the last out was called. I wanted to talk with Willie's catcher, Terry Marshall. They were pretty close. I never got the chance."

Richardson made a note in the little leather-bound notebook he carried. Dante focused on Barry's gambling angle.

"How much do you know about the New York bookie scene, Mr. Zajac?"

Barry studied the lieutenant's face, trying to decide how forthcoming he should be at this juncture. He was a tough one to read, played his cards close to the vest. "Less than I wish I did right now," he lied. "I hear things. I see the same faces here and there, boxing down in Atlantic City, some of the bigger races out at Aqueduct and Belmont Park. They show up in the halls outside the skyboxes at Shea, Giants, and Yankee Stadium, too.''

"Faces but not names." Dante didn't ask it as a question.

"I'm sure I could find out who most of them are."

Dante's expression softened as he continued to meet Barry's gaze. "If you have any entrées into that world, they could be useful, Barry. Our directive is to keep it quiet, to poke around and see what we stir up. You should feel free to do the same." It was Barry now, not Mr. Zajac. "If it's indicated, we'll bring our Organized Crime Control Bureau into it, but that's down the road. First, let's spend a few days seeing where we get on our own."

"The commissioner must be even more afraid of publicity than I thought," Zajac observed. "Aren't elections a wonderful thing?"

Dante smiled. "Homicide or no homicide, there's no going back and replaying that last game, Barry. The Yanks are in and K.C. sits home in front of the tube. But yeah, adverse publicity is something the city would like to avoid."

"Especially during an election year."

"There's that, too. But here in this room, all three of us have the same objective. Richardson and I want to know if someone murdered Willie Cintron because it's our job. You? You want to know because Willie Cintron was your friend."

Zajac remained cautious. "I guess I could hook up with a few people, see what they know. I've got a buddy here does investigative features. Mitch Shimizu. He's good. Maybe he'll have an idea or two. What about your end?"

"We can probably find something to keep us busy," Dante replied. "You uncover anything suspicious, don't do anything stupid. Got it?"

Zajac bristled. "Like what, Lieutenant?"

"Like deciding to John Wayne it. Those were blanks the Duke was dodging. Someone was desperate enough to kill once, he'll kill again. The second time it seems to get easier."

Chapter ▪ 5

ANY THREADS OF CONTINUITY RUNNING THROUGH THE last twenty-four hours of Joe Dante's life were not ones he contemplated with joy. His girlfriend had left, just like she had on other occasions over the past five years. This time the parting was friendly, but in her absence, the memories of past partings lingered. Finding willing bedmates was not a problem. It never had been. For Dante, it was a lack of romantic stability that was the problem. Rosa Losada was as close as he'd come to it, but with a history of more ups and downs than a ride on the Coney Island Cyclone. Rosa's departure made a part of Dante feel instantly alone in the world.

Another thread of continuity in Dante's life was homicide. He'd known them in all shapes and sizes, but today's felt different. Yesterday, he'd mourned to see a bright young star fall as yet another victim to drugs. It sickened him to imagine how much Willie Cintron and fans of the game had been denied as a result of that tragedy. Now, if Zajac's suspicions proved accurate, something much worse than sex, drugs, or a gambling scandal had invaded the friendly confines of the ballpark.

When Dante and Richardson called ahead to the morgue, pathologist Rocky Conklin suggested they pick up sandwiches. They arrived at the East Thirtieth Street and First

Avenue medical examiner's office, early afternoon. Now the three men sat eating around Conklin's basement-office desk. Rocky, for years their pathologist of preference, occupied the desk chair, his feet up and ankles crossed. With his sandwich paper spread over the Metro section of the *Times,* he munched contentedly on a liverwurst on rye. Joe and Jumbo occupied chairs out front of the desk, Dante halfway through a turkey on whole wheat and Richardson at work on a salad. The subject was yesterday's rush autopsy of Willie Cintron.

"No sooner do I point to the lack of needle marks than Ottomanelli shrugs it off . . . like it's hey, no big deal, first-time intravenous users die of massive overdoses, matter of routine."

There was a professional's disdain for the unprofessional in Conklin's tone. Dante couldn't blame him. Rocky had his irreverent side—as evidenced by the chunk of human skull he used as an ashtray for his perpetually smoldering cigars—but when it came to sweating the details, he was the consummate pro. Dante knew that Frank Ottomanelli was not Gus Lieberman's choice for whip of Manhattan South Homicide. Years ago, while PC Anton Mintoff was still in uniform, he was boss of the 109 Precinct in Flushing, Queens. Ottomanelli was a young ass-kissing rookie who'd made it clear he was headed for the top in a hurry. Then-captain Mintoff became his rabbi. Big Tony was famous for slotting his protégés into high-profile positions, regardless of their qualifications. Ottomanelli had been awarded his gold detective's shield just six years ago, and Dante knew for a fact that Frank was being groomed for one deputy-chief job or another. He needed a posting like this on his résumé, and the command of Manhattan South Homicide just happened to be handy the last time he came loose.

"So what'd you find once you got Cintron on the slab?" Jumbo asked.

"Along drug lines? Not enough to make me feel any better about them. In beautiful shape, this kid, with a draft horse's heart and not a single internal abnormality."

Dante noticed the way Rocky's brow was knit, and dug in. "What's bothering you, Rock? Other than the lack of needle marks?"

"I found a couple other things, cowboy. Toxicology spotted antihistamines at surprisingly high levels. Right there alongside the opiate and a little alcohol."

"Antihistamines. You mean like Contac?" Richardson asked.

Conklin shrugged. "Maybe. But more likely something along the lines of liquid Benadryl, administered in strength. It made me curious enough to go back in. Take some sinus tissue and have a closer look."

"What would that tell you?" Joe wondered.

"Whether or not he had any significant allergies, the kind that would justify him taking one of those preparations. Nothing. I know allergic tissue when I see it. He had none."

Joe waved what remained of his half sandwich in the air between them. "So, at least so far as you can tell, Cintron took antihistamines for no apparent reason."

"You got it."

"In levels high enough to do what? Make him drowsy maybe?"

Conklin grunted. "From the blood levels Toxicology measured? They estimate he ingested close to a hundred milligrams. At regular, commercially available strength, that's something like two and a half tablespoons. Drowsy? That much antihistamine, reacting with the alcohol in his system? He had to be semicomatose."

Jumbo had a forkful of salad halfway to his mouth. He

lowered it back to the clear plastic container in his lap. "You think someone else coulda administered it. Without him knowing. What's that shit taste like?"

Rocky shrugged. "Not so bad. Kids'll take it, no problem. The evidence in the room says it was either beer or rum he drank. Rum might mask the taste entirely."

"Wait till he nodded off," Jumbo mused. "Fill a spike. Pop him in the arm with enough to kill him and walk away."

"Here's another thing you're gonna find interesting," Conklin added. "I found what looked like fingernail scratches across the backs of both his shoulders. Nothing heavy, but enough to make me curious. I combed through his pubic hair and put a couple that fell loose under the microscope. Guess what?"

"No shit?" Dante demanded. He felt his interest level surge.

"Yep. Half dozen of them all had the same owner, and it wasn't him. Depending how far you guys get, those loose hairs might come in handy. The lady who left them behind may not be the person who killed him, but she might know who did."

Dante mulled over this pronouncement. "You said it like homicide is a foregone conclusion, Rock. At least in your mind."

"I'm saying something isn't right here, cowboy. How they are killed is my bailiwick. Who killed them is yours. This guy pushed that plunger home on himself, I'd be very surprised. No matter what Frank Ottomanelli thinks."

Debbie DeLong didn't know the word "symbiosis," but she understood give-and-take. That was the key to enrichment and survival.

Freddy Mendoza had her standing, face to the full-length mirror alongside his bed, as he watched himself caress her breasts from behind. He liked mirrors, liked watching himself. He took pains to direct her, making sure he always had the best possible vantage.

"What you think he'd do, he could see us right now?" Freddy spoke in a whisper, his lips close to her right ear as he lifted one of her breasts to hold it in his open palm.

"The same thing you'd do if you were him," she replied. "Kill me and cut your balls off."

Freddy chuckled. "But he ain' gonna find out, is he?" He dropped the breast to grab her hips and grind his loins against her. "Turn sideways an' bend over."

At least he was predictable. She moved to comply, reaching for her ankles and closing her eyes. "How much longer you gonna let him run open throttle, Freddy? He's outta control."

"Long as he's useful. You like this?"

"Oh God, yes."

"Freddy Mendoza, he fuck like bull."

Almost exactly like a bull, she thought. And mercifully, with as much haste and as little ceremony. Those goddamned fingernails of his, as long and sharp as a woman's, bit into the flesh of her hips as he jammed himself against her. Suddenly his breathing became labored. Then, just as quickly, he was spent. One violent shudder and he backed away to head for the bath. That was also predictable. As soon as Mendoza did his business, he had to wash all trace of it away.

Debbie opened her eyes and straightened to survey herself in the mirror. Not too much the worse for wear, reddened nail marks along her pelvic bones notwithstanding. Once she heard the shower door click closed and the water start to run, she got down on her knees and dragged the cardboard carton from beneath the bed. It was packed with bundles of large bills, more than most bank tellers see in a year. Mendoza dumped his skim from cartel receipts here, and his greed was stronger than his accounting methods. Debbie first suspected he had this stash when she saw him sneak a bundle of hundreds from the daily take six months ago. She'd let Mendoza seduce her so she could find his cash. It took a month of visits to find it, but once she did, she'd built her nest with the patience of a bird. One trip after another to the twig pile. At last accounting, she'd fucked this clown fourteen times, to the tune of seventy thousand dollars, or five grand a shot.

By the time the shower shut off, Debbie was dressed, today's packet of fifty one-hundred-dollar bills stuffed into her panties. She slung the strap of her handbag over her shoulder as she advanced on the bathroom door to knock. "Gotta go, Freddy."

Mendoza jerked open the door, his long curls dripping water while he toweled his most prized possession dry. "So soon? Why not you stay for a drink?"

"I've got a go-see and I'm already late. *Ciao*." She leaned in to kiss him, darting a hand beneath his towel. "You've got my number."

One trip to the twig pile at a time.

Midafternoon, Dante and Richardson found themselves back in their SID cubicle office. While Dante had a copy of the Cintron file spread before him and scribbled notes to himself, Jumbo was on the horn trying to locate Kansas City Royals catcher Terry Marshall. So far Jumbo had spoken to the American League office here in New York, the Royals front office in Kansas City, and finally the Royals director of player personnel. To avoid raising anxiety, he'd spun a yarn about routine follow-up questions in preparation for the medical examiner's inquest, busywork mostly, but standard operating procedure.

After eventually obtaining Marshall's home number in the Overland Park suburb of Kansas City, Kansas, Richardson took a break. He replaced the receiver in its cradle, rubbed his phone ear vigorously, and heaved himself to his feet to fill his coffee mug. "How you set?" he asked Dante.

Joe looked up, saw Richardson cup in hand, and shook his head. "I'm fine. Thanks. Sounds like you're making headway."

"If he ain't gone off somewhere to lick his wounds." Jumbo stopped at the coffee machine and poured himself half a cup. Last physical, the doctor said he was drinking too much coffee. Cutting back was easier said than done. Richardson was meeting him halfway. In the subsequent weeks the fight against creeping fatigue had been a constant one. "This morning, Bernice mentioned Rosa's leaving for the month. Told me to have you check your schedule, invite you out to dinner."

Joe was back with his nose buried in that file. "Sounds good."

"How 'bout Thursday?"

"Fine." Joe was writing another note to himself and didn't bother to consult his schedule. "I want to interview the hotel staff, Beasley. Check out the comings and goings on that floor. Willie might've ordered room service. I want to poke into that early dinner he had, too. The one his agent, the president of the food label, and the ad sales exec from the network had with him."

Jumbo resumed his chair. "Zajac mentioned a public-service campaign. What you s'pose that was about?"

"Doesn't say in the file. Ottomanelli and his crew didn't find it all that interesting, I guess."

"It say anything about who, besides his brother, partied with him later?"

"Just that Marshall claims he had a beer and stayed less than half an hour. A couple of other unidentified Hispanic males were in the room, too."

"Really went all out, didn't they?"

Dante dropped his pen and eased back. "To investigate a suicide? One they caught early Sunday morning while the rest of the world was either sleeping in or reading the funnies? This is Frank Ottomanelli we're talking about. How'd you make out with the catcher?"

"About to call him now."

Monday morning, when Royals catcher Terry Marshall had stepped into the bathroom to empty his bladder, he experienced a burning in his urethra that nearly sent him through the roof. Because his wife Tina was still asleep in the adjoining bedroom, he'd bitten his tongue bloody and resisted screaming. At nine o'clock he complained about the discomfort he was feeling in his injured little finger and announced he was going to have the team doctor take a look at it. That was five hours ago. He'd since gone to see the doctor and endured a lecture about having unprotected sex in the age of AIDS. Especially in New York, of all places. Terry couldn't say for sure that New York was where he'd picked up his current case of gonorrhea, but it was a good bet. When he wasn't on the road, Tina kept him on a tight leash. It was the price he paid for having an energetic, community-minded wife and model family situation to come home to. Tina packed and unpacked his bags when he went on road trips, so he was forced to cop condoms somewhere en route.

All the way home from the doctor's office in downtown Kansas City, Terry kicked himself for not picking up any rubbers before Saturday night. Like most pro athletes, the Magic Johnson news of a couple years back had shaken Terry. Still, after the team's game-five loss in K.C. on Friday and the hurried trip back to New York, he'd had other things besides rubbers on his mind. Of course, they'd also slipped his mind before the opening game of the series in New York, ten days ago. So who knew when he'd actually contracted this bug? What he did know was that a peck on the cheek wasn't the end of it when he and Tina got in bed last night. Any bug of his was now a bug of hers, and he was in no position to afford a divorce. He made too damned much money.

Tina was out when Terry returned home, midafternoon. As he tried to figure how he was going to break his news, Marshall grabbed a Coke from the icebox—no alcohol for the next fourteen days—and took it out to the table beside the pool. It was a nice day for mid-October, with temperatures hovering in the high seventies. For a moment his thoughts ran off to San Francisco, and how it would feel to step onto the field Thursday night for game one of the World Series. If the Royals had won that game in New York, if that fool Willie hadn't gone and killed himself, they would have flown directly from La Guardia to SFO. Could be he might have found excuses enough to avoid sleeping with Tina for the next two weeks. Could be the moon is made of green cheese.

The cordless extension, set on the table at his elbow, rang. Terry picked up, hoping to God it wasn't some local sports reporter calling for his thoughts on how it felt to lose the big one.

"Hello."

"This the Marshall residence?" The voice was deep, the tone self-assured. A brother.

"That's right. Who's this?"

"Detective Lieutenant Richardson. NYPD Special Investigation Division. Is this Mr. Terry Marshall?"

"Speaking. What can I do you, Lieutenant?" Terry was searching his recollection for a Lieutenant Richardson. After he found Willie dead like that, there were an awful lot of cops. Dozens of them. It was hard to keep track.

"I'm doing some follow-up work on Willie Cintron, Mr. Marshall. I understand you were in his room with him and a number of other people, Saturday night before he died.''

"Half hour at most, Lieutenant. No more'n that. One beer and I was outta there.''

There was a pause from down the line. Marshall tried to imagine what his caller looked like. A black New York detective lieutenant. He sounded big.

"Why was that, Mr. Marshall?''

The cops working the scene had probably found traces of the pot smoked in Willie's room. Terry wanted to make sure he established the right distance from it, and the lieutenant was giving him that chance.

"A couple of them clowns was blowing dope in there, Lieutenant. Not an orgy or nothin', but still. Reefer's reefer. I got my career to think about. For the record, it made Willie more'n a little nervous, too.''

"So he didn't join them?''

Marshall snorted. "Willie? He drank a rum and Coke now'n then. That's what surprised me so much, when it turn out he'd stuck hisself like that. It weren't like him. Not the Willie Cintron I knowed.''

The lieutenant moved right on. "Who were the other people he was partying with, Mr. Marshall? Other teammates?''

"Nuh-uh. Friends of his. From the neighborhood up where he from. One was his brother. Hector. 'Nother guy, Felipe, he called his cousin. I think the third one, he Felipe's brother. Can't say for sure.''

"Whose dope was it?''

"The reefer?''

"You saw something else?''

"Not a chance. I did, I'd be outta there faster than that. The ganj was Hector's, I think.'' He stopped to search his memory. "Yeah. He had the bag, and he's the one rolled it.''

"Did Willie say anything about meeting anyone later? A woman, maybe?"

Terry felt a twinge below his belt. "Willie? Nuh-uh. He was always real secretlike 'bout any tail he got. I think he worried 'bout one a' them hooking him for all his bread. You start pulling down two, three mil a year, and you ain't married yet? They swarm, Lieutenant."

Their conversation didn't go much further, with Lieutenant Richardson moving through several items from the statement Terry had given the homicide squad. In the end the cop asked Terry if he would remain available for the next few days, or was he planning a vacation? Terry told him he and Tina had plans to spend a couple weeks in Hawaii early in November. Nothing before that. He'd been planning to play in the World Series right about now.

After hanging up, Terry sat staring at the sparkling surface of his pool and wondered where he *would* be a couple days hence. In intensive care at the local hospital most likely, hoping the microsurgery would take. Once Tina found out she had the clap, she was going to cut his balls off.

Chapter ∎6

AFTER WORKING TWENTY-SEVEN YEARS ON THE SPORTS desk of the *Daily News,* Barry Zajac had developed a Rolodex fat with contacts in every nook and cranny of the New York sporting scene. Late last night he'd called Eric Boone, a onetime across-the-hall neighbor in the early 1970s. At that time Boone was also a law student at NYU who worked his way through school as a midtown numbers runner. During a summer internship, Boone started taking side action on his own at the law firm that employed him, and then with the lawyers' friends, and friends of friends. When Boone eventually passed the New York Bar exam, he decided, rather than practice law, to make book full-time. Through those contacts made as a law student, he'd stumbled on a treasure trove of Manhattan business types, all eager to lay a few bucks on a pro football game, a horse, or a little college basketball. Not much was known about Eric Boone's private life, but Barry knew Boone had moved to an apartment in a high-security Fifth Avenue building. Supposedly, Eric was still single.

At three o'clock that Monday afternoon, Boone called back and suggested Barry visit him at home. Fifteen minutes later Zajac departed a cab on the corner of Fifth Avenue and Seventy-third Street. As he approached the awning of Eric's address the uniformed doorman examined him with a critical eye.

"Yes, sir?"

"Mr. Zajac, here to see Mr. Boone. Seven-B."

The doorman, judged by his demeanor, was a retired member of New York's Finest. Now he sniffed the air, wearing an ornery old beat cop's frown of suspicion. "Knows you're coming?"

Barry nodded. "He does."

"Wait here."

The man moved indoors to lift the receiver of the building intercom and punch a button connecting him to 7-B. All the while he stood with one arm folded across his chest, free hand wedged beneath his other elbow. His eyes never left the supplicant on his stoop. It was easy for Barry to understand why Boone would pick a building like this for his residence. The last thing a bookie needs guarding his first line of defense is warmth and hospitality.

A moment later the doorman emerged to wave Zajac inside.

"Elevator's straight ahead and on your right. He knows where to take you."

The lobby was one of those columned, high-ceilinged affairs with acres of shiny marble, a decor that robber barons and others of their ilk seem to favor. As Zajac strode across it the soles of his beat-down loafers echoed impressively through that cavernous interior. Once Barry stepped out onto the seventh floor, the elevator operator continued to sit perched on his stool inside the car, door open and watching until a maid answered Eric's door. The second line of defense.

The maid showed Zajac through an entry gallery done in water-stained silk and hung with several horse-racing paintings. She led him to an office dominated by six televisions. All six sets were on, each carrying a different sporting event. At the moment Barry counted four horse races, a soccer game, and women's tennis. He found Boone seated at a desk facing them, the walls surrounding covered with museum-quality pieces of sports memorabilia. Eric rose to greet him, his hand outstretched to shake. There was a time, early in Boone's law-student bookmaking career, when he'd let himself get dangerously overexposed taking Stanley Cup action. When the Montreal Canadiens unexpectedly upset the Philadelphia Flyers in 1976, Boone was faced with either paying his debts or having his legs broken. It just happened that Zajac was in a position to lend him fifteen thousand dollars, the money paid Barry as settlement for injuries sustained in a cab accident. That loan saved Boone's legs, and maybe his life.

"Barry, my friend. Please. Make yourself comfortable."

Eric indicated a tufted leather divan set perpendicular to his desk and then took a club chair opposite. "I'm not sure I conveyed my sentiments properly on the phone. I'm terribly sorry about what happened to your young friend. Such a waste."

"You have any luck with your inquiries?"

Boone nodded. "You're right about one guess you made. Too many people had too much to lose if Cintron lived to pitch that game. Still, I found no one with more exposure than the man I mentioned to you earlier."

Last night, Zajac had asked Boone to investigate any possible connection between a party or parties exposed to huge losses and Willie's death. Today, Eric reached Barry before he left his girlfriend's apartment for work. What Eric told him had emboldened Zajac enough to approach Commissioner Mintoff.

"You never mentioned a name, Eric."

Boone smiled and gestured to a tray on a nearby table. It held several crystal decanters and half a dozen glasses. "Something to cut the chill?"

"What chill? It's like Miami Beach in here."

"So they don't have a stiff nip in Miami now and then?"

"A short scotch'd be nice. Sure."

Boone poured them both drinks. "It isn't the *amount* this individual had to lose, but what he could *afford* to lose. That and the nature of certain connections he's said to have."

"I'm listening." Barry sipped at a very smooth single malt that he lacked the experience to identify.

"He's not a client of mine, you understand. I've only heard of him from one of my, ah, copractitioners. The man is owner of an exotic-car showroom on Northern Boulevard in Douglaston. Sells Ferraris, Lotuses, and other rich men's toys. From what I hear, the lingering recession has taken a deep bite into his sales."

"And he's a gambler."

Boone nodded. "Big time. The type who never knows when to quit and always believes the big score is just around the corner."

"How much, if the Yanks had lost?"

"Two hundred thirty thousand."

Zajac whistled. "That he couldn't *afford* to lose, right?"

"Worse than that. He's already up to his ass and sinking further with every step. The people he owes keep carrying him because he's been good for it in the past. Now they're getting impatient. It's not my source who holds the paper, but a larger interest this source often takes action for."

"Larger interest?"

"One you don't want to push too far. By the time the Royals made it as far as game seven, our sports-car purveyor was no doubt shitting little green apples."

"So it's not just what he stood to lose, but who he stood to lose it to."

"Correct." Boone reached to retrieve a single sheet of paper from his desk. As Barry received it he saw that all the information it contained was typed rather than hand-written. "We never had this conversation, Barry. Read that and make whatever notes you need. It can't leave here. If they ever knew I gave you this, Rio wouldn't be far enough to run."

"You mentioned certain connections in his past. What kind?"

"Criminal. It's all in there. We're talking about more than just motive to kill your friend, right? The will *and* the way?"

Zajac scanned the information on the sheet. "I owe you," he murmured.

"No, Barry," Boone corrected. "I've owed you. For almost twenty years. I know how much you cared about this kid. Let's hope this helps."

The car dealer's name was Berga. Miles Berga. Barry wondered what sort of name that was.

To judge by the decor of super-agent Rob Ironstone's offices, Joe Dante could see how much the world of sports agenting had changed in the past twenty-four years. At eighteen, when Dante emerged from a grueling citywide tournament as New York's new Golden Gloves middle-weight champion, he'd been approached by several men interested in sponsoring him in the world of professional boxing. Almost uniformly, they had a seedy, snake-oil-salesman look about them. A couple were young, eager-beaver types. Others had spent years developing high-sheen veneers that were tough as tungsten. Joe passed on them and a pro ring career.

Late Monday afternoon, Dante the police detective re-called that other life as he stood on the sidewalk outside the SoHo building housing Rob Ironstone's agency. Two decades ago there were no sports agents working out of SoHo lofts. This one was situated above a prestigious art gallery. Many of the old lines dividing areas of commerce had been erased or at least obscured now. This was a world in which actors and athletes earned astronomical sums endorsing clothing, where fashion models enjoyed the same recognition as movie idols, where sports stars authored best-selling tell-all books and models graced the pages of the sporting press's hottest-selling magazine issue. It took a new breed of power broker to cut these deals—part huckster, part lawyer, and part financier.

The bright-eyed Ivory Girl behind the reception desk upstairs examined Dante from floor to hairline as he approached.

"Yes, sir. Can I help you?"

He could almost hear her memory click in and begin to scour the banks. He was too old to be a current hot property. Otherwise, he had the look; perhaps a retired player interested in doing endorsement work.

"Detective Lieutenant Dante. NYPD. I spoke with Mr. Ironstone twenty minutes ago."

End of search. He watched an almost imperceptible attitude shift. He was no one *really* important. She could let her guard down a bit. "Yes, of course. He's on a call to Los Angeles. It will be just a moment. Would you like coffee?"

"No, thanks." He eased away to examine more closely a basketball jersey in a glass-covered frame. It was one of New Jersey Senator Bill Bradley's from his former career as a New York Knick. There were other pieces of memorabilia framed around the reception area, and Dante glanced at several more before Ironstone appeared.

Fairly tall, at a shade over six foot, the spare-framed agent wore a Ralph Lauren polo shirt with the tails hanging loose, gray chinos, and high-top Nike "Pump" basketball shoes. His curly dark hair was cropped short, he was deeply tanned and wore no jewelry other than a wedding ring and a wristwatch with a brown leather band.

"Rob Ironstone, Lieutenant." He shook hands as Dante turned. "You said on the phone you're conducting a follow-up investigation of Willie's death? What does that mean?"

He indicated the door he'd just appeared through and led Joe toward it. As soon as the receptionist saw them headed that way, she was on her feet to hand her boss several messages. She'd looked taller seated. Dressed in a short, hip-hugging skirt and flattering cashmere sweater, she cut an attractive figure. It reminded Dante that Rosa had left for nearly three weeks, yesterday morning.

While passing through into the agency's inner sanctum, Joe answered Ironstone's question with a question of his own. "How long did you know Willie Cintron?"

"He was a junior at George Washington High when we first met."

"No kidding? Isn't that unusual? An agent of your caliber meeting with a high-school kid?"

Ironstone walked shoulder to shoulder with Joe down a wide hallway hung with contemporary art. After all that memorabilia decorating the reception area, Dante found the change intriguing.

The agent shrugged. "A little, maybe. Under usual circumstances. But these were hardly usual. Barry Zajac from the *Daily News* was taking Willie under his wing. He wanted to impress the kid with how much he stood to lose by screwing up."

So that was the link. Zajac was proving an interesting study.

"He asked me to take a look at Willie," Ironstone continued. "To tell him what I thought of his prospects."

"At sixteen? Wouldn't that be a little speculative?"

"For most kids? A total hand-job." They reached the doorway to a big, airy office lit by huge floor-to-ceiling windows facing east to the street outside. There were a lot of photographs of Ironstone and his clients on the walls. Dante took it all in as Ironstone waved to a comfortable-looking leather sofa and took a seat behind his desk. "But I respected Barry's opinion, Lieutenant. At least enough to waste an afternoon. Turned out it wasn't a waste at all. Willie Cintron was the most gifted sixteen-year-old I've ever seen. Bar none."

That sofa was comfortable, butter soft. "How does that work?" Joe eased back and hauled one ankle up over a knee. "Did you sign him then and there?"

Ironstone smiled. "I told him he ever decided to get serious, make ten, maybe twenty million bucks, I'd like a chance to represent him. As far as Zajac was concerned, it had the desired effect."

"And later he took you up on your offer? Came to you for representation?"

"When he was eighteen. Right before the annual baseball draft. He'd heard from a number of people, including his buddy Zajac, that he was definitely going in the first round, maybe even the first pick overall. It turned out that's exactly where he was taken."

Dante tried to imagine what that might feel like. To be the number-one draft pick of all the kids in the world who dreamed of playing major-league baseball. "How was your relationship with him, Mr. Ironstone? Good? I understand you had dinner with him and some other people Saturday night."

"That's right. With Jaime Madera, president of Hola International, the Hispanic food packager. Him and a woman from one of the network stations here in New York. I *liked* Willie, Lieutenant. And I won't bullshit you, claiming I feel the same about all my clients. A lot of them are a prima donna pain in my fanny. That doesn't mean I don't work just as hard for them. I do."

Dante had read plenty of negative press about several of the celebrities Rob Ironstone was posed with on the surrounding walls. He also had a pretty good idea what sort of money they made. He didn't doubt the agent's claim for a minute. Ironstone was famous for getting his clients top dollar for their talents, no matter what their personality flaws.

"Why the president of Hola International?"

"Willie had an endorsement contract with them."

"Ah. Joe Montana does diet Pepsi, Magic Johnson does diet Coke, and Willie Cintron does Hola."

Ironstone smiled. "You're thinking, not in quite the same league, right?" He reached across to his desk for a pack of chewing gum, offered Dante a stick, which Joe declined, and then peeled and popped one into his mouth. "You have any idea how many Hispanics there are in the U.S. today, Lieutenant? Twenty million. Every Hispanic in America knew who Willie Cintron was. Not just because he threw a baseball, but because every Hispanic neighborhood and TV station in the country has a Hola billboard and runs Hola ads."

Ironstone chewed furiously for a moment while Dante noted the name of Hola's president in his notebook. "I see what you're getting at."

"You increase a client's visibility, you increase his overall worth, Lieutenant. That's what I'm getting at. In his prime, a top performer in any major sport can make as much or more off the field as he does on it. It all depends on how his handlers market him. Willie Cintron was goodlooking, affable, and had his whole life in baseball ahead of him. The sky was the limit for that kid."

"Is there anything you saw that told you this might happen? That something wasn't right in his life?"

Ironstone snorted. "You mean did he seem suicidal Saturday night? If Willie was suicidal, I've got a twelve-inch schlong. That dinner meeting was set up to discuss a WRBS community-service broadcast campaign. Specifically, Willie's participation in it, acting as their spokesman.''

''That's why this woman from the network was there?''

Ironstone nodded. ''From their local station. To create a stay-in-school campaign that Hola had agreed to sponsor.''

''Local kid from the neighborhood makes good and wants to give something back.''

''Exactly. It didn't hurt that we were set to renegotiate our Hola endorsement contract, Madera was already talking good numbers. We weren't planning to dicker. Willie liked the idea of doing public-service work, so it was a nice, friendly dinner.''

''So if he killed himself, you believe he hadn't intended to.''

''Why would he, Lieutenant? You heard what I jus—'' Ironstone stopped. ''What do you mean *if* he killed himself? I didn't think there was any question.''

''You mentioned Barry Zajac, Mr. Ironstone. You know, to hear it from him, there's no way Willie Cintron would have willingly stuck a spike in his arm.''

Dante watched Ironstone's face closely. One thing that bothered him was the agent's failure to express any deep sense of loss.

''Barry thinks he was *murdered?*''

Dante didn't reply.

''Look, Lieutenant. Barry's an idealist. I'm a pragmatist. Why would anyone want to murder Willie Cintron? Look, I deal with people who are products of that kind of upbringing every day. Some forces are stronger than they are. I'm a student of human weakness. I need to be to survive in this business. Believe me. I've seen it all.''

''We should compare notes sometime.''

Ironstone smiled. ''You know what I'm talking about? The weakness that comes when a ghetto kid gets more money dumped on him than he's ever dreamed about. It's like being hit by a truck. Willie made a mistake Saturday night, Lieutenant. It's the same mistake a lot of them make, and it only takes one. Saturday night, Willie thought he was invincible.''

Chapter ▪ 7

RATHER THAN SPEND THAT FIRST AFTERNOON OF THEIR INvestigation searching Central Records for every Hector Cintron and Felipe Doe with a sheet on him in the five boroughs, Jumbo Richardson decided to take a drive. He went on the theory that most of Willie Cintron's homeboy pals hadn't drifted far from the roost, and guessed he would waste a lot less time by going up to the old neighborhood. Willie was raised in Washington Heights, an area in the northern reaches of Manhattan with a largely Caribbean Hispanic population. If Hector Cintron and his pals once engaged in car theft, the detectives at the Three-Four North station house would have their sheets already on hand.

It was late in the day by the time Jumbo aimed it north. At the convergence of the FDR Drive with the Triboro Bridge, rush-hour volume had built to a snarl. Jumbo spent an eternity listening to callers jawing with the jocks on all-sports WFAN radio, the majority of them elated that the Yankees had made it into the Series, the tragedy of Willie Cintron's death notwithstanding. The flow of traffic up the Harlem River Drive past the Triboro Bridge proved more agreeable. Rather than push his luck all the way to the George Washington Bridge approach, Richardson left the drive at 155th Street and drove the remainder of his journey inland.

The building at Broadway and 183rd Street that houses the Thirty-fourth North Precinct looks to be constructed from that same batch of brown brick used to construct the One Police Plaza headquarters building downtown. It is of that same contemporary design, with a fortresslike facade setting it apart from the colorful storefront decorations of the surrounding neighborhood. While parking out front, Jumbo observed a group of fresh-faced young uniforms lining the rail above the front-entrance access ramp. The scene had a discomforting us-and-them feel to it that was unfortunate. Those guys up there lining that rail were visitors to this neighborhood, sent here to keep the peace. While they ogled passing women, local residents kept an uneasy distance. Up here in Washington Heights, tension between the citizenry and the police had been cinched a turn or two tighter by a line-of-duty shooting a couple of years back. There were conflicting stories about its justification. Several nights of rioting were the immediate upshot. It created an ugliness of which all parties involved were still very wary.

Lieutenant Karl Lulevich, whip of the Thirty-fourth North detective squad, was located in the upstairs men's room after a brief search. He emerged into the hall outside buckling his belt and complaining about last night's dinner.

"I shoulda fucking known it. Minute I ate that first fucking forkful. You tell these people easy on the heat, they still figure your gut is lined with asbestos. Jesus. I been on the pot nonstop since I rolled outta bed this noon."

The balding, heavyset whip led Richardson into his office off the squad. He had fingers so short, Richardson wondered how he did the simple things in life like tie his shoes. From the chair Jumbo took, he could see out into the room through a glass partition. There were three four-to-midnight detectives assembled around the table, all in shirt sleeves with jackets hung over the backs of their chairs. One read a file while two watched the five o'clock news.

"So what brings you up this way, Lou?" Lulevich asked. "It ain't often we're visited by one a' you SID guys. What is it? The Dominican and Chinese not gettin' along again?"

In recent years a citywide joint federal and local narcotics task force, run out of the new DEA headquarters at 99 Tenth Avenue, had noticed increased cooperation between a Dominican street distribution network and an Asian supply cartel. Their drug of preference was heroin, imported from the Golden Triangle by the Chinese gangs. The relationship was always tenuous at best. When conflicts between the two factions erupted, they were generally quick, vicious bloodbaths.

"Not today, thank God," Jumbo replied. Lulevich had some rough edges, but Richardson knew of his reputation as a day-in-and-day-out, lunchbox-and-shiny-elbows cop who gave a shift's work and more for his pay. Orders to conduct this investigation on the quiet notwithstanding, it wouldn't be a good idea to leave anyone that streetwise out of the loop. Sometime later, when the Thirty-fourth North squad might be able to help him, Jumbo knew a decision like that could come back to haunt. He took a moment to bring Lulevich up to speed.

"So what we'd like to do now is isolate this brother and cousin," he concluded. "Find out who the cousin is and then figure who the third guy in the room visiting Cintron was."

Lulevich nodded, stood, and tugged open his office door. He called to one of the three detectives seated at the table outside. "Guitan. C'min here a sec." He turned back to Jumbo. "I got the most time up here of anybody in the station house. Five years in blues and ten more in plainclothes. Pete's only been here five and knows twice as much as me. It's his turf."

Pete Guitan was the detective seen scanning that file outside as Jumbo first sat. Now, when they shook hands, Richardson was surprised by the strength of the slender Hispanic man's grip and the intensity of his flashing dark eyes.

"Lieutenant Richardson is wonderin' what we know about some mutt name of Hector Cintron, the dead ballplayer's brother. He's also curious about a cousin of theirs. First name Felipe." Lulevich returned to his desk. When he sat he peeled cellophane from a cheap cigar and began twirling the cigar against his tongue.

"You're gonna light that thing, I hope you do it outside in the hall," Guitan growled.

"Hector Cintron, Pete."

"Long on balls, short on brains," Guitan replied. "Couple years older than Willie. We busted them two for joyriding five, six years back. Before that white knight from the *News* took Willie under his arm. Too bad Hector couldn' throw a baseball for shit. If anybody need guidance, it was *that* stupid fuck."

"It sounds like you've run into him on more than that one occasion," Richardson observed.

"Hector? The term 'repeat offender' was invented for mutts like him. He was upstate in Fishkill till 'bout six weeks ago. First bust for sales the DA could get to stick. Sixth or seventh one we drag the mutt in for. Did a couple pretrial stretches on Rikers before that, but nothing heavier." He paused, his brow furrowing. Lulevich had introduced Richardson as an SID investigator. "This 'bout the Chinese again?"

Jumbo shrugged. "Not sure what it's about yet. Just want to talk to him. Why?"

"You mention his cousin Felipe. That would be Infante. Hector and the Asians are tight as two tits in a bra, but word we're getting? Felipe's got himself wedged crosswise with the Chinese somehow."

"I wouldn't know about that," Jumbo told him. "The two of them and another man partied with Hector's brother the night he died. Any idea how I could find them?''

''Hector'd be easiest. Through his PO, I imagine. You want, I'll call and get an address for you.''

Twenty minutes later Jumbo left the station house with an address one block east and eight blocks south, on Audubon and 175th Street. He stood at that rail overlooking the litter-strewn Broadway sidewalk and glanced at his watch. A few paces away another pair of uniforms ogled passing skirts. It was six now. His wife Bernice would be getting home from work any minute. He was still an hour away from their Fort Greene, Brooklyn, home. Time to call it a day. He would get after Hector Cintron first thing in the morning. At the hour Jumbo planned to come knocking, the man would probably still be asleep.

By now, the hookers working the corner of West Twenty-seventh Street and Eleventh Avenue outside Joe Dante's warehouse loft were accustomed to seeing a cop pull up and park his battered company car at the curb. There was a time when they would drift off a dozen yards in either direction when he appeared. Tonight, his arrival caused hardly a ripple. There were four of them working in pairs. Two stood directly outside the entrance to his building, the others standing in sneering defiance down on the corner. The black pair outside his door were transvestites, both too high to know or care what day it was. The two on the corner, one black and one white, were women. The fleshy, bleached-blond white woman dressed in a green lace bustier, garter belt, and stockings looked as hard-ridden as any Joe had seen. The black woman was younger and slender, but it wouldn't be long before the life-style caught up with her, too.

''Evenin', Officer,'' one of the transvestites purred as Joe passed. ''Anythin' I could do for you?''

''Sure,'' Joe replied. ''Watch my car.''

Dante's upstairs neighbor Diana Webster had invited him to a gallery opening in SoHo that night. The wife of Joe's landlord and best buddy, Brian Brennan, Diana was the lead singer of the hugely successful rock band Queen of Beasts. Her husband was a sculptor of some reputation, and that night's occasion was an exhibition of new paintings by their friend Charlie Fung. The mad Chinese neorealist was famous, among other reasons, for a series of stunning nudes done of Diana several years back. The opening was set for six and would go on indefinitely. Diana had suggested a seven-thirty arrival. She hated to get anywhere on time, and later suited Joe just fine.

Six o'clock was long gone by the time Dante stepped off the elevator into his still-unfinished living room. He'd had the loft space for over a year now, inheriting it raw from the earlier warehousing tenant. While he'd made great strides, completing his kitchen, the first of two baths, two bedrooms, and an open workout area, he'd left the living room and second bath for last. All of the drywall was hung and most of the built-in shelving and cabinetry complete. Among the rough edges remaining were an unfinished floor, no fixtures in the second bath, and the absence of paint.

Joe's cat, Toby, stood to stretch when the security gate over the freight elevator doors rolled back. In either an uncharacteristic show of affection or a characteristic show of hunger, he bounded down off the sofa to greet Dante as he advanced into the room. A totally deaf white Turkish Angora, Toby was a gift from Diana after Joe's former cat was killed in the firebombing of his last address. A kitten then, Toby had since grown to weigh a hefty fifteen pounds, according to his vet. Still, every time Dante saw him, Toby complained bitterly that he hadn't been fed for a week. Dante was wise to his lies.

With the contents of a cat-food can conveyed to the bowl on the kitchen floor, the phone rang. Joe straightened from scratching Toby between the ears to grab the wall-phone receiver.

"Yeah."

"Heard the elevator," Diana Webster replied. "Gimme an estimated TOD."

"Fifteen minutes? I'm too well dressed. Come on downstairs and have a beer."

Joe knew from experience that two sorts of people attended these openings: the affluent collectors of art, who dressed up, and the insiders on the SoHo scene, who dressed down. Most of the former kept the finery low-key, while the art crowd tended to take slovenly to extremes. Grime-smudged T-shirts and paint-flecked pants were too typical to make any kind of rebellious statement anymore. Dante's comment to Diana was more a jab at this trend than an announced intention to emulate it. He'd keep the sneakers and even the tweed jacket, but wanted to get out of his slacks into a pair of Levi's. Maybe change his shirt.

Diana, dressed in boots, faded jeans, a T-shirt, and navy blazer, arrived less than five minutes after her call. Forgoing the elevator, she used the backstairs and her cat-feeding key to enter and grab two bottles of beer from the kitchen. She found Joe emerging from the bedroom, handed him one bottle, and raised her own in toast.

"To our respective lovers, wherever they are."

Dante grinned and took a swig as he advanced into the living room. Before taking a seat, he punched the power button on his stereo and the play button on his cassette deck. The air was instantly filled with the scat singing of Betty Carter. Joe had always liked jazz, but considered himself a rock-and-roll kind of guy before partnering with Beasley Richardson. They'd worked together five years now, and while Dante still had a lot to learn, he was becoming a jazz devotee.

"You heard from Brian?" he asked.

Diana collapsed slouching into one of the room's several comfortable armchairs. Tall, at close to five-ten, she had an ordinary face made special by a goofy smile, and a body that made men drool. Unlike Dante's own cool, slate-blue eyes, hers ran a shade lighter.

"The Hollywood glitterati turned out in force last night. Apparently, everyone wondered where I was hiding."

Brennan was on the West Coast for the opening of a show at the Getty Museum in Malibu. He'd been there a week, supervising the installation, and was scheduled to fly to San Francisco for the first game of the World Series on Thursday. Diana was releasing a new album in two weeks and was resting up before hitting the road for a twelve-city national tour.

"How long you planning to stay tonight?" Joe asked.

Diana shrugged. "Charlie said there'll be food, but you know what that means. Depends on how hungry we get . . . and how the people-watching goes."

Charlie Fung painted women almost exclusively and ran through an extraordinary number of models. For reasons Dante couldn't fathom, a bewildering number of those models remained devoted to Fung for years afterward. Maybe it was the *way* he painted them. Joe was looking forward to the prospect of people-watching, too. Fung openings always made for an interesting mix.

They took a cab, arriving downtown on Broome Street at seven-twenty to find the opening in full swing. Fung's dealer was another of the heavy hitters in the downtown art market. That meant most of the men in Armani suits and women in Chanel outfits were sporting originals, not knock-offs. The affair was by invitation only, somewhat limiting the number of slovenly dressed wannabe art stars. A disappointed Dante thought they at least added color to these gatherings. Tonight, the SoHo contingent consisted of the artist's own ragtag circle and, of course, his models.

As a rock star and wife of a sculptor whose work was shown at a prestigious Madison Avenue gallery, Diana Webster was the sort of celebrity over whom the art set fawned. No sooner did she enter than several collectors spotted her and hurried to descend. She flashed Dante a little dismayed look and kissed his cheek.

"Rescue me?" she begged.

He grinned back. "Isn't that why you dragged me here?"

She squeezed his hand and turned away to be swallowed whole.

"This is a surprise, Lieutenant."

It came from behind Dante, a familiar voice he couldn't quite place. He turned. Facing him with a glass of red wine in one hand and a very attractive ash blonde at his side was Rob Ironstone. The agent extended a hand to shake.

"Meet Sherril Meyer. She's the woman we spoke about this afternoon. The sales rep from WRBS."

If Ironstone was surprised to meet Dante here, Joe was less surprised to see him. It was a safe bet that a sports agent who made millions and had his offices in the heart of the city's art community had interests in that direction. While walking down that hallway to Ironstone's office earlier, Joe had seen an impressive hanging of contemporary artists. He was confident there were others, hung elsewhere.

"Miss Meyer? Joe Dante," he introduced himself. "We spoke on the phone. Made an appointment for tomorrow morning."

Her handshake was firm, businesslike. Several inches shorter than the statuesque Diana, slender and handsome, the sales rep wore a short, pleated black skirt that showed off terrific legs. Joe enjoyed the direct way her intense brown eyes met his.

"This *is* a surprise, Lieutenant. And escorting the heart-throb of rock-and-roll America no less. What is it? Death threats from radical feminists?'' She gestured at the surrounding walls as she spoke.

Joe chuckled. ''Nothing that dramatic. Fung, Diana, and I are friends.'' He pointed to her near-empty glass. ''I was just headed for the bar. Refill?''

She handed the glass over. ''White wine. Thanks.''

Dante speculated on the wedding ring Ironstone wore as he collected a beer for himself and Sherril Meyer's white wine. The body language suggested Ironstone and the sales rep were more than just business acquaintances. When he returned, he found the two of them in conversation with the artist of the hour, Charlie Fung. When Joe handed Sherril her glass, Charlie registered surprise.

''You know this guy?'' he asked her.

''As a matter of fact, we just met,'' she replied.

''Well, be careful,'' he warned. ''Last year my pal Brian Brennan was working on this commission from Nissan and I lend him this beautiful model I'm crazy about. She falls in love with the Marlboro Man here and gets herself killed. Some bastard who hated his guts blew up his building.''

Sherril's eyes widened. ''*That's* how you know each other?''

While Fung explained that Dante was Brian and Diana's downstairs neighbor and close friend, she gave the subject of their discussion a closer look. To divert this attention, Dante turned to Ironstone, changing the subject.

''I noticed some of your collection in that hallway outside your office, Mr. Ironstone. That David Salle's especially nice.''

''Thanks. And call me Rob, Lieutenant. You're a collector?''

Joe grimaced. ''I wish. Charlie gave me a painting of Diana that was lost in that bombing he mentioned. So were a couple of Brian's bronzes. I'm afraid they aren't the kinds of things I can afford to replace on a cop's salary, even if they *were* replaceable.''

"He wasn't joking?" Sherril asked. "Someone really *did* blow up your building?"

"Afraid so."

Joe took a pull off his beer and let his eyes wander around the room. He saw a dealer spot Ironstone and approach to cut him from the herd. Rather than follow her date, Sherril remained behind.

"Rock stars, art stars—you know a lot of people here?" she asked.

He shook his head. "Not really. When Brennan's away, Diana drags me to these sometimes—more for the company than because she knows I'm dying to go."

"Not the regular beat for the kind of cop I'm familiar with. You keep some pretty heady company, Lieutenant."

"The way you said that makes it sound like you know a fair-size sampling."

She got a distant look in her eyes. "My daddy was a New York cop, disgraced by the Knapp Commission in 1972. A week after they forced him and his partner to put in their papers, he ate his gun. Sixteen years on the job, Lieutenant. My early childhood was filled with cops, most of them just like him."

"Jesus."

Sherril nodded. "Three months after he died, my mama married the partner. The three of us moved to Florida."

"What's your stepfather done since?" Joe's own father had also been a cop. Deceased now. He'd retired, not been drummed from the corps. Still, Joe remembered the Knapp bloodbath vividly. His dad was once ostracized by his fellow officers for refusing to go on the pad while they took money under the table as a matter of course. The worst offenders paid dearly for their sins while hundreds and maybe thousands of others received fair warning to clean up their acts. Rumor had it that Intelligence Division still had files filled with names. Many were urged to take early retirement rather than face the sort of disgrace that had prompted Sherril Meyer's father to take his life.

"He started a construction company, made a small fortune developing low-cost housing in south Dade," she replied. "In 1988 the state contractor's council named the company Builder of the Year. Then, in 1992, Hurricane Andrew blew the roofs off most everything they built." As she said it she glanced at her watch. "I'd better pry my date away from his wheeling and dealing. We've got a dinner reservation at the Union Square Café for eight."

She stuck out a hand and shook Dante's with that same firm, vigorous grip she'd used earlier.

"Nice meeting you, Sherril," he said.

"Call me Sherrie, Lieutenant. See you in the morning."

So it wasn't just a gallery stopoff on Ironstone's way home. It was dinner, too.

Chapter ■ 8

LATE MONDAY EVENING, *DAILY NEWS* INVESTIGATIVE RE-
porter Mitchell Shimizu called Barry Zajac and suggested
they link up for an early-morning run in Central Park. After
suffering chest pains ten years ago, Barry was frightened
just enough to give mortality its first real consideration. To
that point he'd played a little racquetball, but that was it.
Dispirited by an ugly divorce, he was content to drag along
from one day to the next. The chest-pain scare—later di-
agnosed as stress-related heartburn—had changed his life.
He now dragged himself from bed early every A.M. to put
in three miles around the Central Park reservoir. At least
three nights a week he hit the health club to work out. It
helped slim him some, and while he would never be a chis-
eled Greek god, his outlook on life had improved. He'd
since started the sports-clinic project, taken an interest in
the future of the city he loved.

Tuesday, when the alarm on his girlfriend Rebecca's
nightstand went off at five forty-five, Zajac killed it and
crawled from between the sheets. He dragged on his sweats,
hit the living-room floor for fifteen minutes of stretching
out, and by six-oh-five was stepping out onto the sidewalk.
From Rebecca's West Seventy-ninth Street and Central
Park West building he started east into the park. When he
returned after his run, she would be up and gone. A com-

modities trader who worked the floor of the World Trade Center exchange, Rebecca did everything in a rush. That included getting herself out the door in the morning.

Even at this early hour there were dozens of runners already on the track circuiting the reservoir. When Barry arrived, Shimizu had a foot planted high on the trunk of a maple. The compact, powerfully built Japanese-American grunted as he tried to loosen his hamstring.

"Morning, friend. This leg's *never* going to be right after that pull last year. Think I've just about got it now." Shimizu dropped the leg, stood shaking it, then nodded. "Let's do it."

They started off shoulder to shoulder, with Barry letting the investigative reporter set the pace. It was a nice crisp day, with clear skies and temperatures in the high forties. Perfect running conditions.

"So what did you learn?" Barry prodded.

Yesterday afternoon, on returning from bookie Eric Boone's Fifth Avenue digs, Zajac had asked Mitch to meet him in the *News* building's cafeteria. After receiving the scant information Barry had on exotic-car dealer Miles Berga, Mitch called later to say he was making headway. Zajac guessed he'd put in more hours since. Once Mitch got his teeth into something, he was relentless.

"Interesting story, your Mr. Berga. Queens-born, but moved to Pensacola, Florida, in his early teens."

Barry knew it would be at least one complete 1.7-mile circuit before Mitch betrayed the slightest strain. Even then, his breathing wouldn't be labored.

"His father was a New York City cop. Put in his twenty and headed south to buy a shrimp boat."

"Strange retirement career for a Queens guy, isn't it?"

Shimizu glanced over at him. "Not when you've got Knapp hot on your tail. Berga Senior's wife was from down there. They met during the Korean War. He was a gunnery instructor at Fort Rucker, Alabama. She was an army nurse.''

''Knapp. On his tail?''

''Let's just say they agreed to disagree, and he put in his papers. Him and a whole slew of others. Anyway, little Miles fell in with some fast company down there. Teenage kids with families who all owned boats. The temptation to borrow them and ferry drugs ashore along the gulf from out of the Caribbean was too strong to resist. By the time he was twenty, Miles and his pals had boats of their own. That's when the state cops in Louisiana dropped the hammer on them.''

''Louisiana? I thought you said Pensacola.''

''I did. They were using a little hidey-hole in the bayou near Morgan City . . . as a way station. Miles caught one to five at Angola. Did two.''

As they pulled abreast of a pair of fashion slaves running shoulder to shoulder, Shimizu scowled. Each wore gear worth hundreds of dollars, from electronic pulse monitors to matching head-and-wrist-bands. Mitch's only concession to current technology was a pair of good shoes. He wore faded cotton shorts and a ragged gray sweatshirt.

''When did Berga move back north?''

''Nineteen eighty-six. Just in time for the Wall Street yuppie boom. That Louisiana bust was in seventy-nine. He was out in late eighty-one. Moved north four years later with enough cash to open his fancy-car emporium.''

''Why is it even the dumbest guys seem to get a little smarter in stir?''

Mitch nodded. ''Or at least better connected. But that isn't it in his case. Not necessarily. I talked to a friend at the *Pensacola News-Journal*. He says nobody's been able to prove it, but Berga's daddy was suspected of trafficking, too.''

''With Miles?''

"Nuh-uh. By comparison, Miles was strictly minor league. The father started out with one shrimp boat and ended up owning a whole fleet. When he died, somebody Cali-cartel-connected bought Miles and his mother out. It wasn't like they had a choice."

Barry's respiration rate was starting to climb. He concentrated on keeping his hands and shoulders loose as he pulled deeper for the oxygen his muscles craved. "Care to elaborate?"

"Story is the father was washed overboard in calm seas. Dead calm. Soon as Miles had his half of the estate in hand, he packed his bags and all but *ran* back to Queens."

"Anything about his gambling habits here?"

As a pretty brunette passed them in the opposite direction, Mitchell flashed a broad grin and nodded. "I've only been on this four or five hours, Barry. Hopefully, that'll come clearer in the rinse cycle. Today, I'm thinking about heading over to Douglaston, see what a new Testarossa might run me."

Zajac grunted. "Keep dreaming."

"It never hurts to ask. He *won* that bet your friend told you about, right? Maybe he's feeling generous."

"I doubt it. The way I understand it, he had other obligations."

The neighborhood through which Beasley "Jumbo" Richardson drove at six forty-five Tuesday morning, leaving his house, was one that gave him hope for the future of New York. Ten years ago Fort Greene, Brooklyn, had been reclaimed from the ravages of urban decline through a process of so-called gentrification. Dilapidated old row houses were given face-lifts by speculators and sold to people from the Manhattan work force who couldn't afford Manhattan rents. Neither Jumbo nor his wife Bernice—who worked for the city's library system—felt much like gentry.

They'd recently sent a daughter through college. Their son was currently attending the state university at New Paltz. The debt incurred educating their children left them perpetually strapped for the last nickel needed to make their monthly mortgage payment. Still, this town house they bought two years ago was a half hour closer to One Police Plaza than their old apartment in Brooklyn's East New York section. The new neighborhood was also safer. Like many other neighborhoods in the five boroughs, it was proof that entropy didn't win *all* the battles in the inner city, proof that citizens of like mind who took the trouble to band together could win a few skirmishes, too.

Richardson's strategy this morning was simple. Rather than stop by the office first, he was headed straight for Washington Heights. That way he could roust Hector Cintron while the man still had sleep fuzzing his brain. Traffic off Long Island was relatively light as he started north into Queens on the Brooklyn–Queens Expressway. Eventually, he caught the Grand Central Parkway going west toward Manhattan via the Triboro Bridge.

It was seven-thirty when he arrived at the corner of Audubon Avenue and 175th Street. The sidewalks were still all but empty at that hour, with the roll-up steel barricades over most storefronts remaining secured. The majority of pedestrians were people out walking dogs. As he sat out front of the address Hector Cintron's parole officer supplied, Jumbo thought back to the last time he'd seen Hector's dead brother pitch. It was via network telecast, game three of the ALCS. Out there on the mound in his Kansas City Royals uniform, Willie Cintron was in total command. It was hard to imagine him being from anywhere but the pages of a storybook. He was every inch the confident young conqueror, a warrior god deserving the adoring fans' love and awe. The world Jumbo witnessed now was far removed from any storybook.

It was hard to tell how long the lock on the door to Hector's building had been broken. The splintered wood surrounding the striker plate in the doorjamb had grayed slightly. It saved Richardson having to press Cintron's intercom button for access. The button panel bore more dents than the front fenders of Beasley's job-issue Plymouth Fury.

The building was a five-floor walk-up, four apartments per floor. Hector's number fifteen was on the fourth, facing the street. There wasn't a single light bulb in any of the fixtures on the landings Richardson passed. As he climbed up through the gloom his nostrils were filled with a stench of urine mixed with frying grease. The cracked linoleum covering the stairs underfoot was littered with discarded fast-food wrappers and broken children's toys. When he passed the second floor, a dog barked behind one apartment door. Seconds later several other dogs on the floors above took up the hue and cry. Somewhere he heard the muffled strains of salsa emanating from a stereo. Again, a picture of Willie Cintron on the mound in his clean Royals uniform flashed before his mind's eye.

There was no audible stirring behind Hector Cintron's door for close to five minutes after Jumbo first raised a fist to hammer on it. Still, if his experience as a street cop had taught him anything, it was persistence. He had gotten himself out of bed at a miserably early hour, driven all the way up here. So why cut Hector any slack? The man wanted to sleep in, he could go back to bed once he answered some questions. Sleep all day if he liked. Right now Jumbo was going to make sure he got no sleep until he answered his door.

Five minutes of near-incessant pounding finally evoked a bellowed "Whaa?" It was as clearly female as it was angry.

Richardson held his shield up to the security peep. "Police, ma'am. Open up, please? I'd like to talk with you.''

From inside the door a shadow moved over the peephole. Seconds later a chain rattled and dead bolts were thrown. Jumbo heard a Fox police bar removed from the middle of the door and saw the knob turn. When the door came open an inch, an eye appeared in the opening to regard him.

''Talk 'bout what?''

''Is Hector Cintron home, ma'am?''

''You know what time is it?'' she complained. ''It seven-thirty in the morning. What Hector done, you come 'round beat on my door like this?''

''Thought this might be a good time to catch him. His parole officer says hello.''

The woman tugged the door open. She was dressed in an oversize man's double-breasted jacket, mustard yellow, the front hugged closed around her and her hands lost in its sleeves. ''You got a cigarette?''

''Sorry. Don't smoke.'' Jumbo surveyed her and then the room behind her. She was that typical Caribbean mixture of African and European, maybe a little Indian mixed in, too. Barely five feet tall, she had chubby legs and a chubby, unlined face. Her hair was cut close to her skull. Her eyes looked tired beyond their years.

The room behind her was half cramped kitchen piled high with dirty dishes and half living room. The two areas were separated by an old tubular-frame dinette table and four chairs. The vinyl cushions on the chairs were cracked, the cotton batting poking through. The primary focus at the living-room end was a brand-new thirty-two-inch Toshiba television.

''What is it you wan' with him?'' The weariness was so heavy it pulled down the corners of her mouth when she spoke. ''I mean, what *now?*''

''I'm conducting a follow-up investigation into his brother's death. He was one of the last people to see Willie alive.

I need to ask him some questions."

It surprised her enough to infuse some life back into her expression. "You *gotta* be shitting me. At seven-thirty?"

"Who the fuck's there, Yvette?" It came from behind a doorway dead ahead, the only doorway Jumbo could see from where he stood. It was a male voice, sounding at least as apprehensive as it did irritated.

"Policeman, Hector. Wan' to ask you some fucking thing about Willie." She continued to eye Jumbo, her disdain dripping from her words. "I'm gonna tell him to come back at a decent hour, baby. There ain' no law says anybody gotta answer no questions at seven-thirty in the fucking morning."

She'd raised her voice loud enough for anyone in the back room to hear her clearly. Richardson moved to match her. "But there *is* a law says a man on parole can be revoked, he tests positive for a controlled substance. I don't want to bust your balls, Hector, but this woman of yours keeps hammerin' on mine? Could be my only choice."

Jumbo heard a rustling of bedclothes. Shortly thereafter Hector Cintron emerged from the back room tugging the waistband on a pair of bright blue warm-up pants. Still bare-chested, he stopped on the other side of the dinette and hit Beasley with his best cool con's disdain.

"Step in an' close the door, Officer. I don' need my neighbors in on *all* my business." He turned to the chubby little woman wrapped in his jacket. "Go put on some clothes."

Jumbo advanced to ease the door shut behind him. "Nice TV, Hector. You buy that with your dishwasher's pay?"

Hector jerked out one of the chairs from the table and slumped into it. "I did my time, man. Why you rousting me like this?" His tone was sullen and, if Jumbo wasn't mistaken, relieved. About what, he couldn't tell.

"I've got some questions I gotta ask you, Hector. That's

all. This ain't no roust. It was a roust, you'd be answerin' back in the bathroom, your head in the toilet.''

Hector was bored now. ''So ask, Officer.''

''You partied with your brother Saturday night.''

''Partied? I don' think so. Couple others'n me stopped up to have a few beers.''

''And smoke a little ganj.''

Hector shrugged. ''Whatever, Officer. It weren't no party.''

''So where did your brother get the dope he killed himself with?''

Now Cintron snorted outright. ''Wait a minute. You think it was *me* sold him that shit?''

''I don't know. Maybe you gave it to him.''

''Bullshit! My brother wouldn't even smoke it no more. Rum an' Coke was as high as he went. Besides, Officer, I'm *clean.* An' even if I had that shit, why waste it on Willie? He wouldn't shoot it, man. He'd throw it back in my face.''

Jumbo stood considering Hector's brand of pent-up disdain, pitying the man for how it crippled him. For all practical purposes, he'd taken himself out of the bigger picture years ago, content to live and die here in this narrow little world. Jumbo had seen too much of this self-destructive rage.

''Any idea where he did get it?''

Hector gave him a lazy roll of the shoulders, his eyes never losing their deadpan sullenness. ''Not the dope, not the works, not nothing. Only thing I know is whoever did it musta *wanted* to see him dead.''

''Your mother and father still live around here? Somewhere in the neighborhood?''

''You kidding? With Willie making all that good bread? He buy them a crib on the beach in Baní, the village where they both was born.''

"In the Dominican Republic?"

"You got it. They honchos in the D.R. now. Or *was* honchos. Ain' quite so big a deal, now Willie is dead."

"What about your cousin Felipe? Where can I find him?"

Jumbo watched Hector's expression close down, an instant suspicion turning him cagey. "What about him?"

"He was with you Saturday night. So was some other friend or cousin of yours. I want to talk to both of them."

"It wasn't them sold him no dope . . . or give it to him neither."

"So let them tell me that, Hector." Jumbo pointed toward the telephone. "You want we can both sit here and wait for your parole officer. When she shows up, you can pee in a cup."

Hector's jaw muscles bunched visibly, all that useless rage in him charging the bars of its cage like a trapped animal. "They got a place at Wadsworth an' One Seventy-third. On the corner there. Felipe and his brother Antonio. Them an' Antonio's bitch. The three of them live there together."

The woman who had answered the door emerged from the bedroom in a tight T-shirt with the Dominican flag emblazoned across her breasts and denim jeans that fit her like a second skin. Jumbo didn't see it as the sort of body in need of graphic definition, but his was only one man's opinion.

"Antonio's *bitch?*" she demanded. "What I *tell* you 'bout that, Hector?"

She and Cintron locked eyes.

"You say it wasn't a party," Jumbo interrupted them. "What time did whatever you wanna call it break up?"

Hector's eyes remained on the woman, still locked in a battle of wills. "Aroun' eleven. Willie, he threw us out on account there was some *pussy* he need to meet."

"He happen to say who the lucky lady was?"

Hector apparently decided he'd won the war of wills with his woman. He dragged his gaze back around to regard Richardson. "To Willie, pussy was pussy. Some *puta,* mos' likely."

Jumbo had no other questions for Hector, at least for the moment. He wanted to spend the afternoon interviewing Marriott Marquis staff. He obtained the address and apartment number of the Infante brothers without further coercion. The threat of calling in Hector's PO did wonders.

It was a few minutes past eight when Richardson descended the litter-strewn flight of stairs to the lobby of Hector's building. As he started along the first-floor hall toward the door, he saw a young Oriental male bound up the stoop steps outside. Without bothering to grasp the knob, the man shoved the door open to hurry ahead. He was almost upon Richardson when Jumbo realized he had no intention of slowing down and no intention of surrendering the middle path. The brown paper sack he carried was shifted from one hand to the other as he tried to bull Beasley aside with a forearm thrust.

Another man might have been knocked into the wall, but Jumbo had twenty years of working the street under his belt. He'd trained himself to see things other men didn't see, and saw this one coming a mile off. When that forearm shot out at him, Beasley planted his away foot to pivot. He then grabbed the arm and used the kid's own momentum to advantage. Surprise, mixed with anger, registered in the kid's expression as he hit the wall hard.

"Hey! What *fuck,* you!" The kid spun off the wall to set in a crouch, his face a mask of fury. It was then that he took his first good look. Richardson had his jacket pulled back so the gun on his hip and tin clipped to his belt were both visible.

"You push it any further, I'm your worst nightmare

come to life, little man.'' Beasley barely whispered it. He then watched the crouching man's eyes. Almost as though a switch had been thrown, all that fury suddenly died.

''You mind I get by?'' the kid growled.

Jumbo stood aside, one wary eye still on the young Asian's hands. ''Be my guest.''

As the kid inched past and continued on toward the stairwell, Richardson watched him with keen interest. Black leather jacket. Skintight black jeans. Sharp-toed boots and hair greased back into a duck's ass. Last year he and Dante had done work on a series of protection-racket killings in the huge Queens Chinese community. What they'd uncovered was a turf war between two groups of transplanted Hong Kong tong members. Both factions were manned by young toughs who dressed and carried themselves exactly as this one did. The jacket, jeans, and boots were like a uniform. Jumbo doubted what the kid carried in the brown bag was takeout from a local Chinese eatery.

Thus occupied, Richardson walked into the brilliant sunshine of that crisp October day and onto the front stoop. There he saw a late-model Mercedes 600 sedan, double-parked at the curb. From inside it, three more Chinese men watched his progress with more than passing interest. All looked to be about the same age as the kid inside. All had the same *West Side Story* haircuts and leather jackets.

Once he climbed behind the wheel of his battered job sedan, Jumbo made a note of the land yacht's plate number.

Chapter ▪9

THE CORNER OF WADSWORTH AND 173RD STOOD AT THE north end of a large intersection where Broadway also passed through, slicing diagonally across Washington Heights from northwest to southeast. The address Hector Cintron supplied for Felipe and Antonio Infante belonged to a building much larger than Hector's own. Lined with a chaos of colorfully decorated storefronts at street level, it ran north and south on Wadsworth for half a block, facing west into the heart of the intersection. It was nearly eight-thirty before Beasley Richardson approached the lobby door. By that time the streets around him had come alive. Shopkeepers hosed down the stretches of sidewalk in front of their businesses, washing debris into the gutter. Out in the intersection, horns blared with each signal change. Here and there he could see proprietors unlocking security gates and hear the rattle of them being rolled up out of sight.

Jumbo knew he'd be kidding himself to expect Cintron hadn't called to warn the Infantes. Unless, of course, they didn't have a telephone. Once again he found a lobby door with the lock broken. This one had the entire lock set removed, and judging from the discoloration of the surrounding wood, that hardware had been missing for months or maybe years. The building directory was in no better shape. The glass once covering it was long gone, and many of the residents' names with it. There was no one listed as occupying 3-L.

The layout of the lobby suggested the building had once been a hotel. The concierge desk area was converted to enclose a row of mailboxes. Another stretch of wall was sheathed in cheap veneer paneling, probably where the front desk once stood. Both elevators had Out of Order signs taped across their doors, edges curling. The names "Infante" and "Rosario" appeared handwritten on a gum label affixed to the 3-L mailbox.

Noise emanated from behind many of the closed doors along the third-floor hallway. People were up now. Jumbo heard radios, televisions, babies crying, and dogs barking as he advanced to locate 3-L in the gloom. When he knocked, dogs barked louder, up and down the hall.

"What is it?" A male voice this time.

Jumbo repeated the routine of holding his shield case up to the security peep and once again watched shadows darken the glass of the little convex lens. "Police, sir. I'd like to talk to you a minute."

Locks rattled as Jumbo waited. When the door panel swung inward, he was confronted by a large, heavyset black Hispanic with a Pancho Villa mustache, muscular arms covered with tattoos, and a shaved head. Rather than try to face Richardson down, the man impatiently waved him ahead.

"C'mon, c'mon. You stan' out there waving that fucking thing in your han', you ruin my reputation with the whole fucking neighborhood."

Jumbo advanced into a room maybe twenty-by-twenty square, with an open bathroom door on his right. Across one end a rope was rigged from wall to wall, suspending blankets to divide it into two sleeping areas. Out front of them were several molded plastic patio chairs and a worn sofa losing its stuffing. A faint odor of marijuana smoke hung in the air, and a woman lounging on the sofa already looked pretty far along for this early in the day. She wasn't quite so well nourished as Hector Cintron's companion, but wore the same sullen expression. This must be Antonio Infante's "bitch," as Hector called her. So which Infante was this? And where was the other?

"It was nice of Hector to call ahead," he growled. "I'm Lieutenant Richardson. Special Investigation Division. I assume he's already told you what I'm here about?"

"His brother Willie. That's what he tol' me. My brother Felipe an' me, we don' know shit about that. Dude was alive as we are when we left him. An' no, I din' sell him that dope, I din' give it to him, an' I don' know where he get it."

Jumbo once again glanced around the room. "I see. And where *is* your brother Felipe, Antonio?"

"A man have his needs. I 'spect he taking care of his."

"Uh-huh. And Willie Cintron was your cousin? Is that right?"

"You got it. My mother an' his mother are sisters."

"So where can I find his mother?"

Antonio snorted. "C'mon, Officer. Why you jerk my chain? You already ask Hector that. An' he already tol' you—Willie, he buy them a house down in the D.R."

Richardson smiled. "You know how devious us Five-Oh scumbags can be, Antonio. Hector says Willie threw you guys out, that he had to meet someone. What time was that?"

Infante fixed Richardson with the same cool con's stare Hector had used. Jumbo wondered where he'd done his time. A man didn't often develop a build like the one Antonio sported without finding himself with a lot of time on his hands—exercise-yard time.

"Same time Hector say it was."

"Fine. And who is it Hector said his brother had to meet?"

"Some bitch. An' no, he din' say who. Willie, he never did much talking, least not about his pussy. But with the money *he* make? I 'spect he got all he wanted."

"Hookers?"

Antonio closed his eyes and smiled. "How would I know, Officer? Why would somebody, a big star like Willie Cintron, have to pay?"

"Because it's less complicated?" Jumbo guessed.

Antonio shrugged. "I thin' maybe Willie, he like it a little complicated. I watch him play out at the stadium last summer? I seen the bitches practically cop his knob in the parking lot."

It had been several years since Joe Dante had visited any of the television-network headquarters buildings. They were all located in midtown and clustered within a few blocks of each other on Sixth Avenue. As he entered the lobby of the Republic Broadcasting System building at Sixth Avenue and Fiftieth Street, not a whole lot seemed to have changed. Security was still tightly controlled, with three staff in neat blue blazers monitoring lobby traffic to and from the elevators. During yesterday's phone conversation he'd learned from Sherrie Meyer that both the national and local station sales staffs shared office space here, on the nineteenth floor. The local station also had its newsroom here, right alongside studios housing the network's popular morning soft-news program and the evening news broadcasts.

Dante found Sherrie's secretary waiting to greet him as he stepped off the elevator upstairs.

"Lieutenant Dante?" Smiling brightly beneath masses of permed chestnut hair, she stepped forward, hand extended.

"I'm Terry Land, Miss Meyer's assistant. She was right. You *are* hard to miss."

Joe was led back through a warren of offices staffed by women in dresses and suits and men mostly in slacks and shirt sleeves. The more stylish men sported suspenders and flamboyant neckwear. Young and old alike, they seemed to be of a sort—slick-packaged corporate eager beavers. He knew from various sources that advertising time sales was the lifeblood of radio and television. Individuals fortunate and talented enough to land positions on a network sales staff were treated as the fair-haired. Joe guessed that Sherrie Meyer, as a sales account exec at the network's New York flagship station, probably pulled down three or four times what an NYPD detective lieutenant made in a year.

"Lieutenant. Nice to see you again." Sherrie Meyer emerged from a doorway to greet him as Dante was led up a wide hallway. It was fronted by an open secretarial area. Her assistant disengaged with another bright smile and started for an empty desk. The sales exec shook Dante's hand with her usual firm grip and led him into a spacious office with windows looking out at several of the landmark spires looming over the midtown landscape. Dominant among them, the Empire State Building stood mammoth against the downtown skyline. Its owner, Harry Helmsley, had lately begun lighting its spire again since his tax-cheat wife was released from federal stir. The twin towers of the World Trade Center, away to the south, had sustained a terrorist bombing just a year ago.

"Nice digs," he complimented his host. In a subtle way she looked even better than she had last night. Today, she was ever so slightly softer. Instead of last night's crisp and efficient business suit, she now wore a silk dress. Her ash-blond hair was pulled back in a French braid, setting off her face. Her makeup highlighted those big brown eyes.

The edges of her mouth, prone to give her too determined a look, were softer.

"Have a seat, Lieutenant. Please. What can I get you? Coffee?"

"Thanks," he replied. "I'm all set."

Rather than take the big leather chair behind her desk, Sherrie eased herself onto a divan facing the armchair Dante selected. "So. That dinner Saturday evening. What would you like to know about it? There really isn't all that much to tell, I'm afraid."

"I understand a public-service campaign was being proposed," Dante replied. "Involving Hola foods, with Willie as your spokesperson."

"That's right." She reached to tug the hem of her dress smooth against her thighs. When she sat, it hiked up six inches above her crossed knees. Joe noticed she also had nice hands. "I'm sure you've seen other stay-in-school spots we've run over the years. Not that they seem to help the dropout rate much, but we have to keep trying. Willie Cintron was a natural to help us take that campaign to the Latino community."

"I assume you were asking him to do this work gratis?"

"That's correct."

"And how receptive was Cintron to your proposition?"

She shook her head, her expression conveying a disappointed sadness. "More than merely receptive, Lieutenant. Enthusiastic. It makes his death all the more tragic. It's such a waste."

"Had you ever met him before that?"

"Just once—at a party that Rob threw out at his place in Southampton last summer. The Royals were in town playing the Yankees."

"Is that when this idea of having Willie act as your spokesman surfaced?"

"Last July? Oh no. That particular brainchild wasn't

born until this past week. Hola wasn't advertising with WRBS right then. I didn't land their account until afterward. It happened to coincide with Willie's signing on to endorse them.''

''A happy coincidence all around, it sounds.''

She smiled. ''I bet I know what you're thinking, Lieutenant. And to some extent it's true. Rob helped put me on the inside track with Hola's president, Jaime Madera. But once I got there, I was on my own. The fact that it was Willie's agent who introduced me didn't hurt, but that's how all the best business gets done. Through networking, friends helping friends.''

Dante thought it best to steer the conversation away from her relationship with Ironstone. Unless it was material to his investigation, it was their business. He nodded.

''Okay. So tell me. What sort of frame of mind was Cintron in Saturday night? You said he was enthusiastic about your proposal. What about the rest of his mood?''

She pursed her lips, her gaze frank and direct. ''That's what I found so strange when I heard Sunday that he'd killed himself. The man I ate dinner with Saturday night seemed anything but suicidal.'' She paused and frowned. ''But you know, there was something that happened after our dinner that may have upset him. I don't know what all was behind it, so I can't really guess how much.''

''What something was that?''

''It was after we left the restaurant—Victor's—and decided to go on to his hotel for a drink in the lobby lounge.''

''All of you?''

She nodded. ''The wife of one of his teammates accosted him there, made something of a scene.''

''Oh?'' This was the first Joe had heard of any such incident.

''I guess I'd describe it as a sort of emotional appeal.''

''About what?''

Sherrie frowned, looking for the right words. "She's the wife of this guy, Juan Rojas. You probably read about him last May. It was pretty big news, the Royals player who was arrested for rape . . . during a road trip to Boston."

Dante had read quite a bit about Juan Rojas. The rape charge stemmed from an incident just weeks into the current baseball season. Rojas was charged with inviting a camp follower to his room and having intercourse with her against her will—someone he'd met in the hotel bar. When she fought him, he'd slapped her around. It was big news not because Rojas was a star—he was a utility infielder noted for his defense who hit a miserable .200—but because Willie Cintron was sharing that room with him and happened upon Rojas in the act. When Willie attempted to wrestle Juan off the woman, a fight ensued. Cintron suffered a broken nose. Joe could vividly recall the photos splashed across the back pages of the New York tabloids featuring Cintron with his nose heavily bandaged.

"Willie was supposed to give evidence against him, wasn't he?" Dante asked.

She nodded. "That's right. And the trial is set to start this week. Rojas's wife—Felicia, I think her name is—was upset that Willie was going to testify. She begged him not to, saying he owed her at least that much. I don't know what she meant by it, but she said something about him already ruining her life once. Now he was going to ruin it all over again."

Dante frowned. "*No* idea?"

"Not a clue, Lieutenant. But she was pretty worked up about it. He excused himself to take her aside and finally managed to get her calmed down."

"And after that, you all had a drink?"

"Actually, no. Willie asked us to excuse him. I think his nerves were a little jangled, and he *did* have the game to pitch Sunday. Rob's wife was at home and I had a pile of paperwork I wanted to catch up on. We decided there in the lobby to call it a night.''

After spending a few minutes more in idle conversation, mostly about her and her work at the station, Dante decided it was best he get on with his day. He did learn that her disgraced-cop stepfather had earned enough money as a Florida contractor to send his daughter to Princeton. There, she'd majored in economics. WRBS was her first job out of college. In seven years she'd risen through the ranks from sales assistant to her current position. Like Joe, she lived in Manhattan, was single, and loved her work. Unlike him, she didn't have a cat.

Douglaston, Queens, was about as far east as Mitchell Shimizu could drive on Northern Boulevard and still remain in New York City. The dividing lines out here were fuzzy in his mind, the distinctions between Douglaston Manor, Douglaston, and Little Neck. As far as he could see, those distinctions mattered mostly to the locals. For all practical purposes, this was the beginning of the affluent North Shore or ''Gold Coast'' of Long Island. Beyond, into Nassau County, ran a string of communities that evoked names of the prominent old families who used to summer here. Vanderbilt, Roosevelt, Guggenheim, and so on. Communities like Sands Point, Port Washington, Oyster Bay, Glen Cove, and Cold Spring Harbor. Here, the hilly, lush-landscaped terrain hugged stately houses to its bosom. Northern Boulevard, the main surface artery running west-east through these enclaves, was lined with many familiar shopping emporiums catering to the needs of the fatter pocketbook: Barneys New York, Anne Klein, Bergdorf's. If it was exotic cars Miles Berga hoped to move, Shimizu could see he had a nose for where to put a showroom.

To make this look right, Mitch had called his ex-girlfriend. They'd remained friends after a problem-plagued romance, but she was still a bit suspicious when he asked to borrow her new Mercedes 560 SL roadster. When he explained his reason, she relented. The car would make the right sort of statement. She was an eye surgeon and her MD plates would add a nice touch, too. Mitch guessed that a Japanese physician pulling up in German wheels worth roughly ninety thou would be enough to get a recession-plagued exotic-car dealer salivating.

If times were tough at Prestige Performance, Mitch wouldn't have guessed it from appearances. There were no festoons of colorful plastic pennants flapping in the breeze; no ''Prices Slashed on Every Model'' come-ons splashed across the plate glass. Instead, the building facade was painted a mellow cream, trimmed in British racing green. Inside the huge curbside windows, Mitch saw a Lamborghini, a Ferrari, a Maserati, and a Lotus parked on gleaming checkerboard linoleum among potted palms. The furniture in view was cream-colored leather, arranged around a low table covered with magazines. Two men were seated there, one in a business suit and the other in golf togs, both reading magazines. Mitch guessed they were waiting while their high-performance street machines underwent thousand-dollar oil changes somewhere out back.

No sooner did Shimizu push through the showroom's glass entrance door than a tanned and energetic man bounded out from nowhere, hand extended. ''Morning, Doc. Nice car, that five-sixty. Not exactly a monster, but sweet enough on the open straightaway, am I right?''

Medium stature, trim and health-club well built with a trace of the south in his speech, the salesman wore a brilliant-red polo shirt with the Ferrari logo stitched tiny in white across the left breast, a rampant lion with the lettering beneath. Mitch had made sure to pull the lady doctor's Benz up to the curb, where his arrival would be observed by any interested parties. This guy had seen those MD plates and jumped to the desired conclusion.

"If I wanted a monster," Mitch replied, "I would have bought one of these." He waved a hand at the showroom.

"I understand. Not everything in our lives can have balls big as an elephant's, right? So can I assume you're not looking to trade?"

Mitch's eyebrows shot up. "Trade? My wife'd kill me. She *loves* that little car."

The salesman clucked his tongue and sighed, his expression all sympathy. "The women all do, Doc. Putting your foot in it and knowing it's gonna snap your head back? They just don't get it."

"Tell me about it," Mitch went along. "It's just *one* of the things they don't get. You Miles Berga?"

"Live and in person. Doctor . . . ?"

"Yamaguchi. Russell Yamaguchi. And skip the Doc stuff, Miles. Call me Russ."

"Okay, Russ. What is it caught your eye this fine October day?"

Mitch imagined this was the most polished alumnus in the history of Louisiana's Angola State Penitentiary. Not a hint of time done. He strolled casually away to stand looking at a sleek new red Testarossa.

"Actually, Miles, the thing that caught my eye is a nifty gunmetal-gray Porsche 928. I was just out in it for a test drive last night. Talk about a sweet piece of machinery." He turned back to Berga and smiled. "Still, I could hardly feel like I was acting responsibly if I just wrote that other guy a check. I mean, after all, Ferrari's been the standard for a lot of years."

He watched Berga struggle to hold that smile, his neck muscles swelling. "The 928 is a nice car, Russ. I'd be bullshitting you to argue it isn't. But to talk about it in the same league as Ferrari?" He leaned harder on that smile, worked a little sadness into his eyes, and shook his head.

"I'm afraid I—and a lot of people more qualified than either of us—just don't do that. Of course, if it's money you're concerned about . . ."

Beautiful. First flatter a customer's manhood. Compliment the size of his balls. Then go for his balls by casting doubt on the size of his wallet. A Porsche 928 could be had for slightly under a hundred grand. A Ferrari Testarossa was close to twice that.

Mitch chuckled. "C'mon, Miles. Where you going to get with a dig like that? I got a daily parade of the best-looking women in the world traipsing into my office. What do they want? They want me to make them look even better. A tighter ass, bigger tits, fuller lips, you name it. Time I get done with them, they worship the ground I walk on. You want to sell me a Ferrari, sell me a better car than the 928."

That smile lost its underpinnings and collapsed. "I didn't mean to . . ."

Mitch hurried to brush it aside. "No harm, no foul, right, Miles? And speaking of beautiful women." He nodded toward a big full-color Prestige Performance calendar hung on a nearby wall. "Looks like you've got a fair eye yourself."

Shimizu had no way of knowing just how much his stock had risen with that compliment. The calendar photo depicted a blond swimsuit model in a thong bikini draped across the hood and windshield of a black Lotus Esprit Turbo. Mitch did notice how Berga's chest swelled with satisfaction as he nodded.

"Hot stuff, isn't she? For next year we've got her riding the nose of a new 512 TR."

Mitch steered the conversation back around to what he was ostensibly after. "Things I'm interested in are what sort of service you offer here, what your bottom line is, and how much below that you'll go in order to make a deal. And don't get me wrong. As sweet a machine as the

928 seems to be, the Ferrari logo on the hood and name back there on the ass end might just be enough to see me go the extra eighty grand.''

Berga's confidence was all the way back now. ''Our service department is second to none, anywhere east of L.A., Doc.''

''Russ.''

Miles nodded like a puppy begging him to throw a tennis ball across the yard. ''State-of-the-art diagnostic equipment. Mechanics trained in Italy, by the factory. You got a busy schedule and need a car picked up for servicing? All you got to do is call us.''

Forty minutes later, laden with literature and next year's calendar, his fingers still tingling from gripping the wheel for an exhilarating test drive, Mitch Shimizu climbed back into his borrowed Mercedes roadster. As he pulled away from the curb into Northern Boulevard traffic, he waved so long to Miles Berga, standing out there on the sidewalk in front of his showroom. That smile was showing the strain of trying to support an hour-long sales pitch. No matter how sincere his declared intention to return, Dr. Russell Yamaguchi—plastic surgeon to the bold and the beautiful—was driving away.

As Mitch swung the Benz around in a U-turn at the next light and started back toward Manhattan through the eastern reaches of Queens, he ran what he'd just heard and seen back through his mind. He only half noticed the champagne-colored Honda Accord and a navy Subaru Legacy that made that U-turn right along behind him. Berga was firm with his price: $189,000 for the new Testarossa Yamaguchi claimed to desire. It boggled Mitch's mind to think of someone paying that much for a car—*any* car. Out back behind the showroom he'd been shown the service bays and given a fee schedule for work done. The hourly labor rate alone was $125, the same rate his attorney charged three years ago to handle his divorce. One thing that piqued his curiosity was an additional metal building behind the service garage. Twice, while inspecting the service facility, he noticed a mechanic with a blond ponytail and baggy coveralls slip in and out of that other building through a side door. The roll-up door out front of it was closed, but he was sure he heard the guttural burp of an air-powered impact wrench back there. Once, as that mechanic emerged from the side door wearing a respirator mask, he saw the blue flash of an arc welder. If they had a body shop, why hadn't Berga bragged about that facility as well?

Mitch was so preoccupied with his train of thought that he failed to notice the Accord and Subaru still following him until the Honda suddenly pulled out to shoot past. In the next instant it cut back sharply into the lane ahead and Shimizu saw brake lights flash on. He barely had the reaction time to slam on his brakes, and when he tried to swerve left around the Honda, he found the Legacy blocking him. He had no choice but to stop. The instant he did, a man wearing a ski mask leaped from the passenger side of the Honda and ran back toward him, brandishing an automatic pistol. Mitch saw the dark hole of the muzzle leveled directly between his eyes and froze. Right here in broad daylight on Northern Boulevard, two carloads of hijackers were stealing his ex-girlfriend's car.

He was so focused on the gun that he failed to see a second man emerge from the Subaru until a pistol barrel rapped at the window directly behind his left ear. His hands shook as he depressed the button to lower that window.

"Leave it runnin', Doctor. An' keep your han's where I can see them. Nice an' easy. Open the door an' get out."

Shimizu tried to sort out the tangled impulses that snarled his thinking as he tugged at the door release. He planted one foot on the pavement. Maybe they weren't going to kill him. And what was that accent? Black ski masks and gloves hid any glimpse of skin color. And what real difference would it make if they *didn't* kill him? Dr. Donna Covington was going to anyway.

Chapter 10

Chapter ▪ 10

JOE DANTE FOUND PLENTY TO INTEREST HIM IN SHERRIE Meyer's story of an altercation between Willie Cintron and the wife of accused rapist Juan Rojas. As soon as he returned to his SID office at One Police Plaza, he placed a call to the district attorney's investigation squad in Boston. After explaining what he was after, he was passed along to the DA's Sex Crimes Unit. A Captain Patricia Reilly spearheaded the prosecutor's investigation efforts in that sector. She sounded harried.

"What can I do for you, Lieutenant? And please make it quick. I'm due in court in twenty minutes."

"I'm investigating the death of Willie Cintron, Captain. I understand he was scheduled to appear as a witness in the Juan Rojas rape trial."

A heavy sigh was audible from down the line. "The *star* witness, Lieutenant." Her tone was weary now. "With his testimony, we had Rojas cold. Without it, we're in a whole different ballgame. Willie was the one who walked in on them. Our single eyewitness."

Dante digested this information thoughtfully. "Are you saying that Rojas might skate without Willie's testimony? What about physical evidence?"

"Once it was clear Rojas wouldn't back off, the victim stopped fighting him physically." There was disgust in

Captain Reilly's tone. "He slapped her around with an open hand. We've got pictures of a little redness in her face. If I know my juries, it's not enough—hardly gut-grabbing stuff. There's evidence he had intercourse with her, but he doesn't dispute that. His defense also has evidence of her long history as a sports groupie."

"Another version of the Willie Smith story."

"It's an older story than that, Lieutenant. She went willingly to his room. Right now what went on up there is her word against his."

"What about Cintron's deposition? Under mitigating circumstances, can't that be admitted?"

"Strictly up to the judge. If the prosecution tries to get it entered, the defense will howl like holy hell."

"Juan's wife Felicia was in New York Saturday night," Dante told her. "Mid-evening, she accosted Willie Cintron in the lobby of his hotel."

Captain Reilly remained cautious. "Her presence in New York is no surprise. That's where she and Juan live. She's from the Miami area, but once she and Rojas were married, she moved north with him. He's from Venezuela originally, but spent a lot of his childhood in some place called Elmhurst. That's in Queens?"

"Uh-huh." Dante knew there was a huge Central and South American population there. "That where they live now?"

"Queens? No. The address we have is somewhere on West Eighty-third Street. In Manhattan. I can look it up for you."

Dante told her he'd appreciate it.

"What's this about, Lieutenant?" she asked. "Why do I smell a possible break for us here?"

"That's *all* it is at the moment, Captain. Remote in the extreme. I wish I could say more right now, but I can't. Is Rojas in custody there or was he in New York, too?"

"I imagine that's where he was. Jury selection ended Friday, and he's been out on bail since May. He'd better be here today, though. With or without the star witness, twenty-four hours is the most the DA could get the judge to postpone."

Beasley Richardson's Tuesday was nearly half-gone, two thirds of it spent behind the wheel of his car, by the time he returned to his SID desk at eleven o'clock. On his way downtown from Washington Heights, the dispatcher reached him with a message from Dante, asking him to call. When he did, Joey gave him an address on the corner of Broadway and West Eighty-third. Ten minutes later Jumbo swung by there to see who was home. It was one of those new high-security apartment towers thrown up in the late 1980s by developers with either deep pockets or good savings-and-loan connections. Apartment sales in most of those buildings had gone south of late, along with a million jobs throughout the northeast. The surplus those units created in the rental market had driven rents down all over the Upper West Side. Bad news for landlords and a real boon for the previously gouged consumer.

"How'd you make out?" Dante asked. Jumbo dropped into his chair. "Didn't answer her bell. Two characters who work the security desk in the lobby don't remember seeing her since Sunday. They say she ain't the type that's easy to forget." He paused, grabbed his coffee cup, and shoved himself back to his feet. Doctor's advisory or not, he wanted a cup badly right now. "Felicia Rojas. Who the hell is she, Joey? What's this about?"

Dante took a moment to outline the story he'd heard from Sherrie Meyer and to relate the gist of his conversation with Captain Reilly of the Boston DA's Sex Crime Unit. "It's one motive for wanting to see Willie Cintron dead that I doubt Zajac thought of, Beasley. One part in particular of what Sherril Meyer overheard strikes me as interesting.''

''You mean the bit 'bout him already ruining her life once?''

''Exactly. Don't you want to know what she meant by that?''

Richardson carried his brimming mug back to his desk and sat down to sip gratefully. Left cooking in its carafe since eight o'clock, it still tasted good to him. ''If she's the one killed him, I doubt she'll be willing to explain.''

''If she won't, maybe Juan will. I just checked the schedule with Delta. If I hurry, I can catch the eleven-thirty out of La Guardia, be at the Bean Town courthouse by two.'' Dante stood to grab his jacket from the coat tree. ''Captain Reilly tells me Rojas and his wife are practically newlyweds. Been married a little more than a year. I'm wondering what stories the other players on the Royals might be able to tell us. Stories about her. About him. About the two of them together.''

''You want, I can try Terry Marshall again.''

Joey nodded. ''Captain Reilly says Felicia's from Miami. I'd like to know how she and Rojas met—and she and Willie, for that matter.''

''During spring training, be my guess.''

Dante was at the door. ''And mine.''

Beasley wished him good luck. ''Anything else need doing? I was gonna try and see if I could make it up to the Marquis, start poking around there.''

Joey paused, remembering something. ''Yeah. Zajac called. That investigative reporter he mentioned yesterday? Mitch Shimizu? Seems he got a Mercedes five-sixty SL hijacked out from under him in Queens this morning. Belonged to a girlfriend or something. She's howling mad. Barry's wondering if we can put a word in with the Queens robbery squad.''

"You told him the car's prob'ly halfway to Ghana by now?"

"Not per se. I told him I hope she's insured."

If there was a silver lining to the cloud hanging over Mitch Shimizu's head, he guessed it was one of those perverse occupational things. He was an investigative reporter for the *Daily News,* something the cops at the One-Eleven Precinct in Bayside, Queens, hadn't failed to miss. They smelled a rat, but were unable to determine what kind. Luxury-car hijackings were a hot item with the press. Lieutenant Dante's scrape at JFK had gotten big coverage in the *News* on Monday, and the Queens cops refused to believe Shimizu when he swore he hadn't been trolling. And who could blame them? The car wasn't his. He was driving around an affluent part of Queens after rush hour, but wouldn't say where he'd been or why he was there. The fact that he'd managed to get a car stolen out from under him could generate just the sort of ink a mayor, three weeks from an election, would hate. That made the duty captain at the One-Eleven and the detective squad commander both edgy. The conversations Mitch had with them were barely cordial.

It was noon now and Shimizu was recently arrived back at the *News* building. Rather than respond to the urgent summons from his editor, no doubt to discuss this morning's enterprise, he slipped quietly into Barry Zajac's office. While word of the hijacking had spread like wildfire throughout the newspaper, Zajac got it before anyone. Shimizu had called him from a pay phone, even before calling the cops. With the adrenaline still raging, he'd asked Barry to sit tight.

Shimizu was considerably calmer now as he sat across from Zajac, hiding out of sight of the sports room behind the columnist's closed door.

"*Donna*'s car, Mitch?" Barry still had trouble believing it. He'd witnessed bits and pieces of his pal's abortive affair with Dr. Covington. She was wound as tight as they came. Her professional accomplishments earned Mitch's respect, but none of the awe she felt they should inspire.

"What would *you* drive, shopping for a Testarossa?" Shimizu demanded. "That beat-up piece-of-shit Corolla you've had since your divorce? Me? I wanted this man to take me seriously."

"And did he?"

Shimizu accentuated his smile with a mischievous wiggle of his eyebrows. "We practically unzipped and compared genitalia. That's how he thinks, this scuzzbucket. I would have offered, but I didn't want to embarrass him."

"What do the police say, Mitch?"

"That inside five minutes, the car had other plates on it. Within ten, they had it tucked out of sight somewhere. By this time next week it will be in a container and loaded on board a ship, probably right across the Hudson in the port of Newark."

Zajac turned his head to stare out through the office partition glass. "My guy? Dante? He hopes Donna was insured. Says he'll be happy to make a few calls, but doubts it'll do you any good."

"Don't sweat it," Shimizu replied. "I already *know* who stole it. Who, and how. Now all I gotta do is prove it."

Zajac's gaze returned to contemplate Mitch with a look of puzzlement. "You've told the police this?"

Shimizu smiled. "Nuh-uh. This one's mine, slugger. Some bastards pull me over, stick a gun in my face, and threaten to blow my brains out just to steal a *car?*" His face was set hard now. Anything remaining of his characteristic happy-go-lucky demeanor had turned to stone. "I was too jacked up to see it at first. Once I took a couple breaths, it all came crystal clear."

Nothing had come any clearer to Barry. "*What* did?"

"The whole clever scam. When Dr. Russell Yamaguchi pulled up to park out front of Prestige Performance, that prick Berga's eyes lit up. Another pigeon come to roost."

"Wait a minute. You think Berga was behind it?"

Shimizu drummed his fingers against the arms of his chair, tapping out a steady syncopated rhythm. "I *know* Berga is behind it, Barry. The special task force the cops have working on these hijackings? They think it's a ring of black Africans, from either Ghana or Nigeria. Could be that's true, but not these guys. The ringleader of the guys who did me was Hispanic."

"I still don't get it. How's that connect them to Miles?"

"They were waiting for me when I left, Barry. But instead of taking me right then and there, they waited until I'd driven over a mile away, *then* made their move. It wasn't until the cops mentioned shipping containers that it clicked into place."

"Whoa. Back up."

Instead, Shimizu plunged forward. "There were two of them, lined up along the back fence behind the service garage at Berga's place. And why not, right? It's probably how they receive their cars, too."

"Exactly. So what does that prove?"

Mitch stopped tapping his fingers. The palms of both those hands met in front of his mouth. He blew between his steepled fingers, cheeks puffing as he formulated his words. "They pulled away from the curb about half a block behind me. I had to make a U-turn at the next light to get myself headed west again. If I'd been paying more attention, the fact they made the turn with me might've triggered something. I wasn't, and it didn't. Still, part of me saw it, remembered it later."

Zajac could visualize the scenario. He had trouble believing Mitchell hadn't picked up on it right away. "Don't tell me Berga *sold* you something."

Mitch chuckled. "On what I make? Fat chance. I was too preoccupied thinking about what I'd seen out behind the service garage." He told Barry about the shop with the doors kept closed.

"This was besides their regular body shop?"

Mitch shook his head. "That's just the thing. They don't *have* a body shop. Berga told me they send everything up to a custom carriage outfit near Danbury. Claims they're the best in the east, so why not take advantage?"

"Then I don't get it."

"That's just the point. Neither did I. It's what I was trying to figure out when the hijackers came flying up on me. I'd let my guard down."

"You think Berga's running a chop shop back there?"

It evoked more finger drumming. "Yeah, that's what I think. I'm going back there tonight, have a look around. Depending on what I see, I'd be interested to know how many of Berga's customers have had their wheels stolen. Be an interesting twist, wouldn't it?"

"What's this got to do with Willie Cintron, Mitch?"

Shimizu shrugged. "Once you start digging, you find what you find. If I'm right, Berga's got somebody speaks Spanish who's willing to point guns at people, hijack cars, and pull any other manner of wild-ass stunts. The man's done time in one of the most notorious prisons in the south. You're worried these people aren't *capable* of killing your friend?"

Once Beasley Richardson dialed the number of Terry Marshall's home in Overland Park, Kansas, the phone at the other end rang for just an instant before someone picked up.

"I told you to rot just five minutes ago, you low-life sonofa-bitch! Stop calling me! As soon as I find a lawyer, you can talk to him!'' The voice was female, high-pitched, and clearly irate.

"Maybe I don't have the right number," Jumbo rumbled, caught off guard. "I'm trying to reach the Marshall residence."

There was a long, pregnant pause. "Who is this, please?" Cool now, and straining to sound southern-belle sweet.

"Detective Lieutenant Richardson, New York Police Department, ma'am. This *is* the Marshall residence?"

"That would depend on which Marshall you're trying to reach, Lieutenant. If it's my soon-to-be-ex-husband, you missed him by half a day."

For an instant Jumbo wondered if it was because Marshall hadn't made it to the World Series. Then he took into account the level of scorn he heard in her voice. "I see. If I missed him there, where can I find him, ma'am? It's important. I'm conducting the investigation into Willie Cintron's death."

"Oh." Another protracted pause. "All us wives still can't believe it. He was such a sweet guy. Cute, too."

Jumbo tried to figure where the accent was from. It was definitely southern, and nowhere near where she lived now. A bona-fide belle would never betray the depths of her anger as she had. Not to a stranger. A certain sense of propriety was bred in so deep that dynamite wouldn't budge it. So where? Texas? Florida, maybe?

"Your husband told you he's the one discovered him?"

"Ex-husband," she corrected. "Yes, he did. It must have been quite a shock. They were close, you know. Not that I care all that much. Not anymore."

"I spoke to him yesterday afternoon about some of the particulars, ma'am. There's a few more that I still need to go over. Things that've come up since. Do you know where he's staying?"

"I do. One of the team has a condo in Shawnee Mission. That's just north of here."

"You wouldn't have a number by chance?"

She read it to him. "But I doubt you'll reach him. He just called me from his car."

"How about *that* number? And if I don't reach him and you do, could you give him a message?"

"Sure," she replied. "Right after that one I gave you by mistake."

Chapter ▪ 11

HER BUSY SCHEDULE NOTWITHSTANDING, CAPTAIN PATRI-
cia Reilly had graciously offered to collect Dante when he
arrived on the twelve-thirty shuttle at Boston's Logan Airport. It was a journey of five miles, part of it beneath Boston Harbor via the Sumner Tunnel, which brought them to
the courthouse building on Somerset Street. As Reilly drove
she brought the visitor from New York up to date. The
captain wore her hair in a short, no-nonsense cut. The air
of confident competence she exuded declared her a law-
enforcement professional to the core. If she betrayed even
a hint of vanity, it would be in her clothes. Her pale gray
suit and cream silk blouse were beautifully cut garments
that flattered her long, lean lines. Dante judged the commander of the Sex Crimes Investigation Unit to be roughly
his own age.

"It's days like these that make me hope there's a hell,
Lieutenant. The Rojas defense filed a motion for dismissal
this morning, right after we talked. It's based on the prosecution's inability to produce their only eyewitness."

"What's the victim?" Joe asked. "Blind?"

"It's her word against his now. He isn't disputing anything but *how* he had intercourse with her. That makes the
forensic evidence pretty weak. It's all going to hinge on
whether the judge will allow Willie's videotaped deposition

to be entered. We won't know that until late this afternoon.''

''I don't get it. Why would he grant a motion to dismiss?''

A cab ahead of them cut across their bow toward a couple of businessmen hailing it from two lanes away. Reilly had to hit the brake and swing the wheel hard to miss clipping it. Dante saw her eyes narrow and focus to memorize the plate number.

''It's been Juan's contention all along that Willie resented Felicia Rojas for marrying him, that Willie resented Juan, too, for stealing Felicia away. He claims Willie was looking for a way to get even, says that's what the fight they had was about. He claims Willie may have even paid this woman to bring charges in a conspiracy to frame him.''

''Why not?'' Joe growled. ''It's the kinda thing jealous guys do all the time.''

She smiled for the first time since shaking his hand at the station. ''You've got to admit it's fairly creative—as these stories go.''

Dante did have to admit it. He wondered if Juan Rojas was really that smart, or if he'd had some coaching. From his wife, maybe? ''The way I hear it, when Mrs. Rojas confronted Willie Saturday night, she said that he'd already ruined *her* life once before. You think she could have helped Juan with his story?''

''That'd be rich, wouldn't it?'' she replied. ''The wife of an accused rapist helping her husband to beat the rap?''

''She's got a lot to lose, too,'' Joe reminded her.

The defense attorney for Juan Rojas insisted on being present during Dante's conversation with his client. Joe was surprised by the Royals utility infielder's absolute lack of presence. The Venezuelan national, in his middle to late twenties, was by no means an imposing specimen, nor was he handsome, nor did he embody what Joe assumed would be a gifted athlete's grace of carriage. Slightly pudgy, he looked like any other guy with a fondness for an extra slice of pie. The only thing that set him apart from most people was the tailoring on his navy pinstripe suit. It probably set him back what most of his countrymen earned in a year. Dante knew the book on this guy. It said he had reflexes like a cobra. If ever appearance belied fact, Juan Rojas was that walking contradiction.

Juan's legal mouthpiece, a dapper middle-aged Hispanic attorney with prematurely snow-white hair and a deep tan, fired the opening salvo. They were gathered in a small room used mostly for small-claims arbitrations, the two interests seated on either side of an old oak table.

"I want to remind you, Lieutenant, that Mr. Rojas answers any questions you put to him only as a courtesy. Considering the prominence of Guillermo Cintron's testimony in the Boston prosecution's case, it's not hard to imagine why you are here. I understand you are conducting an inquiry into Mr. Cintron's death?"

Dante nodded.

"My information says your medical examiner is calling it a suicide, Lieutenant. Or at least an accidental drug overdose. So please, tell us why you are involving my client?"

Dante decided he would get further by seeming agreeable. He offered a slight, conciliatory smile. "We've got some bothersome, unanswered questions, counselor. One of them is where Cintron got the drugs which killed him. Another is who the woman was who visited him in his room after his brother and two cousins left him after eleven o'clock Saturday night."

The attorney scowled. "I'm afraid I don't see what that has to do with Mr. Rojas."

Dante smiled again, letting it linger as he spoke. "That's just what I'm getting to, counselor. You see, the last woman

Willie is known to have had contact with Saturday evening was Felicia Rojas. Your client's wife.'' Joe watched Juan stiffen as he said it. ''They had an exchange in the lobby of the Marriott Marquis. She's reported to have said some things I don't quite understand.''

Joe was sure the sharp glance the attorney shot at Juan was involuntary. So. This was news to him. Good. That meant he was slightly off balance.

''My wife is in Miami,'' Rojas growled. ''Was there Saturday, too. Whoever tell you this other thing is a liar.''

''Where in Miami?'' Dante pressed.

''Visiting relatives.''

''I mean where exactly. I'd like to fly down there tomorrow and talk to her.''

Rojas snorted with contempt. ''Maybe she no want to talk to you.'' He turned to his attorney, irritation flashing in his dark eyes. ''This is bullshit. This man come here an' insult the honor of my wife.''

Counsel glanced over at Dante, still unsure of where he stood.

''I've got witnesses, including the president of Hola Foods, an executive from the local TV station airing the championship series, and Willie's agent, all who can place her there,'' Joe told him. ''Your client knows his wife wasn't in Miami and so do I. Fact is, with him set to go to trial here yesterday, I have to wonder why she isn't here by his side right now.''

''Who said she isn't?'' the attorney countered.

''He just did. He told me she's in Miami, which I suspect is a fabrication.'' He turned back to Rojas. ''So let me ask you another question, Juan. It's your claim, at least so far as I understand it, that Willie resented you for marrying your wife, for stealing her from him. That's interesting. I've got three witnesses who distinctly remember her accusing Willie of ruining *her* life. What do you suppose that

means?'' He had stretched the truth earlier in claiming anyone but Sherril Meyer could identify Felicia Rojas at the
Marquis. On the other hand, why shouldn't he assume the
other two present could pick her up out of a lineup as well?
And why not make them all good listeners while he was at
it?

''She is *puta*,'' Juan spat. ''As soon I leave, she go
where she want. How do I know where she is?''

Dante let it hang awhile, gathering ice crystals. ''I see,''
he said at length. ''You were home in New York this weekend, Mr. Rojas?''

Juan shook his head, his expression despondent now.
''Felicia, she s'pose to meet me here. She does not come
an' I call her. There is no answer. Not Saturday. Not Sunday. Not yesterday an' not today.''

''So for all you know, she *could* be in Miami.''

Rojas turned back to his attorney, his expression sullen
again. ''No more, Tico.'' He scraped back his chair and
pushed to his feet. ''I thin' I already say enough.'' Before
starting for the door, he aimed those lifeless dark eyes back
at Joe and almost seemed to smile. ''So who have the last
laugh, huh, policeman? Willie is dead. I am alive to spit
on his grave.''

After trying the numbers given to him by Tina Marshall
for the better part of two hours, Beasley Richardson was
relieved when the phone in Terry Marshall's car was finally
answered.

''Baby? Before you say a word, I need you to *listen* to
me. I blew it, okay? I know I fucked up. These bitches,
they *throw* theirselves at a man. It's hard enough being on
the road all the time, but you find me any man can say no
when some hot-to-trot bitch rubs it in his face. Shit, Tina.
I'm flesh and bloo—''

''Mr. Marshall,'' Jumbo interrupted. ''I doubt you want

me to hear any more of this."

The silence that greeted him in return was all-absorbing. "Jesus," Marshall muttered. "Who is this?"

"Lieutenant Richardson, NYPD, Mr. Marshall. You thought it was dial-a-confession, right?"

"I don't *believe* this," the catcher groaned.

"They say it can be good for the soul," Jumbo replied. "I wouldn't know, myself."

Marshall must have seen the humor in his situation. Beasley heard him chuckle. "I got me a case of dickrot, gave it to my wife, Lieutenant. She throw my ass out, say she be filing for divorce."

"You think she's serious?"

Marshall sighed. "I don't know. Might be best. A thing like this, she got me by the short hairs forever. You don't know my Tina, Lieutenant. Crazy bitch won't *never* let me live it down."

"I ain't preaching morality here, but you've heard there's a virus going 'round? One that'll kill you?"

"Like I say. I fucked up."

"Uh-huh. It's your life, Mr. Marshall. But considering how often you've called each other since she threw you out? My money's on it all blowing over. Meanwhile I got a few questions. They're different from yesterday's, and you're the only guy I know to ask."

"What about, Lieutenant?"

"Juan Rojas."

"Ah. Thought that was a Boston thing."

Just before Jumbo finally managed to reach Marshall, Dante had called with an update from Boston. They now had two conflicting stories regarding the relationship between Willie Cintron and Juan Rojas. To Joey, the quickest route toward getting them straight was Juan's wife Felicia. Unfortunately, she still proved to be elusive.

"You hear anything of Mrs. Rojas accosting Willie in

your hotel lobby Saturday night?''

''Nuh-uh. But that don't mean she didn't. Just like somethin' *that* silly bitch might do.''

''Any guesses what it was about?''

Jumbo heard Marshall grunt. ''Sure weren't nothin' what Juan might tell you. Rojas, he couldn't get it outta his head he'd sucked Willie's Johnson by proxy. You hear what I'm sayin'?''

Jumbo heard him. According to Joey's information, Felicia Rojas and Willie had had some sort of prior relationship. ''How long was Cintron involved with her before she married Rojas?''

''Involved's sorta strong, Lieutenant. Problem with Felicia, she give a man one taste, he s'pose to act like she give him the keys to the kingdom of bliss.''

''Where did all this happen?''

''Spring training. Two years ago. Willie'd just signed a contract for a million five.''

Jumbo tried to visualize it. ''I've never met the woman. What kinda package we talking about?''

''Hot enough, I s'pose. Hardly any ass. Night she first showed on the scene? She wore this blouse you could see right through to the bare titty.''

''So Willie was the first of you to take the bait?''

Another grunt. ''Shit, Lieutenant. We *all* took the bait. Willie the only dude she let bone her. One roll and she acts like she took a mortgage on his ass.''

''And that didn't go over too well.''

''Not hardly. Willie had a little mean streak with bitches, 'specially he smell them after his bank balance. He strung her along a couple weeks, let her play her game.''

''Rojas is claiming he stole her away from Willie. That's why Willie tried to frame him for rape.''

''He pulling your dick, Lieutenant. Willie dumped her. When he did, everyone in camp, they know about it.''

"So when did Rojas enter the picture?"

"Juan? He be tryin' to get into her picture the whole time. It wasn't till after Willie give her the push that she give Juan the time of day."

"The second string."

"You got it. Difference 'tween six hundred thou and a million five. 'Sides, Juan always actin' like he got something to prove. Got a chip on his shoulder. Till Willie dumped her, Felicia *like* how he act so aloof, like he don't care. It said he was cool."

"Until it proved true."

"Oh yeah. Then Juan forced it on some groupie bitch an' Willie walks in. Felicia, when she heard Willie was gonna testify? Well, that was her gravy train, headed south."

"You mean, if she didn't have reason enough to hate him already . . ."

"I seen this one in action, Lieutenant. She ain't just crazy. She's *dangerous* crazy." There was a pause. "Wait a minute. I see where you're headed with this."

"I didn't say I was headed anywhere."

"You don't have to. Bein' a dumb nigger who catches baseballs for a living don't mean I can't add. I *know* the sum of one and one."

Hector Cintron had paced the floor of the Infante brothers' apartment for nearly an hour before Felipe eventually wandered in through the door. Antonio and his woman had left to deliver a package for him, shortly after he arrived. Left alone in their little hovel, Hector had started to feel the way he often felt in stir. With each passing minute the size of the room seemed to shrink. He felt caged.

"Where the fuck you been?" he demanded. Hot anger flashed in his eyes as he rushed Felipe to grab him by his jacket lapels and throw him hard against the wall beside the door.

"What's with you?" Felipe protested. "Why you always think you can push me aroun' like this?"

Hector held his face just inches from his cousin's. "Why?" He sneered. "Because you always fucking up, Felipe. Because Lin T. Wah come to my door this morning an' tell me you got jus' forty-eight hours to come up with his money or he gonna cut your *cojones* off."

Felipe tried to squirm away, but Hector, equal to him in size, was made stronger by the iron he'd pumped in prison. He held fast. "What I tol' you las' night, Hector? I tol' you no problem, no? I got it all covered."

"You spend it again, din' you?" The minute he said it, Hector was sure it was true. Felipe could not meet his eyes.

"My *cojones* are my problem," he murmured.

Hector released Felipe's lapels and shoved off in disgust. "Oh, that is good, Felipe. They yours the last time you fuck up, too. Only then, my brother, he was alive. He buy them back for you. Some of *this* money, you promise him you use it to pay him back."

Felipe sneered. "An' he would take it, too, no? Saint Willie Cintron, who hates the drugs that kill his people? He would take the money I get from selling the drugs, no problem."

"He save your life, Felipe."

"But he wan' his money back. How I'm gon' get ahead, I got to pay him first?"

Hector stared at him in amazement. "What? He should *give* it to you? Why, Felipe? You would give it to him, you were in *his* place?"

Felipe shrugged. "Sixty thousan' dollars? What it is to him? I tol' him to lighten up. Relax. He get it soon enough. But Willie? He got to be a prick about it. A *moralista*."

Hector had known Felipe since they were both tiny children in the Dominican Republic. All his life Felipe had never changed. He believed the world owed him something. "I don' give a *fuck* what sixty thousan' was to him. To you, it was your life."

"You think he don' remind me of this? So many time I wan' to grab him by the throat an' choke him."

"What makes you so angry, Felipe? That he was right? That it *was* his money?"

"Fuck you, Hector." Felipe thumped himself on the chest. "Willie is dead. It *is* my money now. Lin Wah wan' his money, you tell him he *get* his money."

"How, Felipe?"

Felipe leered, tapping his temple with a forefinger. "You say I spen' it, Hector. Not me. I say I *invest* it. By midnight tomorrow? I double what I invest, an' give Lin Wah his piece back."

Hector stared at him and shook his head. "Not through me, Felipe. I finish with you. You wan' to commit suicide an' join my brother with the angels, you do this thing on your own."

Beasley Richardson struck out at the Marriott Marquis and was preparing to call it a day when a Sergeant Dougherty from Operations reached him by beeper at five-thirty. Both the bell captain on duty Saturday night and the room-service waiter assigned to the Royals' floor had Mondays and Tuesdays off. No one he interviewed could tell him anything about the altercation between Cintron and Felicia Rojas in the hotel lobby or of any comings and goings on the sixteenth floor late Saturday night. As he called Dougherty back he hoped the sergeant had better news. Earlier, Richardson requested not only that Operations run the plate on that Mercedes seen outside Hector Cintron's building, but that Central Records do a follow-up on the owner. Dougherty apologized for being so late getting back.

"The president was in town this morning, Lou. Addressing some business circle-jerk at the Waldorf. We been up to our ass down here."

"So what've you got for me, Sarge?"

"That car is registered to a Lin T. Wah. That's W-A-H. Middle initial as in 'tong.' The sheet we got on him? Nothin' compared to his federal file. Kid ain't thirty yet, but his suspected connections read like a Golden Triangle Who's Who. You heard of the Tung-on?"

"Sure have." Last year when he and Joey had worked that protection-murder case in the Queens Chinese community, they learned more than they wanted to know about the new Chinese gangs. The Tung-on, along with the Flying Dragons and the Fuk-Ching, were primary among the Chinese interests importing heroin from Southeast Asia to New York. As they began to dominate the heroin-trafficking scene they started getting bolder, flashier. That 600 Mercedes fit the new profile. Like their Colombian brethren in the whiff trade, the young ones really liked to strut it. "This particular mutt, what is he? Native or import?"

"Born and raised, Lou . . . or he wouldn't still be here. Anywhere else you want us to go with this?"

"Not right now, Sarge. Thanks." Jumbo said it slowly, his expression thoughtful. "I just saw him someplace I didn't think he belonged. Now I ain't so sure."

Chapter ▪ 12

By the time Joe Dante reached La Guardia on the return leg from Boston and fought his way back to Manhattan through rush-hour traffic, it was after six o'clock. Throughout the drive home to West Twenty-seventh Street, Dante considered what he'd accomplished that day. It had started out on a positive note. Not only was Sherril Meyer easy on the eye, the information she imparted opened a whole new avenue of inquiry. Felicia Rojas's actions the night Willie Cintron died, combined with her disappearance, made her an obvious object of focus. Regardless of what Beasley had since learned about her romantic past, she had good reason to hate Willie. A year ago she'd hooked herself a major-league ballplayer pulling down nearly three quarters of a million dollars. Felicia was on easy street. Then along comes the rape indictment, Willie agrees to testify as an eyewitness, and Felicia is back to square one. Juan himself had called her a whore, which meant even he recognized a certain avarice in her. But was Felicia's avarice strong enough to motivate her to murder?

Toby the cat was batting a dead mouse back and forth across the living-room floor as Dante stepped off the elevator into his loft. This was the second year of Joe's residence here, and last fall, same as this one, there had been a noticeable up-tick in the mouse population as soon as the weather outside turned cool. Joe had tried Havahart traps, but Toby went mad attempting to get at the live animals caught inside them. Brian and Diana employed old-fashioned wood-and-wire traps to swift and sure effect, but Dante couldn't. While mice were a food-chain matter with Toby, Joe was driven by no such instinctive urge. Deep down he was a live-and-let-live kind of guy. His twenty-five-hundred square feet of loft space was more than enough for him, one deaf cat, and a small rodent population. Rather than pry little dead carcasses from traps every night and flush them into the sewer, he tried to look the other way.

There were two message blinks on his machine. The first was from Diana.

"You got any frustrations you want to work out tonight? I just agreed to let the record label add three cities to the tour, and I'm in a fighting mood."

The largest room in Dante's loft was a wide-open space furnished with a heavy bag, free weights, and a dojo mat. A year ago Diana had expressed an interest in learning some tae kwon do conditioning routines. A dedicated gym rat with her own private Nautilus circuit upstairs, Diana showed promise as a fighter, and Dante agreed to teach her. When she was home and he wasn't, she often let herself in to use the bag and mat. Joe hit the stop button and then the speed dial for the loft upstairs.

"I heard the elevator. No rush. My nails are drying."

"The cat's glad to hear that," he replied. "He's about to chew my left foot off."

"I've got to warn you, I'm plenty pissed off."

"Good. That tends to blind you. Makes you easy meat."

"In your dreams, copper. Lucky you're my friend. I've been wanting to kick somebody in the balls all day."

Joe chuckled. "Maybe I better take a rain check."

"Oh, sure. I bet you're terrified. I'm there in five or ten." Diana broke the connection.

Joe glanced down at Toby as he depressed the start button to retrieve that second message from his answering machine. After returning the receiver to its cradle, he opened an overhead kitchen cabinet used to store cat food.

"What say, bub?" Toby was threading in and out between his ankles in a figure eight. The culture that had come up with the symbol for infinity knew something about the nature of feline hunger. "Liver and chicken, or sliced beef? Your choice. Both in gravy, of course." The answering machine whirred and clicked into play. The cat said nothing.

"Lieutenant Dante? It's Sherrie Meyer."

How the hell had she gotten his home number?

"Listen. My schedule's open this evening. I'm wondering if you'd like to meet for drinks? I realize this is late notice, but if you're free, give me a call. Oh, it's three-thirty and I'm at the office." She left both her work and home numbers.

Joe found something appealing in an aggressive, self-assured woman. This one had the added appeal of being fun to look at, too. Rosa had been gone what? Fifty-five hours? So much for avoiding the occasion of sin. Joe usually avoided those occasions by burying himself in his work, helping Brennan around the studio, or hitting the mat in his workout room. Tonight he planned to help Diana perfect an off-balance sweep kick. He dialed Sherrie's home number.

"Hello. You've reached four-seven-eight—" It was interrupted by a squeal that made his teeth ache, followed by, "Damn! I'm sorry. Hello? Hang on a sec." He waited until the answering machine on the other end clicked off. "There. Hello?"

"It's Joe Dante, Ms. Meyer. How'd you get my home number?"

"Oh! *Hi*, Lieutenant." She sounded immensely pleased. He wasn't sure whether it was with herself or with the fact that he'd returned her call. "I used feminine wiles. First I called Charlie Fung's gallery and told them I was a model who had lost his number. Then I called him, said I'd met you at his show, and had lost *your* number." She paused to chuckle. "He gave it to me *and* asked me out to dinner."

"Figures. Did you accept?"

"Took a rain check. No sense burning bridges, right?"

He grunted. "You're asking the wrong guy. Some say I'm a master at it."

"So are you free tonight?"

"Sorry, but *I've* gotta take a rain check. I just this minute walked in the door from Boston and I'm whipped. But thanks for asking. I'm flattered."

"What about tomorrow night? Dinner. My treat . . . or at least the station's. They hate it when my expenses run too low in a month. You'd be doing me and my career a service."

That brought a laugh. "You're appealing to the altruist in me, Ms. Meyer?"

"Call me Sherrie. And forget the altruist. When was the last time you or any other cop refused a free meal?"

"You got me." He was set to have dinner with Beasley and Bernice at their place Thursday. Tomorrow night his slate was blank. "Okay. All this resourcefulness, how could I say no?"

"You like bistro food?"

"Love it. Where and when?"

"Bruxelles? Seven-thirty? That's only a dozen or so blocks downtown from you, right?"

Fung had given her his number *and* where he lived? "How do you happen to know that, Sherrie?"

"Your address? We've got a Cole's reverse directory in the newsroom. More of that resourcefulness."

"See you there," Joe told her. When he replaced the receiver, Toby stood staring up at him. "Damn, little buddy. This one's the occasion of sin if I've ever seen it." He stooped to set the cat's bowl on the floor. Toby attacked his sliced beef.

The notion that Miles Berga had Willie Cintron whacked was secondary to what now motivated Mitchell Shimizu. Late that afternoon he'd met Dr. Donna Covington back over at the One-Eleven station house in Bayside. After she signed complaint papers and consulted with a detective acting as liaison to the Queens robbery squad, Mitch walked her back downstairs and outside. She refused a ride back into Manhattan with him, preferring to take a cab. Still, she took the time to tell him there was no way she could replace the car with the compensation her insurance carrier would pay. She intended to buy a brand-new one, and Mitch could make up the difference between her compensation and the new car's cost. If he refused, she would sue him. Until that morning, Mitch had entertained hopes of getting back together with her. That idea was all in the past now.

He arrived outside Berga's high-performance emporium just after sundown. A drive-by inspection of the showroom suggested business was finished for the day. Still, he spent the next hour in his parked car on the other side of Northern Boulevard, watching until nightfall inked in every nook and cranny the streetlights couldn't reach. During that hour he saw what looked to be the last straggler leave the premises. That blond ponytailed mechanic in coveralls he had seen earlier now drove through an open gate on 243rd Street, behind the showroom. He emerged from his black Porsche Carrera to shut the gate and lock it. That was forty minutes ago. Mitch hadn't seen so much as a squirrel scurry across the sidewalk since. Time to inspect the perimeter defenses.

Traffic going west into Queens was lighter than that going east on the boulevard past the front of Berga's showroom. Rather than approach from the front, Mitch elected to slip around behind it on Alameda and park near the service entrance on 243rd. Other adjacent businesses along that stretch of Northern Boulevard were also closed for the night, and there was ample parking between Alameda and the corner. In fact, there wasn't another vehicle parked on either side of the street. As Mitch pulled up beneath a huge overhanging poplar, he was both thankful for its shadow and concerned that a solitary car might attract attention. He waited for another fifteen minutes, seated inside his two-year-old Mitsubishi Eclipse. In that span of time not a single car pulled onto 243rd traveling either north or south. He guessed he was relatively safe, but on second thought, pulled his radio from its Benzi Box mounting and locked it in the trunk.

The top of the chain-link fence surrounding the Prestige Performance service area was strung with a concertina of razor wire. As Mitchell strolled casually down the sidewalk inspecting the area inside, he searched the back of the showroom building for surveillance cameras or surface-mounted boxes containing motion detectors. Nothing. He had to assume there was some other sort of alarm system. The showroom housed cars worth more than a million dollars. Customers surely left cars overnight in the service area. There would be expensive tools stored there, too. Berga wouldn't be fool enough *not* to have an alarm installed.

If Berga ran a secondary operation involving the theft of luxury cars, how did he move them in and out? And when? It wasn't likely the thugs who'd hijacked Donna's car had driven it directly back here. So it only made sense that sometime between now and sunup tomorrow would be the best time to make such a move. Even at this early-evening hour, this area was dead as disco. Later it would only get quieter.

There was only one gate in and out of the service yard. Mitch walked from it to the corner and east half a block past the showroom facade until he reached an alley running between it and the business adjacent to it. A pair of Dumpsters were parked there. Farther back he could walk abreast of the perimeter fence, clear back to the southeast corner of the compound. It was in that corner that he'd seen those two shipping containers set side by side. When he reached them now, he crouched to inspect the shipper's code stenciled low on one corner of the ribbed metal box. Headlights swung in to illuminate the gate across the yard.

The light startled Shimizu, sending his hammering heart up into his throat. Thankfully, the container afforded perfect cover from which he could watch without being seen. The vehicle at the gate was some sort of van, towing a long, low trailer. Mitch saw someone emerge from the passenger side to unlock the gate and swing it wide. Once the way was clear, the driver eased into the yard. When the van and trailer came around in an arc and started back toward that mystery shop Mitch had seen earlier, he could read the matching signs painted along the side panels of both vehicles.

PRESTIGE PERFORMANCE RACING TEAM
DOUGLASTON, NEW YORK

These were surrounded by product-endorsement decals from a variety of lubricant and specialty racing component manufacturers.

The gate man guided the driver into a position out front of the bay door, then hurried around to the building's side door to unlock it and disappear inside. Seconds later the growling of an electric motor kicked in. The bay door began to rise.

Shimizu already knew what he would see once the trailer's rear doors opened and a loading ramp was deployed. Donna Covington's silver Mercedes roadster, looking none the worse for wear, glided into view and out again, disappearing into the confines of that garage.

"I knew it," he muttered to himself.

"Knew what, asshole?" It was a woman's voice, tight in her throat, cold, and murderous.

Shimizu whirled as his cardiovascular system experienced the adrenaline surge of a lifetime. Set in a crouch, he was prepared to lunge when the sight of a pistol muzzle aimed at his face froze him. Behind it stood the coveralled mechanic with the blond ponytail he'd seen earlier, only now he realized the mechanic was a woman. He recognized her as the same lady posed half-naked on Berga's calendar. That tiny dark hole at the end of her gun looked as deep as eternity.

"Why aren't I getting it?" Diana complained. She stood erect, trying to catch her breath. Sweat glued her jacket to her back. She bit her lower lip in frustration.

Dante moved behind her, putting his hands on her hips to edge her forward. "You're rocked too far back on your heel when you launch. It destroys your leverage." The loose folds of her ghee disguised Diana's perfectly toned and proportioned body, and Joe was grateful for this.

"What leverage?"

"You've got to create it, use the fact that you're caught off balance to your advantage. Come on. Let's try it again. And try to forget you're gonna fall. Accept it."

He watched the frustration vanish as a look of grim determination filled her eyes. She came at him with a flurry of punches that he parried with fluid ease. Then, when he thought he saw her focus flag, he stepped inside a left hand and used an elbow punch to force her off balance. An instant later he landed hard on the flat of his back, Diana executing a perfect shoulder roll and springing back to her feet beside him.

"Shit," he cursed himself in disgust.

"I got it!"

Joe hoisted himself up on one elbow and smiled. "Yeah, you did. Sucked me right in." He started to rise. "So. Want to hit the shower or you think you can do it again?"

She raised an eyebrow, the grin becoming a leer. "Your shower or mine?"

He pointed to a spot across the mat. "Get your fanny back over there."

The sixty-five thousand dollars Felipe Infante owed the Tung-on for half a kilo of eighty-five-percent-pure Southeast Asian heroin had been burning a hole in his pocket for three days. Tonight, as he shifted from foot to foot against the chill October air, Felipe could think only of the additional thirty thousand dollars he stood to clear on his latest deal. It involved risking less than half the sixty-five in a sweet double-your-money proposition. The man he was meeting to consummate the first step of the two-step deal was late right now, and that was irritating.

As he stood on the corner of Amsterdam Avenue and the 181st Street Washington Bridge approach, Felipe soon recognized the Jaguar Vanden Plas sedan of Oscar Saavedra rolling toward him. It had to be Oscar, because it was followed by a rental truck with a thirty-foot cargo box. The sight of that truck, with the two hundred Panasonic Panafax UF-733 plain-paper facsimile machines it contained, was enough to get Felipe's blood racing. Those machines retailed for $1,499 a pop, deep discount. Any fool who bought full retail could expect to pay up to three or four hundred more. Felipe's price from Saavedra was a dime on the discount rate, or $150 per machine. Hot or not, the guy Felipe had lined up in Jersey would jump all over them at twice that money.

Oscar was out of the car almost before it came to a stop. Felipe saw the heavyset driver eye him as the high-energy Saavedra scuttled toward him along the sidewalk. Oscar in motion evoked the image of a crab.

"You got a place to stash the van, right, amigo?" A hand shot out as Oscar asked the question, fingertips locking with Felipe's. "Like I tol' you, it in't returned tomorrow night, they gonna report it stolen. Once your man unloads, you burn it. *Comprende?*"

"Where I gonna check the load?" Felipe asked. "Not here, I hope."

Oscar leered up at the taller Felipe, the gold cap encasing one of his two front teeth flashing in stray streetlight. "What it is, amigo? If I din' know you better, I say you soun' nervous. Forget checking the load. I got one in the trunk of the Jag. All two hundred you buy from me? They all jus' like it."

Saavedra walked around to the back of his car as the driver released the trunk automatically. The deck lid rose to reveal a sleek-looking piece of hardware that was considerably bigger than any fax machine Felipe had ever seen.

"Fucking carton it come in was too big to fit back here," Oscar explained.

Felipe shrugged and handed over a brown paper sack stuffed with rubber-banded packets of twenties. "Thirty thou. I s'pose to trust you enough not to check the load? You trust me enough not to count the money. *Sí?*" He winked at him. "Don' worry. It all there."

Saavedra tossed the paper bag into the trunk, slammed the lid, and signaled to the driver of the truck. "Like I tell you. That truck due back 'roun' five. They usually give it a couple hours 'fore they call the state police."

Felipe knew that *they* was Oscar himself. He not only worked as office manager for a large truck-rental firm in the city, his wife worked as a dispatcher for one of the largest overland freight haulers in the country. Oscar rented the trucks from himself with stolen credit cards and fictitious driver's-license information. Felipe suspected his own physical description was entered on the rental agreement papers, making him the most obvious fall guy should he and that truck run afoul of the law. There was nothing stupid about Oscar Saavedra. He ran a high-risk, high-profit operation and knew that the best way to survive was to minimize his risks.

"I meet my man at nine," Felipe replied. "I know your rental place, they got their rules, but maybe they don' get 'roun' to calling for *four* hours, huh?"

Saavedra shook his head. Behind him, his truck driver opened a backdoor and slid inside the Jag. "Always got to cut it fine, don' you, amigo? You fuck it up, you never met me. An' forget 'bout turning evidence. I got people could find Elvis. You don' want me to sen' them looking for you. Trust me."

Chapter ■ 13

WEDNESDAY MORNING WHEN JOE DANTE ARRIVED AT HIS SID task-force office early, he found Beasley Richardson already there. The Mr. Coffee carafe was brimming full of fresh java, but Jumbo was too preoccupied with the file in his lap to have poured himself a cup. Joe hung his jacket on the coat tree, poured both their mugs full, and carried them across.

"What has you here so bright and early?"

Jumbo glanced up and accepted the mug of coffee. "Thanks." He nodded to part of a forensic report in his other hand. "Our mystery woman. I'm try'na find reasonable cause for a judge to authorize search of the Rojas apartment."

Dante frowned. "To what end?"

"A comparison of the pubic hairs Rocky found and any we might recover."

"Ah. You think maybe it was her who was with Willie?"

Beasley eased back in his chair and raised his mug to his lips. As he sipped he shrugged. "I don't know what I think. It sounds to me like she had a motive, Joey. At least of a sort. And from what Terry Marshall tells me about her, it sounds like she was driven."

"Good. You got him again."

"Yeah. Late yesterday afternoon." Jumbo went on to describe the conversation. "He thinks she was after the best cash deal she could get. Plain and simple as that."

"Her husband did call her a whore," Joe mused.

"Uh-huh. And then there's another thing Marshall said that gets me thinking in a slightly different direction. He said Willie had a little bit of a mean streak with women, especially if he knew it was his cash they were after." He went on to detail Marshall's description of Cintron and how he often engaged hotel staff to procure whores for him. "So. Saturday night, him and Felicia Rojas get into something in the hotel lobby. He takes her to a neutral corner and manages to get her calmed down. What is it you think he said to her?"

"She knows his act and plays to it," Joe replied. "Makes herself available. Asks if they can get together later, just like old times. She knows that because he's got this little mean streak, he'll take the bait."

"It ain't so farfetched, Joey. She's thinking with the wiles of a woman scorned and he's thinking with his dick. Who do *you* think'd have the upper hand?"

"Rhetorical question, Beasley." Dante pointed to the paperwork in Jumbo's lap. "So what've you found us?"

"Nothing. Them pubic hairs is the *only* evidence there was a woman in the room with him. Last I checked, women comprise better'n half the general population, something like fifty million between the ages of eighteen and forty. With what we got right now, that's as narrowed down as I can get it."

Instead of taking his chair at the desk opposite, Joe remained on his feet. He stood with his coffee cup cradled in those scarred and callused hands, his brow furrowed and lips pursed. "How'd you make out at the Marriott? We need to place Felicia Rojas on that sixteenth floor."

"*If* she was there. I pretty much struck out. After the

weekend, everyone I wanted to talk to takes Monday and Tuesday off.''

"What about your buddy Marshall? Couldn't he help us any?"

Beasley grunted. "My buddy? Nuh-uh. He had a big game the next day and was lights out by eleven. Found himself someone downstairs in the lounge to tuck him in and keep him warm. Went home to Kansas City with a case of the clap.''

Dante registered surprise. "He told you this?"

"His wife's thrown him out, Joey. I was half a day tryin' to get his sorry ass on the phone. You ask me, if he's feeling the pain now, he got that dose earlier than this past weekend.''

"We need to make contact with the bell captain on duty that night. He's probably our best bet.''

"I know. They tell me he comes back on duty today.''

"Be handy if we had a picture of the Rojas woman.''

Jumbo set the file on his blotter and his coffee cup atop it. "There's something else come up you should know about.''

"Yeaaah?" Jumbo would swear he saw Dante's eyes start to glaze over.

"Hector Cintron did his time for heroin sales. Yesterday, I ran into this skinny little mutt from the Tung-on gang downstairs in his building.'' Jumbo described the incident and how he'd seen three more gang members parked in the Mercedes outside. "I want to head on up to the Three-Four North again this morning. I think it's time to put Willie Cintron's own finances under a microscope, too.''

Dante frowned. "Because his *brother* might be mixed up with the Tung-on?"

"That was a heroin overdose he died of, Joey. He was a young kid who made an awful lot of money. Who the hell knows what he did with it? Could be he had his finger in the wrong pie, that a whole shitload of blackbirds took offense.''

Joe regarded Beasley with a look of heightened interest, his glazed-over reluctance vanished. The idea that Willie Cintron might have been mixed up in a criminal activity that had backfired on him was a new ingredient. ''Kinda contrary to the picture our crusading columnist paints, ain't it?''

''He wouldn't be the first do-gooder had the wool pulled, Joey. Be an easy enough matter to have Gus request his banking records.''

''Consider it done. And I'll see if we can scour up a picture of Mrs. Rojas somewhere. What was the upshot of that call you made to Queens Robbery? They any help to Zajac's pal?''

Beasley closed his eyes and took a deep breath as he shook his head. ''Damn. I knew there was somebody I forgot to call.''

Captain Greg Newell, skipper of the tug *Judy Blue Eyes,* was lost in thought that crisp October morning when his ruminations were interrupted by a shout from the bow. His vessel's position was just east of the Throgs Neck Bridge, technically in the waters of Bronx County, and headed out into Long Island Sound. They'd just finished towing a string of barges loaded with rock to a runway extension project at La Guardia Airport and were headed back up to Norwalk, Connecticut, to pick up another. Newell was in the wheelhouse, standing alongside his quartermaster at the helm. To the south, they were running just opposite Kings Point, Long Island.

In his twenty-four years since graduation from the U.S. Merchant Marine Academy, Newell never ceased to be stirred by a wave of what-ifs each time he passed his Kings Point alma mater in the course of his work. In 1965 the war in Vietnam was heating up. Newell had never met an Asian and couldn't see why he or any other American should feel threatened by an agrarian culture eight thousand miles away. To Greg, the domino theory of John Foster Dulles failed to take into account the thousands of miles of Pacific Ocean in between Asia and North America. Greg's means of avoiding the draft turned out to be Kings Point.

He did eventually go to Vietnam. As a civilian third officer on a tanker, he'd delivered JP-4 helicopter fuel to the port of Da Nang. Later he signed on with a tug outfit in New York harbor. On mornings like this one, when he passed Kings Point, the same old guilts broke over him. He wondered how much of his humanity would have survived had he not attended the academy. How many people were saved by that fuel he delivered to the port of Da Nang? And how many more were crippled or killed by the machines it fueled?

Newell stood drifting in that same old mental backwater, no closer to any answers now than before, when he was brought to the here and now by bo'sun Pat McIntyre's shout. He focused forward to see Pat wrestling with the end of a boat hook and two more crew hurrying to the bow to help him. Greg ordered his quartermaster to cut the growling twin diesels, and he stepped outside onto the starboard catwalk. McIntyre had hooked into something out in the water and dragged it alongside.

Newell started down the starboard wheelhouse ladder toward the deck. Long before he saw that first arm flop over the bow rail and its dead owner wrestled onto the deck, Greg knew he had a floater on his hands. Lousy luck. As skipper, Greg would have no choice but to hold position and radio the coast guard. Depending on how they chose to handle it, his boat could be tied up in red tape for the rest of the morning, or even the day.

Newell was no more than ten feet away when McIntyre

rolled the corpse over onto its back. One of the crew—a kid named Carlson—lurched backward a step, stumbled, and fell to his knees, puking. Greg saw the normally walnut-brown coloring of his face go almost gray. Oh Jesus God.

The floater was male, maybe thirty-five and maybe sixty. It was hard to tell after a few hours in the water. Stocky. Oriental. Greg had seen a number of bodies pulled from the waters surrounding New York over the years, but never an Asian. The last Asian he'd seen pulled from the drink was his first floater ever, a Viet Cong saboteur caught by a concussion grenade in Da Nang harbor. The man was killed trying to plant explosives on the hulls of enemy shipping. Greg had no idea what this man's transgression was, though there was no doubt he'd been murdered. His head was nearly severed from his body by one clean slash of a knife. The cut stretched like a second mouth, gaping from ear to ear.

"Where's that prowess we're so proud of, speed?" Debbie DeLong asked Miles Berga.

The two of them and three other cartel drones had worked like slaves through the night to clean out Prestige Performance's clandestine body shop. When Debbie finished with the snoop she'd caught, she let the three Colombians deal with dumping him. It wasn't because she found the task particularly distasteful, but she was the only one of them with a Class-2 driver's license. She had to make the run in the semi rig, shuttling anything that could incriminate them, packed into one of the shipping containers, to safekeeping.

"Just give me another minute," he begged. "I'm a little distracted, that's all."

The frame of her big brass bed squeaked as she turned away from him in disgust and reached for the hand mirror on the nightstand. Propped on one elbow, she drew coke from the pile on the mirror into two lines with a single-edged blade. "I've given you the past half hour, speed. This was your big idea, coming here, not mine. I'm fucking dead." She leaned into the mirror, the tubed bill held to a nostril, and snorted deep. "This shit won't keep me with you forever, hotshot. Another few minutes of this, you're on your own."

Berga rolled onto one side and reached to run a hand across her flank, tracing the curve of her waist and up along her hip and fanny. Generally, it felt good to be touched like that. Right now it irritated.

"Every time I close my eyes, all I see is blood," he murmured.

She returned the mirror to the nightstand and lay with her head thrown back, the drug starting to rev up her synapses. "You didn't have to watch. I thought you were a tough guy, all that time you did at Angola. What was it you did down there? Run the ladies' auxiliary? I've got a go-see at three. Let's try to get some sleep, huh?"

She knew the ladies'-auxiliary crack would get him going. Suddenly he was alive and on her, limp at first but getting hard fast as he dry-thrust himself against her, his face a mask of fury. "I've got all the tough guy you need," he snarled. "Hanging right . . . *here.*"

She grinned back, her own eyes alive now. With the coke roaring like a runaway freight through her consciousness, she reached to rake her nails across his tight, flexing butt and back. When she closed her eyes, she could see the blood, too, like a veil draped before her mind's eye. To watch the terror in that stubborn little reporter's eyes had flushed her with the same sort of excitement she felt now.

"Lick me, you sorry bastard," she growled. And as Miles moved with purpose to comply she dug fingers into his curls and forced his face hard against her. He'd been some big buck's girlfriend in stir. She was sure of it. Every time he crawled into the sack with her, he was consumed with proving he was no pansy. She knew his buttons. He was as predictable and as wild as a carnival ride; just push start and hang on tight.

Teetering on the edge of ecstasy, she jerked his head up and met his fevered gaze with a grin. ''That's more like it, speed. Now get your ass up here.''

As he mounted her Debbie closed her eyes and rode with the flow. She drifted back twelve years to when she was fourteen and in the backseat of a Jaguar SJ sedan. That was in her daddy's Hayward, California, body shop, and her lover was the best hand with a torch, body grinder, and bondo in the west. He'd taught her one trade afternoons, and shown her another move or two nights. Two years later he was stabbed to death in a Bass Lake bikers' brawl. She'd sat huddled twenty yards away and watched. A month later she seduced the guy who stuck him. Once he fell asleep, she slit her first throat. The next day she packed and left to travel east. In the past ten years she'd come a long way. Her modeling career was less than she wanted, but it was how she'd met Miles and Mendoza and landed her current moonlighting gig. Life's early lessons were proving a nice fallback. With Debbie, body-and-fender mechanic meant more than the usual array of skills.

A gasp from Miles, coupled with a sudden stiffening along the entire length of him, brought Debbie back in a rush. He shuddered and thrust with the purpose of an animal possessed.

Beasley Richardson had just departed the task-force office, headed for Washington Heights and a conversation with detectives at the Three-Four North, when Dante received a call from Chief Lieberman. Joe was preparing to head up to the Marriott Marquis with a photo of Felicia

Rojas faxed from the DMV, but Lieberman's news stopped him cold. Earlier, he'd called Gus, asking him to intercede with Queens Robbery on Zajac's friend Shimizu's behalf. Now Gus told him the *Daily News* investigative reporter had been found floating in Long Island Sound by a tugboat crew. Special Operations' Harbor Unit *George* was on the scene, along with the coast guard. There was no doubt this was a homicide. Gus was departing the building immediately for *George* unit's landing in College Point, Queens. Dante met him downstairs in the garage.

The Chief's mood inside his Buick sedan was markedly darker than the dazzling October morning he emerged into from the interior gloom. The driver eased the magnetized red gumball light onto the roof and put his foot into it as Dante regarded his boss across the backseat.

"I was on my way to Boston yesterday when Zajac called. I didn't give what he'd told me enough thought. Now that I'm not so distracted, I don't like anything that's occurring to me."

"A reporter for the newspaper with the largest circulation in America? Found with his throat cut? I don't like it much either." Lieberman was frowning down at his nicotine-stained hands. He didn't see Joe shake his head.

"It's more than that, boss. It's *why* he got his girlfriend's Mercedes stolen."

Gus looked over now, his eyes clouding. "I *know* I ain't gonna like this."

"Monday, Zajac offered to contact Shimizu, thinking he could be helpful probing any gambling connection to the Cintron investigation. We gave him the green light."

Gus covered his face with one hand and groaned. "I don't believe this."

"Yesterday, when he called? He sounded . . . I don't know . . . anxious? Like I said, I didn't have time to think about why. Not until now."

"You mean like why he was driving around Queens in a borrowed, ninety-thousand-dollar car?"

"Or where he'd been. Yeah. If I wanted to look like a player in the world of high-stakes sports wagering, that's just the kind of car I would drive."

Barry Zajac caught a ride from two *News* reporters and a photographer, heading out to College Point as soon as he heard word. It wasn't quite ten o'clock when he arrived outside the EDO Seaplane Base at the foot of Fourteenth Avenue. That same facility, situated directly across the mouth of Flushing Bay from La Guardia Airport, also housed one of NYPD's harbor units, one of six such outposts located around the city's waterfront. He saw the street outside the gate already jammed with vehicles from at least a dozen area television and radio stations, along with a fleet of police cars, both marked and unmarked. Reporters crowded outside the gate, held back by a cordon of uniformed patrolmen. This was no ordinary murder they'd been called to cover and their demeanor betrayed it. One of their own had fallen.

Almost simultaneous with his own arrival, Barry saw Lieutenant Dante and Chief Lieberman emerge from a black Buick. As soon as the news hounds recognized the chief of detectives, they found focus for their restlessness, nearly trampling each other in the rush to reach him. It was interesting to watch Dante anticipate this surge and sidestep around it to the other side of the throng. Zajac let his two *News* comrades have the chief. He hurried to fall in step alongside Dante. As soon as Dante saw Zajac, his expression clouded.

"What is it you *didn't* tell me yesterday, Barry? I get complaints from friends about their friends and car thefts all the time. You forgot to mention why this one was different."

Barry didn't know whether he should be surprised or relieved to be confronted so bluntly. ''You know something I don't?'' he asked. It was impossible to hide his anxiousness.

''I'm the one should ask *you* that question, mister. All I know is your buddy got someone else's wheels stolen yesterday, and today he shows up with his head barely attached. I'd be a complete idiot I didn't wonder if those two incidents aren't somehow connected.''

There was another knot of reporters still waiting expectantly outside the cordon of uniforms who had the gate sealed off. They looked on with irritation as Dante showed his tin and hustled Barry inside. Several recognized Zajac and hollered out to him.

''Cat's gonna be out of the bag now,'' Dante growled. ''You're finished holding out on me, Barry.''

Rather than lead him toward the dock area, jammed with emergency vehicles, Dante found a bench alongside an outbuilding. It was drenched in sunlight and out of a wind-cutting cold across the compound from off the water. Zajac sat as Joe loomed over him, his hands shoved deep in the pockets of his slacks.

''I'm only gonna ask you this once, Mr. Zajac. I want to know what your friend was up to and what your connection to it was.''

''Or what, Lieutenant?'' Barry was a newspaperman, for godsake. He was surprised a cop with as much experience as this one would try to strong-arm him like this. ''You'll arrest me?''

Dante's right hand flew from his pocket to slap Barry hard across the face. By the time Zajac recovered, the hand had disappeared.

''Don't fuck with me, Barry. You came to us because you *think* your friend Willie was murdered. Well, I *know* your friend Mitchell was. I want to know what you two were up to.''

Barry blinked and sputtered. ''I d-don't *believe* this! You can't—''

''Save your civil rights for cocktail parties,'' Dante snarled. ''I'm waiting.'' His eyes said he felt no remorse. In fact, he just might slap him again.

Barry swallowed hard. He was angry at himself for submitting so easily to the icy fear that suddenly got hold of his guts. ''A bookie I know fingered a guy named Miles Berga for me. He sells exotic sports cars out of a showroom on Northern Boulevard in Douglaston. Mitch went out there yesterday morning pretending he was interested in buying one.'' He went on to relate how Berga had wagered a quarter million dollars on the Yankees in the ALCS, how the car dealer was already in deep to some very unsympathetic people and couldn't afford to lose another nickel. He told Dante about Shimizu's background check on the man and the drug trafficker's past he had uncovered. ''He was sure those guys who hijacked him were part of a setup engineered by Berga, that they followed him when he drove away from Prestige Performance. He went out there last night to poke around some more, see what he could find.''

Barry watched Dante glance skyward. His hands came back out of his pockets to finger-comb his hair. ''He's the Lone goddamn Ranger and who were you, Barry? Tonto? A guy who did time at Angola, who's running a luxury carnapping ring, and your pal was gonna *peep* them? Jesus. And what did *you* say? Don't forget the popcorn and Milk Duds?''

Barry shut his eyes and swallowed again. A lump had suddenly formed in his throat. ''You didn't know him like I did, Lieutenant. Every ball he caught, he ran with himself. No matter what or who was involved. He was fearless.''

''And you were stupid, letting him run with this one.

This was *my* ball to carry, Zajac.''

When Dante's voice seemed to fade on the last few words, Barry opened his eyes to see the lieutenant walking away from him. Chief Lieberman was just now coming in the gate. ''Wait a minute,'' he called after him. ''What are you going to do now?''

Dante's reply reached Barry on the breeze, thrown back over the lieutenant's shoulder. ''My job, Mr. Zajac.''

When Jumbo Richardson pulled up before the Thirty-fourth North station house on Broadway and 183rd, yet another flock of young uniforms lined the rail out front like roosting gulls. Since Monday, the weather had turned cool enough to cut deep into any loitering outside the adjacent storefronts. While there was still plenty of sunshine, gone were the card tables surrounded by old men playing dominoes. The people Jumbo did see were all in motion, rushing to and fro wrapped in coats and jackets. He imagined it was hard on a native of the Caribbean to adapt to the New York winter. He didn't like the prospect much himself, and so far as he knew, his ancestors had been trying to acclimatize here for at least eight generations.

When he called from downtown, he learned that Lieutenant Karl Lulevich and Detective Pete Guitan were working the eight-to-four shift for the rest of the week. All the better, as far as he was concerned. Driving up here now beat doing it later in the day and fighting rush-hour traffic again. He found both Lulevich and Guitan upstairs in the squad, waiting for him. The younger Guitan, dressed like a street punk, offered coffee. With a steaming paper cup of it in hand, Jumbo joined them at one end of the squad table.

''Petey here makes a good cup of coffee, Lou. Roasts the beans himself.''

Jumbo sipped and couldn't argue. He liked his coffee dark and oily, even if his doctor didn't. Squad coffee was notorious for tasting like hell, mostly because the guys who made it knew nothing about what coffee should taste like. "Exceptional," he complimented Guitan.

"He might dis my threads, but ask him who runs the snitches that feed us *quality* goods in this godforsaken neighborhood." There was good nature in Guitan's tone. "Lieutenant Squarehead here? I don' think so. Even the semicomatose junkies see him an' his brown suit coming a mile off. Me? I got the psychology of the street on my side."

"And your right hand full a' your own dick," Lulevich growled. He made a jerking-off motion and shook his head. "And my old lady keeps askin' me why I won't retire. Hell, it's to keep shit-for-brains guys like Petey here from trampling their own organs every time they leave a urinal." He turned his attention to Jumbo's visit now. "So what brings you up here this mornin', Lou? You manage to find Citizen Cintron yesterday?"

"Had a nice talk with him. Yeah," Jumbo replied. "Then a funny thing happened on the way out of his building." He told them about running into the Chinese punk and the Benz registered to Lin T. Wah.

"You actually physically touched this guy?" There was awe in Lulevich's voice. "And he didn't try to gut you?"

Guitan grunted. "C'mon, boss. Look *close* at this man. Not everyone works downtown is a pussy. This be a dude could break most Tung-on punks in half."

"So what gives," Richardson pressed. "A high-visibility Chinese presence up here must mean the inroads are pretty deep."

"Strongest new drug alliance in the Apple," Lulevich replied. "Chinese gangs on the import end and Dominicans controlling distribution. In the poppy-dust game, they've cornered the market."

"No more of that Eyetalian-French connection bullshit,

Lou,'' Guitan added. ''They got fat an' lazy. The skinny, hungry crowd moved in.''

''Hector Cintron did time for heroin sales. What's *his* connection to the Tung-on?'' Jumbo asked.

''Ah.'' As Guitan said it he rose to pour himself another cup of his brew. Beasley had to admire the authenticity of his getup, from the thin, black leather necktie knotted loose at the open collar of a canary silk shirt, to baggy black pants made of some shiny, space-age material and ultra-white Nike high-top basketball shoes. The S&W ''Bull-dog'' .357 tucked in at the small of his back was the only thing that gave him away. A street punk would carry an automatic. Thus far, New York cops without special clear-ance still weren't allowed. ''That's this month's sixty-four-thousand-dollar question. You see, Lou, Hector—it is known for a fact—took a fall this las' go-roun' for one of Lin Wah's fuck-ups.''

''Not like he had much choice,'' Lulevich growled. ''Do the time with a smile or eat his own dick. It ain't *my* idea of options.''

Guitan finished filling his cup and returned to his chair. ''No matter. Hector made a delivery for the Tung-on, and that weren' his usual function. He was a money collector. An' not jus' that, it was outside Hector's regular network. He work up here with other Spanish people like himself. This delivery was to a black dude in Harlem. It was a con-nection Wah made through someone else. Turned out the man on the receiving end was one of ours, working deep. He wan' Lin T. but got Hector. When Cintron wouldn' turn state's, they had to settle for him.''

''A money collector. At what level?''

''Strictly middle management,'' Lulevich explained. ''Sorta like a regional sales manager. Hector takes orders, has other guys make deliveries, and handles the cash. So far as we've been able to learn, he never actually touches the product himself.''

"He lives in a shithole," Jumbo countered. "What gives? He does this outta the goodness of his heart?"

"He's on parole now, Lou," Guitan reminded him. "Can't have it look like he's doin' no more than washing dishes, or whatever the fuck he pretends. It in't the way he lived before the fall, an' it won't be for much longer, after."

"Where do Felipe and Antonio Infante fit in?" Richardson asked.

"They're a pair of junkies spend every cent they make, but nepotism works in *low* places, too," Lulevich told him. "They're blood-related to the regional manager. That means they get thrown a bone now'n then. Nothin' too major, 'cuz Hector can't really trust them. They're a coupla fuck-ups. You saw where they lived, too?"

Jumbo nodded.

"Well, they *ain't* on parole. What you seen is who they are."

Richardson sat back in his plastic bucket chair, his brow knit in consternation. What was he missing? "So I got one major player in the Chinese-Dominican alliance and two major fuck-ups, all partyin' in Willie Cintron's hotel room Saturday night. The residue they analyzed from the spoon on Willie's nightstand says the poppy he popped was the straight shit, no cereal fillers. If it was one a' them three that did him, I still ain't got a motive."

"How much was Willie pullin' down a year?" Guitan asked. "Million five? That's a lotta Play-Doh."

Jumbo nodded. "We've thoughta that. I've asked the chief to have his money dealings checked out. We should have something soon." He paused to glance back and forth between the partners. They presumably had a finger on the local pulse. "You mentioned snitches, Pete. What about them? If Willie *was* in on something that turned sour, could be it's leaked out through the cracks.''

"I got some places I could ask," Guitan replied. "They keep a pretty tight asshole 'bout the Chinese, mostly outta fear of them. Up here, the Caribbean Spanish don' get what all the *rush* is about. The Chinese gangs are the 'xact opposite of relaxed, you know what I mean?''

Beasley had plenty on his plate today and needed to get on with it. He finished his coffee as he started to rise. "I'd appreciate your asking anyway.'' Another thought occurred to him as he adjusted his weapon in his waistband. "And while you're at it you might ask around about a Felicia Rojas, wife of one a' the other Royals players. See if that name rings any bells. Good-looking woman, from what I understand. Sounds like anybody's seen her ain't likely to forget it.''

Chapter ▪ 14

WEDNESDAY AFTERNOON, DANTE AND RICHARDSON CON-
vened in C of D Lieberman's thirteenth-floor office to discuss the investigation's immediate directions. Beasley,
returned from uptown, had been brought abreast of developments on the Barry Zajac/Mitchell Shimizu front. Now
Dante sat on the sill of a huge window overlooking the
Brooklyn Bridge, the East River, and Brooklyn beyond. He
had Gus facing him from behind the desk and Jumbo in an
armchair out front. The chief shook a Carlton from his pack
and tapped the filter end against his blotter.

"This thing sprawls any more, I'm gonna have to call
the ringmaster from the Big Apple Circus," Gus complained. "How you want to cut it up, Joey?"

Dante ran a hand back and forth across his chin. "Best
way to make things worse is to start people stumbling into
each other. Beasley's running with the Dominican lead. I
say we leave it that way." He turned to Richardson.
"You're waiting on Willie's financial workup. What else?"

"I've asked the guys at the Three-Four North to nose
around. I'll chase anything they toss my way."

"And I'm gonna stick with Juan and Felicia Rojas," Joe
told Gus. "Head up to the Marquis and dig in where Jumbo
left off last night. That means we'll need a couple bodies
to work the stakeout on Berga."

"I've already talked to Detective Borough Queens. They're setting up the surveillance rotation as we speak. What kinda numbers you need crunched?"

Dante frowned. "With the northeast economy in the shitter, Berga's sales must be way off. We need to know how he's paying the rent."

"I'll get Support Services to crunch some numbers," Gus replied.

"And maybe contact the DMV," Joe added. "See if they can isolate all the Ferraris, Lamborghinis, and Lotuses owned in the tri-state area. Once they supply a list, we can see how many are reported stolen."

Richardson picked up his drift and made the connection. "Interview those owners. See where they bought them or have them serviced."

"Ah," Lieberman murmured. "Berga sells them, steals them back, and ships them overseas. I *like* it."

Joe faced Gus again. "Anything else we think of, we get Support Services to run with it. Shimizu was onto something. I'm convinced of it. Maybe Berga will panic—move something he's afraid to have found there and tip his hand."

"We need to find Shimizu's car, too," Jumbo said. "If Berga's got it or moved it, I'd like to know where." He glanced at Lieberman. "What's holding up Cintron's banking records? I thought we had a rush on 'em."

Lieberman's eyes narrowed slightly. "You ain't noticed that traffic seemed lighter than usual this morning?"

Beasley thumped his forehead with the heel of his hand. "Shit. It's Yom Kippur." Half the civilian personnel in Fiscal Section would have taken the day off. His expression turned amused. "So why ain't you at home, Gus? Atoning for your sins?"

"What sins?" Lieberman growled. "I spend my adult

life wading through everyone else's. When've I got time to commit my own?''

Captain Patricia Reilly had endured one of those days that made her wonder why she bothered. As she sat with the phone receiver wedged between cheek and shoulder, a huge wave of fatigue washed over her. The call she was making was to NYPD's Lieutenant Dante. He'd seemed a decent enough sort, conscientious enough to come all the way to Boston just to better understand a character peripheral to his investigation. Anybody that thorough would want to know the outcome of a disastrous day in court.

''SID Special Task Force. Lieutenant Richardson.''

''Dante there?'' she asked. ''This is Captain Reilly at Boston. Sex Crimes.''

She heard Richardson's half-muffled, ''Joey—phone,'' and seconds later Dante picked up.

''Yeah. Dante.''

''Pat Reilly, Lieutenant. I thought you'd want to know. Judge Coffelt set Juan Rojas loose about an hour ago.''

''Jesus. Why?''

''The exact same reasons we talked about. He partially bought in to Juan's story, that Willie Cintron held a grudge against him. Given that, there was no way he would allow Willie's deposition to be admitted.''

''The story is bullshit,'' Dante protested. ''My partner talked to another of the Royals yesterday afternoon. He claims it's Juan who held the grudge, that Willie dated Felicia first. Long before she ever gave Juan the time of day.''

Patricia ran her free hand over her face and bit her lower lip, the rage swelling within her. ''You're familiar with the term 'gender bias,' Lieutenant? Judge Barney Coffelt's got one in spades. Juan's accuser is a wanton woman. From Judge Barney's point of view, you play with fire often enough, sooner or later you *deserve* to get burned.''

There was a brief, heavy silence before Dante next spoke. "I'm sorry, Cap. I truly am. A lotta damned good that does you, right?"

"Or the justice system in general," Pat agreed.

"Where's Rojas now?" he asked.

"Free to go wherever he chooses. If I were him, I'd get far away from Boston in a hurry. There's an element in this community that's none too pleased he walked."

No sooner did Jumbo Richardson hand that call over to Dante than he fielded another from Detective Pete Guitan.

"I know you already been up here once today, but what you got on tap tonight?" Guitan asked. "'Bout eight?"

"I was seriously thinking about eating dinner," Beasley replied. "Why? What's up?"

"I got a guy you can talk to. Jumpy bastard, but mostly his info is solid gold. You want, I can put you together. He's a Hector Cintron runner, low-level mostly, but he hears shit."

"Name the place," Jumbo told him.

"Okay. You know the Highbridge Park? Off Amsterdam along the Harlem River? There's a thing called Highbridge Tower there, right opposite a Hundred Seventy-third Street. Meet me at eight."

"Kinda dark and desolate, ain't it?"

"That's the point, Lou. Me? I'd carry it locked and loaded, shoot the first thing that says boo."

As Dante headed his Fury north on West Street, headed for the Marriott Marquis on Times Square, he couldn't escape the tone of frustration in Captain Patricia Reilly's voice. There was little doubt in his mind and none in hers that a rape had been committed in Boston last May, that Juan Rojas was the perp and was guilty as sin. Joe had plenty to be frustrated about, too. Monday, Willie Cintron's possible homicide was little more than an irritation, a thorn trying to pierce the flank of Captain Ottomanelli's quick-wrap hot-air balloon. Now Joe had an innocent man dead on his watch. A probe that started out small just three days ago was threatening to go ballistic.

Times Square on Yom Kippur was only a bit quieter than it was most weekday afternoons. Traffic was lighter, with much of Fashion Avenue to the south and all of the Forty-seventh Street diamond district to the east taking the day off. An abnormal cold for mid-October was driving much of the loitering riffraff into the area's video arcades and sneaker emporiums. There were still a few frail joy boys looking hopeful, curbside. A knot of scantily clad trans-vestite hookers huddled together on another corner, and the usual crack and sinsemilla dealers muttered to passersby. On this day of atonement, one thing he didn't see was the usual stream of Hasidim skulking in and out of porn video and live peep shows.

Dante parked at a No Standing sign in the Marriott Marquis guest arrival area and saw a doorman eye him as he flipped his vehicle ID card onto the dash. The activity level was fairly subdued, probably because it was now several hours after checkout. Two limousines were pulled up, back-doors and trunk lids open as men and women in business attire supervised the unloading of their luggage. Down the way, idle cabbies clustered in conversation outside their cars. The hotel's atrium lobby was located eight floors above Times Square. Once Dante arrived there via a futur-istic elevator, he skipped gaping upward in awe. Instead, he approached the bell captain's desk. The uniformed man on duty gave Joe's lieutenant's gold a glance and met his gaze with nonchalance. Big and barrel-chested, the captain reminded Joe of older desk sergeants. If there was any doubt about him being a retired cop, his greeting removed it.

"Do for you, Lou?"

"Dante. I'm running an SID follow-up on the dead ball-player." He read the man's nameplate. "You have the duty here Saturday night, Mr. Cole?"

The bell captain nodded. "But only till eight. Damn shame, ain't it? Kid with that kinda talent?" He stopped, brow furrowing. "Dante? Any relation to Tony Dante, used to work outta the Brooklyn Six-Nine?"

Joe nodded. "My dad."

Cole's expression livened some. "No shit? Great guy, your pop. How the hell is he?"

"He drowned about ten years back."

Tony Dante and several friends had been fishing in rough water off Montauk Point when one of them was washed overboard. The senior Dante and another man jumped in to save him. None of the three came back alive. Dante's mother had since remarried.

"Damn, I'm sorry to hear it." Cole focused closer, sizing Joe up, and brightened again. "I remember hearin' it that Tony had a boy—a pretty good ballplayer."

"That was a long time ago. Listen. I need to talk to somebody who worked the late Saturday-night shift. Preferably the one who's got a few girls' numbers."

A gate came down. "This ain't that kinda hotel, Lieutenant."

Joe smiled. "I know that. But it doesn't stop one man from doing another a favor, strictly between the two of them." He leaned closer and lowered his voice. "I'm not here to bust anyone's balls, Cole. And I'm not here for a hand-job, either. You give me a name, my conversation with him goes only that far. You people had an entire major-league ball club here Saturday. I *know* how strange-tail-crazed those guys can get. I need your man who had his thumb on that pulse."

The gate came up just high enough for Cole to peek out

from beneath. "He knows I fed him to you, he'll kill me."

"Who?"

"I get no cut, no nothin'."

"Fine, Mr. Cole. Who?"

"Name's Hull. Frank Hull. Matter of fact, he's across the lobby on the other side of the elevators there." He pointed to where lift cars in modernistic pods operated from a cluster similar to a circle of covered wagons. "In the Broadway Lounge. He don't come on shift till five, but he always comes in a couple hours early. Likes to keep tabs."

"I don't imagine he's in uniform yet, right?"

"Nuh-uh. But ask the bartender. Ain't much of a crowd in there this time of day."

As Dante turned away his beeper went off. He scanned the message window and headed for a pay phone.

Because the request was made by the chief of detectives to the Department of Motor Vehicles commissioner in Albany, it was less than an hour before Support Services started getting results. New Jersey and Connecticut would be a little longer replying, but for fifteen minutes before Dante returned the Request Section's call, their fax terminal had been spewing data. Meanwhile, a call was placed to the marketing director of Ferrari North America in Cypress, California. Ferrari had sold nine hundred sixty units in the U.S. last year, at a cost of $189,000 per. Plus or minus twenty percent of that number were sold in the metro area. There are only a handful of authorized dealers, and that was less than two hundred cars between the lot of them.

After reporting on the Ferrari findings to Dante, the Request Section commander explained that he'd asked the DMV to go back eight years, to 1986. "We're talking about a thousand cars, more or less, Lieutenant. To simplify matters, we're seeking to isolate only Ferraris."

"Why not one of the others?" Joe asked. "Maybe the numbers are even smaller."

"They are, but so's the resale demand. Maserati had a serious registration falloff during that period, and the Lotus numbers are way down, too. Ferrari's the hot one to own and the hottest one to steal."

"Any chance the Ferrari people can get us names of people who bought through Prestige Performance?"

"The request has been made, Lieutenant. The DMV list is compiled by model year. We've started off with the last two, all the registered owners of 1992 and 1993 Ferrari 512 Testarossas in New York State."

"How many is that?"

"One hundred sixty-eight."

"Be a good idea to run them by Central Robbery while you're waiting on Ferrari," Joe suggested. "See how many are reported stolen."

"One step ahead of you there, too, Lou. I'll be in touch."

The lounge at the far east end of the Marriott Marquis lobby was as slick in its design as everything else about that John Portman creation. Perched up eight floors above Times Square, the Broadway Lounge had a bird's-eye view of midtown, a forest of brick, steel, and glass spires with Broadway cutting its course across Seventh Avenue below in a concentration of commercialism second to none in the hemisphere. Behind the floor-to-ceiling glass, the lounge interior was cut up into dozens of cozy seating arrangements, clusters of plum tub chairs where patrons could relax. There was also a large, central bar area rimmed with upholstered bar chairs, where the more outgoing could mix and mingle.

As Dante approached the lounge area late Wednesday afternoon, he found it all but empty. Here and there he saw businessmen and women in conversation, a notepad and pen in evidence. Otherwise, any action was centered at the bar. A woman bartender leaned against the central backbar cabinetry while three patrons seated before her pored over a sheet of paper set between them.

"I don't care *how* good Dallas is this year. Ain't no fucking way they can cover a spread like that. Not against the Vikes. They'll play them tough. Guaran-fucking-teed."

Dante gave the speaker a quick glance as he stepped to the bar and nodded to the barkeep. A stocky character with a heavy beard shadow and an awful toupee, he was probably correct in his analysis. That morning, Joe noticed oddsmakers had the Cowboys winning this Sunday's contest by thirteen and a half. He believed Dallas would win, but not by more than a touchdown. The other two there at the bar weren't so sure. One, a young kid in a dark blue suit with flakes of dandruff on his shoulders, shook his head with vehemence.

"Bull-dookie. The Vikes ain't played nobody but cream puffs so far."

The bartender, a slender blonde with her hair treated a touch too brassy, pushed off the back bar to sidle over. She had the tired eyes of a woman old beyond her years, of someone who'd heard and seen it all and come away none the happier for the experience. Joe guessed she'd been a genuine beauty once. He didn't want to know how life had failed her.

"Hi. What can I get you?"

"Frank Hull?"

The discussion between the three sports fans died abruptly as she shot a look over. Her eyes then came back to Joe, more guarded now. "Who's asking?"

Dante assumed that all three men at the bar were off-duty hotel employees, killing time before or after their shifts. The kid in the suit was some variety of desk help. Joe had noticed others dressed in the same conservative manner at registration, across the way. The bad rug wasn't Hull either. He didn't have enough polish for a man who performed Hull's function. That left the last man. Joe stepped toward him now, producing his shield case as he moved.

"Lieutenant Dante. Special Investigation Division, Mr. Hull. You think I could have a word with you in private?"

Hull, a slender, neatly turned-out man in a gray worsted jacket and razor-creased tan slacks, looked more like a Washington lobbyist than a pimp. His neat-trimmed hair was graying slightly at the temples and worn straight back. He was maybe fifty at the outside and looked fit.

"Who tipped you to me?" he growled. "Jimmy Cole?"

"Relax, Frank," Dante replied. "I don't know this Cole, but your name came up in conversations with three different Kansas City Royals."

Hull grunted as he slipped off the stool to stand. "Figures. You do these kids a favor, and that's the thanks."

Dante led him toward a nearby pair of deep chairs with a low table between them. He took one and watched as Hull sat. "The way it sounds to me, you do lots of people favors, Frank. It's kinda your specialty here."

"Is this a roust, Lieutenant? Because if it is, I think I'd like to call my attorney."

"I told you to relax, Frank." Joe handed across a faxed photo of Felicia Rojas from her driver's license. "You recall ever seeing this woman?"

Hull took the sheet of paper, unfolded and frowned at it for a few seconds before shaking his head. "Not a very good shot, is it?" He handed the sheet back. "I'm pretty good at remembering a face, and that's not one I know. Are you asking if I ever got her dates?"

He made it sound so civilized. "Just if you'd ever seen her," Joe replied.

"Not that I recall. No."

"Okay." Dante tucked the photo away in his jacket. "I'm investigating Willie Cintron's death, Mr. Hull. I understand he preferred the sort of *date* you could get him to picking up a stray in a bar. The Royals arrived here Friday for Saturday and Sunday games. You got him a date Friday night." He didn't ask it as a question, taking a shot in the dark instead.

"Maybe I want to call my lawyer anyway. I'm not sure I like where this is headed."

The shot had hit the target. Joe eyed Hull steadily. "You're an uptight guy, Frank. Didn't I say you could relax?"

"Same as Hitler told Stalin *he* could relax."

Dante smiled. "Public morals is some other lucky stiff's bailiwick, Mr. Hull. There's a demand; you provide a service. That's all I know on that count and all I *want* to know. But I do need to know if you got Willie Cintron another date Saturday."

"I never said I got him a first."

Dante's eyes went hard, framed by a face that said he was done playing games. "I advise leaving the stroke-jobs to the people being paid for them, Frank. You keep messing with me, you *will* need your attorney. I promise you. Right now you still don't."

Still annoyed, Hull relented. "Saturday night? No, I didn't."

"You talk to him at all, Saturday?"

"Nope. They don't come to me, I stay out of their faces. This isn't a whorehouse the Marquis is running, Lieutenant. If they even knew what I was doing here, they'd fire me in a New York minute. Nuh-uh. This is strictly between me, some of the other help here, and the guest with the special need."

"You write your own material?"

Hull blinked. "I beg your pardon?"

"Forget it." Joe thought this guy might make the perfect mortician should he ever tire of his current line of work. "Any chance Cintron made Saturday arrangements with his Friday date? Without your knowledge?"

Now Hull smiled. "Considering how they all seem to fall for her, he probably tried, Lieutenant. But Saturday she already had another obligation."

"No chance she might have finished early?"

"Not in this instance. The other gentleman makes regular visits to the city on business. They have a standing arrangement."

"Our evidence says Cintron spent part of Saturday night in the company of an unidentified woman, Mr. Hull. Any light you could shed would reflect what a civic-minded guy you are."

Hull barely suppressed a sneer of derision. "Sorry. Can't help you, Lieutenant. But believe what I told you. She wasn't one of mine." He leaned forward in his chair. "You want my opinion? You're pissing into the wind. The minute a pro ball team shows up here—or at *any* New York hotel—it's like the word goes out on some universal grab-ass grapevine. Last Saturday night we had tits hanging out by the ton up here. Willie Cintron wanted his pipe cleaned? He was a good-looking kid, he was rich, and he was a star. He would have had them lining up."

Chapter ■15

DOUGLASTON, QUEENS, WASN'T EXACTLY ON DANTE'S way home, but he wanted to get a good look at Miles Berga's operation up close before he called it a day. He'd arranged with Jumbo to meet him there, and at four-thirty that Wednesday afternoon, Joe parked three blocks away on Northern Boulevard and sauntered toward Richardson's car up the sidewalk. En route, he passed the regular surveillance team put in place by Queens Detective Command. He shot a sideways glance through the passenger-side glass to see a pair of plainclothes female officers lounging with cans of soda, their feet up on the dash. It looked a whole lot like a stakeout to him, and probably to Berga as well.

Beasley was behind the wheel, at work on a deli salad in a clear plastic container, when Joe slid in beside him.

"Much trouble spotting our team?" Dante asked.

"Why don't they hang out a fucking flag?"

"Probably against some regulation." Dante brought Richardson up to date on his conversation with Frank Hull, then pulled his notebook from his inside jacket pocket. "Just off the horn with Support Services. There are seventeen late-model Ferraris on the state-police reported-stolen list. One from Queens, six from the near North Shore of Long Island, and seven more from greater Long Island. Only three from upstate."

Jumbo nodded toward the showroom across the boulevard. "How many sold by Berga?"

"They haven't isolated them yet, but I'm taking bets. Half were stolen within ten miles of where we sit." His eyes followed to where Richardson was looking. "Anything interesting?"

"I think the dude in the red polo shirt must be Berga. He's the only salesman I've seen. The tall blonde there with the manila envelope must be some sorta secretary. Seems she's getting set to call it a day."

They watched the blonde toss the manila envelope into a briefcase on a magazine-laden coffee table. After closing the case, she shrugged into a light coat. The polo shirt carried the case while walking her to the front door and out onto the sidewalk. Joe noticed the blonde glance diagonally across the street to where the surveillance sat parked. No question they'd been made. He got a better look at the secretary's face then. It was pretty in a sharp-featured, brittle way, but he doubted that was what men noticed about her. He'd gotten a good look at her body while she was in the showroom.

With her escort, the woman crossed the sidewalk to unlock the driver's-side door of a black Carrera Porsche. As she climbed behind the wheel the polo shirt remained behind. When she drove off, he returned to the showroom.

"Pretty nice set of wheels for a secretary," Joe commented.

"You talking about her or the car?" Jumbo lifted a forkful of greens to his mouth and shoved them in to chew thoughtfully. "I'd say most everything I've seen of her is nice, wheels included. Maybe Berga goes in for profit sharing. It makes a good performance incentive."

"Stop it," Joe complained.

Minutes later the polo shirt emerged again from the showroom to lock up and head for the service-area gate.

"Kinda early to be calling it a day, ain't it?" Beasley asked.

"Man like that can set his own hours," Joe supposed. "Especially when he's got cops watching him and blood on his hands."

Less than two minutes later a red Testarossa appeared through the gate and the polo shirt hopped out to swing the chain-link closed behind him. He punched a code into the alarm-system keypad.

"So that's Miles Berga," Dante mused. "I had him pictured different. More imposing, I guess. Probably because of that stretch he did at Angola."

Jumbo reached for the ignition key. "I don't know about you, but I'm ready to call it a day."

The restaurant Sherril Meyer suggested for dinner was an old standby from when Dante lived a few blocks away on Perry Street in Greenwich Village. He'd lost his rent-controlled garden apartment to fire, but Bruxelles remained a constant. Their selection of Belgian beers made by Trappist monks was extensive. Joe liked the informal bistro atmosphere. As soon as he entered tonight and the bartender lifted a hand in recognition, he felt himself start to unwind after what had been too long and ugly a day. Suddenly he was among restaurant patrons who had none of his cares, who'd only heard vaguely about a *Daily News* reporter found murdered and had no idea how or why. Tonight he wished he could be one of them. If he couldn't, he'd try his damnedest over the next few hours to forget Mitchell Shimizu's second grin.

Before Joe could say anything to the hostess, she flashed him a bright smile.

"Lieutenant Dante?"

He frowned. "Yeah?"

"This way, please."

He followed her to a table in a corner at the back of the dining room, all the while wondering how she'd known him. The restaurant had a good crowd that Wednesday night, most of the clientele still wearing work clothes, but a few in more casual attire. Sherrie Meyer was seated with a view of the whole place, one finger tracing patterns in the dewy sheen coating a full champagne glass. She had an ice bucket set alongside, the telltale neck shape of a Dom Perignon bottle protruding from beneath the cover towel. She beamed brightly at Dante's approach and half rose to extend a hand. Joe forgot about the strength of her grip until she applied it again.

"Am I late or are you early?" he asked.

"I could just about set my watch, Lieutenant. I got away from the office a few minutes early."

"You should probably call me Joe."

Their waitress appeared as Dante got himself seated. "A glass of champagne, sir?" she asked. "Or something from the bar?"

Dante nodded toward Sherrie's glass. "D.P. no less. What's the occasion?"

"Join me," she urged him. "I'm celebrating tonight. The network's just promoted me to station sales manager."

Dante told the waitress he'd join Sherrie and watched her eyes glisten as the wine was poured. "Congratulations. It's the next step you wanted to take?"

She lifted her own glass to sip. "Oh God, yes. New York is the network's flagship station. The king of the whole hill? His office is just down the hall. New York's a monster market. At this stage in my career, this is right where I want to be." She reached across to click her glass with his. "Considering the World Series package I put together, there's hardly a way they could have given the job to anyone else."

Dante drank to her continued success and considered

what he found so attractive about her. This was the third time he'd seen her in three days. He realized now, on close examination, that she didn't have a classic physical beauty. She was pleasant to look at, but the energy she exuded was what drew him into her sphere. It was rare to meet a woman so confident—not just intellectually, but physically, too. It gave her a unique strength of presence. The French braid of yesterday morning was gone tonight. She still wore her hair away from her face, but secured it loosely now with combs set behind her ears. Both combs bore the same geometric shapes present on a whimsical-looking plastic bracelet. Instead of a suit or dress, she wore a beige skirt and slate-blue jacket over a white silk blouse. On her, they looked elegant and sexy at the same time.

"Sounds like you want to be queen of the hill sometime yourself," he observed.

She took another sip and savored it, eyes closing briefly before swallowing. "Why shoot for anything but the bull's-eye, Joe? By the way, have you ever had the calves liver here?"

"It's good. And the fries in the paper cone are excellent."

"Pommes frites."

"They'll always be french fries to me, I can't help it. I'm from Brooklyn."

"But you've become a downtowner. SoHo art openings and all."

He smiled. "Downtown Manhattan is as far as I could risk moving without losing my soul."

She chuckled. "I see. The soul of a Brooklynite."

"It's a very delicate thing."

"Uh-huh. I'm guessing it's the *only* delicate thing about you."

His smile hurried to match hers. "So how did the waitress know who I was when I walked in here?"

She reached across the table to pat the back of his hand and winked. "Never mind, Joe. It's a woman thing."

Amsterdam Avenue fronting Highbridge Park was all but empty by the time Jumbo Richardson reached it at seven-fifty Wednesday night. From a tiny tail down at 156th Street to its head at 201st, the park ran as a verge separating Washington Heights from the Harlem River. Two bridges and a viaduct crossed through it and over the river, connecting upper Manhattan to the Bronx. It was at the base of that viaduct that the Highbridge Tower rose to dominate the surrounding landscape. Jumbo had no idea of the history behind its construction, but there was no question that someone, once upon a time, had meant it to make a statement. He wasn't a good judge of heights, but it had to be ten to fifteen stories tall. It was built of stone blocks, the trunk rising sheer to an overlook punctuated with elongated Gothic windows and crowned with a funnel-shaped roof.

Access to the tower was gained through a gate and via a paved path running back through the Highbridge Park Playland. A public facility, the playland was home to the immense Highbridge Park pool, a gymnasium, outdoor basketball courts, and other sports structures. On a hot summer night, Richardson imagined the basketball courts would still be seeing action. Now, in the gloom of an early nightfall, the whole facility appeared abandoned as he parked his car and climbed out into the chill night air. Up and down the park side of Amsterdam he could make out the hulks of stripped cars every forty or fifty feet, many tipped onto their sides. He could only imagine what went on in the deeper shadows of the park's interior. Detective Pete Guitan's locked-and-loaded advisory echoed in his memory as he reached to the small of his back for his service weapon and slipped it into his jacket pocket.

The broad paved area surrounding the tower appeared

empty as Richardson stepped into it. Then a figure materialized from beneath a perimeter tree, signaling Jumbo forward. With one hand eased into his jacket pocket, fingers wrapped around the butt of his revolver, Beasley advanced.

"Evenin', Lou," Guitan greeted him. He turned his head to speak over his shoulder. "C'mon, Manny. He ain't gonna bite you. Let's all three of us take a walk."

A slender, jumpy-nervous Hispanic man emerged from shadows to join Guitan. He only let his eyes barely brush Richardson before forcing his attention elsewhere.

"Manny Lupo, Lieutenant," Guitan introduced them. "This ain't his idea of no walk in the park, but maybe a little fresh river air help put him at ease."

Richardson let Pete lead them toward the viaduct and riverbank beyond the tower. The three of them stopped when they reached the stone bulwark, the lights from buildings across the river reflecting off the water below. Away to the south, the Manhattan skyline glowed like some remote fantasy kingdom. Jumbo imagined that for a man like Manny Lupo, a fantasy was all mid-Manhattan would ever be. He could visit, but it was as far removed from his grasp as winning the lottery.

"Manny, he got an interesting story to tell you, Lieutenant." Pete Guitan stared off to the south. "Go ahead, m'man."

"You say there is a hundred in this for me," Lupo murmured. "I don' see it, Pete."

Guitan dug into the pocket of his shiny black slacks and produced a roll of bills. From it, he peeled five twenties and handed them across. "So talk."

Lupo turned to Richardson, really looking at him for the first time. "Pete, he say you wanna know what gives with Felipe Infante an' Hector Cintron. What I know is this. Felipe, he already fuck up once. Real bad. Barely got his ass *outta* that jam. Now his ass is in one again, an' this time he ain't got no rich cousin to bail his ass *out*.''

Beasley was lost. "So *how* did Felipe fuck up?"

Lupo glanced to Guitan, who nodded. "He s'pose to pay the Tung-on for half a key of product, man. Only instead, he take most the money from that deal an' play it on this sure-thing horse tip he get. When the horse dump the jockey in the stretch turn, Felipe? He walk away with his *cojones* on the edge of a straight razor.''

"So to save him from Tung-on retribution, Hector Cintron bailed him out?" Jumbo concluded.

Lupo shook his head. "Not Hector. Hector was in stir. His brother Willie. Dude that jus' bought it t'other night. Willie, he buy Felipe's balls back from Lin T. Wah. Pay him the sixty-five gran' Felipe lose.''

"I expect Willie wanted his cousin to pay that money back to him?" Jumbo asked.

Lupo nodded. "But last I hear, Felipe still hadn'. Willie? He was getting pissed. It weren' like Willie couldn' afford it, but that wasn' the point. It was a loan, like.''

Richardson had seen how Felipe and Antonio Infante lived. Sixty-five thousand dollars was a lot of money for anyone to owe. To a fuck-up who lived in a one-room apartment and was prone to betting the farm on a horse, it probably looked like he owed the moon.

"I don't imagine Felipe will be having to pay that money back now," Jumbo surmised. "You?"

Lupo shrugged. "It don' make no difference to a chump like Felipe. Word on the street? He owe Lin Wah for *another* half key now. I know he did the deal 'cause I know a man took half his action.''

"What's Felipe done with *this* money?" Jumbo asked.

"Beats me, man. Prob'ly bet the whole wad on the fucking Royals.''

■　　■　　■

During his dinner conversation with Sherrie Meyer, Dante felt the ground beneath him constantly shifting. Her ability to keep it moving lent her an air of playful mystery that he found incredibly appealing. They'd finished their entrées and ordered coffee when he finally asked the question that he'd been wanting to ask since first meeting this woman Monday night.

"Maybe I'm being too personal, but I'm curious." He looked directly into her eyes. "What is it between you and Rob Ironstone? He's married, isn't he?"

"Which question are you asking?" Again, she was frank and straight with him.

"Maybe I shouldn't ask either," he replied. "Sorry. It's the nosy cop in me."

"Why not?" she replied. "If it wasn't something you wanted to know, you wouldn't have asked." She paused, her gaze still locked with his. "Yes, he is married. Her name is Jillian. My relationship with him is pretty uncomplicated. We're fuck buddies."

Dante managed not to betray the fact that she'd landed one flush. "Fuck buddies."

Her lips stretched in the slightest of smiles, those big brown eyes sparkling. "That's right. Two people who enjoy a friendly fuck now and then. Nothing more complicated than that. You find the idea shocking?"

The notion wasn't so shocking, just the fact that she'd so freely admit it. "You and Jillian. You're friends?"

She shook her head, her gaze trying to measure his level of discomfort. "No. I wouldn't say that. I've met her, of course. I mentioned that party out at their place last July? There and other places. Similar situations. And if you're wondering how I *feel* about her?" She shrugged. "I don't, really. If I did, I'd probably sleep somewhere else."

"But seeing as you don't, why not?"

Again, the unwavering frankness that was almost a challenge. "I've never met an honest man—or woman, for that matter—who could claim they were monogamous by nature. The occasional change of venue keeps the blood moving."

"Good-looking guy, Ironstone. That can't be his real last name."

That slight smile of hers showed a touch of frost at its edges. "What are you implying?"

"Nothing. What was it? Eisenstein? I'm just curious to know what he hoped to accomplish by changing it. Eisenstein sounds real. Ironstone sounds like something out of D.C. comics."

"It's done all the time," she replied. "I don't know why you find it so unusual."

Dante eased back in his chair and lifted his coffee to his lips. At tables around them, other diners were engaged in their own conversations. He hoped they were enjoying themselves as much as he was. "I don't. Just curious. That's all. I'm not making any judgments."

She stared hard at him, clearly trying to decide if he *was* making a judgment. "All relationships between people are political alliances, Joe."

"Made for whatever reasons," he replied. "We're being frank here, right?"

She nodded, a wariness in it.

"Okay. Frankly, I feel flattered when a woman as attractive as you are invites me to dinner. And when you start talking about how you and some guy are nothing more than a couple of happy-go-lucky fuck buddies, a certain part of me—the part that would do *most* of my thinking if I let it—gives me a nudge in the prostate and starts wagging its tail. Gee, Joey. Maybe she'll be our fuck buddy, too. It forces me into asking all sorts of questions. Maybe it's a defense."

She couldn't help but chuckle. "You make it sound like

being sentenced to a year at hard labor. Keep it up and I may withdraw the offer.''

''I didn't know you'd tendered it.''

She snorted with mock contempt. ''I'm supposed to do what? Submit it in writing? I may be a woman with healthy appetites, but a taste for masochism isn't one of them. You're worried about my motives? There's only one. The nosy cop in you aside, I liked what I saw Monday night, and again yesterday morning.'' She paused to grin while shaking her head. ''Heck, I still like what I see. I bet we could really enjoy getting acquainted.''

The strip mall off Route 503 in Hackensack, New Jersey, was almost completely dark by the time Felipe Infante pulled Oscar Saavedra's pirated box van into the parking lot. Way down at one end, a liquor store was still doing business. Halfway along, a Laundromat was open. Felipe could see several dryers tumbling clothes in there, the patrons reading magazines or looking bored. At the end of the mall toward which he drove, the front doors of Compu-Mania—GUARANTEED ROCK-BOTTOM LOWEST PRICES *ANY*-WHERE!—lay in the shadows of an overhanging roof canopy. The only lights were those illuminating the parking lot and several security spots set atop the building facade.

When making tonight's arrangements, the owner of Compu-Mania instructed Felipe to meet him around back, using the delivery driveway at the east end of the complex. Before Felipe did that, he wanted to make sure he wasn't driving his two hundred Panafax UF-733s into a state-police sting net. He eased the truck up to park it in front of the Laundromat with the several other vehicles clustered there. After locking up, he strolled down past the end of Compu-Mania and turned into the service drive, his eyes alert for trouble. To his relief he found the owner sitting alone in a parked Mercedes 300 turbo diesel. The man jumped almost a mile when Felipe sneaked up to rap at the window glass behind his left shoulder. Seconds later the owner stood outside his car mad as hell, an automatic pistol gleaming a menacing blue cradled in his right hand.

"What the *fuck?* What kinda shit-ass stunt is that? You're trying to give me a heart attack?"

Felipe patted the air between them apologetically. "I'm *sorry,* man. But I s'pose to what? Jus' drive back here, not check the scene *out* first?"

The Compu-Mania proprietor, pudgy and pasty-faced with a moth-eaten beard, rolled his eyes in exasperation. "How much business your pal Ramon done with me, huh? For crissake. You think I'd be sittin' out here with my finger up my ass, I didn't know from him your deal was straight goods? Why you fucking with me? You think I *need* this bullshit?"

Ramon Espejo was a friend of Felipe's from the neighborhood. He did a lot more trading along this line than Felipe did. In fact, this was Infante's first such foray into the world of black-market high-tech hardware. He couldn't believe this. The fat-ass doughboy expected him to ride in here on a cloud of goodwill and trust? Felipe pointed to the gun.

"I be more comfortable you put that thing away, amigo."

"Sure thing, amigo. Soon as I see the goods and we get this deal done. I expect you want your money and I expect I ain't showing you shit until I see the machines."

Felipe was getting cold, standing out there in the stiff breeze that was funneling down that back alley. Already he was contemplating being picked up by his brother Antonio in his warm car out front. The heater in the box van didn't work for shit. He'd be glad once he was rid of it. He headed back to the parking lot, returning minutes later with the fax machines. He hopped down after killing the engine and found the store owner still waiting, his gun now tucked out of sight.

"Ramon, he tell me you take care of losing the truck, yes?"

The other man grunted. "What? You planned to stick around, wait for me to call my people and have them unload two hundred machines? Just open the fucking cargo door. Let's have a look."

Felipe inserted his key into the padlock, securing the door-latch handle. No sooner did he heave the door upward than the store owner was playing the beam from his flashlight over the stacked cartons.

"Help me get one a' them down, huh?"

Felipe wondered what had happened to all that straight-goods garbage as he climbed up to lend a hand. They were big suckers, those cartons, at least two feet high and nearly three feet long. No wonder Oscar couldn't get one into the trunk of his Jag.

Once they eased a box to the pavement, the Compu-Mania man produced a carton knife and used it to cut the factory seal. Felipe watched while he removed Styrofoam bracing and then slit the clear plastic wrapping surrounding the machine itself.

"Why you do that?" he asked. "Factory fucking carton, seal tape still there on the top. Machine right there inside. What else you need?"

The man did not reply. He triggered a latch on some sort of cover. Raised, it revealed the machine's innards. "Why? Because we got us a little problem here, amigo."

Felipe stiffened. "Wha'? I tell you two hundred. I deliver two hundred. Where the problem with that?"

The buyer straightened to point down into the guts of the machine. "Some of these, they ship with the print processing unit inside, and some they ship separate. You see that empty space there?"

"Yeah?" Felipe said it warily, panic suddenly gripping his bowels.

"But you don't see nothing *else* in the box, right? Just the one machine. For it to be any good to me, I need the developer unit, drum unit, and toner cartridge that goes with it."

Felipe was fast seeing his panic fuel anger. "What the fuck you saying, man?"

"I'm saying we ain't got a deal, amigo. Not with the print process units missing, we don't. Them suckers go a couple hundred apiece, wholesale. Everything but the telephone on this machine is useless without it."

Felipe's anger turned to panic again, pure and clear. "Without that thing—whatever you call it—what you give me for them? They gotta be worth something, bran' new in the box like this."

The buyer retracted the blade on his carton knife and shoved it back into his hip pocket. "Not to me, they ain't. How's it gonna look, I call up a supplier and tell them I need print process units for two hundred UF-seven-thirty-threes? I'd have state and federal task-force cops crawling up my ass before I could hang up the phone."

Felipe only half heard the man. He was suddenly dizzy. Two minutes ago he expected to walk out into that parking lot and wave to his brother Antonio, his wallet thirty thousand dollars fatter. Now Antonio would collect a condemned man. When Lin Wah had pronounced his death sentence, he was given forty-eight hours to appeal. Tomorrow morning his time was up and he'd failed to make his case.

"Hey! Where the fuck *you* going?!"

Felipe had started to walk away zombielike, headed for the service access and parking lot out front. He only half heard the man's words and tendered no reply.

"Wait a minute, amigo. You ain't leavin' *me* with this truck. What the fuck am *I* s'posed to do with it? Hey!"

Felipe stopped and turned. "What you gonna do if I don' take it? Shoot me? Go ahead."

Chapter ∎ 16

THE TWO MEN SITTING PARKED IN THE TAN PLYMOUTH Fury sedan across the boulevard from Prestige Performance were obviously cops. Miles Berga was seated beside Fernando Mendoza in the Colombian's borrowed Chevy Caprice Yellow Cab. They'd watched the cops come out from the side alley between the showroom and the business next door, twenty minutes after a hidden surveillance camera in the yard picked them up outside the back fence. The minute they appeared, Mendoza started reaching for the iron, checking the magazine and action of the Ingram MAC-10 machine pistol shoved beneath his seat. Miles went into a near-blind panic. You could kill a troublesome lawman in Colombia, but here in the States, you killed a cop, they hunted you to the ends of the earth.

"They back there for close to half an hour, Miles. What they *doing* back there? An' why they jus' sitting there?"

The cops had circuited the entire service yard, but hadn't tried to breach the fence. Miles was trying to view these developments more calmly than Mendoza. "They've been there all day, Freddy. How many times I got to tell you? Soon as we caught that sneak last night, we cleaned out *everything*. Got rid of his wheels. Got rid of the other wheels. They could bust in there right now, tear it apart, and all they'd find is an empty garage."

They'd worked that reporter over pretty good last night before Debbie cut his throat. Not that beating him had done much good. If it hadn't been for the identification found in Mitchell Shimizu's wallet, Miles wouldn't have known who they killed until today, when he and the rest of New York heard about it on the news. For the cops to be onto Prestige Performance so soon after Shimizu was discovered floating in the sound, Miles assumed the reporter had kept some sort of notes. But he couldn't imagine what could be in them. Shimizu had shown up yesterday morning for the first time. He'd gotten his car hijacked within ten minutes of leaving, but what could that produce? Conjecture, maybe, but nothing concrete. Miles had to believe this second surveillance team, like the two women earlier, was on nothing more than a fishing trip.

"The people in Cali? They ain' going to like this interruption, Miles. Not one fucking bit. An' you still telling the same story. You got no *idea* how that man, a fucking reporter, come to be poking aroun' here in the first place?"

"The hijack is all I can figure, Freddy. Other than that? *Nada.*"

"I wan' fucking answers, Miles," Mendoza growled.

"Well, I ain't *got* any answers. My guess? One of the people got his car stolen started throwing theories around. They landed on Shimizu's desk on a slow news day."

Mendoza turned enough in his seat to regard Miles with half his attention while keeping the rest on those cops in the car across Northern Boulevard. He slowly shook his head, that damned machine gun still cradled in his lap. "You know what I thin', Miles? I thin' you got a leak somewhere."

"Bullshit!" Miles spat it back.

"I thin' maybe you been a little distracted lately," Freddy continued. "Like by how much you owe the fucking goombahs, 'cause you got no gambling sense."

It hit Berga like a hammer. How could Mendoza know such a thing? Miles kept his business and his private affairs separate. "Wait a minute," he murmured. "How—"

Freddy cut him off. "You thin' we all a bunch of stupid spics, don' you, Miles? Jus' like your father did. A man like Lucho Esparza, who runs a pipeline brings him four hundred million a year, don' know where the weak spots are? Please."

Miles realized he'd half soaked the shirt beneath his jacket with cold sweat. "I scored pretty good, just this last weekend," he defended himself. "Paid down a big chunk of what I owe. I'll make the rest of it square inside the month. Just a little streak of bad luck. That's all."

Fernando clucked his tongue. "Miles, Miles. What if the Yankees *hadn'* won? You were one ballgame away from having your *cojones* cut off. An' how you going to pay the rest? Make more shitty bets? We are shut *down* here. We got *cops* parked at the curb. You know I got no choice. I got to contac' Lucho. This is going to make him *very* unhappy."

Mendoza caressed the gleaming weapon in his lap.

Dante was about to drive Sherrie Meyer home to her Upper East Side apartment when his beeper went off. It was nearly nine-thirty and they were crossing the sidewalk outside Bruxelles. Joe snatched the unit off his belt to scan the message display. It bore the all-too-familiar number of the operations desk downtown.

"Saved by the bell?" Sherrie asked.

Dante looked back toward the restaurant, remembering where the pay phone was. "Sorry," he apologized. "You want to wait in the car for me or back inside?"

When she motioned him on to the restaurant door, Joe hurried to an alcove midway between the bar and dining room. As he dropped a quarter and dialed he watched Sherrie settle into a bar chair.

"Operations. Lieutenant Crowell."

"It's Dante, Dick. What's up?"

"Chief Lieberman's got a corpse he wants you to look at. A suicide. Twenty-two eighty-two Broadway. Nineteenth floor. That's the corner of West Eighty-third."

Broadway and Eighty-third sounded familiar. Dante scrambled, trying to think why.

"It's one of those new luxury high rises up there. Dead lady's name is Rojas. Felicia M. The chief said to tell you Conklin from the ME's office and Chip Donnelly from the Crime Scene Unit are en route, too. Sounds like a party."

This was Wednesday night and Felicia Rojas hadn't been heard of since Saturday at the Marquis. "Any word on how and when?"

"Drug overdose is the early word. I gather it's been a few days. You're on your way?"

"Ten-four, Dick. The chief calls, tell him I can hardly wait."

Sherrie was engaged in conversation with a dapper middle-aged businessman when Dante returned to collect her.

"Sorry," he apologized. "Something's come up and I've got to run." He reached for his wallet. "Let me at least pay for your cab."

"Which way you headed?" she asked.

"West Eighties and Broadway."

She started down out of her chair. "You'll make out better if I catch a cab from there. It's a cheaper ride across the park."

Dante started for the door while Sherrie shook the disappointed businessman's hand. The ability to establish an instant rapport with almost anybody was the most valuable weapon in a good salesman's arsenal. Joe wondered how many hearts she broke in the course of a week.

Sherrie was intrigued by her surroundings as Joe eased his job-issue sedan away from the curb and into Fourteenth Street traffic. She looked confused as she took in the bare-bones instrumentation of the dash and the cracked-vinyl-covered bench seat they both occupied.

"You're disappointed," he observed. "It's hardly what you imagined a ride in a cop car would be like. Right?"

"You don't even have a radio."

"It's a hand-held unit. In the glove box. The latest high-tech scrambler technology in a format no bigger than one of those wireless phones."

"What about a siren?"

"You bet. But not tonight. I'm not in that kind of rush."

"Where are you going?"

"Someplace I wish I wasn't going on a full stomach."

Jumbo Richardson was on his way south from his High-bridge Park rendezvous, headed for the Triboro Bridge interchange on the Harlem River Drive, when he received his own beeper summons from Operations. Instead of going on toward the bridge, he exited the drive at Park Avenue and found a pay phone at the corner of East 131st Street. When he arrived outside the Rojas building twenty minutes later, he saw Joey's car pull in to park at a bus stop across the intersection. Dante emerged into the crisp night air as a blond woman Jumbo didn't recognize climbed out on the Fury's passenger side to join Joey on the sidewalk. When he reached for something in his back pocket, she gave him a playful shove and shook her head. Joe then flagged her a cab and she gave him a brief kiss before disappearing into the night.

Dante joined Jumbo to head for the revolving door to 2282 Broadway. Richardson tilted his head toward the de-parting taxi. "*How* long's the cat been away?"

"So far I've escaped with my virtue intact," Joe replied.

"Just a nice, friendly dinner."

"So far?"

"I'm playing hard to get, Beasley."

Richardson got his laugh caught sideways in his throat and choked. Dante slammed an open hand between his shoulder blades.

"You okay?"

"Don't *do* that to me, Joey."

A number of police vehicles and an EMS wagon were parked out front of the building. The partners flashed tin at the two uniforms standing with a security guard inside. Another guard manned the security desk alongside the entrance door, one eye on a bank of video monitors.

"Nineteen?" Dante asked the cops.

"Yeah, Lou. C of D's on the scene. Showed about ten minutes ago."

When the doors of their elevator car closed, sealing them in privacy, Richardson voiced the question that was also on Dante's mind. "If it was her who popped Cintron, why would she turn around and pop herself?"

"Would tend to eliminate her as a suspect, wouldn't it?"

"Maybe so," Jumbo agreed. "Unless she left a long, rambling note about unrequited love."

The doors parted and they found themselves walking into a hallway heavy with aerosol air freshener and cigar smoke. It could only mean one thing, and Jumbo braced himself. One means of determining time of death, once a corpse had a chance to cool, was by the quantity of maggots hatched out on it. The common housefly reproduces with astonishing speed, given a proper host for its eggs. Rotting flesh is one of the best. As comely as Felicia Rojas may have been in life, she'd be a thing of horror to behold tonight.

The four-to-midnight shift at the Twenty-fourth squad were the first detectives to catch this call. Two of them loitered in the hallway outside the door to apartment 19-

M, and Jumbo nodded in recognition. Tom Schneider and John Ozbek were two veterans he'd run into over the years.

"As ugly as it smells?" he asked Schneider.

"Worse. There's a picture on the living-room wall of what she used to look like. Bears about as much resemblance to the nightmare on that bed in there as week-old roadkill."

The sickening-sweet smell of decay was so cloying that Richardson covered his nose and mouth with a handkerchief as he pushed through into the apartment proper. Dante, leading the way, had accepted a fresh-lit cigar from John Ozbek and walked with his head wreathed in a cloud of smoke. He spotted Gus Lieberman standing with Lieutenant Tim Crary, whip of the Two-Four squad. Behind them, another detective Jumbo didn't recognize sat with a distraught Hispanic man on a low, black leather sofa.

"Joey. Richardson." Gus waved them over. "You guys all know each other, right?"

They all nodded and shook hands. "Got lucky and recognized the name when I called the op desk for the evening report," Gus told them. "We've got Conklin in there with her now. Donnelly and his Crime Scene crew'll be here any sec. We ain't touched a thing in there. I want you to have a look. Tell me what your first impressions are."

"I *know* what my first impression's gonna be." Dante spoke it around the cigar clenched in his teeth. "Stench like this? So what's up? You think there's something outta whack?"

"You tell me. And I hope you ate light tonight."

"Thanks. I ate like a starved dog."

Together, Richardson and Dante started down a hall toward the master bedroom. They found pathologist Rocky Conklin alone with the corpse in there, a Dutch Masters going pretty good and his hands in surgical gloves. Jumbo knew that Conklin preferred a better brand of cigar at quieter times, but why waste them at the rate he smoked at a homicide scene? As much as he tried to steel himself for the spectacle of a woman dead for days in an overheated apartment, the sight of Felicia Rojas forced his stomach into an involuntary back flip. He *hadn't* eaten a heavy dinner, and had never been more thankful. The odor of bug spray mixed with decay and cigar smoke suggested the place had recently been thick with flies. The white carpet underfoot was littered with them now. Thousands. All dead. On the bed, the Rojas woman's rotting flesh crawled with so many maggots it appeared to be moving in tiny, undulating waves.

Jumbo watched Joey pinch the bridge of his nose up high and close his eyes a moment to gather himself. "Beautiful evening, Rock. Who's your patient? She don't look so good to me."

Conklin looked over, beads of perspiration trickling from his hairline into his eyebrows. He wiped at them with the back of his forearm, careful not to burn himself on the lit end of his smoke. "Weirdest feeling of déjà vu I'm getting here, cowboy. She's even got a picture of the other guy."

Dante frowned and stepped closer, Jumbo on his heels. The picture of the "other guy" was Willie Cintron's photo torn from the back page of Friday's *New York Post*. It depicted the young hurler on the mound in midwindup, and was set at rest on the coverlet just inches from the dead woman's left hand. One leg from a pair of panty hose was draped loose around her upper arm on that side, presumably employed to tie it off. An empty syringe, plunger run home, was still in her right hand. The rest of the works were on a nearby nightstand.

"Can't tell about additional needle marks once they're this far gone," Conklin continued. "But the setup's kinda spooky . . . with all the other similarities."

"How about the time of death?" Dante asked. They all

realized it would be a rough guess.

The pathologist straightened and stepped back. "They tell me the thermostat was set at eighty here when they first responded. That tends to accelerate the breeding speed some. And the chief mentioned she was seen alive Saturday night. Say sometime later that same night, maybe? Early Sunday at the outside."

Dante turned away, his eyes meeting Jumbo's. Beasley knew exactly what he was thinking.

"Do us a favor," Joey told Conklin. "Have Toxicology keep an eye out for that heavy antihistamine-alcohol mix. I think we'll go have a look at her kitchen and liquor cabinet."

Antonio Infante couldn't believe it when his brother told him he hadn't made the sale. They were on I-95 in Antonio's eight-year-old Nissan Maxima now, headed toward the George Washington Bridge. Felipe slunked down in the passenger seat, shoulder wedged against the door. His were the eyes of a condemned man.

"An' you jus' fucking *leave* them there! What you thinking, Felipe? The man won' pay you, so you *give* them to him? For free?"

"Saavedra, he already report that truck stolen," Felipe murmured. "I get caught driving it back to the city, all that stolen shit in it? I'm busted hard time. What I'm s'pose to do?"

"Busted is better than dead, little brother. Lin Wah, he ain' gon' to listen. Not to no hard-luck story."

Felipe straightened some in his seat, his eyes ahead on the looming bridge structure. "Fuck Lin Wah, Antonio. The sixty-five I owe him? I still got half. For Lin Wah to kill me, he got to fin' me first."

Antonio slammed the steering wheel with an open hand, his teeth clenched in anger. "Where? That's fucking *estú-*

pido! Where the *fuck* you gonna run?''

Felipe heaved a sigh heavy with fatalism. ''Not that I don' trust you, but I tell you? Then it one more thing you got to keep from Wah. I thin' it better you don' know.''

Antonio flicked a scowl at him. ''How long you thin' thirty thousan' gonna hide you in the D.R.?''

''Thirty-five. Jus' take me home so I can get my passport.''

Chapter ■ 17

WHEN DANTE RETURNED TO THE LIVING ROOM, HE FOUND Gus and local squad whip Tim Crary in conversation with Juan Rojas. Instead of the tailored suit he'd sported yesterday in Boston, Juan wore casual slacks, expensive-looking loafers, a silk shirt, and double-breasted jacket. There were at least a half-dozen gold chains strung around his neck. His right wrist glittered with the shiniest gold oyster case Rolex money could buy. He recognized Dante as Joe stepped into the surrounding circle.

"... and stayed down there all weekend?" Crary was asking.

Juan's gaze left Dante and returned to his interrogator. "Like I tol' you, my attorney, he wan' to go over some last-minute shit on Saturday. I din' see no sense in coming all the way back down here jus' to turn aroun' again, go back the next day."

Gus backed away, touching Dante's elbow. Joe followed him to another corner of the room as Jumbo loitered behind.

"What do you think?" Lieberman asked.

"That picture of Willie, torn from Friday's paper, was a nice touch. It's just too big a coincidence, Gus. Two people seen talking together early Saturday night both wind up dead by the same means within hours of each other?" Joe tilted his head in Rojas's direction. "He's claiming he came home tonight and found her like that?''

"You got it. Judge cut him loose a little after nine this morning. He took until after lunch to wind up his affairs down there and check outta his hotel. Caught a one-fifty train that got him into Penn Station around quarter to six.''

Dante was puzzled. It was after nine o'clock when he got the op-desk call. ''And waited three hours to report what he found?''

"He's claiming he went from the station straight to his agent's office, that they had a date for drinks. I know. It sounded like bullshit to me, too, but Crary checked it out.''

"Who represents him?''

"The same guy who represented Cintron, if *that* ain't rich. Rob Ironstone. He told Crary he contacted Rojas up in Boston soon as he heard the news. Wanted to talk game plan. It seems the Royals ain't likely to renew Juan's contract. Too much controversy. Rojas says they talked about where he might be able to make a deal as a free agent, and the remote chance a Japanese team might want him.''

"A two-hundred hitter?''

Gus grunted. "Ain't fucking likely, right?''

It made sense to seek a deal before the media heated up the debate over whether or not the charges against Rojas should have been dismissed. Still, all this coincidence was eating at Dante. "What about Juan's claim that he never returned here to New York over the weekend?'' he asked.

"That's gonna need to be checked out. You want it?''

"Might be best. I've already made a good contact up there. Meanwhile, I'll be interested to see what the Crime Scene Unit and Rocky's toxicology analysis turn up. That picture in her hand is screaming melodrama, Gus. I've seen bulldozers with more subtlety.''

"I know,'' Lieberman agreed. "Rubs me all wrong, too. No note, but a picture layin' there like it's this dyin' broad's final declaration of *un*dyin' love? Someone's pulling my pud.''

Dante noticed Richardson had wandered off somewhere. Seconds later Jumbo emerged from the kitchen doorway across the room, beckoning in Joe's direction. Dante slipped away to join him.

"What've you got?"

"You tell me," Richardson murmured. "When's the last time you ran your dishwasher with only two glasses in it?"

Joe stared at him. "You're sure?"

Jumbo nodded. "Found the lock lever in the 'on' position, the only two items inside both sparkling clean."

"Glasses. Two," Joe repeated. "Like a couple people might use to have a friendly drink together."

"Yep. And one could use to slip the other a nice Mickey Finn. It's all the rage right now in certain circles."

"There goes this contestant in our mystery-woman sweepstakes."

"Maybe not," Jumbo argued. "Say Felicia Rojas *did* do Willie Saturday night. Dismissed charges or not, we already know her husband Juan's got a violent streak. We also suspect he's jealous as hell of her past relationship with Cintron. There's that, and the fact that Rojas could probably get both of them to have a drink with him."

Dante nodded. "One out of guilt and the other out of duty."

He looked over at Juan Rojas, still seated on that low, black sofa. He masked his emotions with a lot of macho posturing, and it was hard to guess what he was thinking. The pimp threads he mistook for the cutting edge of fashion made him even less sympathetic. Still, he appeared genuinely stunned.

"I suppose running a dishwasher with only two glasses in it is something an undomesticated guy, away from home a lot, might do."

"You think he can *prove* he stayed in Boston?" Jumbo asked.

"I don't know. It's something I aim to find out. And I'll be curious to see what Rocky's comparison of the pubic-hair samples proves. They don't match? It blows our whole theory out of the water."

When Antonio Infante pushed in through the front door, he saw his woman Milisa sitting directly opposite in one of their molded plastic chairs. While struggling to appear normal, her face was a mask of terror. He started to follow to where her eyes looked past him, to his right, when he heard the metallic click of a hammer pulled into firing position. It happened just as the cool metal of a gun muzzle touched the back of his jaw, below his right ear. Frozen, Antonio watched peripherally as his brother Felipe walked ahead into a gun butt. A man with a machine pistol, lurking on the other side of the threshold, clubbed Felipe to his knees from behind.

"You move, I blow you face off!" It was the voice of Lin Wah, hissed so close to his ear he could feel the moist warmth of the air propelling it. Wah kicked the door shut behind them. "Okay," he growled. "Slow now. Over to chair. Next to girl."

As Antonio started ahead a cold sweat trickled down his sides from his armpits. He watched his brother roll over onto one side and draw his knees up to his face, his eyes squeezed shut. Felipe was too frightened even to moan with the pain of his blow. Milisa, too, was frozen with fear. Her expression did not change as Antonio eased into a chair alongside and glanced at her face. He saw a bluish welt between her left eye and hairline.

"Where my money, Felipe?" Wah demanded. He pronounced it "Fleep." He then launched a skip kick into the middle of the downed man's back.

Felipe's moan of pain was muffled by his knees.

"Where?" Wah snarled.

"Tomorrow," Felipe gasped.

That got him kicked in the head. "I no think so. Tonight, Felipe."

Antonio's anguish overwhelmed him. "You know he don' got it, why not jus' kill him?" he begged.

Lin was winding up to kick Felipe a third time, taking aim at the exposed coccyx area below his jacket tails. He stopped in midexecution to turn, aim the noise-suppressed muzzle of his Beretta Model 92 F, and shoot Antonio Infante in the chest. The impact slammed Antonio backward out of his chair. When Milisa opened her mouth to scream, Wah shot her, too.

An hour and a half after arriving on the scene of Felicia Rojas's doubtful suicide, Dante and Richardson were back on the Broadway sidewalk, preparing to go their separate ways. Dante was grateful for the crisp, clean bite of this October cold snap. The weather people were calling it abnormal. Joe called it refreshing. He gulped at it, savoring every frigid molecule.

"Full plates tomorrow, huh?" Jumbo commented. "Ain't exactly funneling down the way it's s'posed to, is it?"

"Not hardly. But they can't *all* have killed him."

Jumbo chuckled. "Be some kind of wild party, wouldn't it?"

They said good night. Dante started off for his car across the Eighty-third Street intersection. As he approached he was surprised to see Sherrie Meyer rapping on the glass of an eatery and bar across the sidewalk. She was seated on a stool at the end of the bar. He watched her grab her handbag, hop down, and head for the door.

"Didn't I put you into a cab?" Joe leaned across the roof of his car as Sherrie emerged from the restaurant. "Or has it been such a long day, I'm starting to lose my mind?"

"You're not losing yours," she replied. "I changed

mine. I got about a block across town and said wait a minute, Sherrie. You've got this gorgeous guy right where you want him and the night is *over?* Just like that? I decided I wasn't giving in . . . at least not that easily." She leaned over the other side of the car, facing him, her eyes bright with mischief.

"Have you *always* gotten exactly what you want?" he asked.

"Ask me that tomorrow morning. If you have to phone it in, the answer will be no."

Dante stepped back to unlock the car. He climbed in and leaned over to unlock her side. Maybe he *was* losing his mind. It was eleven o'clock, he was exhausted.

"You think I'm just a little crazy, don't you?" Sherrie buckled her seat belt as she spoke. "I'm sorry. Maybe I'm being too impulsive. If you want, you can just drop me off and call it a night. I'll understand."

Joe twisted the key in the ignition as he studied her face. "Oh, you will, eh?"

She nodded. "I was having such a good time, and when I climbed into that cab, I didn't want it to be over yet. But I know you've had a long day."

Dante started the car away from the curb. "Where to?"

"Eighty-fourth and East End."

That was the southwest corner of Carl Schurz Park, or Gracie Square, as it was called, the grounds surrounding the Mayor's Mansion. Joe started east toward the Seventy-ninth Street Central Park transverse. "How about you invite me up for a nightcap?"

Her address was a stately building from the affluent pre-Crash 1920s, set midway along the south side of the park between East End Avenue and the river. Farther east, the FDR Drive disappeared into a tunnel at Eighty-first Street, affording residents of Sherrie's block an unobstructed view of the water. Joe knew she was making good money. He wondered whether she owned her apartment here and guessed, with the doorman and the rich mahogany lobby decor, that her monthly maintenance alone would be a couple thousand bucks.

The apartment turned out to be a duplex, covering half of two entire floors. On the entry level it had a large living room, a library, formal dining room, big kitchen, and maid's quarters.

"Amazing what money can buy in a depressed housing market, huh?" She said it as she swept in to shrug off her coat and throw it across the back of an antique Victorian settee. The room was furnished with such period pieces, the parquet floor covered with a huge Oriental carpet. "Make yourself at home, Joe. What's your pleasure?"

"What've you got by way of whiskey?"

"No bourbon, I'm afraid." She headed for a marble-topped breakfront. After swinging a pair of doors wide, she began reading labels. "Arberlour, Glenfiddich, Black Bush—"

"Stop right there."

"With water? Ice?"

"Just a splash. No ice. Thanks. How long have you been here?" He surveyed his surroundings. Before his apartment on Perry Street was destroyed, he'd done some reading on period furniture and cobbled together an eclectic and eccentric collection over the years, nothing particularly valuable on a cop's pay, but all of it fun. Sherrie's collection was in a whole other league.

"A year this Christmas. It belonged to a film producer's crazy widow. She'd spent herself into a hole so deep the bank was going to foreclose. It would make you sick to know how much I paid. Less than half of what it would bring six years ago."

She poured a couple fingers of Black Bush into a tumbler and led the way to the kitchen. There, she splashed water into the glass and handed it to Dante before pouring herself a white wine from a bottle in the refrigerator. Dante waited to click glasses with her before taking his first sip.

"I'll risk sounding like a cliché, but I've been in these clothes since seven o'clock this morning," she told him. "I'm going to disappear for a minute and change. If you'd start a fire in the living room, I wouldn't mind."

She ascended the staircase off the entry hall while Joe examined the grate. After ensuring that the damper was open, he crumpled newspaper from a basket alongside and stacked some kindling atop it. Soon he had a cheery little fire crackling and was standing before it, glass in hand, when Sherrie reappeared.

Barefoot, she descended into the entry hall in an emerald-green silk dressing gown tied loosely at the waist. The front was left open enough to give Dante a glimpse of the slinky chemise beneath. She smiled, retrieved her wineglass from a side table, and moved to the sofa. With her feet tucked beneath her, she patted the cushion at her side.

"Join me?"

Joe took another sip of his whiskey and shook his head. "I don't think so, Sherrie. Like you said, I've had a long day. It's a lovely offer, though."

She frowned, her expression puzzled. "Something I said?"

"Nuh-uh. Something I *didn't* say. More romance in my life isn't what I need right now. I need to make the romance I've already got work." He drained his tumbler and set it on the mantel. "I'd better say good night."

Sherrie sat wordless as Joe crossed to lean and kiss her on the forehead. As he turned away he didn't fail to notice how her nipples strained against the thin fabric of her chemise.

Chapter ■ *18*

AS PROMISED, THE MAN SUPPORT SERVICES SPOKE WITH at Ferrari North America faxed them a list of Prestige Performance's recent Ferrari sales. Both Dante and Richardson arrived at the Big Building at eight o'clock to discover the list in an envelope delivered to their office. While Richardson scanned the fax, Dante started coffee.

"What have you got?" Joe asked. He picked up another envelope and found it to contain surveillance photos of a single rust-splotched shipping container.

"I think we've got our link," Beasley replied. "Those seventeen late-model Testarossas stolen in the area? I'm only a quarter way through this list of Berga's customers and already I've found three. So where've they gone and how did he send them there?"

Dante brightened. "Which makes these all the more interesting." He held up the surveillance pictures. "I think we should find somebody to show these to over at Port Authority."

Jumbo crossed to scrutinize them more closely. Sitting there in the Prestige Performance service yard, that turquoise-painted container was suggesting a number of questions. "Same thing occurs to me. Could be he's receiving car shipments in one direction and smuggling the stolen jobs out the other way."

Dante sat at his desk watching coffee drip too slowly into the Mr. Coffee carafe. He rubbed his face and yawned. "You know, something hit me in the shower I hadn't thought of before. My subconscious must've been mulling it all night."

"What's that?"

"Rob Ironstone. I find myself wondering how many other players on the Royals and Yankees teams he represents."

Jumbo thought that one over a moment. "I'm not sure I follow."

"The extra bucks earned in postseason play. To say nothing of the endorsement money. The winners of the World Series, especially the big-name stars, must bank a bundle."

Richardson's expression changed. "Jesus, that's cold."

Dante nodded. "Most premeditated murder is."

"You're talkin' the potential overall take versus one high-paid dude's. He represented Willie, but represented Rojas, too."

"That's the basic drift. How heavy is his client list with Yankee stars?"

"I bet the players' association could tell us. Or better yet, since we want to keep the lid on this, maybe they could tell Barry Zajac."

"Good idea." Joe reached for his phone while flipping through his notebook with his other hand. "I'll give him a call as soon as I get in touch with Captain Reilly in Boston. We need to run a check on Juan's weekend alibi. This morning, I plan to have a face-to-face with him. Be best to do it while the stink is still fresh in his mind."

Richardson checked his watch. "I'm gonna go goose the people in Fiscal about Cintron's banking records. When did Conklin say he'd have the toxicology report?"

"He put a rush on. Noon at the latest, at least for analysis of the heroin traces in the spoon. That, and the antihistamine check. He promised to do the pubic-hair comparison himself, first thing.''

As Joe dialed, another line rang and Jumbo grabbed it. "Yeah." He paused. "Hey, Karl. What's up?" He listened for a moment and asked, "When?" He cradled the receiver a half minute later, his face sober.

Dante cupped his receiver, glancing over. "Problem?"

"That was Lulevich up at the Three-Four North. Half hour ago a citizen found Felipe Infante tied to a lamp pole on Amsterdam, his cock in his mouth. We just busted into his apartment. Found both his brother and brother's girl-friend shot to death. I'd better take a run up there."

"Christ. You want company?"

Beasley was thoughtful as he shook his head. "You got plenty working already. Besides, whether he owed Willie money or not, I got a feeling this is something else. The snitch I talked to last night? He called Felipe Infante a fuck-up. Word on the street said the Tung-on gave him forty-eight hours to come up with some cash he owed them.''

Juan Rojas never considered spending the night in that apartment. Not where his dead wife had lain undiscovered for four days. He couldn't even get himself to go back into the bedroom for clean socks and underwear. He'd arrived at the apartment with bags packed for his stay in Boston, and that's how he left. Two detectives from the Twenty-fourth Precinct drove him south thirty blocks and across the park to the Pierre. He'd checked into a room there at twelve-thirty A.M., but was unable to get to sleep for an-other two hours. Every time he closed his eyes, he saw maggots.

Juan was awakened from a deep, hard-won slumber at nine-thirty by an insistent hammering at his door. He sat bolt upright in a cold sweat as he tried to remember where he was. When he did, his anger boiled.

"Wha'?" he roared. "You can' read the fucking sign?"

His caller continued to thump the panel. In a rage, Juan threw back the blankets and stalked naked to the door. Yesterday evening, Rob Ironstone had told him it wouldn't be long before the media vultures found him. When they did, they'd pick out his eyes. He hadn't been acquitted of rape; the charges were dismissed. He jerked open the door, set to tear a reporter's throat out. The sight of that cop who questioned him in Boston and again last night stopped him cold.

The cop handed him the Do Not Disturb sign. "I can read the sign, Mr. Rojas. I've got immunity." Lieutenant what was his name? Dirtbag? Dante? He paused to survey Juan's condition of undress. "I *wondered* if you slept in your gold chains."

Rojas tried to slam the door, but the cop was quick. He got a foot jammed between the bottom and the threshold, then planted both palms against it for good measure.

"We need to talk, Mr. Rojas. Now, while things are still fresh in your mind. Why not grab a robe?"

Two minutes later Juan sat on the suite's floral-print sofa with a cigarette going. Lieutenant Dante sat across from him on the end of the bed.

"I give you ten minutes," Juan snarled. "What it is you wan'? This is how New York treat a man jus' fine his wife dead from suicide?"

"Nice hotel, the Pierre."

Juan lifted his chin, his face set in a scowl of disdain. This cop made as much in a year as he did in a month. "I like the Four Season hotel chain. It got good service. Get to your poin'."

Dante shook his head. "No point, Mr. Rojas. Tuesday, when we talked in Boston, you told me at first that your wife was in Miami. Then you told me you didn't know where she was and called her a whore. It turns out she was here all along. You were angry. Why?''

"I don' thin' that's none of your business.''

The lieutenant sighed and hung his head. "Maybe I'd better explain something here, Mr. Rojas. Until your wife's death has officially been ruled a suicide, it's a homicide. Until the investigation can confirm your alibi, you're a suspect.''

Propelled by indignation, Rojas sat up straight. "Wait a min'. I was in Boston all fucking weekend. Call my hotel. Four Season. Two hundred Boylston Street. That right across from the fucking Common. I order room service Saturday night. Breakfast Sunday.''

"When was the last time you spoke to your wife, Mr. Rojas?''

Juan slumped back into the sofa in a huff. "I don' know. Saturday after I talk to my lawyer, I think. She call to say Willie, he wan' to talk with her.''

Juan saw the policeman frown. "Wanted to talk about what? Testifying at your trial?''

"How the fuck do I know? Willie? He don' even have the balls to call her himself. He have some bitch of his do it.''

Dante was on his feet, staring down at Juan, his hands in his pockets.

"What bitch, Juan?''

"I don' know.''

"And what did she say?''

"Only that Willie, he still have a sof' place in his heart for her. That he don' want to hurt her, but he got to do the right thing. That maybe they could talk.''

"Felicia told you this?''

"That what I say, in't it?''

"And what did you tell her?''

"I say I don' believe this shit. I ask her why she telling

me this if she ain' gonna do nothing about it, anyway.''

''And she told you maybe she was. That's why you called her a whore on Tuesday.''

''I couldn't believe she do this to me. Not after what *he* done to her.''

''Do what to you, Juan?''

Rojas threw up his hands in frustration, his cigarette tumbling onto the table before him in a shower of sparks. ''C'mon, man! Willie din't wan' to *talk* to her. He wan' to *fuck* her. Get her someplace alone with him so he can sweet-talk his way back into her pants.''

''Aren't you being a little paranoid?''

Juan was agitated, unable to calm his gesticulating hands. He thumped his chest. ''Me? *Me* paranoid? I *know* this bastard. He like to play games.''

''Like having some strange woman call your wife, invite her someplace to talk?''

Juan nodded emphatically. ''To the lobby of his fucking hotel. Where every other player on the team can see them together there. I tol' her, he wan' to make her beg. She won' listen to me. She say she don' care who see her, it was the only chance we have.''

''And you didn't hop on a train? Rush down here to New York and try to stop her?''

Juan stabbed the butt of his smoke into an ashtray. ''I tol' you. Call my hotel. Ask when I call room service.''

The cop decided to change directions. ''Did your wife use drugs, Juan?''

How many times had he answered this question last night? ''You mean heroin? Stick herself in the arm? Jus' like I tol' a hundred cops las' night. No. Maybe she smoke it once in a while. Not heroin. Not crack. A little weed. I think her an' her friends snort coke sometimes when I'm not aroun'.'' He realized he was referring to his dead wife in the present tense and closed his eyes. ''Lissen,'' he murmured. "I tol' you I give you ten minutes. I think your time is up now."

Juan barely heard the policeman thank him. He sat there with his eyes closed long after he heard the door click shut.

Back in his Special Investigations office, Dante spoke with the director of the marine terminal, port of Brooklyn. Joe had the pictures of that container spread before him as the man explained what he was looking at.

"Each of those things has a seven-digit code unique to it."

Joe found a series of white numbers and letters stenciled against the box's turquoise background.

"And that particular shade of blue you described?" the man continued. "That, or whatever color it might be, is the identifying color of each shipping line."

"Wouldn't that code be easy enough to change?"

"You bet," the director allowed. "That's why most of the bigger lines have bar-code plates now. No matter what the stencil says, it's the plate that a scanner reads as the container comes off the ship."

"So, who does our baby belong to?"

"From the way you described it, I'm guessing an outfit called Sea-Trans. Main East Coast offices across the harbor in the port of Newark. Your best bet would be to go straight to them. They could tell you everything. Punch it up on their computer and tell you where this thing's been, what cargo it carried, and who it was shipped to."

"You got an address?"

Jumbo Richardson was happy to arrive in Washington Heights *after* the ME's men had bagged the Tung-on gang's handiwork. One corpse, whether mutilated, ruined by decay, or otherwise, was more than enough for any single day. Lulevich and Guitan were at the Three-Four North station house when he arrived. They'd returned there with Hector Cintron, dragged in for questioning. Jumbo joined them in one of the squad's bare-bones interrogation rooms.

Hector glanced up in recognition as Richardson was shown in. Pete and Karl nodded in greeting.

"Message for you from the chief," Lulevich told him. "You made a financial-records request on this mutt's brother? He said to tell you that sixty-five grand from a cash account was wired to a bank in Nassau, the Bahamas." Karl was watching Hector's face, not Jumbo's, as he spoke. "They got disclosure laws down there protect good guys and scumbags alike. Still, Fiscal ran a DEA check and found out that the account is just a transfer point. Most everything that goes in gets funneled back out again to a bank in Kuala Lumpur, Malaysia."

Jumbo focused on Hector. "You mind?" he asked Lulevich.

"Be our guest, Lou."

"You remember me, right, Hector?" Jumbo advanced slowly to stop less than a yard from where Cintron sat at a heavy, olive-green metal table. "I'm the dude you told you were clean, your brother was the straightest of the straight arrows, and who knows what other bullshit. So what's your straight-arrow bro doing wiring money to Malaysia, Hector? Maybe he was investing in mineral rights, huh? Or beachfront property, on the Gulf of goddamn Siam."

Cintron glowered back at him. It was obvious from his rumpled hair and wrinkled shirt that he'd been rousted and dragged in with no warning, probably from bed. "My cousin Felipe owed some people money. They was gonna hurt him bad if he din' pay. Willie helped him, to save his life. That's all I gon' to say."

"You mean wiring money to Southeast Asian dope lords

was like a Christian act?'' Lulevich interjected. ''A Mother Teresa kinda thing?''

''It was a loan, like,'' Hector growled.

''Something Willie was expecting to get back?'' Jumbo pressed.

Hector gave it a lazy shrug. ''What you expect? My brother was no pussy pushover. Sure he wan' it back.''

''Did Felipe pay it?'' Richardson asked.

Hector grunted, shaking his head. ''Felipe? I don' think so. Soon as one problem, it was solved? Felipe, he go out an' make another.''

''When you left Willie Saturday night, did Felipe come back uptown with you and his brother?''

Hector's face said he knew right where this was headed. ''You askin' if Felipe stay downtown after we leave the hotel? Go back upstairs an' kill my brother?'' He closed his eyes and snorted through a smile of derision. ''I don' think so. I think he wen' to Roseland. Felipe? He love to dance.''

Pete Guitan changed the direction. ''It *was* Lin Wah who killed him, right?''

Hector looked over at his fellow Dominican, freezing him with his cool con's disdain. ''Who you think you kidding, asshole?''

Guitan smiled back. ''Not a streetwise homeboy like you, Hector. Shit no. You way too smart. That why you're sitting there an' your cousin's in a bag, sucking his own cock? You dudes? You got it *all* figured out.''

Jumbo steered it back his way. ''Who did your cousin go to Roseland *with?*''

Hector was still projecting his hatred Guitan's way as he replied. ''His bitch mos' likely. He say that her an' her friends was meeting him there.''

''Who?''

''The bitch? Carmen Guzman.''

Beasley made a note of the name and glanced up, pen poised. "Where can I find her?"

"Carmen? Somewhere in the neighborhood. I don' know. Why don' you look it up?"

When Joe Dante wandered into the morgue basement that morning, Rocky Conklin was expecting him. The pathologist had been up late and had returned to his office early to get to work on Felicia Rojas. First thing, he'd done the pubic-hair comparison Dante requested.

There was a time in his career when Conklin couldn't have cared less about what they did with his results. His job was to slice and dice and leave everything but the how and when to the Detective Bureau. Then, over time, Rocky had started thinking a bit like a detective himself. He liked Dante because Joe was always interested in his opinion, if and when he had one to offer. Conklin took pride in his work, and Dante knew that. They'd developed a mutual respect. When Rocky happened to notice something like barely visible fingernail scratches on Willie Cintron's back, he went the extra mile for the man he called "cowboy." Those pubic hairs he'd found were the key to Dante's current case. Rocky was damned near sure of it.

"Pull up a chair, cowboy."

Dante tossed a white paper deli bag onto Conklin's desk and sat. "You look about as tired as I feel, Rock. How's your coffee today?"

Conklin nodded toward the machine. "Fresh, anyway. Help yourself. We struck out on one count and hit a home run on the other." He opened the bag and extracted a wrapped bagel. "I called a man owed me a favor at Toxicology. Got him out of bed to do that antihistamine check for you. Right over the center-field fence."

Dante filled a paper cup with coffee and paused. "That must mean the pubic hairs don't match."

"Nope. But everything else does. The antihistamine-to-alcohol ratio in the bloodstream is roughly the same. The purity and alkaline structures in the two heroin samples? Identical."

His bagel, sliced in half, had a nice thick smear on it, just the way Rocky liked it. He broke off a piece and saluted Dante with it after taking a bite. "Thanks for this. The shoemaker's kids go barefoot, and here I sit, a refrigerator full of meat and nothing to eat."

That night, at eight P.M., the president of the United States would throw out the first ball of the World Series in San Francisco. Five days after Willie Cintron's death and in the wake of Mitchell Shimizu's murder, Barry Zajac couldn't get enthused about going west. He'd made a reservation on the latest possible flight he could take and still make the game. Thursday morning, as he awaited Lieutenant Joe Dante's arrival at his office, he was still debating whether or not to take that plane. Mitchell's body had been released by the medical examiner. It was being flown home to the dead man's family in Hawaii, but *News* management planned a memorial service for tomorrow at ten. It was hard to imagine not being there. Shimizu was headstrong and independent, but Barry couldn't shake the feeling that he'd gotten him killed.

Dante appeared midmorning. He looked tired. After yesterday's harsh words, there was an air of caution as they shook hands and Dante pulled up a chair.

"Did your inquiry ruffle any feathers?"

In reply, Barry handed across several sheets of shiny fax paper. "Not particularly. A week after the Series ends, writers all over the country start speculating about free agency. Who will declare and who's happy where he is. Agents are the primary conduit for obtaining player comment. This request? It just makes me look like I'm doing my homework early.''

Dante took the list and scanned it, recognizing names of players from every club in baseball. Some were marked in yellow.

Zajac pointed. ''I've highlighted his players on the Yanks and Royals for you.''

In addition to Willie Cintron and Juan Rojas, Rob Ironstone represented one other player on the Kansas City Royals. Of the three, Cintron was the only bona fide star. Rojas and the other were journeymen players, currently earning at the peak of their salary curves. The group Ironstone represented on the Yankees was a whole other story. The super-agent represented seven players, or nearly one quarter of the names on the New York team's roster. Five of them were *big* names, players commanding an average of two million dollars per annum. Barry nodded to the list in Dante's hands.

''If you're headed where I think you are, it's Machiavellian.''

''Where am I headed?'' Dante asked.

''You're checking what kind of motive Ironstone might have.'' He shook his head. ''That would be like killing the goose that laid the golden egg.''

Dante extended the list toward him. ''How bad could that be when you've got another dozen in the barnyard? If the Royals went on to the Series and won it, how much would he have gained?''

''Last year's winning share per player was a hundred and twenty-five thousand.''

''Not to mention special-performance clauses in individual player's contracts, right? Another fifty thousand for a hundred RBIs, twenty or more homers, that sort of thing?''

As off base as he thought Dante was, Barry was encouraged by his creativity and tenacity. ''We're still talking peanuts, Lieutenant.''

''An additional two, maybe three million between all his Yankees, if *they* make the Series? That's peanuts? You're kidding, right?''

''His players might get that, but not Rob,'' Zajac explained. ''Sports agents don't command the same fee percentage as, say, film or literary agents. Depending on the agent or the client, they take a commission of between three and five percent. Rob's cut? We're talking about a hundred fifty grand here. Tops. If Willie had lived to renegotiate in the three-to-five-million-a-year range? Rob's take on that deal alone would be easily as much as you're talking about, or more.''

Dante sat a moment, absorbing this information.

''You knew Cintron as well as anyone did, Barry. Any indication he wasn't completely satisfied with his representation?''

Zajac didn't even have to think about it. ''He loved Rob, Lieutenant. Thought he had style. When Willie was in town to play the Yankees, Rob would invite him out to his place in East Hampton, introduce him to movie stars and money managers, make him feel like he belonged in that world. He was making more money than he'd ever dreamed of, and he was represented by one of the true class acts in the business.''

''Tell me what you know about Ironstone's wife.''

Barry wondered where this came from. ''Jillian? What about her?''

''I'm wondering what sort of parties Ironstone throws for his clients. Whether they're weenie-and-marshmallow roasts with his wife, or the kind where the boys all bond, mostly with blond bimbos.''

''I've only been invited to one,'' Barry replied. ''Just this past summer. It was grilled lobster, not weenies. Jillian was there and so were their two teenage daughters. All three of them and a handful of the others were blondes, but I wouldn't term any of them bimbos.''

Dante smiled and eased back a little farther in his chair. He left his notebook and pen in his lap as he folded his arms. ''I think I heard about that party from the new sales manager at WRBS. Sherril Meyer. She tells me it's where Willie first met Jaime Madera, the president of Hola International.''

''That's right. Does this have something to do with them all having dinner together Saturday?''

''Beats me. I'm just throwing shit at the wall. Willie spent time with a woman sometime late Saturday night. We know from a teammate he didn't like picking up camp followers, that he preferred whores. A bellman at the Marquis tells me he provided Willie with a woman Friday, but never heard from him again. I'm trying to figure out who that Saturday-night woman was.''

''Could be he made a date with the same woman two nights in a row.''

''We checked. The bellman claims that particular item was otherwise engaged.''

''So you wonder if Rob might have fixed him up with someone?''

''He was with him,'' Dante replied. ''It's another possibility.''

Zajac thought a moment about the Rob Ironstone he knew before offering his two cents. ''Let me tell you why I doubt it, Lieutenant. It's got to do with how I see the man. He's a business animal to the core. Pimping for a client is something that could blow up in his face. It isn't a risk he would take, because he doesn't have to. There are already plenty of pimps in this world.''

Dante moved on. ''Tell me what you know about Jaime Madera.''

"Just met him that once. I hear he's a pretty decent tennis player."

"Married?"

"A widower, I think. Kinda quiet." Barry watched Dante unfold his arms to pick up his pen and make a note of some sort. "Aren't you wasting your time on this, Lieutenant? Isn't Mitch turning up dead in the sound enough for you? I don't understand why this Berga is still running around free."

Dante remained unruffled. "There's no question that Berga's dirty. The question is *how* dirty. Do I believe he slit your buddy's throat?" He nodded. "You bet I do. All I need is proof. Do I think he killed Willie, too?" He dropped his pen to spread his hands in a gesture of surrender. "Based on what evidence? That he made a risky wager? It looks to me like everything he does is risky. I've got two men in the field right now doing everything but crawl up his ass. We'll get him for Shimizu, sooner or later. But Willie Cintron? I'm not at all sure he isn't a whole other matter."

Chapter ∎ 19

WITH PETE GUITAN ACTING AS HIS NATIVE GUIDE, BEAS-
ley Richardson finally located Felipe Infante's steady
squeeze. It was late morning when the two detectives approached a SRO hotel on St. Nicholas Avenue just north
of the Columbia-Presbyterian Medical Center at 169th
Street. It was a neighborhood not unlike the others Jumbo
had visited here in Washington Heights. The day's warming
trend had brought the card tables and their domino games
back out onto the sidewalks. The colorful storefront decors
of mostly red, yellow, and green seemed more alive now,
with clusters of loiterers all posturing and jiving out front.
As they walked toward Carmen Guzman's place of residence, he could hear strains of salsa leaking from small
businesses up and down the block.

After a climb up creaking stairs to the third floor, Guitan
hammered on Carmen Guzman's door. A woman's enraged
voice screamed back, "You wake the baby, you fuck!"

Jumbo guessed that if Pete hadn't, she just had. The door
flew open and a chubby woman, pale with fury, confronted
them. The air behind her quickly filled with plaintive wailing.

"Who the fuck are you?" she snarled. "This baby, he
up all night crying. I jus' now get him asleep."

Jumbo saw Guitan flinch. He stepped up to take the brunt of the woman's wrath and held up his shield case. She was opening her mouth to continue her tirade when the shiny gold, flashing in the light, stopped her.

"We're sorry about waking the baby, ma'am. You're Carmen Guzman?"

She got cautious now, her scowl changing. "Wha' about it? If this abou' the crying, I don' hit my kids."

Jumbo could smell the stink of dirty diapers and felt pity for her kids, whether she hit them or not. "It's about Felipe Infante, Carmen. You mind if we talk inside?"

The room behind her was chaos, a squalling infant in a chipped bassinet set along one wall and another baby on the floor before a television. There were dirty dishes piled to overflowing in a Pullman kitchen sink. The garbage pail alongside ran over onto the floor with greasy fast-food wrappers and Styrofoam cartons. The countertop swarmed with roaches. A divan with yellow-stained upholstery was torn and oozing stuffing. Hector Cintron's remark that Felipe was a loser gained new credibility.

Once they stepped inside, Guitan flipped open his notebook and uncapped his pen. "When was the last time you saw Felipe, Carmen?"

"Night before las'. You arrest Lin Wah yet?"

"Not yet," Guitan allowed.

Her eyes narrowed. "I tell you one thing, Mr. Cop. You better find him before I do. I find him firs', I gonna cut *his* cojones off. He kill the father of my baby."

Which one? Jumbo wondered. "We understand Felipe owed his cousin Willie money." He stepped to one side of the closed door and eased himself up against the wall behind. "Money Willie gave him to pay a debt he owed Lin Wah."

"That wan't what this about," she retorted.

"But he did owe Willie money."

She wasn't long on patience, her short fuse sparking her powder all over again. "Felipe, he owe Willie shit! Willie *give* him that money."

"People we been talking to say it was a loan," he countered.

"*Who* say?" she demanded. "Hector? Felipe, he see Willie last Saturday, before he meet me at Roselan'. He tell me Willie, he say not to worry about it."

Jumbo's gaze drifted around the room again, taking in an open bedroom door and more squalor beyond. There was also a bathroom door, left slightly ajar. "You two didn't happen to go by there again after you finished dancing?"

"Where?" There was suspicion in it.

"Willie's hotel. You know. Smoke a bone. Have a nightcap."

She snorted with contempt and turned away to retrieve the squalling infant from its bed. Jumbo watched the way the fabric of her jeans stretched taut across the breadth of a heavy posterior. "Nice try, Mr. Cop. It was four o'clock, time we left Roselan'. Willie, he have a game to pitch next day." She hefted the baby onto one hip and jostled it none too gently.

"Mind if I use your bathroom?" Jumbo asked. "While Detective Guitan asks you a couple questions about last night?"

"Go ahead." Her focus was already turned toward Pete. "I don' know fuck-all about last night. That bastard say he be here by eleven, that he bring me money for Pampers an' baby food."

Jumbo had gotten a good look at the inside of her left forearm when she opened the front door. He doubted Pampers were the first thing on her wish list.

Earlier, Richardson had used a phone at the Three-Four North station house to try to catch Joey at the morgue. Rocky Conklin reported that Dante was long gone, and updated Jumbo on the latest forensic findings. The pubic hairs recovered from the corpse of Felicia Rojas had failed to match those found on Willie Cintron. Jumbo only had Carmen Guzman's word that she and Felipe hadn't paid Willie another visit late Saturday. Judging from the tracks on Carmen's forearms and the business Felipe was in, they'd certainly had the means to overdose Cintron. How Felicia Rojas could end up dead the same way was troubling, but perhaps she'd been lurking outside the room and saw something.

Once inside the bathroom, Jumbo closed the door and flipped on the overhead light. The tub was brown with encrusted filth. Above it, baby clothes and Carmen's undergarments hung on the shower rod to dry. The commode and surrounding floor were heavy with scum and cockroaches. Just as Jumbo hoped, the floor was littered with stray hairs. Why Willie would want to screw Carmen Guzman was nothing he wanted to think about. Beasley failed to understand why people did much of what they did, but after twenty-three years on the job, not much would surprise him anymore. He stooped, handkerchief in one hand, and picked out a dozen random hairs. As he worked, a wave of sadness and disgust washed over him, accompanied by that baby's insistent wailing.

Before he left the *Daily News,* Dante made an appointment to see Hola International president Jaime Madera. That was where he was headed as lunch-hour traffic started to build through the Midtown Tunnel. Joe was assuming that Madera, like Willie, was Hispanic. It occurred to him that in the heat of Willie's impassioned exchange with Felicia Rojas in the Marquis lobby, something may have passed between the former lovers that neither Ironstone nor Sherrie was linguistically equipped to catch. It was also possible that during their dinner together Willie had intimated to Madera, man to man, what kind of plans he had for later that evening.

Hola was located in south Brooklyn, a block inland from the Port Authority Grain Terminal, on Bryant Street opposite the Gowanus Bay estuary. It was an odd neighborhood, where the old port of Kings County backed up to a desolate residential and light-industrial area dominated by the huge tower blocks of the Red Hook Public Housing Projects. As a rookie in uniform, Dante had become intimately familiar with this neighborhood while assigned to the Seventy-sixth Precinct station house on Union Street. That was eighteen blocks north of where he now parked. Back then, area crime was an even mix of domestic violence, break-ins, pilferings along the waterfront, and disputes turning into brawls between longshoremen working the area docks. Today, the port area and that ranging directly south of it were active as ever, but most of the freight handling was done by machine. The ranks of the Longshoremen's Union had been laid waste by mechanization. Truck traffic was heavier, and Joe was sure that pilfering, like drug trafficking in the streets, had seen a steady upswing.

As Joe approached the plant to park at a hydrant on Bryant and head for the entrance on foot, he passed the gate to Hola's shipping area. He saw six shipping containers lined up against a wall past the loading bays. Two were painted that telltale Sea-Trans turquoise.

The women who worked the busy phones in an office pool behind reception were uniformly the high-school-graduate, tight-skirt-and-tortured-hair breed of the outer boroughs. The cacophony created by their conversations was a primal chorus to Dante's ear. It was the music of his youth, of Remsen Avenue social clubs, cafeteria cliques, and summer days in Canarsie Beach Park.

"Can I help youse?" the receptionist asked.

He told her he had an appointment with Mr. Madera and identified himself. It got him a second, closer look and a nervous smile. She asked him to wait after making a call. Mr. Madera's secretary would be right with him.

This secretary turned out to be a very good-looking Hispanic woman who reminded Joe just a little bit of Rosa.

"I'm Maria Ayala, Lieutenant." She approached him with her hand extended to shake. "How do you do?"

"Fine, Miss Ayala." He saw her eyes widen slightly when she gripped the rough texture of his karate-tempered hands. She was about Rosa's age. Late twenties or early thirties. Sherrie's age, too.

He was led down a hall to an elevator. They rode it upstairs three floors to the company's executive offices, where corporate president Jaime Madera occupied a large corner suite with windows overlooking the Bush Terminal docks across the estuary. Once introductions were performed, Maria Ayala retreated to her desk outside with a clearly flirtatious parting smile.

"Make yourself comfortable, Lieutenant. Please." Madera gestured to a furniture-grouping around a low table in one corner of the room. He was a tall, carefully groomed man of aristocratic bearing in a beautiful suit, maybe sixty. "When you said on the phone this was about Guillermo, I'm afraid I was baffled. But of course I will help how I can."

As he took a seat Joe moved to shed some light. "There are some inconsistencies we're trying to clear up, sir. One involves an incident that occurred after the dinner you had with Cintron Saturday night."

Madera adjusted his cuffs while continuing to stand. "What is it you want to know? We ate at Victor's, at the invitation of Miss Meyer. I believe she had several motives for extending it, but primary was her public-service campaign. You've heard of it, no doubt?"

This was a slight sidetrack, but Joe followed. "Several motives? I thought the public-service campaign was the only motive."

Madera smiled wryly. "Sherril Meyer sells advertising time, Lieutenant. Last week it looked like Kansas City, and not New York, would be playing in the World Series. Not just the local station, but all of RBS was in a panic. They paid close to one billion dollars for the rights to broadcast major-league baseball."

"And faced taking a bath. Interesting."

"Very, Lieutenant. If the Yankees hadn't won, incentive for someone like me to buy advertising time in the New York market during the Series would be somewhat diminished. I would be airing ads to half as many viewers, and that time is expensive. I am sure Hola was not alone, thinking this way."

It made perfect sense. At least part of it did. "But I'm still not clear what other interests Miss Meyer had on Saturday night. Other than to nail down Willie for that public-service campaign. He played for the Royals."

"But he was a New York hometown boy," Madera reminded him. "Before Guillermo and Rob Ironstone arrived at the restaurant, Sherril took pains to point out my unique position in the marketplace should the Royals emerge victorious. Hola has a half-dozen spots featuring the Royals star pitcher as our spokesman."

"So no matter who lost, you were still a winner."

Madera chuckled while slipping his hands into his pockets and strolling the carpet before Dante, a picture of power at ease. "At least that's what she *tried* to sell me, Lieutenant. I'll admit, I did enjoy her creativity. It's what I found appealing about her from the start. It seemed like a breath of fresh air after all the turmoil WRBS had put us through."

This was another sidetrack, but again Dante's interest was piqued. "What sort of turmoil was that?" he asked.

A sadness filled Madera's expression. He stopped pacing and stood backlit by those huge windows overlooking the bay. His brow knit as he chose his words. "They were forced to let their sales manager go, you know. Last summer. I was interested to learn yesterday that Sherril was promoted to fill the vacancy. There are other people there more senior, and it surprised me, to be honest. But perhaps they, like I did, recognized how much better she is than the rest. She would have to be, in order to get Hola back the way she did."

Dante knew how good she was at closing a deal, but didn't understand this other reference. "Got you *back?* I thought it was a new account."

Madera stopped. He shook his head. "Our second time around," he corrected. "Trent Blevin was the former sales manager, and Hola's original account executive. We terminated with them when Mr. Blevin sent us a series of critical communications we found offensive, about how we were handling our time-slot strategy. They were near-incoherent diatribes."

"By communications, do you mean phone calls? Letters?"

"Fax transmissions, actually."

"It sounds like the man went off his nut."

Madera had started to pace again, clearly uncomfortable. "I don't believe in spreading rumors, Lieutenant, but it is pretty much public knowledge that RBS let Mr. Blevin go because of an alcohol problem. It was interfering with his work. It's a great pity. The man had a lot of talent once."

"When was all this?" Dante asked.

"Early last summer. The corporate VP sales has been acting as local manager in the interim."

"That's the turmoil you're referring to?"

"It is. Alcoholism is a terrible disease, Lieutenant. As you may know, one of its symptoms is denial. Mr. Blevin denied sending those communications to us and others. He claimed someone was trying to destroy him.''

"Any idea why RBS took so long to replace him?"

"Perhaps to give the dust time to settle. We weren't the only account they lost. Lost accounts mean lost revenue. Corporate management had to be very upset.''

Dante moved on. "Back to that dinner, Mr. Madera. After it, I understand you continued on with the others to the Marquis. I'd like to hear your version of what happened there.''

Madera stopped behind a wingback chair and laid those perfectly manicured hands across the top of it. He frowned. ''It was very strange, Lieutenant. We were going to have a drink in the Broadway Lounge. We'd just stepped off the elevator when Guillermo was approached by a distraught woman. He seemed to know her, but didn't want to see her. There was an exchange that I would term pathetic, at least on her part.''

"How's that?"

"She wanted to know why, if he didn't want to talk to her, he had some woman call her. He claimed he didn't know what she was talking about.''

"Was this in English or in Spanish?"

"Almost entirely in English. When he insisted he didn't have anyone call her, she became very upset. Guillermo took her aside and tried to calm her. I've no idea what was said, but she was still very angry when she left.''

Dante digested this, comparing it with other versions of events he'd heard. Madera's story seemed to substantiate what Juan Rojas had told him earlier. Some woman, claiming to represent Willie, had contacted Felicia, saying Cintron wanted to talk.

"Was Willie angry, too?" he asked.

Madera thought a moment and shook his head. "He seemed more shaken than angry. It rather destroyed the mood. We all had other places we needed to be. We decided then it would be best to call it a night.''

Dante chose his words carefully now. "We've got reason to believe Willie spent time with a woman late Saturday. For a while we thought it might have been the woman who confronted him in the Marquis lobby. Now that doesn't seem likely. Do *you* have any idea who that woman might be?''

Madera pushed off from the back of the chair as he shook his head. "I'm sorry, Lieutenant. I don't. I assume he had every young man's appetites, but I have no idea how he indulged them. Perhaps you could speak to Robin Ironstone, Guillermo's agent. They'd known each other for a number of years. I have the impression they got on well.''

"Mr. Ironstone's on my list, as a matter of fact." Joe rose, hand extended. "Thanks for your time, Mr. Madera. I know you must be a busy man." Those containers on trucks in the shipping yard downstairs came to mind. He was tempted to mention them, but thought better of it. That was the ball he and Jumbo intended to run with next.

"Your visit can mean only one thing, Lieutenant." Madera's eyes tried to probe Dante's. "That you suspect Guillermo's death was not a suicide.''

"Careful," Dante cautioned. "There's no question it was a drug overdose, sir. We're only trying to determine if anyone else was in the room with him when he died. If that someone was a participant, it would make her an accomplice.''

Chapter ∎20

ROB IRONSTONE HAD SOUNDED ANXIOUS WHEN HE CALLED Sherrie Meyer at her office to ask her to lunch. Last night after Dante left, she'd picked up two messages from Rob on her machine. The first said he was staying over in the city, that some negotiations might go late. He hoped he could see her afterward. The second wondered if she'd tried to reach him. He'd been tied up until later than expected.

They sat across from each other now at the Union Square Café, Rob looking a bit fidgety as he adjusted his napkin for the third time.

"You look great," he complimented.

"Thanks, Rob. What's on your mind?"

"I tried to call you last night. Twice."

"I wasn't home."

He tugged at the corner of that napkin again, not the picture of cool he usually projected to the sports business world. "Since Jillian started getting suspicious, I don't get to spend many nights in the city anymore. I'm disappointed we couldn't get together."

Sherrie flashed him a bright smile and reached for a roll. "Jillian's not my problem, Rob. She's yours. If you've got to know, I had a date last night." As she broke and buttered the roll she watched his face muscles stiffen.

"You mind me asking who?"

"I do. You're the one who's married, Rob, not me."

"Did you fuck him?"

"That isn't any of your business, either. I don't ask who else you fuck."

"You don't have to. I don't."

She smiled, took a nibble of her roll, and chewed. "No, I didn't fuck him. Feel better?"

Ironstone's face relaxed. Suddenly he was confident again. "Horny as hell is how I feel," he replied. "The idea of another guy screwing you makes me crazy, Sher. I know that isn't our deal, but I can't help it."

She reached across the table to cover one of his hands with hers and pat it. "I told my assistant I have an appointment after lunch. We could go back to your office, tell your receptionist to hold your calls." She squeezed his hand and sat back, her eyes holding his. "Tell you the truth, I find that possessive streak of yours kind of touching. It makes me horny, too."

"What possessive streak?"

She snorted and turned to catch the waiter's eye. "Let's eat, shall we?"

The Sea-Trans offices in the so-called port of Newark were located on the New York Harbor side of the city of Bayonne. To reach it that Thursday afternoon, Dante and Richardson had to exit lower Manhattan via the Holland Tunnel and take the Jersey Turnpike extension. Sea-Trans was located off Red Hook Road about two miles south of the huge Military Ocean Terminal. The partners found a no-frills office complex there, in an area filled with freight yards, railroad sidings, and hundreds of idle semitrailers parked shoulder to shoulder behind chain-link fences. In the near distance, where land met the Kill Van Kull waterway separating New Jersey from Staten Island, huge cargo off-loading apparatus loomed against the skyline. Sea-

Trans, not to be confused with the giant Sea-Land, looked to be a midsize outfit by comparison. When they parked their car out front, Jumbo noticed another national flag flying alongside an American one on poles outside the building.

"Whose flag is that?" he asked.

Divided into four quadrants, a solid red and solid blue on a diagonal and the other two white, one with a red star and the other blue, it flapped lazily in a breeze that had shifted direction overnight. Today's breeze was decidedly warmer than it had been of late.

"Looks familiar, but beats me," Dante replied.

On their approach to the building they watched a tractor-trailer ease up to a nearby yard gate. A uniformed guard swung it open and the truck pulled out into the roadway. It towed a container almost identical to the one they had found last night in Miles Berga's yard.

"Looks like we've come to the right place," Joe murmured.

Inside the front doors, in the lobby of the building, they got the answer to their question about the flag out front. There on one wall, in a world-map mural, Sea-Trans world headquarters in Panama City, Panama, was prominently featured, with smaller Panamanian flags painted across the globe to indicate the company's regional offices. Besides Bayonne, the map indicated Sea-Trans had American outposts in Miami, Corpus Christi, San Pedro, Oakland, and Seattle.

They identified themselves to a receptionist and were met moments later by the northeast U.S. regional sales director, Jorge DiSalvo. Diminutive in stature, DiSalvo had thinning black hair combed straight back from a pronounced widow's peak and fine, aristocratic features. While slightly accented, his English was perfect.

"Gentlemen. What is it I can do for you? When Tracy

said you were from Special Investigations, I was afraid there had been a hijacking.''

The Detective Bureau's Special Investigations Division was also home of the job's Safe, Loft, and Truck Squad, the unit that investigates truck hijackings, among other things, in the city's five boroughs.

Dante moved to put him at ease. ''Nothing we're handling. It's one of your containers. We'd like to do a background check on it, see what was shipped in it last and who it was shipped to.''

DiSalvo's face clouded in confusion for an instant. ''One of our containers?''

Beasley handed him a still slightly damp photograph, withdrawn from an envelope he carried. ''That's one of yours, isn't it?''

DiSalvo studied it only briefly. ''It is. Indeed. Come this way, please.''

They were led back through a pair of double doors and a labyrinth of partitioned offices to DiSalvo's office suite. There, DiSalvo had a computer terminal on a stand behind his desk. The two detectives were invited to take seats while he sat in his swivel chair and kicked around to face the monitor screen.

''May I ask where this is?'' he asked. ''The location where you found it?'' He punched the seven-digit code from the photograph into the computer.

''Man I spoke with at the Brooklyn Marine Terminal told me it's easy to alter those codes,'' Dante replied. ''We've got a close-up of the bar-code plate, too, if that'd be any help.''

Without an answer to his question, DiSalvo watched a block of data appear on his screen. He tapped a key and traced a finger down a list that now appeared. ''We don't have a scanner here at the office. They read the codes dockside as the containers are off-loaded from the ships. It says here that unit six-NS-seven-two-eight-F is under long-term lease to Roastmasters Incorporated. They're a coffee importer."

Richardson was taking notes. "Where they at?"

"Just up Kennedy Boulevard from here. In Jersey City."

"Can you tell us when they used it last, what it carried, and from where?" Joe asked.

DiSalvo tapped more keys. "It carried coffee, I expect. They import from all over South America and the Caribbean basin." He paused to scan a new set of data. "This container was the last part of a shipment they received from Limón, Costa Rica. It is often the case that their coffee is cluster-shipped from one port like this."

"Means what?" Jumbo wondered.

"That a company maintains larger warehouse facilities in central locations to collect smaller shipments from all over."

"And this Roastmasters outfit has theirs in Costa Rica?" Dante concluded.

DiSalvo smiled. "They have three, actually. Another in São Paulo, Brazil, and their biggest facility, in Barranquilla, Colombia."

"Sounds like you people do a lot of business with them," Beasley observed.

"We are their only shipper." He stopped, an expression of concern deepening. "Perhaps I could be more helpful to you if I knew what this is about."

Dante again ignored his request for more information and changed direction slightly. "So what happens to these containers on the return leg, Mr. DiSalvo? They wouldn't ship them back empty, I don't imagine."

"Some of that is necessary," DiSalvo replied. "But you are correct. Roastmasters, in this case, has collateral deals with a number of U.S. exporters. They sublease the bulk of their empty container space. Off the top of my head? I can think of one who ships raw cotton from Corpus Christi to South American textile manufacturers. There is another, I believe, who supplies paint to one of the big three's truck assembly plants in Venezuela. It can get very creative, this back-scratching.''

''Do you help them with it?'' Joe asked. ''Finding people to take their action, help fill the empties?''

DiSalvo turned completely away from the monitor to regard the two detectives across the top of his desk. ''I wish I knew what it is you are digging at.'' He shrugged. ''But let me try to explain it like this. The rates they would pay if we handle those administrative aspects are much higher than if they do it. It would almost pay to ship the leased containers back empty rather than ask us to make those arrangements. When they lease, they get a volume discount. It's considerable.''

''I think we're getting your drift,'' Dante told him. ''If they can find cargo to fill their empty containers on the return leg, they're lowering their costs even further.''

''Exactly. They still pay the freight, but they share the cost of the containers themselves.''

Joe and Jumbo looked at each other. It seemed their next stop would be Roastmasters. Just the name got Richardson thinking about the cup of coffee he couldn't have.

With Rob Ironstone nuzzling between her breasts, his tongue tracing cool wet trails back and forth from one to the other, Sherrie stared at the office ceiling, her hands behind her head. She liked the tension and urgency along the entire hard length of him as his hips ground slowly against her thighs. She wondered if his wife Jillian knew that the beautiful butter-soft sofa opposite his desk turned into a queen-size bed, or that he kept a set of satin sheets in one bottom file-cabinet drawer.

''Mmm,'' she purred. His tongue traveled down across

her belly now to flick in and out of her navel. Slowly, she closed her eyes and eased her knees apart. Rob was more than eager to please, and a smile stretched across Sherrie's lips as she let herself go. Her fanny muscles tightened as his tongue sent delicious shivers through her. "Come up here and fuck me, you stud."

He entered her too quickly.

"Ow!" she complained. Not only did it hurt, it destroyed the escape route she'd conjured up, transporting herself away from him and into herself. When her eyes opened, Rob's determination confronted her, his breathing coming quickly as he thrust again with purpose.

"Sorry," he gasped. "God, that's good!"

"Slow down, Rob. *With* me."

"You haven't been here since we started," he growled. Instead of slowing, his rhythm became more labored, each quick pelvic thrust taking him as deep as he could go within her. "Who got you Jaime Madera and Hola International, Sher?" He stiffened suddenly and came in a series of spasmodic shudders before collapsing atop her, his mouth close to one ear. "You were just another wannabe before me." He was panting hard. "Remember that."

Something Dante heard in his conversation with Jaime Madera had nagged at him all the way out to Bayonne. After stopping with Jumbo to grab a sandwich en route to Jersey City, he found a pay phone and called the RBS network. He learned from the secretary to the vice-president of the sales division that her boss was away from the office.

"This is Lieutenant Dante, NYPD Special Investigations. Maybe you can help me, Miss . . . ?"

"Henderson, Lieutenant. Is there some problem?"

"I don't think so," he assured her. "A name has cropped up in an investigation I'm conducting. I understand a Trent

Blevin recently worked for your local station. As their sales manager?''

''That's correct, Lieutenant. Mr. Blevin is no longer with WRBS.''

''So I understand. Any idea how I can get in touch with him? It's important.''

''I believe Mr. Blevin is working at Saachi and Saachi now, Lieutenant. I can connect you to our pension office in personnel. They may be able to give you his home number.''

Dante thanked her. Minutes later the pension people at RBS gave him the most current number they had. He called Saachi, learning from them that Blevin worked there on an independent-contractor basis. They had the same number he'd just obtained from personnel. When Joe dialed it, he got Blevin's voice mail and left a message, asking him to return the call. It was a good policy in any investigation to get both sides of a story.

Located near the intersection of Kennedy Boulevard and Danforth Avenue in Jersey City, Roastmasters Incorporated maintained a specialty coffee-roasting facility in one building and their shipping annex in another. The whole complex was nowhere near as large as the giant, recently closed Maxwell House plant in Hoboken, four miles farther north, but neither Dante nor Richardson expected it to be. A rage for gourmet coffee was currently sweeping the country. Smaller than the name-brand-coffee giants, outfits like this one were thriving. From what Jorge DiSalvo described of the operation, Roastmasters had managed to carve a nifty niche in the marketplace. The company's buildings were contemporary concrete structures, well maintained. The offices fronting the roasting plant featured lots of glass, with elaborate landscaping planted away from the building to the Danforth Avenue sidewalk. The loading bays of the shipping annex were lined with trucks of various sizes. The partners observed three carrying Sea-Trans turquoise containers.

On making inquiries at the front office, they were directed to the shipping manager's office in the warehouse out back. A woman working in customer service offered to lead the way. As he followed, Beasley inhaled the mouth-watering aromas from the surrounding air.

"Damn. There ain't no justice in this life."

Joe grunted. "How long did it take you to figure that?"

Richardson turned to the mahogany redhead in the too-tight knit dress who guided them. "How do you stand it? If I worked in a place like this, I'd be forever wired outta my skin."

She smiled, shoved open a door, and led the way onto an expanse of asphalt separating the front and back buildings. "Believe it or not, you get so you hardly smell it after a while. Not like I did when I first came to work here."

They were halfway across the trucking access, following the customer-service rep's mincing high-heeled progress, when Dante's elbow caught Jumbo's attention. Richardson focused a sideward glance at his partner to catch the direction of Joey's nod. Toward the far corner of the shipping building, he saw a half-dozen cars parked against a chain-link fence. Among them stood a sinister-looking black Lotus Esprit coupe and a black Carrera Porsche. The Porsche had New York plates. Jumbo's gaze slid back to make contact with his partner. Two cars in the eighty-to-ninety-thousand-dollar range. It felt like they were getting warm.

The shipping manager's office was situated above the warehouse floor, behind a catwalk running the length of one wall. The detectives were led up access stairs. From the landing they could see the entire operation below. Lift trucks shuttled cargo into trailers backed up to loading bays. Deeper into the building, pallets stood shoulder to shoulder, stacked high with gunnysacks bulging with unroasted green beans and cartons of roasted product. That same aroma, slightly less intense than on the roasting-room floor, pervaded the air up here, too.

The shipping manager could be observed inside a glass partition separating his office from the catwalk. He sported a Mets cap, was bull-necked, and had dark eyes set in a lantern-jawed, deeply tanned face. The customer-service rep entered to announce the NYPD visit, and while she stood in conversation with him, he glanced at his visitors. Beasley watched him look at his watch before nodding to the redhead. She turned to wave them ahead.

Inside, the rep asked them if they needed anything else. Dante didn't think so and thanked her. The manager invited them to take chairs.

"Monica said something about shipping containers, Officers. What's this about?" He was introduced to them as Tony Lopes. There was a slight accent to his speech, barely discernible.

Joe presented his tin and introduced both himself and Richardson. "We understand from Mr. DiSalvo at Sea-Trans that you have subleasing agreements on the containers you rent from them—with people who ship in the other direction. We'd like to know who those people are."

Lopes frowned. "You mind me asking why?"

Joe shook his head to the negative. "It's part of an ongoing homicide investigation. That's all I'm at liberty to say."

The word "homicide" got Lopes's attention. His hands moved from his lap to the desk before him and he hunched forward, his expression cautious now. "I don't understand why the front office sent you to me. Isn't this information they can give you?"

"Not according to them," Joe replied. "We're trying to

pinpoint a specific container. They told us you handle routing.''

''Uh-huh. And you said homicide? Was this a hijacking? Why haven't I heard about it?''

Dante removed an eight-by-ten photo of their container from its envelope and laid it on the desk between them. Leaning over, he tapped the seven-digit code number with an index finger. ''This is the unit we're interested in, right here. You think your computer could tell us something about it?''

Beasley watched Lopes eye Dante with barely concealed impatience before swinging around in his chair. ''If it's one of ours, it should be in here,'' he grumbled. ''It's a Sea-Trans unit. You ain't wrong there.''

He flicked the power switch on his machine and waited a moment for the screen to light while Jumbo studied him further. He seemed an odd type for this job. He had a tough demeanor, better suited to working downstairs on the loading dock than up here pushing a pencil. He didn't seem at ease with the keyboard console of his computer. He acted like any use of it was an affront to his masculine prowess.

''Six-NS-seven-two . . . what?''

''Eight-F,'' Dante said.

Lopes finished punching the code in and sat back to wait. Seconds later a cluster of code numbers appeared on one side of his screen, with some sort of printed information opposite. Jumbo leaned closer. He'd made sure the correct code got typed into the keyboard and read it now among others on the screen.

''Not ours.'' There seemed to be a degree of satisfaction in the way Lopes said it. He eased back away from the screen. ''By that I mean not one of ours *here*.'' He pointed to a firm name, Timber-Tech, and an address, the names of several people and contact numbers in Aberdeen, Washington. ''Beats me what they do.''

As Dante digested the information he betrayed neither satisfaction nor disappointment. "Any idea how one of their containers could wind up here on the East Coast?"

Lopes shook his head. "That ain't the kind of thing we're likely to screw up. Not at this end, anyway. We keep pretty tight control, what comes in and what goes out. Maybe you should check with the cops out west . . . and this Timber-Tech. Could be it was stolen from them."

There was another office farther down the catwalk from Lopes's that Richardson had glimpsed on arrival. An adjoining door between them opened now and a woman's voice called out from behind it.

"Benjy just called, Tony. Says they're ready."

Jumbo wondered what was behind the panicked look Lopes tried to mask quickly with an irritated scowl. "I got company here, hon. You handle it."

A tall blond woman dressed in coveralls and a Ferrari ball cap with her hair tucked beneath it poked her head in to meet Richardson's gaze. Beasley had trouble concealing his own surprise, but had better luck than Lopes did seconds earlier. He'd been in a car outside Prestige Performance the last time he saw her. She was the tall, lanky blonde who was escorted to the curb by Miles Berga last night and then drove off in that Carrera Porsche. It was probably the same car parked at the fence downstairs.

"Sorry," she murmured to Lopes. "They're all set in the yard. I'll get right on it."

Minutes later, as the partners descended the catwalk stairs, Jumbo spoke to Dante's back. "You *did* see what I just saw?"

"Bingo, huh?"

"How we gonna play this?"

"Set up outside and watch for her. Sorry, buddy. Could be another long night."

Chapter ▪ 21

THE LANKY BLONDE EMERGED FROM THE ROASTMASTERS warehouse in the company of a dark-complected male. She climbed into one of the trucks towing a Sea-Trans container, and to the relief of both Dante and Richardson, she embarked on a very short haul. With the blonde behind the wheel, they rolled just half a mile west down Danforth Avenue to the shipping bays of Allied Paint Manufacturing: CUSTOM SERVICE TO THE AUTOMOTIVE INDUSTRY, WORLDWIDE. There, Joe eased to the curb across the avenue, fifty yards back, and shut his engine off. From where they sat, both detectives had a view of the entire loading-dock area, a concrete platform and two huge roll-up doors set into the side wall of a no-frills metal commercial building. They watched as the blonde backed the rig around to the dock and hopped down to climb a short flight of steps.

"Best-looking truck driver I've ever seen," Beasley commented. "What's goin' on here, Joey?"

Dante dug under the seat for binoculars and trained them on the loading dock. There were three men up there: a heavyset bearded guy with huge, tattooed arms and a Harley-Davidson cap pulled low on his brow, a shorter Hispanic man in a satin Jets jacket, and another Hispanic seated aboard a forklift. As soon as the container-trailer was in position, the big biker advanced to tug at the rear-door release. When he heaved both doors wide, one partially blocked Joe's view of the platform. Still, he could see the biker step back to signal the forklift driver forward as the blonde crossed the platform to greet him.

"Anything?" Beasley prodded.

"What kind of delivery would a coffee roaster be making to a paint company?" Dante asked.

"Exotic South American pigment?"

Dante grunted. He watched as a first load of bulging gunnysacks rolled into then out of view.

"What was that?" Jumbo demanded.

Joe could hear the frustration in his partner's voice at being unable to watch up close. "It looked like those bags of beans we saw stacked over at Roastmasters. What could they want with coffee?"

"Some kinda overflow storage agreement, maybe?"

They sat and watched as three more pallet loads came off the truck and were shuttled to the building interior. After the fourth load was delivered inside, the forklift driver parked his rig rather than head back in for a fifth. The blonde then advanced to disappear inside the container.

"What now?" Beasley demanded. "This is the last time we roll with only one set of glasses. I can't see a fu—"

"Hang on," Joe cut him off. The front bumper of an automobile nosed into view past the edge of the container door. "Bingo, buddy."

Richardson was leaning as far forward as he could get, peering hard. "What the hell was that? A car?"

"As in Mercedes, partner. What color was that SL the reporter got hijacked from under him? Silver, wasn't it?"

Within half an hour of Dante's late-afternoon update via Securenet radio hookup, Gus Lieberman had the green light from Commissioner Anton Mintoff and had contacted the DEA. He and Mintoff concurred. NYPD had an excellent joint-task-force relationship with the Drug Enforcement Administration. There was no question that the FBI would be eager to jump in, too, but if they could get the DEA into the driver's seat first, maybe the FBI could be kept at bay. The Federal Bureau lacked the finesse a well-orchestrated quick strike demanded.

At five-thirty, Gus called Joe and Jumbo back. Dante reported that they'd seen no further developments. The semi-rig was still backed to the loading dock, and most activity was now concentrated inside the building.

"What about local cops?" Joe asked.

"Drug Enforcement's SAC is handling liaison with all agencies. They'll probably let the state police decide who to call in."

The SAC was Special-Agent-in-Charge Charles O'Roark. Dante knew and trusted him. "Any luck on Allied Paint?"

"Nobody knows shit about them. The feds do have a file on Roastmasters. They got warehouses all over South and Central America, the biggest of 'em in Barranquilla. It's easy to guess what that could mean."

"What about the interstate-traffic-in-stolen-cars angle, boss? Ain't the FBI gonna want to try and grab the reins?"

"I can't keep 'em out, Joey."

"Everything they touch, they fuck up, Gus. I've got some vacation time coming. How about I take some of it now?"

Lieberman could sympathize. Both he and Dante had seen the Bureau step on its collective dicks more often than either wanted to remember. They'd gotten so they would do anything to avoid involving the Federal Bureau in an investigation.

"They're putting this thing together fast, Joey. Anticipate assembling within the hour. Soon as I hang up here, I'm rolling."

"Where's this carnival setting up?"

"Jersey State College has a stadium over there, about half a mile from where you are now. The SAC is using the parking lot behind it as the staging area. He'll send a relief team to take over your surveillance. He needs you and Beasley to help with the briefing."

Lieberman ended the transmission and reached for his jacket, eager to get into the field. The blonde that Joey and Jumbo had observed at Prestige Performance had now tied Miles Berga to the hijacking operation and probably to Mitch Shimizu's homicide. But who was she and how was she involved? Joey was looking for a woman in the Cintron investigation and a lot of the pieces seemed to fit.

Debbie DeLong had a craving for a burger that just wouldn't quit. Now that everything was safely removed from their clandestine body shop in Queens and brought here to Jersey City, she could relax. The truck was mostly unloaded now. Big Benjy and Freddy Mendoza could handle the last of it, decide where to store the rest of her tools. This space was their part of the operation and she was only in the way here. Besides, they'd already had lunch. She hadn't.

"Benjy. Gimme the key to your bike."

A San Quentin alumnus, Benjy Pollock had done time for operating the biggest crystal-meth lab on the West Coast, in San Bernardino. He stood ten yards from her, his huge tattooed arms glistening with the sweat of his exertions. While Mendoza had some of his stooges running the quasi-legit paint-company business as a front, this part of the building behind a double-insulated partition wall was his domain. He'd made no secret about how irritated he was to see it invaded like this. He was a neatnik by nature. It made him crazy to see two stolen cars and a pile of body-and-fender-working equipment off-loaded into his space.

"Debbie," he snarled in reply. "Sit on my face."

She laughed. "In your dreams. You be good, when I get back maybe I let you sniff the seat."

She'd noticed the current Prestige Performance calendar hung opposite Benjy's desk. When he first learned she was from Hayward, he tried to imply some kinship between them, that they were both from California cities with strong biker traditions. She'd laughed in his face.

The ever-optimistic Pollock unclipped his keys from his belt and tossed them to her. "One fucking scratch and I break your neck. Bring me back a strawberry malted."

"Please."

"Get the fuck outta here."

Benjy's 1955 knucklehead was a West Coast import, traveling east with him when he made the move eight years ago. It was a year newer than the one Debbie's first lover had owned, but every bit as lovingly customized. She preferred the gooseneck style of his handlebars to the less practical butterflies that were part of too many chopped and chromed packages. She *hated* all that trim crap favored by today's law-abiding biker, trying to look dangerous. Debbie loathed the East Coast helmet laws, too, and only grudgingly strapped on Pollock's Nazi-style lid.

Like all knucklehead machines, it took a Herculean effort to kick this old Harley-Davidson started. But a day didn't go by that Debbie didn't do at least three circuits of the Central Park reservoir and put in another half hour on the Soloflex machine in her spare bedroom. While a beer-guzzling slob relied mostly on the weight he could throw to get the job done, Debbie could depend on strength of leg and will. She crouched up high over the kick pedal, gathered herself, and rammed down hard with a quick, pistonlike thrust. On the fourth try, the engine coughed, barked twice, and quit. The next time it caught and roared to life with the bellowing snarl of an enraged bull elephant.

The Burger n' Shake was a few blocks west on Route 440, less than a two-minute ride. As Debbie pulled into the lot and eased into a narrow nonparking space, one of the two cops from Tony Lopes's Roastmasters office emerged carrying a tray loaded with bulging paper sacks. He didn't recognize her as she quickly averted her face.

Debbie didn't freeze or do anything else stupid. Instead, she reached to twist the key and kill the engine. The cop headed for a beat-up Plymouth Fury sedan—navy blue— while she took her time setting the kickstand. Lopes had been in a near panic when they left, saying they had a picture of the last remaining container in the Prestige Performance lot. They were asking questions about it. Like all the containers delivered to Miles, care had been taken to alter at least one of the letters or numbers in the seven-digit code. Lopes tried to sell the idea that their container was supposed to be in the Pacific Northwest. Yesterday, when cops were seen staking out the showroom, Debbie was amazed they'd been able to get so far, so fast, on so little information. Maybe she shouldn't be. Freddy Mendoza contended that Miles had a leak somewhere.

To her great relief, the cops in the Fury didn't stay to eat in the lot. She had no idea how long she could sit on that bike without taking her helmet off, and once she did, a pile of blond hair would cascade to her shoulders. She was afraid even to stand and walk, fearful that something in her gait might tip them, something they'd observed earlier. Instead of lingering, the cop behind the wheel took off almost as soon as the black cop's passenger door swung shut.

Her hunger forgotten, Debbie switched the ignition key back on as soon as the unmarked car cleared the lot. It was an hour and a half since those two had left Roastmasters. She could guess why they were still in the area. The bike's engine was warm now, and maybe that adrenaline surge she experienced helped. The first kick did it this time, and after rocking it off the kickstand, she walked it backward into the lot with purpose. A straight-pipe knucklehead made nearly as much noise as an attack helicopter. Not the ideal pursuit vehicle.

The Plymouth headed south along 440 to Danforth. Then, instead of turning left toward the paint plant, it went right toward Newark Bay. Debbie hung back far enough to let them make the turn. Once they got another hundred yards along, she followed. It wasn't a track that took them far. A quarter mile down, they pulled into the parking lot of the local state-college stadium and started around to the back side. Out on the street, Debbie rode far enough north to be able to just glimpse what was going on back there, away from the public eye. Those two cops and their fifty friends parked around back probably weren't there to watch football practice. Men in bulletproof vests and windbreakers emblazoned with FBI and DEA in huge block letters loitered in knots, many brandishing automatic weapons.

Debbie didn't care who could hear her anymore as she gunned the bike around and started back down Danforth. Any question of whether or not the cartel had a leak was irrelevant now. Somebody had screwed up somewhere. There was enough incriminating evidence stacked in that paint plant to get them all sent up until they were old and shriveled. It was a low move to screw Benjy out of so beautiful a bike, but he wouldn't have much use for a knucklehead Harley where he'd be going. Right now it was every woman for herself. She twisted the throttle hard, opened it up full bore, and jammed.

Gus Lieberman wondered if the jackass on that chopped Harley doing seventy down Danforth Avenue knew there were at least fifty cops less than half a mile away. As that bike roared past, going in the opposite direction, the noise was deafening. Gus and his driver hadn't made good time, hitting a late rush-hour snarl in the Holland Tunnel. Gus hoped the combined federal forces of the DEA and FBI didn't get impatient and decide to go on without them.

On his approach he found the parking lot behind the stadium teeming with enforcement personnel. Dante and Beasley were sticking close to the DEA agent-in-charge. He was NYPD's original contact and the ranking force in the field. In Lieberman's experience, these joint local and federal operations usually involved a lot of ego butting. The New Jersey state people were likely to feel a little left out. The FBI was sure to flex whatever muscle it thought it had. Dante's main concern would be to make sure none of those hot dogs shot him or his partner in their eagerness to throw down. The adrenaline charge of an op like this could warp a man's perceptions. Everyone went in on the nerve.

Dante eased up alongside Gus as he met with DEA Special Agent-in-Charge Charles O'Roark.

"Looks promising, doesn't it?" Joey murmured.

"Any idea yet who the woman is?" Gus asked.

"Nuh-uh. But she's definitely the link. Got her finger in the pie, both ends of the plate."

Gus turned to O'Roark. "Who's got an eye on the paint plant?"

"Couple of my people, Chief. One of the suspects left the premises on a motorcycle fifteen minutes ago. Caught my guys by surprise. The rest are all still there."

Lieberman frowned. "Big, showy chopped hog? Guy in a Nazi helmet?"

"That's right. Why?"

Gus turned to address Dante and Jumbo as well. "My driver and me just passed him on the way here, coming from this direction like a bat outta hell. He must've seen this circus and had the fear of God put in him."

"Christ." O'Roark snatched the bullhorn from atop his

car and raised it to his mouth. "All right, people. Mount up. Slight change of timetable. They might be tipped off. Same approach, but we may meet resistance. You go on word from me."

Lieberman and his two detectives left in a caravan of over twenty vehicles. It exited the stadium parking lot moving at speed.

Benjy Pollock was wondering where Debbie had gone with his baby. Twenty minutes was longer than it should take to make a four-minute round-trip to the burger stand. It didn't help enhance his mood either to have everyone else around him on edge.

"This is the DEA! You are surrounded! Walk out of the building and into the middle of the parking lot with your hands on your heads!"

Benjy and his Colombian assistant Enrique were back at the work they were paid to do when that bullhorn voice penetrated the partition wall of the lab. The Colombian's eyes bugged as he froze, a thirty-kilo gunnysack hoisted on one shoulder. Benjy was anything but paralyzed. When they first built this lab, he and cartel boss Lucho Esparza had foreseen this possibility. Before installing the equipment needed to process a ton of cocaine a month into crack cocaine, they'd cut a trapdoor into the floor of Benjy's office and dug a crawl-space tunnel out beneath the Allied Paint building. It opened into the basement of an older building to the west. The Cali cartel owned it and two more beyond. Thus they'd created an egress from their crack factory, midblock, to a garage with an escape vehicle disguised as a plumbing contractor's van.

"Don't just stand there, you fucking moron!" Benjy snarled. "Get your ass into the tunnel!"

Almost on cue, the door to the loading bay flew open and Freddy Mendoza burst in. He was followed by his six paint-company workers. By that time Benjy had the trap-door ring in his hand and was jerking up hard. "You get the damned doors down?" he demanded.

"They ain' gonna hol' them for long," Freddy replied. He got the gun cabinet open and handed over the first AK-47 assault rifle. "Mus' be a hundred out there. Where the fuck is Debbie?"

"I think we just discovered our leak," Pollock replied. "She puts a scratch on my bike, I'm gonna personally cut out her heart and feed it to my dog."

Special-Agent-in-Charge Charles O'Roark's demand for surrender failed. He then ordered a team of agents onto the roof, where they dropped tear gas into the ventilation ducts. So much military C-S tear gas went into the building that it started pouring back *out* the vents. Still no response. O'Roark figured the building occupants must have gas masks, so he relented and let New Jersey State Police take down one of the two big metal loading-bay doors. A special SWAT assault team was loaded into a rubber-tired armored personnel carrier fitted with a twenty-foot ram. The bay door buckled and caved with a great whoosh of trapped gas, but the action drew no fire from inside. All was quiet.

"What gives?" Jumbo murmured to Joe. "Suicide pact?"

"Why do I doubt it, Beasley? Something's not right. Maybe the guy on the bike managed to get them word."

"Then who lowered them doors? Where the fuck did *he* go?"

Dante surveyed the street to the west and east. "I wish I knew." To the east, the avenue stretched a quarter mile to the next intersection. Behind them, the state-college campus sprawled past an open lawn and parking lot. Going west, three more buildings stood between Allied Paint and the corner. They were all old brick structures with no gaps between them. Adjacent to the much newer Allied building, fifteen feet of paved alley was lined with Dumpsters. O'Roark had stationed a half-dozen men back there. So far as Dante knew, no one had been placed on the intersecting side street, fifty yards farther along.

''C'mere with me a sec.'' He started away toward that intersection at a trot.

Everyone else was engrossed in the Allied Paint loading dock. No one but those isolated in the side alley noticed Dante and Richardson jogging toward the corner. Joe indicated the three older buildings off his shoulder in passing.

''The basement vaults of a lot of these old places were built to interconnect.''

''A tunnel?'' Jumbo asked.

''How far is it from the paint plant under that alley?''

They rounded the corner. Behind the corner building, they found a garage. It had a pair of heavy wooden doors swung wide onto the sidewalk. The interior was empty.

''Fuck me,'' Richardson muttered in disgust.

A subsequent move on Allied Paint turned up Dr. Donna Covington's stolen 1992 Mercedes 560 SL and Mitchell Shimizu's Mitsubishi Eclipse. Also found were three pallet loads of gunnysacks bulging with cocaine hydrochloride—total weight 5,800 pounds—a crack-cocaine laboratory capable of large-quantity processing, a heliarc welding rig, and various body-and-fender-working tools. The DEA and state police were calling it the second-largest cocaine confiscation in New Jersey enforcement history. Dante and Richardson were calling it a puzzle. While others milled around the laboratory and examined the tunnel, Joe stood before the hijacked Mercedes roadster and opened the passenger door.

He noticed that the gleaming stainless-steel-rocker-panel cover was cut carefully away from the threshold. It was set aside on the floor mat. Gene Hackman as Popeye Doyle in the *French Connection* came immediately to mind—him discovering the cache of heroin secreted in the rocker panels of a car he'd otherwise torn completely apart. The panel from the driver's side was also cut away.

It didn't make sense that they would use such relatively small compartments for smuggling drugs. Besides, these cars were presumably headed out of the country, not into it. He noticed the keys were still dangling from the ignition and removed them to pop the trunk lid. Inside, he found the deck carpeting peeled back and a whole new floor constructed. An access cover in it was set loose in place. When Joe lifted it, he let out a long, low whistle. The interior of that compartment—a full four feet by three feet and at least three inches deep—was packed tight with one-hundred-dollar bills.

"Hey, Beasley," he called to his partner. "Look what I found."

Richardson advanced from an adjacent doorway. "Trade you," he said. He brandished a cheesecake calendar featuring a bathing beauty reclining on the hood of a black Lotus Esprit. Her body was every bit as impressive as the car she graced.

When Jumbo reached the Benz, he pulled up short. "Holy shit!"

Dante did some quick arithmetic in his head. The bills were bundled in three-inch stacks of a hundred thousand dollars each. He used the rough three-by-eight dimensions of each bill and the total surface area of the compartment to come up with a staggering sum. "My guess is nine million plus."

Richardson pointed at the carpet. "Maybe you best pull that back over. We better let Gus decide how to handle this. We don't, we'll be buying all them FBI assholes new swimming pools for Christmas." He nodded toward his calendar girl. "So?"

"It's her, all right. The one we saw last night and then here today." There was no question that this was their blonde mystery woman, first seen driving away from Prestige Performance in a Carrera Porsche and last seen in a pair of coveralls. For her calendar appearance, she wore little more than dental floss.

"*And* she can drive an eighteen-wheeler," Jumbo said, marveling. "Could be we got lucky here." He shook the calendar. "This'll be a big help tracking her down."

"That and the plate number we got off her car," Joe added. "Any word from Roastmasters yet?"

"The Porsche was gone when O'Roark's people showed. They got our guy Lopes and some company management in custody. Holdin' 'em on suspicion of conspiracy to distribute." Jumbo paused. "They found a chopped Harley-Davidson knucklehead in the lot over there. Sounds like the one Gus saw on his way to the stadium."

Dante pulled the carpet back over the cash, lowered the trunk lid, locked the car, and pocketed the keys. "My suggestion? Let the DEA and Bureau finish up here. I say we focus on the calendar girl . . . and Berga." He beckoned for the calendar and held it at arm's length. "First thing we do? Fax this picture to Operations. Get them to circulate it to every modeling agency in the city."

Chapter ∎ 22

With the World Series set to get under way at eight o'clock, the fate of Sherrie Meyer's advertising package was now in the hands of the WRBS technical crew. Today, she already had her attention fixed on the months ahead. After her lunch and visit to Rob Ironstone's SoHo office, she'd returned midtown to conduct a Christmas strategy session with her staff. Because the session ran late, it was five-thirty before she could think about leaving for the day.

Sherrie wondered if she should be angry that Dante hadn't stayed last night. Men could get funny about stepping out of bounds, but few could resist one of her seductions, launched head-on. He'd surprised her. She ran her attempt over in her head again and was squaring up the work on her desk when the network-sales VP's secretary, Judith Henderson, poked her head in the door, coat in hand.

"Hi, Sher. Glad I caught you."

While Judith was several years her senior and had been at the network when Sherrie came aboard as a new hire, it rankled that a secretary would address her with such familiarity. "I was just getting set to leave," she replied.

Judith stepped into her office anyway. "A strange thing happened this afternoon. Phil wonders if you know anything about it."

Why didn't she say this was official business at the outset? Good old Judith. Once Sherrie was promoted to Phil Guthrie's position, Ms. Henderson had better have her résumé in order.

"Know about what?"

"A phone call he got from the police this afternoon, regarding Trent Blevin. Is Trent in some new trouble?"

"A call from the police? Asking what?" Sherrie guessed Blevin had a wad of parking tickets stuffed in his glove box. The city had been cracking down recently.

"Where they could find him. I told the detective to try personnel, transferred him to the pension office."

What sort of coincidence was this? A detective making contact with RBS sales twice in one week? Sherrie contemplated Judith with new interest. "A detective, no less."

Judith took another step into the room, her tone becoming conspiratorial. "From something called their Special Investigations Division. I heard from Terry that you had a visit from one of them, too. Phil wants to know if this is something he needs to be concerned about. On a corporate level."

Sherrie frowned. Her assistant, Terry Land, talked too much. "Did you say what this detective's name was?"

"I didn't. It's Dante. Like the *Inferno*."

Sherrie opened her desk drawer to retrieve her handbag. Why Trent Blevin? she wondered. How could Dante know who Trent was? RBS had terminated Blevin way back in July.

"Tell Phil it's nothing. They must be investigating Hola International's relationship with Willie Cintron. He's the baseball player who killed himself Saturday night."

"Why Hola?"

Sherrie was on her feet and going for her jacket, hung on a hanger on the back of her door. "Because Mr. Cintron was their spokesman. I'm not clear on what it all involves.

They may think Trent knows something about it that I don't. Hola used to be his account.''

''He lost it, didn't he?''

'' 'Lost' is putting it kindly, Judith. He all but dug the hole and buried it.''

Judith's smile had a patronizing edge. ''Everyone knows how hard you worked to get it back, Sher.''

Sherrie pulled the jacket from the hanger and started to slip into it. ''I doubt it, Judith. Not by half.''

The task of circulating that calendar photo to modeling agencies all over the city was in the hands of Support Services now. Most agencies were closed for the day, which meant running down principals and pressing them to co-operate. While Dante would have liked to be on the scene when the DEA arrested Miles Berga, he knew it was their show now. Back at the Big Building, Joe continued his own effort to locate the mystery blonde. Unfortunately, the Porsche Carrera she was driving was registered to Berga's Prestige Performance Corp. The motorcycle was registered to a Benjamin Pollock, address in Hoboken. They'd struck out there, and when Dante returned to his SID office Thursday evening, he wasn't surprised to learn Berga had gone to ground, too.

A further search at the Allied Paint warehouse had turned up several five-gallon paint cans in the trunk of Shimizu's Eclipse. They were stuffed with another three million dollars in bundled hundreds, bringing the total confiscation to well over twelve million. There were no further traces of the money's owners. When Joe contacted Support Services for an update on progress made with his only lead, he learned that the photo had been faxed to thirty-nine modeling-agency people. As yet, they'd received no response.

Awaiting Dante's attention was a message from Trent

Blevin. Once Joe could clear his slate, he punched the number into his keypad.

"Trent Blevin." It was a deep, resonant voice, with plenty of self-assurance behind it.

"Lieutenant Dante, NYPD Special Investigations, Mr. Blevin. Thanks for returning my call."

"No problem, Lieutenant. I understand you tried to reach me at Saachi today, too. What's on your mind?"

"Nothing as urgent as it seemed a few hours ago," Joe admitted. "I spoke with Jaime Madera at Hola International today and thought it might be useful to talk to you. Now it looks like it won't be necessary."

There was a long, pregnant pause down the line. "I see. Can I ask why you talked with him?"

"It has to do with a case I'm investigating. Or I thought it did at the time."

"A *case* you're investigating. I don't understand how my name would come up."

"It had to do with why Hola terminated its relationship with WRBS, Mr. Blevin."

"Oh, Jesus," Blevin moaned. "I thought I'd put that nightmare behind me."

"I hope you have, sir. It sounds like a rough time for you."

"Let me guess," Blevin said. "Madera told you I'm a drunk, that I conducted myself in so unprofessional a manner they had no choice but to terminate with the station."

"He was a gentleman about it, Mr. Blevin." Dante could hear a barely contained anger set to blow. He was starting to regret returning the call.

Instead of coming unglued, Blevin remained calm and cool. "I'm not a drunk, Lieutenant."

"That's why I thought it important to call," Dante replied. "To get your side of it. Now other developments suggest that entire inquiry was irrelevant."

"You've no doubt heard of a woman named Meyer, that she was promoted yesterday to fill the vacancy, Lieutenant?" Joe heard him sigh. "God knows what other treachery she had to engage in to manage that little coup."

Dante frowned and sat a little straighter in his chair. This was not the ranting of a paranoid alcoholic. It was controlled. "Other treachery? What are you suggesting, Mr. Blevin?"

The former WRBS sales manager chuckled. "That clever young woman did everything but castrate me, Lieutenant. She engaged in deliberate acts of sabotage. Madera told you about a series of fax messages he received, written on my stationery?"

"He mentioned them. Yeah."

"I didn't write them *or* send them, Lieutenant. I don't drink Gilbey's gin, either. That's the brand of pint bottle Phil Guthrie, the network sales VP, found in my bottom desk drawer. So tell me something, Lieutenant. Dead end or not, what was it you *thought* you were investigating?"

Dante dodged a direct reply to the question. "Are you surprised that it was Miss Meyer who was chosen to replace you?"

He heard Blevin grunt. "Not as surprised as the three people senior to her on the sales force must be. It had to be that World Series package I hear she delivered. Then again, if the Yankees hadn't beat the Royals last Sunday, she and everyone *else* at RBS would be in a panic right now."

"Because of the money they stood to lose?"

"Ah," Blevin replied. "So you *do* understand."

"Understand what?" Dante asked.

"What that package of hers must mean to them. The way I hear it, she better than doubled the revenue generated by their next-most-productive salesman. It was practically all she worked on the past six weeks. Two of my old staff with whom I spoke called it grandstanding. Me? I call it an unbelievable stroke of luck.''

''You're implying her eggs were all in one basket?''

''I know it for a fact, Lieutenant. I've got some friends there who still keep me up to date. The backup sales she'd made, for a San Francisco–Kansas City Series? Barely a quarter of the slots she filled for the scenario which ultimately prevailed. After game six last Saturday, she must have been ready to kill.''

As offhand as Blevin no doubt meant it, his choice of words set Dante's mind reeling.

''You don't think she's *that* driven, do you, Mr. Blevin?'' He tried to keep it light, jocular in tone.

Again, Blevin grunted like he'd been jabbed by a sharp object. ''The woman is poison, Lieutenant. A back-stabbing Medusa.''

Their exchange was interrupted when Jumbo hurried into the crowded office cubicle. He handed Dante a sheet of paper.

''We got her, Joey.''

''I'm sorry, Mr. Blevin,'' Dante apologized. ''Something's come up. I've gotta run. Can we get together tomorrow? Say, in the morning?''

''I'm in meetings till noon. How about lunch?''

''Gimme a number where I can reach you. I appreciate what you've said. It could be important.''

''You never told me what this is regarding.''

''Tomorrow, Mr. Blevin. I promise.'' Joe scribbled as Blevin gave him his reach number. When he hung up, he sat face-to-face with Richardson's excitement. ''That was fast.''

''We got lucky. The folks at some outfit called Mermaids were working late. Had a whole flock of their models out at Jones Beach. Doing swimsuit-catalog work. One of the staff remembered our gal because she was booked for that job—called this morning to cancel. Name's Debra DeLong. Address way east in the seventies.''

"Swimsuits in October?"

"Sparkling blue skies and no people for miles of white, sandy beach,'' Jumbo replied. "Anyway, they've represented this Debra DeLong for close to three years. Still don't seem to know much about her. Just the basics—social security number, phone, and address.''

All Dante wanted to know about her was what one single hair could tell him. They still hadn't tied Miles Berga, Debra DeLong, or their operation to Willie Cintron. Berga had wagered a huge sum on the success of the Yankees in the ALCS, a sum he couldn't afford to lose. But in view of the nearly thirteen million in cash recovered in today's raid, Joe could only conclude that Berga was a relatively insignificant front man, a cartel stooge on a leash, fed peanuts.

Meanwhile, Sherrie Meyer was definitely at the Marquis the night Willie died. If what Blevin said was true, she was much more than just aggressive; she was ruthless.

"You ready?'' he asked.

"Gus has got a couple detectives from the Nineteenth squad meeting us up there. We're s'posed to keep him posted. First sign of resistance, we call in backup. He's promised not to alert the feds until we've got the cuffs on. This one's ours.''

Now that everything had come apart, Debbie DeLong knew that no one she'd considered a friend yesterday was a friend today. Cali boss Lucho Esparza had lost two and a half tons of coke and better than twelve million in cash. The dope was worth ten times the cash, and that was too big a hit for Esparza to take without exacting reprisals. While Debbie had never met him, she guessed she didn't want the pleasure. And Freddy Mendoza? The leak theory was his in the first place. She wanted to be gone. Far away.

After recovering her car, Debbie called Miles while en route to Manhattan. Whoever sold out Allied Paint would finger Prestige Performance, too. That's where the damned reporter had showed up in the first place. She kicked herself now for being unable to make him so much as squeak before she cut his throat. It made her wonder how much he knew about this afternoon's impending disaster.

She was in her bedroom, just finished packing, when Miles was announced downstairs by the doorman. She carried her Louis Vuitton garment bag and the first of two valises down the hall and was setting them on the parquet foyer floor when Berga's knock came at the door. If Miles was as predictable as he'd always been, he could make this flight easier than it might be. She couldn't get to her nest egg in the safe-deposit box at this hour, and the five hundred dollars she could get from a cash machine wouldn't get her far.

When Debbie opened the door, Miles strode in, a bundle of jangled nerves. "How the fuck did it happen?" he demanded.

"What car and where?" Debbie demanded back.

"That Taurus wagon I use for service calls. It's parked at a meter, around the corner on Second. What the hell happened, Deb?"

"The lid blew off is what happened." She started back down the hall for her other valise. "Who *cares* how? You got a snort? I'm dying for a fucking snort right now."

In her bedroom she jerked the last bulging bag off the bed. When she arrived back in the foyer, Miles had his stash unfolded in the palm of one hand. He used the corner of a matchbook cover to dig a little mound of the drug out and extend it toward her. She held her hair away from her face with her free hand and gave a quick sniff.

"How much cash got delivered today?" she asked.

"Little over two hundred thousand."

While the cartel's operation was running smoothly Berga was the daily cash drop for all the monies collected in the metro area. Out back of Prestige Performance, Debbie was employed to skillfully create storage compartments for that cash in hijacked luxury cars. Two hundred thousand was light, less than half the daily take that went into Berga's reinforced showroom safe. They shipped a car south roughly twice a month, allowing the Cali cartel to funnel home more than $250 million per annum. If Freddy Mendoza or Lucho Esparza ever suspected Miles of stealing so much as a nickel, his death would only be a matter of when.

"I still don't get it. I expect they got Benjy and Freddy, but you got away."

Debbie dropped her bag and gestured toward the paper in his hand. "Again."

Miles dug another little pile onto one corner of the match cover and held it out to her. She snorted with more vigor this time, drawing the drug as far into her sinus cavities as she could. Already, the first hit was kicking in, her body starting to tingle in all the right places. "I got lucky," she replied. "How much more of this shit you bring?"

"A couple ounces is all I had. We've got to figure a way to get that bread to Lucho, babe. I like my balls right where they are."

Debbie had a headful now, the psychoactive elements of the drug charging her from the soles of her feet all the way up the length of her fine, slender physique. She was a high-strung woman by nature, but this stuff put her energy on a whole other level. There was nothing she couldn't manipulate, bend to her will. Right now she sought to twist fate in her favor. Yesterday's plan was used goods. It was pathetic that Miles still thought he could play the same old game. She wondered if his father had been equally dense, or if he'd at least known that shove overboard was coming.

She checked her watch. "We've got a few minutes. Let's

live dangerously. Work off some of our frustration.'' The tip of her tongue wet her lips. She stepped in close to rake her nails across the bulge of his crotch and plant an eager wet kiss hard into his mouth. With her face then pressed to his neck, she could feel Miles swallow, feel the heat rising in him as he moved against her hand.

''Now I *know* you're crazy.'' It was throaty, half-strangled. ''Freddy's patience has gotta be mighty thin right now.''

''Freddy's in jail, Miles. Relax.''

He tugged at her blouse, trying to get the tails free from the waistband of her jeans. She stopped him with a restraining hand.

''Wha?''

''Wood floors give me bruises. Let's try a bed.''

With new eagerness, Berga led her down the hall. He never saw the gravity knife come out of her back pocket, or how the four-inch blade was deployed, expertly, with a flick of her wrist.

Chapter ∎ 23

WHILE DANTE AND RICHARDSON WERE EN ROUTE TO DE-
bra DeLong's address on East Seventy-first Street, they got
a Securenet radio call from Gus at headquarters. After
twenty-two years of seeking out pay phones, Dante was still
getting used to this new freedom.

"I just got word on those inquiries you asked Support
Services to make, Joey." They were rolling up Third Avenue through a snarl in Midtown Tunnel traffic. Lieberman's voice came at him loud and clear through the tiny
speaker of Dante's new hand-held. "So far as they can tell,
this Debra DeLong appeared outta nowhere three years ago.
New driver's license and social security number. The
county in Illinois she claims she's from? Never heard of
her."

"The birth certificate was a fake?" Joe supposed.

"That's their call."

"Which means, if we don't find her fast, and she isn't
stupid enough to buy a plane ticket with a credit card, we'll
never dig her back out of the woodwork."

"O'Roark's raid on Prestige Performance came up
empty, Joey. Somebody tipped Berga. He cleared out. The
door to a floor safe in his office was open, the one car in
their service bays left up in the air on a rack. It's like they
just set their tools down and walked away."

"I assume someone tried his house?"

"Wife says she ain't heard from him all day. They went in with a warrant, tore it apart anyway. *Nada.*" Gus paused. "Oh, by the way. Tell Jumbo that Rocky called. Them pubes he shipped him from the Guzman woman were negative."

"It was a long shot," Joe replied.

Beasley had the wheel, and even with the flashing red gumball stuck to the roof and an occasional burst of siren, he wasn't happy with the speed they were making. When a motorist in an Audi Quattro failed to yield, blocking the intersection ahead, he flipped the siren switch and snatched up the public-address hailer hand mike. "*Move* that fuckin' thing," he roared.

The driver jumped in his seat and lurched forward, slamming hard into the back of a delivery van. Jumbo took advantage of the narrow opening astern to slip through. The irate driver of the van erupted onto the pavement and started pounding on the windshield of the Audi with his fists.

"You might call the Seventeenth station house," Joe told Gus. "They've got a little fender bender, corner of Thirty-five and Third. Could get bloody, any second now."

The doorman, seeing Debbie struggling with three bags, helped her get them out to the curb. There, as Debbie kept an eye on them, he stepped between parked cars to search the street for a cab.

"Taking a trip, Miss DeLong?"

For starters, she was taking a cab around the block to Berga's parked station wagon, but Tim the doorman didn't need to know that. She flashed him a bright smile. "Lucky me, Tim. A swimsuit shoot in the Caribbean. I can't wait to hit the sand and soak up some sun."

"Sounds nice. Bring a little back with you. I got a feeling

it's gonna be a long, cold winter."

Not for some of us, Debbie thought. Southern California wasn't exactly the Caribbean, but it would be warm enough. The highway patrol and Madera county sheriff probably still had a file open somewhere, looking for Blondell Debra Radford. But Blondell had been dead for years. She died just like Debbie DeLong died half an hour ago; when Deborah Louise Turner flushed Debra DeLong's cut-up credit cards and ID down the commode.

Benjy Pollock didn't know what he was angrier about, the bitch giving them the slip, her being the leak, or the fact that she'd stolen his bike. It made him sick to sit across the avenue from Roastmasters and watch those FBI geeks circle his baby like a pack of excited dogs. He half expected one of them to lift a leg and pee on it.

"We going to do this my way," Freddy Mendoza murmured.

It was an hour later now, and Benjy was double-parked with Mendoza three buildings east of Debbie DeLong's address. They'd dropped the other seven who'd made the tunnel escape with them at a cartel safe house on 101st Street in Spanish Harlem. Almost as soon as they pulled up to park here, they saw Debbie emerge onto the sidewalk, the doorman helping her with heavy pieces of luggage.

Like hell he'd do it Freddy's way. This bitch might think she was better than the rest of them, but she was nothing more than a gutter-crawling rat. She had to be insane to mess with Lucho Esparza. Her double cross had blown an operation worth a quarter billion a year to the Cali cartel. Did she actually think she could run somewhere?

"Lookit her," Benjy growled. "Fucking bitch thinks she's pulled it off."

Mendoza reached around from the passenger seat into the back of the van. He lifted an assault rifle from beneath a pile of drop cloths, his practiced fingers checking the action to make sure it was clear after that crawl through the Allied Paint escape tunnel. He tripped the clip release, checked the spring tension on a load of cartridges, and slapped the clip back home. With one eye on the weapon and the other on that doorman, scanning for a cab, he failed to see Benjy ease a big Bren Ten automatic from his waistband. Pollock held it out of sight between the driver's seat and door.

"Roll the window down," Freddy directed. "When I say you go, bring it right in tight. Then lean back out the way."

The DeLong woman's building was at Seventy-first Street and Second Avenue, southeast corner. The majority of trucks making deliveries were gone by that hour, enabling Richardson to park at the curb in a No Standing zone, fifty feet past the intersection. When the Nineteenth squad detectives pulled in ahead, all four cops met on the sidewalk. They'd received a second communication from Gus. A judge had signed a search warrant, authorizing access to Debra DeLong's apartment. To effect that access, the Nineteenth squad guys carried a Hydra-Force III forcible entry tool in its tote bag.

Dante pointed to a cluster of Dumpsters overflowing with construction debris parked outside the building's Second Avenue service entrance.

"You guys ring the bell and get them to take you up the back way. She's probably got a door accessing the service elevator. One of you station yourself outside it."

"I'll take it," the older of the two offered. "Tommy'll meet you in the hall with the hardware."

Dante nodded toward Jumbo. "Beasley's gonna stay downstairs in the lobby, wait for us to give him the word. He'll keep an eye out, make sure she doesn't have a friend working the intercom switchboard. Once we break the door, don't let that cheesecake pose fool you. Keep your heads down. No telling what sort of firepower she's got in there.''

''*If* she's there at all,'' Richardson reminded him.

The squad cops started for the service entrance as Joe and Jumbo went north along the Second Avenue sidewalk toward the corner. With many local residents stepping out for dinner, pedestrian traffic was heavy. As the partners proceeded both were on the lookout for that black Carrera Porsche. Dante spotted it, parked at a hydrant, kitty-corner to the intersection.

''I'm surprised,'' Richardson said. ''Tell you the truth, I figured she'd be halfway to Baltimore by now.''

''Ain't arrogance a wonderful thing,'' Joe replied. ''Probably thinks her friends are cooling their heels in some Jersey lockup, that we don't even know who she is yet.''

They were starting to turn the corner when Dante threw an arm out to stop Jumbo's progress. He grabbed a fistful of Beasley's jacket and pulled him back out of sight behind the edge of the building.

''What?'' Richardson asked.

''Speak of the devil . . .''

Jumbo looked. Sure enough, there she was at the curb beneath the entrance awning. Ahead of her, a uniformed doorman stood in the street scanning to the east with a whistle in his mouth.

''Easy pickings, Joey.''

Dante dug for his shield case. ''Just watch her hands,'' he cautioned. ''Matching suitcases and designer outfit or not, this is no lady we're taking down.'' Joe had his tin in his hand now. He pulled his weapon from the clip-on holster at the small of his back and slipped it into his waistband up front. Jumbo did the same and buttoned his jacket over it.

''You ready?'' Dante asked.

''Can't wait.''

■   ■   ■

Tim the doorman had been in the street ahead of Debbie for less than a minute when a free cab appeared down the block. He'd lifted a hand high and blown his whistle to flag the cab when a tradesman's van pulled out into traffic and nearly hit it. The cabbie was forced to slam on his brakes, tires squealing and horn blaring in anger as Tim hurried to grab Debbie's two heavier bags.

"Just what you need, huh?" he said to her. "A driver in a mood to kill."

She shrugged, hefting the remaining bag herself. "As long as it isn't me."

The van slowed rather than hurry ahead to make the green light. Debbie was too busy watching the cab to pay much attention. Then she heard a kissing noise and looked over in irritation.

The van was directly abreast of where she walked, lugging her bag between parked cars. She froze with the impact of recognition. There in the driver's seat, leering out at her over the muzzle of an automatic pistol, sat Benjy Pollock, tattoos and all. Time stood still.

The blow came before her conscious processes could click another turn. The pavement came up at her with absolute abruptness as she was hammered face-first into it and nearly knocked cold. So this was what it felt like to be shot. She hadn't felt the bullet at all, but hitting the pavement sent a searing bolt of pain all the way through her.

Dante was on automatic pilot. The second he saw that van slow instead of making the light, he moved. Something wasn't right. The sign on the side of the van said LEO LOCATELLI PLUMBING AND HEATING CONTRACTORS INC. JERSEY CITY, NJ. He heard the driver kiss at Debra DeLong and saw the look of recognition on her face. He and Richardson were less than ten feet from her then. Jumbo must have seen the gun muzzle, too, and maybe the other man in the passenger seat, trying to aim an assault rifle out the window.

The sweep kick he aimed at Beasley's ankles tripped Jumbo and sent him sprawling. Dante was a step closer to Debra DeLong's back now, and from there, he launched. In setting himself and going hard off his plant foot, he hyperextended and felt something give in his right knee. He concentrated on keeping his head up anyway and drove through his target.

Before the van driver could get off a shot, Joe slammed the woman and her garment bag to the street, her body cushioning his landing. He rolled hard to the left, collided with her luggage, but managed to clear the Walther P-5 from his waistband. His momentum took him onto his belly, hands coming together on the street before him. Overhead, he heard the snarl of a full-automatic discharge. He forced his focus to the open driver's window of the van, lifted his gun, and fired.

No sooner did Richardson hit the sidewalk than the world overhead exploded in a cacophony of gunfire and a hail of shattered glass. He was up on his knees, balance regained and pistol tugged free, when he heard the report of a different weapon. Once, then a pause, and then twice more in quick succession. Shielded by a parked car, he scrambled head down to the front bumper.

The first thing Jumbo saw when he peered out was the van driver slumped over the wheel, his head a bright red pulp. Then he saw the door on the opposite side hanging open, a pair of feet in sneakers running away from it toward the rear of the vehicle.

"Coming at you on your right!" he yelled. He could see Joey down there on the ground with the gagging blonde and her garment bag between him and any clear line of fire.

Richardson surged to his feet and threw his body across the hood of the car, gun out before him in a two-hand grip. When a heavyset Hispanic male wielding an AK-47 assault rifle leaped out from behind the van, Jumbo drew bead and fired. His first shot took the target dead center of the chest and threw him backward onto the terrified cabbie's hood.

By the time the two Nineteenth squad cops rushed onto the scene in response to gunfire, it was over. Both occupants of the plumbing van and the doorman from the East Seventy-first Street building were dead from gunshot wounds. Dante had either torn or badly sprained his right knee, while the woman he tackled had a broken collarbone and several cracked ribs. The fact that Dante had probably saved her life did little to subdue her anger. Even the news of Miles Berga lying dead of a cut throat on her hallway floor didn't evoke much more than a malice-soaked sneer. When more detectives and uniforms from the Nineteenth station house arrived to secure the scene, Dante pushed his pain aside to isolate Debra DeLong in one corner of the building lobby.

"You can't keep me here like this," she seethed. "I'm hurt."

Joe sat across from her on an upholstered bench, his injured leg stretched throbbing before him. He had the identification from her purse fanned in one hand, and was studying these documents. "If you die, we'll all send flowers, Ms.—what is it today? Turner? I like the Deborah Louise. It has a nice all-American ring to it."

The driver's license was from the state of Nevada, the address Las Vegas. Her several credit cards and automated-teller plastic had been generated by a Las Vegas bank. Facial bruises sustained in her collision with the street notwithstanding, there was no question that she was the woman on the Prestige Performance calendar.

"Kiss my ass!" she hissed in reply. "I know my fucking rights!"

Joe nodded. "Sure you do. I heard Lieutenant Richardson read them to you myself." He raised his eyes to study his subject. Tall, at close to six feet, she had a great slim-hipped, angular build, but the face was too ordinary for high-fashion work. The body was perfect for the sort of cut-rate catalog-and-calendar work she did. "So tell me about Willie Cintron, Ms. Whatever-your-name-is. Are he and Mitchell Shimizu why you did your pal Miles? So that he couldn't implicate you in killing them?"

For an instant her eyes betrayed something other than utter contempt. "I don't know what the fuck you're talking about."

"Sure you do. You're the one cut Shimizu's throat, same as you cut Berga's. A killer gets the hang of something, they tend to stick with it."

Anything attractive about her was erased by the unfathomable emptiness Dante saw in her eyes. They were a deep green, and utterly dead. He'd observed that impenetrable gloss before, the windows to the soul of a sociopath.

"I've got no fucking idea what you're talking about, bud. I read about the Jap reporter in the paper. Who's the spic?"

When Gus Lieberman arrived to assume command of the scene, Jumbo got some help persuading Dante to see a doctor. With three people dead downstairs and one up in the apartment, there was a large crowd of rubberneckers outside the cordoned-off area. Inside the yellow plastic tape, dozens of lab techs, detectives, and federal agents milled around getting in each other's way. Dante needed less convincing to leave now than he did before his talk with Debra DeLong/Turner.

"I called Bernice," Richardson told him. "Canceled our dinner plans." They were together in Dante's car, Jumbo behind the wheel. He steered them toward Lenox Hill Hospital.

"Oh God. That's right. What time did you get her?"

"No problem. She was late getting home from work. We'll do it another night. Once we get you home, you'll need to stay off that leg."

"What do you think, Beasley? Is she our gal?"

"You saw what she did to that poor bastard upstairs, Joey. Jesus, that's cold."

"You take a look at her eyes? There's nobody home."

Richardson shivered as he nodded. "Scary, ain't she?"

"Oh yeah." Dante shifted in his seat, trying to get the leg comfortable. For the most part it was a losing battle.

Jumbo had crossed to Park Avenue via Seventy-first Street and now turned them north. His expression was thoughtful as he settled into the middle traffic lane. "She wanted it to look like an accidental overdose. So no heat came off it to spook the bookies, make 'em cut off the action. This way Berga won his bet, just the way he placed it."

Dante toyed with the idea, examining it from several sides. "Makes sense, sure. Still, it feels like a reach to me."

"It *is* a reach, Joey. But we're running outta possibilities."

"True, but if it was Berga she was trying to help in the first place, why turn around and butcher him now?"

"What good was he to her anymore? His whole world crashed and burned today. Maybe she decided to cut her losses."

Dante groaned. "Please. Is *that* what we're stooping to now?"

Richardson smiled. "Don't lose any sleep, Joey. First thing tomorrow, Rocky orders a DNA probe. Either that hair sample is a lock or it ain't."

Debra DeLong's bathroom was so spotless that the only

hair they recovered was from a brush in her handbag. The difference in textures between pubic and scalp hair made microscopic comparison less conclusive than DNA testing. That more sophisticated process employed the latest state-of-the-art forensic technology. It would eliminate even the shadow of doubt.

"And what if it isn't?" Joe asked. "That would mean someone else killed Willie, and probably Felicia Rojas, too."

"Like I said, partner. We've run out our string there."

"Maybe," Dante murmured. His expression was thoughtful as his eyes scanned the avenue ahead. He was probing something other than the steady stream of traffic.

"If something's bugging you, Joey, spill it."

"Probably just another dry hole. A thing I heard today. Twice, in fact. It's got me thinking in a different direction." He shook his head. "You're right. Debra DeLong, or Turner, or whatever the hell her name is, will either be a lock or she won't. Why waste time now spinning my wheels?"

"Speaking of wheels, how's yours feeling?"

"Burns, buddy. Like I've been branded."

Chapter ∎ 24

TRENT BLEVIN HAD RETURNED HOME THURSDAY EVENING to his East Sixty-third Street apartment both physically and mentally exhausted. Still, he felt better about life than he had in recent memory. His Saachi project was a television ad blitz aimed at winning their client a bigger share of the interactive-video-toy market. The competition was stiff, and their client was small potatoes compared with outfits like Nintendo. Blevin loved this sort of challenge. He was performing up to his level of talent for a change, and it made him feel at least a decade younger than his fifty years.

The message waiting for him from that detective lieutenant came like a knuckleball from nowhere. It was a rare thing, in his experience, to get an opportunity to set the record straight, and Trent felt like he'd done pretty well. His story would doubtless go no further than the eternity of dead files that police amassed, but Blevin felt better for getting it off his chest. The lieutenant seemed sympathetic, or at least interested. Maybe Sherril Meyer's game had reached some higher-stakes level where her good looks and charm could no longer cover her treachery. Trent never stopped hoping he might live to see the day.

An inveterate bachelor who enjoyed the solitude of nights at home with a good book or old movie from his extensive film library, Blevin had ordered in Chinese and settled on the sofa to eat and read. The rest of the city would spend the next week or two wrapped up in Yankees mania, but Blevin couldn't care less about baseball. The fact that it was Sherril Meyer's World Series ad package that put her over the top with RBS management made the prospect of watching the games that much more distasteful.

Blevin had returned to his tiny kitchen to scoop more shrimp with black bean sauce onto his plate when the intercom buzzed. It was nearly eight-thirty and he wasn't expecting visitors. With his plate balanced in one hand, he picked up the receiver to the house phone.

"Yes?"

"Bicycle messenger for you, Mr. Blevin. Got a big envelope for you from an advertising agency. Can't leave it here at the desk. Says you're s'posed to sign."

Trent knew nothing of an envelope being delivered to him here tonight. Something must have come up, a new angle the account exec wanted him to consider. She lived somewhere up in the wilds of Westchester and probably hadn't had the opportunity to call him yet. Some nights that commute could take forever.

"Which ad agency?" he asked.

There was a pause where he could hear the doorman's muffled voice. Seconds later he was back on the line. "Sahshi something?"

"Send him up. Thanks."

Blevin cradled the receiver and moved back into the living room to set his plate on the cocktail table. He had another sip of his wine. They had a promo they wanted to shoot that involved several kids competing against a recognizable sports celebrity. Trent had nailed down every aspect but the talent. The list was down to four possibles. This must be something new.

His doorbell rang, and Trent crossed to the entry hall. He answered his door to a female messenger and the muzzle of her gun. As she came at him he faltered back, speechless. When she lowered the gun to motion him farther into the apartment, he recognized Sherril Meyer. She had her hair tucked into a Yankees cap pulled low on her brow, wore faded jeans ripped at both knees, dirty sneakers, and a windbreaker sizes too big. If he hadn't seen her every day for several years, he wouldn't have known her.

"Yell and I shoot you right here," she warned.

"Good God, Sherril. What is this?"

Once he'd stepped far enough back, she reached around behind her to ease the door shut. "This is you and me having a little heart-to-heart, Trent. And this"—she nodded toward the gun—"is to ensure you tell me the truth."

"About what, for godsake?"

She motioned him toward the living room. "Go sit down."

They sat, him on the sofa and Sherril in a chair across the way. She pointed to the remaining food on his plate. "Finish your dinner, Trent. We'll talk while you eat."

There was something spooky in her tone.

"I don't understand, Sherril. First you try to destroy my career. Now you come to my home with a gun? Why? What did I ever do to you?"

"A police lieutenant tried to reach you today."

How the hell did she know that? He nodded. "Less than two hours ago. What have you done, Sherril? He wouldn't tell me."

"What *did* he tell you?" she demanded.

Blevin pushed his plate away across the coffee table and folded his napkin. "Hardly anything, actually. Mostly he asked questions."

"Regarding?"

"Why I was terminated at WRBS, the circumstances leading up to it."

"And what did you tell him?"

He met her eye dead-on now. "The truth. That somebody set me up. That I'm no more an alcoholic than you are. That I didn't send those fax transmissions to my clients and that the gin found in my desk wasn't mine."

"How did he react? Did he believe you?"

"I think he had his own suspicions already. What have you done, Sherril? You've screwed up big time, haven't you?" He couldn't conceal his pleasure.

She stood and started to pace the floor before him. "Not unless they can prove it."

"Prove what?"

"That I killed Willie Cintron."

Blevin wasn't a baseball fan, but Cintron's drug overdose suicide was big news that past weekend. "Jesus," he murmured. "And I know why. My God, woman. You *are* insane."

She stopped before him and shook her head. "Why, Trent? Because I want things? History is *made* by people like me. No one calls Andrew Carnegie insane. Half the towns in America have a library named after him."

She'd murdered a man to gain a promotion at a local television station and was talking about making history? Blevin felt like the lone skier on a slope where an avalanche has started, miles above him. The rumbling he had heard when he first saw that gun was now a deafening roar in his ears.

"You need help, Sherril. It must be all the pressure you're under. Believe me, I know how bad it can get. It can warp your perspective, bend it all out of whack."

"I've never thought more clearly in my life," she replied. As she spoke she moved closer to where he sat. The knapsack she carried came off her shoulder, and she unzipped the top. When she reached inside, her hand came back out holding a large potato. "You think I'm crazy?" She hefted the potato as she asked it.

"What's that for?" Trent asked.

"Something I saw in a movie. Here, let me show you."

She held the potato before his eyes, placed the muzzle of the pistol against the back of it, and pulled the trigger.

The noise the gun made, suppressed by that crude, make-shift silencer, wasn't so bad. Sherrie had heard louder champagne corks. At the last instant she shifted her aim to hit him in the right temple for the more authentic angle: Trent was right-handed. The slug from the little .25-caliber automatic didn't have enough zip to create an exit wound in the back of his skull. For that, Sherrie was grateful. Her work here wasn't finished yet.

As soon as Blevin's corpse stopped twitching like high voltage was being run through it, he started to topple. Sherrie caught him. She'd taken care not to leave any finger-prints since her arrival and now pulled latex gloves from her knapsack. Once she put them on, she stripped out of her windbreaker. Underneath, she wore a Kevlar vest that she'd purchased after work, ostensibly as a birthday gift for a policeman boyfriend. To make this look like a suicide she needed to get discharge residue on Trent's hand. That meant firing a second shot and replacing the spent bullet in the clip. She also needed something to fire that shot *into*. The Kevlar bulletproof vest was a stroke of sheer genius.

The potato Sherrie packed back into her knapsack was looking a little worse for wear after she fired the second shot into the propped-up vest. A suicide note deploring the lie Trent lived as a closet alcoholic was a simple matter of slipping a disk of precomposed text into his computer and letting the printer spit it out. With that huge windbreaker pulled back over the bulky vest, no one who saw her de-scend the elevator or ride off on her bike would suspect she weighed less than a hundred fifty pounds. To make it look like her victim had all his affairs in order, Sherrie carried his plate to the kitchen, scraped it into the garbage, and set it in the dishwasher. Perhaps her old corrupt-cop stepdaddy wouldn't be proud of her—especially considering how *their* relationship had ended—but she was damned grateful for all he'd taught her over the years.

She left the apartment hungry. Maybe she would stop on the way home, pick up some Chinese food.

By the time Dante reached his loft after his pit stop at the Lenox Hill emergency room, the president had thrown out the first ball. The World Series was well under way, with the Giants at bat in the bottom of the third. Jumbo offered to stick around and help get him settled, but after one ceremonial beer, Joe sent him home to his long-suffering wife. The painkiller an emergency doctor had prescribed was kicking in and Dante didn't know how far into the game he'd last anyway. This had been a brutal day. Right now he was feeling nearly as exhausted as he was apprehensive.

Before Richardson departed, Diana called from upstairs. She'd heard the elevator. Learning Dante was lamed up, she stopped down as Beasley left. The singer had just finished her workout. Her hair wet with sweat and leotard glued to her torso, Diana stood in the kitchen pouring them both glasses of seltzer.

"Only a knee sprain and not a gunshot this time? So what is it, copper? You losing your sense of the dramatic or just getting old?" She carried the two glasses in and handed him one.

"Getting old. What do you hear from our boy? I'm keeping an eye out for him in the crowd."

Diana continued to stand while Joe sat with his bad leg extended out across his coffee table. She took a huge gulp from her glass and smacked her lips. "He called this afternoon from San Francisco. It's Giants mania there. You heard anything from Rosa?''

Dante realized he hadn't checked his machine. It had been four days since he put Rosa on that plane to Brussels. He knew she'd been busy this first week and wondered how it went. "Not yet," he replied. "But you know what a romantic she is. Probably thinks I'm busy. Out chasing skirts.''

Diana chuckled. "With a leg like that? They better not run too fast. So what gives, Joe? You two *ever* gonna get serious?''

"I did once, and look where it got me.''

She pointed her glass at Dante while shaking her head. "You wanted to change her, and that isn't how it works.''

"And now I'm not trying to change her anymore. So, I guess we'll see.''

"I guess she's as pigheaded as you are.''

"You gonna sit down or wear out that spot in my carpet?''

Diana smiled. "I'd like to stay and watch the game, but I need a shower and don't even have milk for coffee in the house. You need anything when I go out?''

Dante reached over to pick Toby the cat up off a cushion alongside. He pulled him into his lap and gave him a playful scratch behind the ears. "Naw, we're fine. You want to have breakfast tomorrow? It looks like I'll be available.''

"You bet. Give me a call when you're up and around.''

She finished her drink and left as the Yankees were taking the field in the bottom of the fifth, the score tied at two runs apiece. It was going on nine-thirty and Joe realized he hadn't eaten anything since lunch. At a commercial break he grabbed his new crutches, hoisted himself to his feet, and hobbled toward the kitchen. He had a little nine-inch color set on the counter in there and switched it on before rummaging in the refrigerator for sandwich components.

When the picture blinked to life, WRBS was airing a local spot for Citibank. Dante set deli-wrapped packets of salami, provolone, and mortadella on the counter while thinking again of Sherrie. That ad was part of her package. He wondered how the exec with the Citibank account had fared in her clutches. If that person was male, Joe guessed he'd made out just fine.

He found a fresh roll in the breadbox and popped it into the oven to warm. He washed some lettuce, dug out mustard, and located a new jar of pickled peppers. Fifteen minutes later, when his intercom buzzed, he was seated in the breakfast nook downing a slapped-together dinner sandwich on a warmed-through kaiser roll.

He hauled himself to his feet and hopped on one foot to the wall-mounted box. No one had called to say they were stopping by. "Yeah?"

"It's Sherrie, Joe. You've got quite the sexual freak show out here. Could you buzz me in, please? Quickly."

Diana Webster exited her building and was heading east on Twenty-seventh Street toward the supermarket on Ninth Avenue when a cab pulled up to discharge a passenger. Because Diana's loft and Dante's were the only two residential spaces at that address, she slowed to glance over her shoulder and see who it was. The woman in Capri pants and a colorful turquoise-and-yellow parka was no one she recognized. Blond hair pulled up and secured with clips. Attractive. No sooner did the woman depress a button on the intercom panel and seem to be identifying herself than Diana heard the electrically controlled lock buzz. At this hour only one person could have granted her access.

Puzzled, Dante reached to depress the door-lock button. "When you get to the elevator, hang on a sec," he told Sherrie. "I need to release the car."

He collected his crutches and made his way through the living room to the freight elevator at the opposite end. After inserting the key to release the car, he unlocked the expanding steel gate covering his entrance. Before stepping off, a passenger had to open that gate when the doors parted. It was a system designed to discourage pilfering when the building had been leased, each floor separately, to warehousing tenants. Brian and Diana still had three such tenants occupying the floors below.

While the winch motor whirred and cables in the shaft slapped each other, tugging the car toward him, Dante wondered how she'd found him, and what this was about. He then remembered what she said last night about the newsroom having Cole's reverse directory. It would tell her his address and even what floor. That answered one question, but what about the other? If she killed Willie Cintron, did she have some perverse desire to walk the edge of the precipice? Or was she attempting to monitor the investigation's progress from an insider's vantage? If Trent Blevin was right about her, then she was just crazy enough not to see how nuts it was to come here.

As the elevator inched toward him Joe remembered the look of blank incomprehension that registered in Debra DeLong's eyes at the mention of Willie Cintron. He already knew the outcome of tomorrow's DNA test. Last night Sherrie had tried to seduce him because she wanted something, needed to find out where his investigation stood. Tonight she was no doubt fueled by the same purpose. Okay, fine. Two could play that game, and to get proof positive, he might have to play it her way. He needed a pubic hair.

The car doors opened and Sherrie registered surprise, seeing the crutches. "What on earth?"

Joe heaved the gate open to allow her access. She was dressed casually, in hip-hugging Capri pants and a cashmere sweater under a colorful ski parka. Her hair was pulled away from her face again, and instead of a handbag, she carried a small blue knapsack.

"Little scrape I got into a few hours back. Bad knee sprain." He was forced to hop a step on one foot as he tugged the gate shut again. "This is a nice surprise. I figured you'd be home watching that ad package you put together for the Series."

"Baseball isn't really my thing," she replied. She glanced over to see he had the game on, and grimaced. "Sorry. I guess I'm interrupting, huh?"

"Forget about it. Come on in." He shifted his crutches to position them comfortably and led the way into his sprawling, half-finished living room. A chair occupied by the cat got a nod in passing. "Meet Toby. My roommate."

Sherrie proceeded, absorbed by her surroundings. "Pretty bohemian life-style for a cop, isn't it? Midtown loft . . . with trolling johns and a horde of hookers out front?"

"Midtown *south*," he corrected. "At least that's what the realtors are calling it now. I apologize for not calling and thanking you for dinner. Circumstances made mincemeat out of my schedule. I barely had time to breathe."

She took a seat on the sofa opposite the television and met his eyes with friendly frankness. "My father and stepfather were cops, remember? I understand. Believe me."

"I had a great time last night."

"Me, too." She gestured toward the crutches and the way he held the injured leg. "So what sort of scrape *was* it?"

"The arrest of a suspect in a drug-related homicide. I've been developing the case all week. You'll hear all about it on the eleven o'clock news."

"I was sort of hoping to be otherwise engaged," she purred.

Joe grinned at her and jerked his head toward the television. "If you'll keep an eye on the action, I'll get us something to drink."

"What action? This is baseball you're talking about? Let me give you a hand."

Joe shrugged as he started away, still getting used to the crutches. "Why not? There's a tube in here, too."

Inside the kitchen he leaned the crutches against the counter to free his hands. Sherrie followed, and before he could ask what she'd like, she produced a bottle of lime juice and a pint of Cuervo Gold from her knapsack.

"I had this wild desire for a margarita. Didn't know what you'd have in your cabinet. A little Triple Sec wouldn't hurt. We in luck there?"

"We?" He kept his expression amused, eyebrows raised. "I'm under a doctor's care. Maybe a beer for me."

She looked disappointed. "I make a mean margarita. Not at all sweet, but just like they do at my favorite bar on Summerland Key. Dry enough to pucker you from one end to the other."

"So this isn't just a drink. You're talking a cultural experience."

"Damn straight, mister. And all I need from you? A little coarse salt and ice."

"And Triple Sec."

"If you've got it. Sure."

Dante's loft still had a few rough edges, but where it counted, he possessed all the amenities. Before producing Triple Sec, salt, and ice, he opened a cabinet and brought forth a pair of shallow-bowl, stemmed margarita glasses. "How's that for equipped?"

She had a wicked little smirk working. "That's teasing, Joe, bragging about being well equipped. The glasses are a nice touch, too." She took them from him, set them on the counter, and unscrewed the tequila cap. "Put confectioner's sugar on your list, if you've got it."

"I thought we were talking dry?"

"I am. But it's nice to have handy, to ease the edges." She set the bottle down and frowned back toward the front room. "I think I'd better use your bathroom before I get started. I won't be a minute."

Joe pointed to the doorway. "It's the next one along, to your left. Crushed ice, correct?"

"That would be lovely."

She couldn't know he was onto her. Not yet. He'd only heard Trent Blevin's story a few hours ago. Maybe this was her idea of a dry run, get him used to her doing something like this, get him to let his guard down. The idea made him cautious, resolved to watch her closely. Joe wondered if she'd brought liquor and mixer to Willie Cintron's room last Saturday night.

When Rosa Losada arrived home from the airport, she'd tried to reach Dante and gotten no answer. So instead of leaving a message, she decided to surprise him. He was probably out eating dinner or maybe watching the first Series game in one of his after-work haunts. If she let herself in and didn't find him home, she could curl up on the couch and read.

It was nine forty-five when Rosa stepped from a cab outside Joe's building. She'd grown so accustomed to ignoring the trade working the sidewalk outside his front door that she missed Diana until she nearly ran into her.

"Hey!" Diana greeted her. "You're s'posed to be in Spain."

"My aunt had a stroke and two uncles flew over from Miami. They didn't need me in the way, and the weather further south was bad anyway. It didn't seem like a good time for a vacation."

"Joe knows you're home?" Diana asked it as she extended her key to open the door.

"He must be out somewhere. I called."

"So come up for a drink. We'll compare notes on Brussels. Beasts did a concert in a soccer stadium there last year."

"I'll leave him a note, tell him I'm here."

Diana had the door open and held it for her. "Why? We'll hear the elevator." She shifted her groceries from one hand to the other to let Rosa pass.

A drink sounded good after seven hours in a plane and fighting airports on both ends. She'd eaten an early—if dreadful—dinner en route and wasn't hungry, but she was a bit wound up. "Maybe a glass of wine," she agreed. "It's been that kind of day."

Sherrie couldn't believe her luck. The second she stepped off the elevator she'd seen Dante's eyes light up. Too bad. He'd had his chance. Sherrie never fucked for fun. Fucking was business, a means to an end. Dante only spoke to Trent this evening, which meant he wouldn't likely have passed on what he learned to anyone. With Trent dead and Dante soon to join him, any trail of evidence from Willie Cintron to her would be effectively eliminated. Sherrie could walk away with her mind at ease and her sights fixed on the next goal in her quest. In two years she would occupy the office of RBS executive VP sales, Phillip Guthrie. She'd be content to sit in his chair a few years, but by the time she was forty, she expected to be running the network.

As soon as she closed herself in Dante's bathroom, a prescription bottle caught her eye. Set right out there on the vanity alongside the sink, it contained Robaxisal in 750-milligram strength. Sherrie guessed it was some sort of pain reliever or muscle relaxant, given to Dante for his injury. She read the boldprint advisory describing side effects. It warned of potential drowsiness and light-headedness. Perfect. What better drug for an autopsy to find in his system?

The drug was in tablet form, and Sherrie used her hair-brush to crush several into a fine, dissolvable powder. She scooped the powder into a tissue, intending to produce it later on the pretense of blowing her nose. The trick would be to keep Dante momentarily distracted. She was confident it wouldn't be a problem.

Joe had kosher salt spread in a saucer and a lime cut into wedges on a board next to a bowl of crushed ice when she returned. Damn, this fool was eager to please. It amused her to feel him so close as she set to work mixing ingredients in a shaker. Just to keep him on track, she shifted her hip to make contact with his and let it linger there.

"This is the first time I've seen you dressed in pants," he mentioned.

"You like it?"

"This pair of pants especially."

She glanced over at him. "How's your game going?"

"Barry Bonds just hit one out with a guy on second. Giants four, Yankees two."

"You have some chips or something we could nibble on with these? Keep them from going straight to our heads?"

"Sure." Dante turned away for a cabinet next to the refrigerator and removed a partially consumed bag of Tostitos. While he hobbled about, getting a bowl to put them into, Sherrie took advantage and reached into her bag for her tissues. As she feigned a sneeze she unfolded the crushed Robaxisal into one of the glasses, its rim glistening with a fresh coating of salt.

"Bless you."

Sherrie blew her nose into the tissue, nodding, while us-ing her free hand to pour the two glasses full. "Thanks. It's only a matter of time when there's a cat around."

Dante had removed a jar of supermarket salsa from the refrigerator and was busy shaking it out into a second bowl. "I've got some decadron a doctor gave me. You take one now, you shouldn't have any problem.''

She shook her head. ''It's never more than a few sneezes. You ready to try the world's greatest margarita?''

In reply, he moved next to her, eyes locking with hers. ''I think maybe we should clear our palates first.'' He leaned in to kiss her, arms encircling and body pressing her back into the edge of the counter as his tongue probed her mouth.

Sherrie was impatient, but she told herself to relax, to act like she was in no rush to do anything but make him feel good. It got pretty hot for a moment. She wondered how far Dante intended to go before he tasted his drink. Then he broke the kiss off, gingerly stepping back.

''All clear,'' he murmured. ''What say we remove to the living room? Get comfortable.''

Sherrie swallowed hard on her revulsion and handed him his Robaxisal-laced drink. ''You bet.'' She lifted her glass in a toast. ''If it's *too* dry, we'll cut it with a little sugar.'' She watched him over the rim as he sipped and she sipped with him. She had to admit it might even be too dry for her own arid taste. ''What do you think?''

''I think mine is just about perfect. Yours?''

''It'll do. Can you manage, if I carry the bowls?''

They adjourned to the living room with Dante employing only one crutch, leaving his other hand free to carry his drink. He waited while she selected a spot on the sofa before taking his place alongside. God, she hoped she'd crushed enough of those damned pills to make quick work of him. If she hadn't, she was going to have to fuck him, same as she had to fuck Willie last Saturday night.

It came as something of a relief when the Yankees staged a comeback, rallying from two runs down to draw abreast of San Francisco in a series of plays that made no sense to her. One Giants player had a ball hit directly at him and seemed to kick it. The batter ran all the way to second base.

The next hitter just stood there while the pitcher lobbed four straight balls into the catcher's outstretched mitt. The man who followed him knocked a ball all the way to the wall in the middle of the field. It caromed crazily off the wall, away from the man giving chase, while the two men on base ran around to cross home plate. While watching all this, Dante sipped his margarita between exclamations of excitement. By the time things settled back to normal, he'd consumed all but the dregs of his drink. It was all over now but the fade and coup de grace.

"You like that enough to have another?" she asked.

"I'd better not. The doctor gave me something for the pain and swelling. I had a beer with my partner when he first brought me home and it made me a little light-headed."

Good news. "But you feel okay now?"

He gave it a waggle of the hand. "I think I've probably taken it as far as I should."

Sherrie rose, her empty glass in hand. "There's more in the shaker that I'd hate to waste. You'll excuse me?"

"No problem. You're over your cat allergy, I see."

She started back for the kitchen, smiling brightly. "Like I said, it's never more than a sneeze or two. I'll be right back."

After swallowing the last of the wine in her glass, Rosa set it on the table before her, stretched, and tried to stifle a yawn. "God, I'm beat."

Brian and Diana's vast living room was hung with more quality contemporary art than many museums owned. They were dedicated collectors, committed to supporting the community that went so far toward supporting them. Across from Rosa, Diana lounged with one leg thrown over the back of a huge leather sofa, her wineglass on the floor alongside. She looked over at her longtime friend, the panic she'd experienced earlier kicking in all over again. Rosa hadn't been here twenty minutes. Joe's ladyfriend had been down there what? Forty-five? For all she knew, the woman could be Dante's new accountant, but somehow she doubted that.

"Have another glass of wine. You'll sleep like a baby."

Rosa yawned again. "I have another glass of wine, I'll pass out. I think I'll head downstairs."

"I haven't heard the elevator. You?" It was lame, but the best she could do.

"Maybe he used the stairs."

"And maybe he was busy and just didn't answer when you called."

Rosa sat up to look straight at Diana, brow furrowing. "What aren't you telling me, Di? You've been acting just a little nervous ever since we met on the street."

Diana dragged her leg off the back of the sofa and hauled herself upright. She took a deep breath and squeezed her eyes shut. "Okay. I saw a woman going in while I was heading out to the store."

"Ah. Not anyone we know?"

Diana shook her head. "I was hoping we'd hear the elevator, which would mean she was leaving. You still going down there?"

Rosa stood and crossed to the wine bottle. "Damn straight I am, right after I have another drink."

How long it would take Dante to fade, Sherrie couldn't answer. Antihistamines administered in the same strength took half as long to put Felicia Rojas out as they did Willie. Willie was younger than Dante, just as tall, and maybe fifteen pounds heavier. Joe, however, had an older man's slower metabolism. She would have to wait and see.

When she returned from the kitchen, Sherrie had her drink glass in one hand and knapsack in the other. Dante was sufficiently curious about the bag to mention it.

"You got any more surprises in there?"

She chuckled, zipped open the top closure, and reached in to produce a .38-caliber Smith & Wesson "Combat Masterpiece" revolver. It was a lot more cumbersome than the .25 Beretta automatic she left in Trent Blevin's hand on East Sixty-third Street, but it was the only weapon she had remaining from her dead stepdaddy's unregistered arsenal. "Just this," she replied.

Chapter ∎ 25

SHERRIE WANTED TO SAVOR THAT LOOK SHE SAW ON DANTE's face for as long as she lived. He was, without question, dumbfounded.

"You were going to figure it out sooner or later, Lieutenant. Maybe not the rest of your department, but you personally. If I let that happen, I'd be letting you fry me, and I can't do that. You see, I've got other plans."

"Figure what out, Sherrie? And it's lieutenant again, I see."

"Give me a break. You think I can't hear those little wheels whirring inside your head? There's a lot you still don't know, but once you had a few more pieces, you would have put it all together."

Dante took care not to provoke her as he gestured between them with an open hand. "I must be missing more than you realize. Figure *what* out?"

Sherrie cradled the pistol in her lap, barrel aimed at his heart through the left side of his rib cage. "I know you talked to Trent Blevin this evening. He told me all about your conversation, the things he said to you about me."

No question, it surprised him. "How?" he asked. "How did you find out?"

"Phil Guthrie's secretary told me you called, trying to find Trent."

"Ah."

She watched his eyes measure the distance between him and the gun. Sherrie had taken care to sit far enough away to make a grab for it too big a risk. He made that determination and seemed to resign himself, but she knew better than to buy this act. She played a mean hand of poker, too. She knew a bluff when she saw one.

"So Blevin was right. You *did* set him up."

"I had no choice, Lieutenant. The RBS old-boy conspiracy was never going to promote me past him, no matter how good I was."

"So you decided to go *through* him, huh?"

"It worked for Genghis Khan."

The bastard smiled. Here he was, about to be shot through the heart, and he had the temerity to humor her. "What was Willie about, Sherrie? Tell me it was more than making sure the Yankees won a ballgame."

Now it was her turn to smile. "I had to fuck him to gain his trust, Lieutenant. He was the wham-bam type, and believe it or not, that actually makes it easier. I don't have to work so hard pretending I'm there."

He didn't miss a beat. "So why Felicia Rojas?"

"The crazy woman was in the hallway outside his room when I left. I'd left him dead on the bed in there, and it was the second time she'd seen me that night."

"So what did you do? Offer to compare notes, woman to woman? Get her to invite you to her place for a drink?"

She nodded. "Something like that. I had a backup set of works with me, in case I got nervous and dropped the first on his bathroom floor. I hadn't used half the Benadryl."

It was what now? Almost ten minutes since he downed that drink? God, *she* was feeling pretty damned tired herself. So *nod,* you bastard!

Almost on cue, Dante's eyelids drooped. He tried to fend off fatigue by shaking his head. "How do you figure you'll get away with shooting me, Sherrie?"

She suppressed a yawn and glanced down at the gun in her hands. "All cops keep at least one throwaway. Even straight arrows like you, for that one time you accidentally shoot an unarmed citizen in the back. Matter of fact, my dear departed stepdaddy kept two."

His eyelids drooped again. "Oh? Your stepfather's dead, too? You never mentioned that."

She shouldn't have started on that second drink after gulping her first so fast. Another wave of exhaustion swept over her. She fought to suppress a second yawn. If she had to, she would shoot Dante with the gun in her hand, but her plan was to give him his own and help him pull the trigger. Every year a hundred cops across America ate their guns. If she made it look good enough, it would never go further than the initial medical examiner's inquest.

"He didn't want me to have more education than he had," she told him. "And Princeton was expensive. His construction company had assets over six million, and Mama got it all. I got what I wanted, too. He wasn't my *real* daddy, anyway."

Sherrie doubted he'd heard more than her first few words. He no longer had the resolve to fight. His eyelids drooped a final time. She eased to within arm's reach and gave him a gentle prod. Nothing.

"Finally, you bastard," she whispered.

Sherrie looked away to scan the room, wondering where he kept his service weapon. She then started to rise, and as she did she caught a flash of movement before the Smith & Wesson was ripped from her hand. A yelp of pain was only half out of her mouth before Dante was all over her. He wrapped an arm around her waist and drove her to the floor, her forehead grazing the edge of the coffee table. The wind knocked out of her when she landed, she saw stars. Still, she could feel the cold metal of the gun barrel jammed up beneath her chin and feel his hot breath in her ear as he rasped:

"You so much as twitch, I'll blow that ugly mind of yours all over the front of my sofa."

Dante had never actually seen the drug hit the glass, but when she had passed the tissue over the top of it like a matinee magician, he knew she'd accomplished her objective. That was when he'd decided to use the distraction of an amorous embrace to reach behind her and switch glasses.

He kept the barrel of the gun tight on her jaw while prodding her to her feet. She hadn't entirely recovered her breath and all the Robaxisal she'd ingested was starting to make her sluggish. That margarita he'd consumed was reacting with the drug in his own system to make him more light-headed than the earlier beer had. Thankfully, he'd eaten. His knee was burning like hell again, too. That kept him plenty alert.

He pointed to the crutch leaning against the sofa. "Hand me that and then put both hands on top of your head."

She stayed stubbornly rooted, her face a mask of hatred. He gave her another none-too-gentle prod with the barrel.

"You lose, Sherrie. Pick it up."

Frightened by his grim determination, she moved to comply. He took the crutch and then nodded toward the door to his bedroom.

"Cuffs are in there on the dresser. Try anything dumb and I'll shoot you."

In the bedroom, Sherrie faced the wall mirror above the dresser, her back to Dante as he fastened the hardened steel bracelets, one wrist at a time. She'd started to cry tears of outrage, and Joe met her eyes. He leaned close to whisper in one ear. "Ain't ambition a bitch?"

■   ■   ■

As Rosa entered Dante's kitchen she saw Toby the cat rise from the floor in the living room, stretch, and amble toward her. There was a half-empty tequila bottle on the counter, along with lime juice and a bowl of melting ice. On the coffee table in the living room she saw a pair of the margarita glasses she'd given to Dante as a housewarming gift when they first got back together. The empty glasses, followed by the sound of low voices coming from the direction of the bedroom, made her blood boil.

"You fucking bastard," she murmured.

She marched into the living room and toward the master-bedroom hallway. When she threw open the bedroom door, she was already speaking before she saw the tears, the blood trickling down the woman's face, and the handcuffs.

"Surprise, you bas . . ."

The way Joe jumped, with that gun in his hand, it was a miracle he didn't shoot anyone.

Chapter ■ 26

By STREET-LIFE STANDARDS, THE WASHINGTON HEIGHTS night was young at ten-thirty. After the examples made of his cousins, Hector Cintron was perhaps more sober than he normally would be; but he understood the law of Lin Wah's jungle. That morning, he'd received a visit from Lin. The Tung-on street lord asked point-blank if they now had a problem with their relationship. Hector was quick to assure him they did not. He would continue to perform his duties as overseer of Wah's distribution network and continue to make cash collections. Privately, he was relieved to have the embarrassment of Felipe's fuck-ups off his back. Yes, blood was blood, and he hadn't been able to deny the Infantes a piece of his action, but it was better to see it end this way than some other. So far as Hector was concerned, he liked his own *cojones* right where they were.

Tonight, Hector's girlfriend Yvette made him promise to take her dancing. There was a social club opposite the Port Authority bus station on 178th Street with a house *típico* band that played hot salsa. Yvette hated to miss a single beat, and the music would be in full swing by eleven o'clock. She also liked to have a couple of rum drinks before the music started, to limber her hips and get the fire burning. Both of them were dressed for the town and ready to go, but Lin Wah was late making his pickup. Yvette was steaming a different, contrary kind of heat by the time the knock came at their door.

"Everything cool?" Hector asked as Wah entered.

Lin appeared distracted. As always, rather than trust Cintron's count, he dumped the bundles of cash onto the table to do a reckoning of his own. Hector had witnessed this process countless times, but was always amazed at how fast the Chinese street lord's fingers flew.

"I get word," Wah said, eyes on his hands. "That bitch of Felipe's, she is on street. Look for me."

"Carmen?" Hector couldn't hide his amusement. She was a big, sloppy cow who would rather shoot dope than feed her kids. The idea of Carmen Guzman hunting Lin T. Wah to exact revenge seemed comical.

Lin scowled. "They say she have crazy look . . . in the eyes." He finished counting the day's take of over seventeen thousand dollars and resecured the bundles with their rubber bands. The money was dumped unceremoniously into a rumpled paper sack and stuffed inside his jacket. "I have people out. They find her first. Until this, I am careful."

Hector was surprised Wah would take such a threat seriously. "You wan' me to have words with her, I'm sure I can find her, no problem."

Wah scowled again as he started for the door. "What is there to say?"

"Can we go now?" Yvette demanded.

Hector shot her an icy look that melted quickly as he turned back to the drug lord. "We are going dancing. You got this crazy Latino bitch stalking you, we walk you to your car."

As they started out the door, the Tung-on leader was no happier to give Hector his back than he was to think about Carmen lurking somewhere with revenge in mind. Lin and his Chinese brethren would always be fish out of water in

Washington Heights. Whether Hector had taken that fall for Wah and done hard time or not, they would never trust each other.

There was rain in the forecast, due to arrive with a new warming trend from the Atlantic off Bermuda. As the three of them emerged onto the building's stoop through that front door with its broken lock, Hector scanned the cloud-heavy sky. It was hard to believe that only yesterday he had been forced to bundle up against the chill. Tonight, his upturned face was caressed by a balmy breeze off the Harlem River.

Wah *was* being cautious tonight. It was rare that the Tung-on henchmen in the Mercedes didn't stay inside the car. Tonight, all three men loitered outside its open doors, smoking and conversing in low tones. As Lin moved down the steps in front of him, Cintron saw them eye him suspiciously. He could feel their anxiousness. When the Tung-on underboss reached the pavement, he turned to face Hector and Yvette.

"I sorry, Hector. There no choice, the stake is this high. I sure you understand."

Cintron stood gaping as Lin turned to walk away. If Hector hadn't come downstairs, Wah would have sent his thugs up. Either way, he'd been a fool not to anticipate this turn of events. If it was true about Carmen at all, the only way Wah could know was by talking to others on the street. He only made such contact when he had business to conduct. Hector guessed that today's business was the establishment of a replacement structure, to handle the action that was once his. He steeled himself for the hail of lead that would, any instant now, tear into him.

Lin Wah stopped in his progress with a spasmodic jerk that seemed to mimic Hector's as the first bullets from a Tung-on gun tore into Cintron. Lin was halfway across the sidewalk, on his way toward the backseat of his Mercedes, when a gaping crimson hole appeared below his chin. He grabbed at it with both hands while the single shot that created it went unheard above the deafening din of a Skorpion machine pistol. Lin's driver was the first to realize his boss had been hit. As he reached for his own weapon the second bullet from that unseen gun hit him in the chest.

The Tung-on shooter with the machine pistol was unaware of any problem until a fat, disheveled woman with wild hair advanced from the basement stairwell beneath Hector's stoop. She gripped a 9mm automatic at full extension as she charged toward him. Her hands were trembling so furiously it was hard to imagine how she'd hit her first two targets. She missed her third as the next shot went wide. A burst from the Skorpion then threw her hard into a row of plastic garbage cans like a discarded rag doll.

In their rush to depart the scene, the two unscathed Tung-on left their fallen leader on the sidewalk to suffocate on his own blood. Unable to coax the driver with the chest wound into the backseat of the car, the Tung-on shooter squeezed off a single coup de grace round to the head.

Once the Mercedes sped away, a quiet descended over that stretch of Audubon Avenue, violated only by the barking of dogs. Hector Cintron and his girlfriend Yvette lay sprawled before the door to their building. Lin Wah and Carmen Guzman lay so close on the sidewalk that her fingers almost touched his face. All five of the corpses lay in spreading pools of blood. Reflected in the amber streetlight, the blood glowed a soft orange, like the edges of flame.

It was nearly four o'clock Thursday morning when Rosa helped Dante limp home from the Tenth Precinct station house and fall into bed. An hour earlier, a groggy Sherril Meyer had been transported downtown to the Manhattan lockup and booked on three counts of second-degree homicide. In her condition, she refused to make any sort of statement, even with her attorney present. A call made to Trent Blevin to build support for Dante's case eventually produced support more grisly and damning in nature. Residue scrapes were done from Sherrie's hands. A search of her apartment turned up a Kevlar vest with a .25-caliber slug snagged in its high-tech weave. Her freezer yielded close to a full ounce of a white powder later analyzed to be heroin. It was still contained in a large plastic evidence bag, once employed by NYPD back when Dante first started on the job.

Gus Lieberman had a more detailed update later when Dante and Rosa joined him and Jumbo for lunch at their favorite Vietnamese eatery in Chinatown. After seven and a half hours sleep, Joe felt almost refreshed. When he first awoke, his right knee was swollen so stiff he could barely move it. After a shower, half an hour of ice, and a Robaxisal, it felt passing fair. Then he tried to make the stairs descending into the restaurant from street level. His crutches would require a period of adjustment, if he didn't fall first and break his neck.

They ordered appetizers to start. While waiting for them, Gus sipped tea and fidgeted with his Zippo lighter. "We ran a check on her father," he reported. Thus far he hadn't dug out his smokes, for which Dante was grateful. "Got caught up in an evidence-pilfering investigation back in seventy-one. A quantity of drugs went missing after him and his partner busted a Columbo runner with two keys of smack in his trunk. Only half of it ever made it to court. They never proved Jim Meyer took it, but enough other shit turned up to brand him and his partner Fred Casey dirty as sin itself. Meyer ate his gun and Casey put in his papers."

"He's dead now, too, right?"

"Yep. And it looks like his stepdaughter's nothing if she ain't consistent. Casey was a closet junkie. Died of an overdose, and the only thing different this time was the pop pricks. An autopsy found them in all kinda clever places.''

''But no antihistamine.''

Lieberman shrugged. ''I'm sure they weren't suspicious enough to look. If you think about it, an entire kilo of ninety-eight-percent-pure heroin, rationed a tiny bit every day, would easily last him the ten years between when he stole it and when he died.''

''And Sherrie walked off with what was left,'' Dante concluded.

''Probably his works, too,'' Jumbo guessed. ''Her mother inherited control of the construction company. Named South Florida Builder of the Year a while back.''

''What about hair samples?'' Joe asked.

Lieberman smiled the satisfied grin of a well-fed cat. ''A pube we recovered from her bathroom is so close, the DNA testing's just a formality. With it and the other shit we've got, the DA will nail her to the wall.''

''And I thought I'd seen it all.'' Joe tasted his own disgust as he said it.

Jumbo gave him a you-should-know-better look. ''You hear about Washington Heights?''

''Just the bare bones. Bad week for Mama and Papa Cintron.''

''You still ain't explained how the Meyer broad wound up at your place, Joey.'' Just as Dante feared, Gus had a fresh pack of coffin nails out now. ''Considering what you went through yesterday, I wasn't gonna press you on it last night.''

Dante glanced to Rosa. ''She came there to kill me, boss. Because I was the last link in the chain connecting her to Willie Cintron.''

''What? You think I'm a fucking putz? I know that much.''

Dante fed him a smirk. ''And it's all you need to know.

You'd hate the sordid details, anyway.''

Lieberman's eyes narrowed as he looked to Rosa. ''The smart-ass is still alive. He claiming he didn't have to compromise his virtue?''

Rosa smiled. ''It's what he claims, and it appears he had the chance. Maybe there's hope for him after all.''

Joe reached across to pluck the pack of smokes from Lieberman's hand. ''I delivered her to you on a platter, Gus. At significant personal risk.''

Gus reached across the table for his cigarettes. ''Gimme back my butts.''

Later, when Rosa parked out front of Joe's building, she switched off the ignition and sat back to look at him beside her. The sun sparkled bright on the pavement from a crisp autumn sky and the hooker traffic had vanished.

''So, she comes downstairs in a slinky chemise. There's a crackling fire on the hearth, and you say good night.''

''And thanks for the drink.''

''Why do I believe you?''

''Because only a fool would expect you to, and I'm a fool . . . for you.''

She closed her eyes, took a deep breath, and grinned. ''So what are your plans for the rest of the day, big fella?''

''Oh, I know this hot Latin lady, looks even better naked than with clothes on. Thought I'd try to con her into my bed.''

''Untie that knot you tied in it?''

''Something like that, yeah.''

Epilogue ■

ONE WEEK AFTER THE YANKEES WENT DOWN IN FIVE
games to the San Francisco Giants, Guillermo "Willie"
Cintron was named the posthumous winner of the American League Cy Young Award. Sportswriters across the
country used the occasion to speculate on what might have
been had the young Dominican left-hander lived to play
another eight or ten years. Perhaps the most touching of
those testimonials, about greatness snuffed in its prime, was
written by Barry Zajac of the New York *Daily News.*

Two weeks before Christmas, Jill O'Brien of Kings-
bridge, the Bronx, stepped outside her front door to look
at the filthy station wagon her husband Bob had purchased
at the city's unclaimed-vehicle auction. A man in a wrecker
from the Ford dealership delivering a new set of keys was
just leaving. Another guy from an automotive-glass place
on Broadway was almost finished installing a new windshield. Bob had washed the car and cleaned the inside,
proving he had a better eye for a diamond in the rough than
she did. There was white paint under all that grime.

"I don't believe it," she called down to him. There was
a mixture of awe and admiration in her voice.

Bob grinned, wiping a soft cloth over the tailgate glass.
"I think all that dirt actually protected the paint. Look at
it. There's hardly a scratch."

"Does it run?"

"Like a top. I think that guy from the dealership was even more surprised than me. I put a new battery in and the oil looks brand new. Records show it was towed just this past October, registered to a car dealer who went belly-up."

"You're kidding."

He shook his head. "It only *looked* like shit, Jilly. Let me see if the spare's any good. If I can change this one flat, we'll take it for a spin."

The glass installer backed away to toss tools into his box and wipe his hands on a rag. "All set, Mr. O'Brien. Fifteen hundred you say you paid? I say you stole it."

O'Brien hoped so. City taxes were killing his little custom carpentry business, and last month he'd been forced to replace his old work truck with a new van. With a family of three kids to feed, he and Jill were strapped.

O'Brien unlocked the rear-deck compartment with his new key. The spare turned out to be full size and not one of those little donut things. When he hauled it out onto the drive, he noticed a nylon duffel stuffed back in the deepest recess of the well. He could tell right away by the weight that it wasn't a tool kit. He poked at the contents with his fingers as he reached for the closure zipper.

When Bob opened that bag, he was thankful he kept his heart in decent shape, running five miles every evening in Van Cortlandt Park. It helped him withstand the shock. What he thought might be old receipt books turned out to be bundles of hundred-dollar bills. Lots of them, each as thick as his thumb.

"Sweet Jesus, Jilly. I think I just died and went to heaven."

A frowning Jill O'Brien gasped when her husband placed one of the bundles of cash into her hands.

"There must be a hundred thousand in here," he guessed.

They would later discover it was over two.

Jill's voice quavered. "Oh my God, Bobby. Should we call the police?"

He stared at her in disbelief. "What? Are you *nuts*?"